The

Challenge has often been a driving force in Adda Leah Davis' life and, ultimately, her writing career. Growing up in a large family with limited resources in McDowell County, West Virginia, she has channeled her life experiences through fiction writing to showcase the indomitable spirit of the Appalachian people. (From an article by Ellen Elmes, an artist and teacher at Southwest Virginia Community College which appeared in the Richlands Press.

If anyone is qualified to tell the story of this place and the wrenching changes it has undergone it is Adda Leah Davis. . . . . While McDowell County, West Virginia, invites song and story, only a keen and careful observer, aware of the unspoken language that passes between people who have lived for generations in places like Panther and Estep Ridge, should dare attempt it. Ms. Davis has found the language to express the ineffable, something that Jack Weller (Yesterday's People) and others of his stripe never quite "got." Her story is a confession of a love affair with home and its people who are linked to one another and the land in a manner seldom understood by mainstream America, frenetic in its zeal to get somewhere else. From the introduction in Lucinda's Mountain by Dr. Jerry Beasley, President Emeritus, Concord University.)

Adda Leah Davis has written a book with characters that are realistic and compelling without being overly romantic or idealized- not an easy task...by Dr. Thomas Keats McKnight, Professor Emeritus of English, Southwest Virginia Community College, Richlands, VA. This appeared in an article by Heather Powers in the Lebanon, News, Lebanon, VA.

"Hey there Lady, Just wanted you to know that I finished (and Loved) The Beckoning Hills. I hope that somewhere in the future we get to read about Lucinda's "Happily Ever After." As always I was pleased as punch with your creative mind. You are a jewel to be treasured!!. (Facebook entry of Vickie Hagerman)

FARTHER ALONG

FARTHER ALONG

By

ADDA LEAH DAVIS

Mountain State Press, Inc.
Charleston, West Virginia

International Standard Book Number: 978-0-941092-67-8

Library of Congress Catalogue Number: 2012944915

1 2 3 4 5 6 7 8 9 0

Cover Art by Rhonda Whited

Cover Design by David C. Brown

Book Design by William Haydon

Mountain State Press, Inc.

2300 MacCorkle Avenue, SE

Charleston, WV 25304

www://mountainstatepress.org

Printed in

The United States of America

DEDICATION

This book is dedicated to my Grandfather, Cicero Wagner, who was the anchor to my soul until he died when I was five years old. He taught me to write.

FARTHER ALONG

CHAPTER 1

"I can't even offer to drive you home, can I?" The tall man with mingled black and gray hair asked with raised eyebrows and a quirky smile. "Your son saw to that, didn't he?" Dr. Jason McCall stood in front of the Whitewood Volunteer Fire Department looking down at Lucinda Harmon Marshall. He was dressed in a gray tee shirt and worn denims, borrowed from one of the firemen and the pants were much too short for him.

"I guess he did. He asked me to drive his car to Welch." Jason looked so ridiculous that Lucinda had trouble not laughing outright. She smiled and Jason reached for her hand. Lucinda hesitantly drew back and Jason dropped his hand. He gave her a puzzled look and then shrugged his shoulders.

When Jason McCall had left Welch that morning dressed in his usual white shirt and tie, slacks, and a sport coat he hadn't once thought that he would go into the river and be baptized in his good clothes. He did though, and now dressed in pants borrowed from a very short fireman, he was standing in front of the woman who had remained in his heart and mind for over twenty years.

Lucinda Harmon had waited for three years for some message from Jason McCall. His wife had been dead for three years and so had her husband. Their last meeting had led to disaster for Lucinda and now she really didn't know how to act. *I don't know what he wants. He doesn't act like I thought he would,* thought Lucinda as she gave him a wary look.

"Well, I guess I can walk you to your car since I'll be following you back to Welch. Are you ready to leave? I want to get out of this outfit."

Lucinda suddenly gave way to a nervous giggle. "You do look funny."

"Look funny. I feel ridiculous. These pants don't even cover my ankles. Are all their local firemen short?"

Lucinda looked down and saw shoes, no socks, and hairy legs, above red muddy ankles. "How come your ankles are muddy?"

He grinned. "I think your dad and Preacher Hiram led me to the muddiest bottom they could find to baptize me."

They both laughed and then he did grasp her hand. "Come on, woman. Let's get on the road before anyone else starts admiring my beautiful ankles."

"I can't go yet. I have to go back to Dad's house first," she said, pulling her hand away.

"Why? Don't tell me you still have to ask your dad's permission to date."

This was the same Dr. Jason McCall that Lucinda Harmon had met when she was sixteen years old, but that Jason hadn't spoken to her in this sarcastic tone. *He thought I was a dumb hillbilly back then and apparently he still does, but he wasn't sarcastic,* thought Lucinda.

Lucinda turned red. "No, I don't have to ask Dad's permission for anything, and I don't like your sarcastic comment. As to a date, I don't know where you got that idea."

Jason stood, looking as if he didn't understand what was being said. Lucinda saw his puzzlement and felt she may have been too quick to take offense.

"Danny and I left our luggage at Dad's. You go on. I'll be fine. I drive over Caretta and Coalwood mountains by myself all the time," she said, trying to assume a cool demeanor. For some reason she felt rather gauche and somehow embarrassed.

"I promised your son I would follow you. Are you tempting a newly baptized church member to break his promise? I didn't mean to sound sarcastic. I think I was remembering the first time I asked you out. I know I had to ask your dad that time," he said and smiled.

Lucinda felt as backward and shy as she had the first time Jason had asked her out. *I should be past that, by now*, she silently chided herself.

"I- I'm- sorry. I just don't know you now. I thought I knew you twenty years ago, but you've changed," said Lucinda, her eyes pleading for understanding.

"We've both changed, Lucinda. Did you think we wouldn't change? Everybody does, you know."

They were standing by the road above the river. The man who had played such a havoc- producing role in her life had just been baptized. He had gone to the fire station and changed his sodden clothes for clothes borrowed from a fireman. A box in the trunk of his car now held his wet clothing.

Soon they were standing beside a new BMW. "What happened to your beautiful black Chevrolet?" asked Lucinda, remembering their first real encounter. The first time she had seen him was when he stopped to ask if she wanted to ride, but the second time was different. She had been walking down Brushy Ridge near a mud puddle when a car came careening up the hill and around the curve, causing her to jump to the side of the road. Jumping wasn't usually a problem, but that day her arms were filled with two bags of groceries. She'd heard a scraping sound as his shiny new black Chevrolet had gone into the ditch line and skidded along the bank.

He laughed. "You caused me to ruin my car by walking in the middle of the road on a curve. When I tried to keep from hitting you I scraped the entire right side. It was never the same and I loved that car."

Lucinda smiled. "I'm sorry. You still had it when . . . Well, the last time I saw you before you got married," she finished in a mumble.

He didn't reply at first, but became seemingly lost in thought. "I kept that car for ten years. I didn't drive it. It was up on blocks in the back of my garage."

Lucinda stood, silently remembering the night he had taken her to the Sterling Drive-In in Welch. It all came flooding back and she thought, *If Nat King Cole were only singing, Too Young it would be perfect.* Their first date passed like a kaleidoscope through her mind.

Lucinda Marie Harmon met Dr. Jason McCall at sixteen when she was like a burgeoning bud ready to burst into bloom. Since then, the storms in life had torn at the petals, leaving anguish and jagged inner scars, but still the rose was resilient and continued on, just as Lucinda was resilient.

At sixteen Lucinda had looked at the grown-up world with dream-filled eyes, seeing nothing but excitement, challenge, romance, and love. Meeting a handsome stranger fit right in with all the many stories of knights and dashing heroes that filled the myriad books she read.

At that time, McDowell County, like all the mountainous counties in West Virginia, was riddled with long, rutted, dusty roads. Brushy Ridge on the top of Bradshaw Mountain was one of those roads. Lucinda had lived on that ridge all of her sixteen years, but the day she first saw Jason McCall the dust and ruts were forgotten. She day-dreamed all the way home after that first meeting. *He stopped and asked me to ride;* she exulted as she made her way in a bemused state.

That first meeting was in August and on the second meeting, still in August, Jason had almost run her down in his car. He ended up carrying her to his car and taking her home.

In the intervening years both Lucinda and Jason had married. Lucinda knew her marriage hadn't been a happy one, but she didn't know about Jason's. She did know that Danny, her son was dating Emily, Jason's daughter and today Danny and Emily had united with her church and like a miracle, so had Jason.

What does he know about our faith? He can't really know, thought Lucinda. She knew that most people joined when they first felt God's spirit in their hearts, but that did not mean that they knew much about what they were uniting with. *I guess he'll learn like everyone else does.*

While waiting for everyone in the baptismal rite to change from their wet clothing into the extra clothing they'd brought with them, Lucinda had walked slowly up the hill from the riverbank thinking, *His being here and uniting with our faith seems like a dream come true - a miracle really. I've had daydreams and night dreams about him for twenty years, but I don't really know him. I was just a backward hillbilly with stars in my eyes and he is the Jason that lived in my dreams,* kept running through her mind.

The others had come prepared, but not Jason. He now stood before her in those ridiculously short pants and she didn't know how to act. She realized Jason wanted to renew their acquaintance, but she was at a loss as to how to respond.

"Lucinda, these hills kept calling me. I thought I'd leave and never return when Janet died, but a voice in these hills beckoned me. It called me in my dreams at night and tormented my thoughts during the day. Finally, I told Dad I had to return. He thought I had lost my mind."

Jason remembered Henry McCall's astonishment. "Jason, you don't have to go back to work. Your grandfather left both you and Frank well-off in trusts and financial investments. Besides Doctors Memorial has closed and your job at Stevens Clinic is in jeopardy"

"I know all that, Dad, but both Emily and I feel that we have to go back," Jason replied solemnly.

Henry McCall was exasperated. "If you feel that you have to work, you know that you have a job with the Mellon Institute anytime you feel ready. Surely, you're not going to give all that up and go back to nothing."

Jason still shook his head. "I still have to go back, Dad. I'll work at the Stevens Clinic hospital as long as it is in operation." He looked at his father without really seeing him, and then said, "I may start my own eye clinic since there is a real need down there."

Now, Jason stood reflecting on his actions. After Janet's death and the devastating revelation he had encountered he didn't know what he really wanted to do, but he did know that the hills were calling him. Emily had helped him make the decision to return to McDowell County as well as his dreams of the woman he had never forgotten. He'd had to explain his motives to his old mentor at the Mellon Institute who had gotten him a position there.

Stevens Clinic hospital had eagerly taken him on when Doctor's Memorial had closed. He was hired with the agreement that he would begin but would be allowed leave for several months due to Janet's illness.

Lucinda stood stock still with her eyes widened, in stunned amazement. She was almost bereft of speech, but finally stammered. "Did. . . did you dream that the hills were calling to you to come home, too?" This was incredible. They couldn't have been having the same dreams.

"Yes, I did, Lucinda. I tried everything, but when any problem arose the same dreams appeared. Did you give your dreams a name?"

Lucinda looked up at the face that had been embedded in her heart and mind for so long and was suddenly afraid. She hesitantly replied, "No, I didn't give my dreams a name."

Jason waited so she continued, "I felt too guilty because I kept dreaming about a voice calling me and it wasn't my husband's."

Jason looked down at her. Her eyes revealed a troubled wariness. *She's afraid of me,* he thought. "Lucinda, we can't control our dreams. I felt guilty too; especially when Janet was so sick, but I couldn't stop the dreams."

They were still standing by his car and now Jason said, "Why don't we just leave my car here and ride together to your dad's?"

"You don't have to go. If you still want to follow me, you can wait here until I get back. It won't take long," replied Lucinda.

"I'd rather go to your dad's house. I'd like to see if I've remembered it correctly."

Lucinda shrugged and opened the door to Danny's car. Jason went around the hood and got in on the passenger's side. Soon they had climbed Bradshaw Mountain and were turning down Brushy Fork Ridge road.

"Well, will miracles never cease? The road is graveled. When did this happen?" Jason asked.

Lucinda grinned. "They graveled it last year. Dad said when the Republicans get in this time, they'll pave it."

"He may have to wait a long time. This is a Democratic county, but that shouldn't have anything to do with whether a road is paved or not."

Lucinda was puzzled, but felt she needed to explain herself. "It does if everybody on this ridge is a dyed-in-the wool Republican. If you're not in with that clique in Welch you may as well bay at the moon as ask for some improvement."

Jason gave her quizzical look. "What do you mean 'clique' in Welch?"

"Well, that's what it is. Jennings Boyd and Doc Whitley are vying for the Democratic chairmanship and even a Democrat is uneasy about who he is seen with," stated Lucinda uneasily.

"I serve on the school board. Does that mean I'm in the clique?" queried Jason.

Lucinda hadn't expected that, but felt she should be honest. "I guess it does since the County Clerk controls the county commission and the board of education. Used to be the Democrats fought the Republicans, but now there are so few Republicans in the county that the

Democrats have started fighting each other," said Lucinda turning to Jason with wary eyes.

"Well, Mrs. Eisenhower, I'll have you know that I'm my own person. Nobody pulls my strings. I'm not a puppet."

"I didn't mean you were, but why does the school board allow the assistant superintendent to pass out cards for a candidate on the school grounds? Or is that not one of your strings?" asked Lucinda while wishing that this conversation had never started. Danny had told her that he worked at Stevens Clinic Hospital and also served on the school board.

By this time they were pulling into the parking place below the home of her parents, Burb and Nancy Harmon. Lucinda shut off the engine and turned to look at Jason who was sitting in bemused silence. Lucinda had a stricken look until Jason smiled and Lucinda realized he was enjoying himself.

Jason knew he looked upset, but he really wasn't. Sure he was shocked, at first, by this far-more-out-spoken Lucinda, but when he saw her red- faced, unhappy look, he laughed. "So, you are also a dyed-in-the-wool Republican, just like your dad?"

"I'm a conservative thinker, Dr. McCall, but I'm proud to be likened to my dad," replied Lucinda in what she hoped was an angry voice, as she opened her door.

Jason opened his door with a grin on his face. "Is it safe for me to come in? If we go in with you mad enough to burst a blood vessel I don't know what Burb Harmon will say to me."

"I'm not mad and Dad doesn't know what we were talking about. Come on in," said Lucinda and dropped her head to hide her own grin.

Burb and Nancy welcomed Jason as the new brother in their church and offered him coffee. Jason realized that they were unsure as to how they should act around him. *They'll get used to me, but right now I'm still the doctor and they are the mountain folks,* he thought pensively.

Lucinda soon came out with two suitcases. She put them down to hug her parents and when she had finished Jason stood with both pieces of luggage in his hands. They said their good-byes and soon had the car loaded.

CHAPTER 2

When Lucinda stopped Danny's car in the street across from Jason's house in Welch she still felt bewildered. She and Jason had talked on the return from the top of Bradshaw Mountain, but they'd tried to pick subjects of a neutral nature and didn't bring up their past relationship. Lucinda didn't know whether she should or not and Jason hadn't seemed to want to.

Instead they talked about how much Burb and Nancy had aged since 1950, about Emily and Danny, about the desolation in the area with houses boarded up, blank windows staring from closed businesses, littered roadways, abandoned cars, neglected houses, and beer joints spilling their excess of unemployed workers onto the sidewalks.

They had agreed that the boom and bust of the coal industry had exacerbated the creeping apathy of the people, which led to the neglect of almost everything.

"Absentee landlords created most of the problems," stated Jason adamantly. He quickly glanced at Lucinda trying to gauge her reaction.

Lucinda had listened to him without interrupting. When he stopped she couldn't hold back any longer. "The union's demands for higher and higher wages and other benefits for miners have forced everybody else to live with a cost of living based on those high wages. That isn't fair. That's like the 'haves and have nots.' Everybody else is really strapped just trying to feed their families and pay their bills. I'd be apathetic too, wouldn't you?"

"You can't believe that all this is caused by the unions. Don't you think the coal companies, that own all the land, should do more than what they do?" asked Jason in a calm manner.

"All I ever hear from politicians is that absentee landlords don't pay their fair share of the taxes. If that is true, why are the same representatives who never mention increased taxes for the "so-called" absentee landlords, sent to the state and federal governments to be their representatives" Lucinda gave him a thoughtful look. "To use your own words from twenty years ago, 'it seems that somebody hasn't been minding the store.'" She grinned mischievously.

"I did say that," didn't I? Jason said, breaking into a wide grin and then asked, "Do you remember everything I said?"

Lucinda turned red. "No," she blurted and then got back to their original topic. "I'll grant you the point that the coal operators have often treated their men unfairly. I'll even concede that their actions probably ushered in the unions, but you can't ever make me believe that a one party system has been good for the state of West Virginia," declared Lucinda adamantly.

"Lucinda, we're not talking about political parties, but the plight of the miners. I know that If miners don't band together and make demands on the companies they will be treated much worse. The mine owners live in the big houses and drive the big cars all on the backs of the men laboring under the ground."

"So, you think that, say for an example, that if I open a store and hire three people to work for me, and these people also needed a job, that I shouldn't buy a new car if I want one. After all, the men wouldn't have any work had I not opened the store, would they, Jason?"

"No, they wouldn't have any work, but you shouldn't put them in harm's way and then begrudge them benefits."

"That's why they need a board of arbitration, made up of miners, owners, a lawyer, a merchant, and an ordinary citizen. They should all be able to vote a secret ballot on all decisions which would hinder any coercion. Doesn't that make sense? The way it is now, miners pay into the unions and then their money is used like our social security funds are used; anyway the unions want to use them. Union dues are used to back any candidate the union officials want to back whether the miners like that person or not. Now, you tell me how fair that is? Are the miners treated fairly?"

Lucinda was so caught up in proving her point that she, at first, didn't even realize they were back at the water's edge. She pulled to a stop and Jason got out of Danny's car to go to his own. He stopped. "Lucinda, I don't know where we will go from here, but I already know that we certainly won't be bored along the way." Jason got into his car and laughed as he motioned for her to follow him.

Lucinda had driven along behind Jason going over all they had talked about. "Well, we certainly have a difference of opinion about the role of unions and governments, that's for sure." She stated this aloud and also realized that there were probably many more things that they would differ on. After all they had only known each other a very short time before he married Janet Washburn and she had married Jeff Marshall. Their paths had crossed three or four times in the ensuing twenty years; each with unpleasant results for Lucinda, and those times were certainly not enough to learn much about each other. The more she thought about it the less likely it seemed that an amicable relationship could exist between them.

She'd followed Jason over Caretta and Coalwood mountains and pulled in behind him when he pulled into a wide spot on the side of the highway when they left Route 16 to take Route 52 toward Welch. Jason got out of his car and came back to her window.

"When I get to my house, I'll put my signal on and you can either pull in behind me or you can park across the street from the house."

"I'll just pull in behind you. Since Danny was only driving Emily back home, he'll probably be ready to leave, anyway," she replied.

Jason raised his eyebrows. "I doubt that. I've seen very few young men who are anxious to leave a pretty girl."

Lucinda didn't say anything, but thought that Jason McCall didn't know her Danny.

Emily and Danny came out onto the carport. "Come on in, Mom. We've made supper."

Jason raised his eyebrows and grinned. "See, you should listen to an older and wiser head."

Before Lucinda could make any comment, a door opened in the house next to Jason's and Rita Bender stepped out onto the front patio. "Lucinda Harmon! What are you doing here? I've not seen you in ages."

Lucinda ran across the driveway and threw her arms around Rita. "Rita, my goodness, how good it is to see you. I didn't know you lived on this street."

"I thought I told you that I lived on Browns Creek," said Rita.

"You did, but I always think of Blakely Field as Browns Creek. I've looked as I drove down that part of the street every time I've been through here." Lucinda and Rita were obviously so pleased to see each other that Jason didn't interrupt. That didn't deter Emily, however. She yelled, "Aunt Rita, we have supper ready and it's getting cold. You two can catch up after supper."

The table was spread with hamburger buns and meat patties, cheese, relish, tomatoes, lettuce, onions, and mayonnaise. "I guess this means I have to make my own, doesn't it?" Jason picked up a plate and began to help himself. When he saw Lucinda standing back, he turned.

"Lucinda, grab a plate. This is supper for everybody, which includes you."

"Sure, Mom, we knew you'd be hungry. We haven't eaten since this morning, remember," said Danny with a smile.

"That's right. I haven't eaten either. It's surprising what one forgets under certain circumstances," said Jason.

Soon everyone had a plate of food and a drink and was settled around a table in the dining room. Lucinda looked around the room and liked what she saw. The furniture looked like pale maple. The walls were papered in a silk textured mauve with a pale green stripe. The drapes were a darker mauve with green leaves.

"Do you like my home, Lucinda?" asked Jason.

"This room is really nice. Your wife must have had good taste."

"She did, but Emily and I redecorated after we moved back."

"Yes, and we argued a lot, didn't we, Dad," said Emily, looking quizzically at Jason.

Jason shrugged his shoulders. "I had no idea that it would look this good. I wanted it in browns and beiges, but Emily wouldn't hear of it."

He laughed. "No need to gloat, Emily, just because you got your way." He looked across the table at Danny.

"Do you and your Mom argue? I'll bet she can be stubborn," said Jason, looking sideways at Lucinda who turned a becoming red.

"Mom's only stubborn about her faith and . . .," to be interrupted by Jason. "She's stubborn about politics, too. I found that out today."

Danny looked puzzled for a moment. "I never thought of Mom as being pro-Democrat or pro-Republican. I've known her to support candidates from both parties."

"Hm-m, I would have sworn she was a hard-headed Republican, just like your grandfather. I know for certain that she is against organized labor," said Jason, looking at Lucinda.

"Unions were started by communists and I don't have communist leanings. I believe in free enterprise. I told you that I felt the men had been treated unfairly many times. It isn't that I don't sympathize with miners. I certainly do. My brother Gordon has been a miner all his life and every time I hear of a mine explosion I quake with fear. I even believe they earn every penny they receive, but I don't believe that unions should have such a stranglehold on the coal industry," stated Lucinda adamantly.

Now, she had everyone's attention. "Dad, I think you're wrong. Lucinda isn't stubborn; she just has strong opinions."

Jason grinned. "Maybe so, but I'll bet money that the devil himself couldn't sway her." He looked expectantly at Lucinda. "Am I right?"

Lucinda looked around the table. "Yes, you are right. The devil couldn't get me to change, but the Lord could. The only thing is the devil believes like you do and the Lord is on my side." She grinned impishly.

"Oh-ho!" She's got you there, Dad. How are you going to combat that?" Emily chortled.

Danny smiled at Lucinda with admiration. "I doubt if the Lord would get involved, but HE is definitely on your side, Mom."

Jason stuck his hand out to Danny across the table. "Let's shake on that, son. The Lord is truly on her side and has been all her life."

Danny sat staring reflectively. "Well, there have been times that she and I have both doubted. We've been there haven't we, Mom?"

"Everybody has trials." Lucinda smiled at Danny. "He's always been there for us, though. He knew what we needed. We only knew what we thought we needed."

CHAPTER 3

Lucinda and Danny were seated at the table facing Jason and Emily while discussing the future. "Mom has sold the house in Rock. She is storing all the furniture that I don't need in Uncle Sam's room over his garage. I don't know what I'm going to do until I leave for college nor do I know what she's going to do," said Danny.

"What are your plans, Lucinda?" asked Jason. "Did you not like teaching in Pineville. Emily told me you had retired."

Lucinda picked up her glass and took a sip of water. "Yes, I really liked working with the children, but I feel rather unsettled right now. I thought I'd stay with Mom and Dad a few weeks until I am more settled. I think Danny's leaving has left me with no responsibility. I don't know what to do with myself."

"Why don't you move to Welch? You know Aunt Rita and Dad. Dad's on the school board. Couldn't you help her get a job, Dad?" asked Emily.

Jason started to speak but stopped when he saw Lucinda's shocked expression. "Move to Welch!" There's nothing in Welch for me. No, I . . . I just need some time to think this through. I may decide to go back to college."

"Not to WVU, I hope," said Danny and all eyes jerked to him. "I mean, I wouldn't feel like I'd finally left home if you were there."

Lucinda looked puzzled. "I didn't know I was that clinging or domineering and I thought you were going to Marshall. Have you changed your mind?"

Danny grimaced. "Gosh Mom, I guess you've forgotten. West Virginia University offered me a scholarship and I decided to go there instead of Marshall. I told you several months ago. I'm surprised that you forgot it, but you had all that business of selling the house on your mind."

Lucinda had a bewildered look on her face. "No, I remember you talking about it, but I don't recall you saying you were definite. I had been thinking of taking some classes, but since you're not going to Marshall and me taking classes seems to bother you, I guess I won't."

"It isn't that, Mom, but it's just that you are pretty old-fashioned," said Danny, giving her a tender knowing smile.

"I . . . I'm not old-fashioned, but I do have a strict moral code. I always thought you did as well, Danny."

"I do have a strong moral compass, Mom. You know that, but young people don't worry as much about appearances as you do."

Jason and Emily had sat watching the facial expressions of first Danny and then Lucinda, but neither of them spoke. Lucinda, aware of their watchfulness said, "Well, we can discuss this later. I'm going on home. If you're going you'll have to come too."

"Don't go! This is getting very interesting," said Jason with raised eyebrows. Seeing Lucinda's disgruntled look, he added, "I think Emily probably feels the same way about me, Lucinda."

Lucinda arose and started clearing the table. "You'll have to discover that from her. She seems a very level-headed girl."

Jason was busily helping to clear the table, as were Danny and Emily. They both spoke at the same time. "We have a . . .," started Emily to be interrupted by Danny. He turned red as he said, "We've been discussing a way to save some money when we go to the University. At first, neither of you will approve, but I'm sure you will see the benefits if you will only hear us out."

Jason stopped with a pile of paper plates in his hand and Lucinda stopped wiping down the table. They stood staring at Danny. Emily hurriedly moved to his side and grasped Danny's hand.

"We've thought about this from every angle and we think it is a very good plan," she said, looking up at Danny for approval.

Jason dumped the plates in the garbage can and Lucinda took the dish cloth back to the sink. They turned together. "What is this plan that you have both thought up?" asked Lucinda, grasping the back of one of the chairs.

"Yes, we'd like to hear what you two have hatched up," said Jason, pulling out a chair and turning to Lucinda, "Sit down, Lucinda. This may take a while."

Lucinda sat down and Jason took the chair next to hers. They sat waiting. Finally Danny spoke. "Emily and I plan to rent an apartment together in Morgantown."

"You're what? Danny, you can't. You know that's . . . Well, not right. I wouldn't have believed that you would even consider such a thing," said a stunned Lucinda.

"Emily had first planned to go to Marshall College with me, but when I got the scholarship she changed her mind also. Then too, her girlfriend decided not to go to college at all and she didn't want to go without knowing somebody. Also, Emily's afraid to live by herself," Danny explained.

"So, you both had several reasons to change your minds about going to Marshall, I guess. I hope this idea wasn't part of it." Lucinda gave Danny a bewildered look.

"It isn't what you people think. We will have separate bedrooms. It is just that it will be a lot cheaper and safer for Emily. She's afraid to live by herself and she doesn't want to live in the dorm and neither do I," said Danny as if Lucinda and Jason hadn't been thinking reasonably.

"Well, that's too bad, but it isn't right. I certainly do not approve and neither will the church," stated Lucinda.

"The church won't know anything about it," blurted Emily.

"What's done in secret will be rewarded openly. Danny, you've read the scriptures enough to know that," stated Lucinda.

Jason interrupted. "That's not the problem I have. I know the nature of young men and young women also and whether you intend for it to happen or not nature will take its course. I'm not sure you two are ready for that kind of commitment."

Lucinda gasped. "Oh, so you think it's all right to sin as long as they are committed to it. I've never heard such nonsense in my life. Church members are to keep themselves unspotted from the world and not cast a slur on the church. That's my main objection."

"Don't you want Danny to be with me, Lucinda?" asked Emily who had thought Lucinda really liked her.

Lucinda was astonished. "This has nothing to do with whether I want you to be with Danny or not except I don't want it to happen without the proper credentials."

"Oh, you mean some preacher saying some words and giving them a piece of paper makes it all right. Well, let me tell you that without loving each other all the papers in the world won't make it right," stormed Jason.

Lucinda dropped her head since she knew that the marriage license she had received when she married Jeff Marshall had brought on years of misery. Thinking back she still knew that she couldn't sleep with a man without being married first. *That's part of my moral compass and it has steered me through,* she thought and felt sad that Danny didn't understand her.

Danny came over stooped down beside her. "Okay, Mom. You're right and I know it, but how else can we solve this problem?"

"Danny, you know that your dad's insurance money was put aside for your education, so there's no question about money," said Lucinda.

"I know, Mom, but that still doesn't make Emily feel safe."

"Did you think about being safe when you first planned to go to Marshall?" Lucinda asked as she looked at Emily.

"Mary Lou Sargent had planned to go to Marshall and she and I were going to room together, but now she is getting married and is not going to college at all," explained Emily.

Lucinda and Jason exchanged a look. "Emily, dear, I do understand, but I'd be lying if I said I approved, because I don't," said Lucinda. "This will take some thought, but surely there is a better answer."

"I know that I have to come to terms with Emily being an adult and I guess this is a test." Jason turned and looked thoughtfully at Lucinda. "I wouldn't have a problem with it if I thought they were ready for a real commitment," said Jason.

"I would," gasped Lucinda. "The scriptures tell us to shun the very appearance of evil and even though they may conduct themselves in a chaste fashion it would still appear unseemly to others."

"Are you worried about what other people will say or about what God thinks?" questioned Jason.

Lucinda turned startled eyes toward him. "Both, I guess," she blurted.

Jason saw her bewilderment and quickly changed the subject. "Well, I think we are going to have to accept that our children are two adults and we can't expect them to live and act according to our beliefs and values. So let's leave them to make these decisions while you and I go over and visit your friend Rita Bender."

Lucinda looked so lost that Jason felt he couldn't stand it. "Come on, Lucinda. You told Rita you would talk to her after we ate."

Lucinda slowly got to her feet and followed Jason out of the room. "Jason, I really don't know if I can visit right now. I'm so torn up on the inside."

Jason took her hand and led her to the sofa in the living room. "Let's sit down here and look at our options."

After a short silence Lucinda spoke up. "I think . . ., no, I'm sure you spoke what I've been dreading. Danny is an adult, isn't he?"

"I'm afraid so, Lucinda. Emily is too and I no longer can make her do anything she doesn't want to do. However, I'm sure that our influence will sway them whether we openly voice it or not. They've heard our values and beliefs from the day they were born and they are both very fine young people. I'm going to try to trust them to make the right decisions most of the time."

"I know Danny is a fine young man and Emily is equally good, but I just can't say I approve of young people living together without marriage," said Lucinda in a defeated voice.

"Listen, why don't we try to put this out of our minds by going over to Kyle and Rita's? A change of topic may be the very thing we need right now," urged Jason, rising from his seat.

Lucinda heaved a heavy sigh and rose as well. "I did tell Rita I would talk to her later, or rather Emily did, so I guess I'd better talk to her or she will think I've forgotten what a good friend she has always been to me."

Rita's joyous greeting helped to lift Lucinda out of some of the cloud which had cast her into the doldrums or whatever mood the past hour had created.

When they went back to Jason's house Emily met them at the door. "Dad, can you drive Danny's mother home. Danny wants to stay a while longer to see if we can work something out? Jason looked down at Lucinda and smiled.

"Sure, I'll drive a pretty woman home every chance I get, but I don't know how this woman feels about it."

Knowing that Danny had seen how disturbed she had been by their decision, Lucinda gladly accepted Jason's offer to drive her home.

CHAPTER 4

Lying in bed that night in an almost empty house, Lucinda felt more alone than she had in twenty years. Her husband was dead and even though it made her feel guilty she wasn't sad. She felt a sense of relief. Danny's leaving, however, seemed almost more than she could bear. *I don't know what he and Emily will do, but I guess Jason was right. We really can't keep Danny and Emily from doing whatever they want to do. I still don't like it, though,* she thought as she tossed and turned.

She'd enjoyed her visit with Rita, but now she was uneasy about her. Rita had never been fat, but now she was very thin. When asked if she was dieting, Rita had revealed that she had a bad heart condition. Lucinda had tried to pray for Rita before she lay down and now she felt she needed to entreat the Lord again on her friend's behalf and once again knelt by her bedside.

Lucinda was still awake when Danny's headlights lit up the room as he passed going to the garage. *I'll not mention anything tomorrow. I don't want our last few weeks together to be fraught with arguments.*

When she awoke the next morning Lucinda put on a bright smile and left her room expecting to see Danny. Instead, she found a note on the kitchen counter near the coffee pot. "I've made coffee, Sleepy Head, so get a cup and perk up. I think we have worked things out to your satisfaction," Lucinda read his note and smiled as the heaviness she had been feeling eased a little.

The phone rang before she could get her coffee poured. "Lucinda, this is Jason. Good Morning!"

"Good Morning, Jason. Is something wrong?"

"Wrong! Why should something be wrong if I called you?"

"Well, you've never called me before," said Lucinda in a questioning voice.

"Well, no, I've not called you, but what kind of reception would a call from me have received while Mr. Marshall was alive?"

"Jeff's been dead almost four years and you never called. That's what surprised me. Why now?"

There was no answer for a minute and Lucinda was almost ready to hang up when Jason spoke. "I was afraid to try to contact you after the way I talked to you at the Pineville Vo-Tech School. I'll never forget how you looked as long as I live. I don't know how I could have said those things to you."

When Lucinda didn't say anything, Jason continued. "The only excuse I have is that Janet was dying with cancer and I had dreamed about you that night. I guess guilt could have caused it, so I lashed out instead of taking you in my arms as I wanted to."

Lucinda stood there with tears creeping slowly down her cheeks.

"Lucinda, Lucinda! Are you there?" asked Jason anxiously.

"Yes, Jason," I'm here," she said softly.

"Are you crying?"

"Yes, I am. I'll never forget that day either Jason, but not as much because of what you said, as that it was the day that I lost my baby."

"Lost your baby!" gasped Jason and stood listening. "Lucinda, may I come over there?"

"I . . . I don't know, Jason."

"Please, Lucinda. I need to talk to you." Jason's voice had such compassion and regret that Lucinda couldn't have refused him.

"All right, Jason. Do you know where I live?"

"Oh yes. I even know when you changed your curtains. I've parked on that hill at the top of your street and looked at your house numerous times. I never got the nerve to come down and speak to you, however."

"What kind of vehicle were you in? An old battered truck used to park there. Danny noticed it first and then I took Jeff's binoculars and looked at it myself, but I couldn't see anyone in it. Were you driving that truck?"

"Guilty! I borrowed Jim Hurley's truck. He was the night watchman at the hospital. Janet was so jealous and suspicious that I feared she would somehow find out if I drove my own car. I'm so ashamed that I did that while still married to Janet, but I did it." Jason waited for a second and then chuckled. "I'm surprised I wasn't reported to the police and charged with stalking."

"If it had been on a regular basis someone would have reported it, but one month it would be there and then it would be two or three months before it happened again," said Lucinda.

"I'd fight the temptation to see you for months and then break down and look for you again," said Jason quietly.

Lucinda was amazed. "Jason, I . . . I don't know what to say. You felt as guilty as I did, didn't you?"

"I'm hanging up, Lucinda. I'll be over there in about thirty minutes," said Jason firmly. The phone clicked and Lucinda stood staring in bemusement.

When Jason arrived, Lucinda hurried to answer the door bell. She unbolted the door and cracked it to make sure it was Jason and then opened the door. Jason stood on the threshold for a moment. *I've dreamed about what I would say if this ever happened and now I'm at a loss, thought* Jason. He drew in a long breath and said, "Hello, Lucinda."

Lucinda turned red and stepped back to allow him entrance. "Hello, Jason," she said in a wobbly voice.

Suddenly Jason swept her into his arms, almost crushing her against his chest. Like a dam breaking open, Lucinda wept while Jason tenderly ran his hand down her hair and murmured softly. "It's okay, dear. It's all over."

Lucinda pushed away and looked up at Jason who also had tears creeping down his cheeks. Involuntarily Lucinda went back into his arms, but this time her arms were wrapped around him as well. They stood holding each other and rocking as if the rhythm of their lives had suddenly changed.

This is the Jason I fell in love with so long ago. Thank you, Jesus, Lucinda prayed silently. She pushed away from Jason and looked up at him again and he tilted her chin and kissed her softly, but when his kiss became more ardent she quickly backed away.

Jason saw her startled expression. "What? You mean kissing is wrong when people aren't married?"

Lucinda turned red. "No, but I don't want to do that."

"Lucinda, are you afraid of me? I'm not going to take advantage of you. I'm not so hard up for a woman that I'd have to force myself on you," said Jason in a puzzled voice.

Lucinda turned and walked toward the kitchen. "Jason, let's go have some coffee and do some talking, okay?"

"It seems like we need to." Jason followed her into the kitchen and took a seat at the table. Lucinda soon had two cups down and came to Jason first with the carafe of coffee. When both had their coffee prepared to their satisfaction, Lucinda took the seat across from him.

Jason took a drink and looked at Lucinda over the rim of his cup. "So, why were you crying this morning?"

Lucinda looked at him steadily for a second. "Last night I was so disturbed about this thing with Danny and Emily and yet I knew you were right."

"You mean you no longer think that a piece of paper makes a marriage," asked Jason.

"No, that isn't what I meant. I meant your saying that Danny and Emily were adults and we no longer could tell them what to do or not to do. I still think people should be married before they move in together, but I can't make someone else see it my way."

"I don't see why that made you cry," said Jason.

"That's not why I was crying. I had lain awake and decided that I would not mention it to Danny again. I put on a happy face and came into the kitchen to show him everything was all right and he wasn't here. Then I found his note saying they had worked it out to my satisfaction. That made me feel easier, but I felt so alone and lost and then you called and told me that you had suffered the same guilt that I did. I was crying because I realized you had really cared after all." Lucinda felt tears in her eyes again and she blinked and swallowed trying to control her emotions.

"Don't cry anymore, Lucinda. I really do care and I always have. I tried not to, but I kept dreaming that you were calling me and that you needed me. Do you need me, Lucinda?"

"Sometimes I tried to pretend I was with you, but I couldn't believe you would ever act like Jeff. Then I'd go to sleep and dream of you and wake up scared to death that I had talked in my sleep or something. Oh Jason, it has been twenty years of such misery."

Jason got up from his chair and came around the table to take her hand. Let's go in the living room. I need to sit beside you while we talk. I've waited too long to hold you close to me."

They sat side by side pouring out their stories of trying to be faithful to their spouses, but being unfaithful in their hearts. Lucinda could not believe that anyone could be so evil as to hide her letters that she had written to Jason and the letters he had written to her as well. "Are you saying that Janet was in on this?"

"She had the letters in a box and she gave me the key and told me to open the box after she was gone. That's when I found your letters and my replies. She also told me how my own mother had been the instigator of the entire thing," said Jason bitterly.

"Sometimes family can cause a lot of anguish even with good intentions. Grandpa used to say that all the evil in the world was started with good intentions, but back then, I thought he meant our welfare program," Lucinda said smiling impishly.

Jason saw her smile and hugged her tighter. "Your grandfather was a smart man."

"Does that mean that you really aren't a progressive liberal thinker? If you don't believe in redistribution of wealth then there's hope for you yet." Lucinda knew she was deliberately bringing this topic up since what he wanted to talk about was so painful and she was trying to avoid it.

"Oh no, my girl. You're not going to get me into another political argument today. I want to know about the baby you lost," said Jason.

Lucinda shivered and sighed tiredly as if the inevitable had happened. She looked up at Jason and then snuggled closer to him. "I was pregnant but I hadn't told Jeff. I knew he wouldn't want it and would probably accuse me of sneaking around and seeing you. Dr. Wright had told me I should tell Jeff and I thought I would on the weekend after that Career Day at the Vo-Tech School in Pineville. I'd been having problems anyway and was scared of losing it."

Lucinda stopped and said, "I need a drink." Jason jumped to his feet and went toward the kitchen.

"Do you want something from the fridge or just tap water?"

"There's a pitcher of iced tea on the top shelf. Get some for yourself if you want it. The glasses are to the right of the sink."

Soon Jason was seated again and after Lucinda had taken several drinks Jason took her glass and placed it on a coaster on the end table. "What happened after I acted like a jerk?"

Lucinda grimaced and looked at Jason with such a forlorn look that he once again took her in his arms. "You can stop if you want to. You can tell me some other time."

"No, I'll finish it. I was already sick before the Career Day event. I hadn't been feeling good all day, but I didn't want to renege after I promised. Jeff even wanted me to make that presentation since some of his union buddies had talked about it. I was going to do that one last session and then go home, but after you walked out I couldn't. It was like I had no more hope or something."

Jason kissed her cheek and once again told her she could stop, but she took another drink of tea and continued. "Two of the boys carried all my stuff to the car and loaded it and I drove away from the school, but I was so distraught that before I actually got to Pineville I headed my car toward the river."

"You what! Oh God no, Lucinda, you weren't thinking of suicide, surely," said Jason in astonishment.

"Jason, you don't know how miserable my life was. Jeff was mentally sick and I felt sorry for him, but I was also afraid of him. Like you, his mother caused a lot of his problems, and she also contributed to what happened that day. Jeff caused me to lose my baby. He slapped me and when I fell I knocked over a lamp and hit my head. I don't know if the fall or the trauma or something else caused me to lose my baby, but that's when I lost it."

"He slapped you! You mean that brute actually hit you?" Jason jumped to his feet.

"Calm down, Jason. He paid for everything he did and more. He died in a motel fire. Did you know that?"

Jason sat down with a solemn look on his face. "How did that happen?"

Lucinda told him how Geneva Clary, with help from Jeff's mother had caused Jeff to be in the motel, not knowing there would be a fire. "Jason, he wouldn't have slapped me if I hadn't shouted that I wished the baby was yours. He left so quickly that he didn't know I was hurt."

Jason snarled. "He slapped you, but didn't know you were hurt. I find that hard to believe. Was he drunk?"

"According to Geneva's father she had come to the union meeting and given him spiked Coca-Colas. He wasn't used to drinking and it made his problem worse."

Jason heaved a sigh. "Poor fellow! That doesn't mean that I approve of what he did, but he must have been a very troubled man."

Jason put his arm around Lucinda and pulled her close. She put her head back against his arm and sighed. "He was, Jason. I felt sorry for him, made excuses for him, hated him, and felt guilty because I couldn't love him like he wanted me to. I'll always feel guilty I suppose since I married him, knowing that I wasn't in love with him."

Jason kissed her brow. "I felt the same way, especially while taking care of Janet and having to watch her suffer. Cancer is such a cruel disease. I hated myself, and hated you, at times, for being there in my heart and in my dreams."

They sat holding to each other, both grieving in their own way, but finally lulled into a soothing quietness. They had both emptied their guilt on each other which somehow gave them peace.

CHAPTER 5

When Danny and Emily came through the door at three o'clock that evening they found Jason and Lucinda asleep on the sofa lying side by side with their arms around each other.

Jason opened his eyes and put his finger on his lips to indicate that they should be quiet. He pointed at Lucinda who was asleep with her head on his arm and a smile on her face. Jason smiled and made an A-okay sign with his thumb and finger. Danny and Emily smiled as well and tiptoed toward the kitchen. Lucinda stirred, stretched and snuggled closer to Jason, but suddenly opened her eyes and sat up.

Her face was crimson. "Jason, what did we do? I . . . I mean did we go to sleep and fall over together. I don't remember lying down."

Jason grinned. "You didn't. I was sleepy and you were too, so I lay down and pulled you down with me." When he saw her red face and shocked look he laughed out loud.

"Lucinda, we both have all our clothes on. We are as innocent as babies, but that doesn't mean I'm anything like a baby when it comes to you."

Danny and Emily came into the room. "Well, Mom, it seems it's all right for you to sleep with a man you aren't married to, but Emily and I can't share an apartment," said Danny with twinkling eyes.

Lucinda jerked loose from Jason and jumped to the floor. "I didn't . . . we didn't do anything. I . . . ." she stammered.

Emily grinned mischievously. "We know what we saw. Don't we, Danny? My dad and Danny's mom lying locked in each other's arms and fast asleep."

Jason sat up, and giving Danny and Emily a warning look, swung his feet to the floor and stood up. "You two stop kidding. Lucinda and I have been filling each other in on our lives for the last twenty or so years. We were emotionally worn out and fell asleep sitting up. I'm the cause of Lucinda lying down."

Lucinda gave him a grateful look and walked toward the kitchen. "You left me a note that was really puzzling, Danny. Where did you go, so early this morning?

Danny grinned. "We've been to Morgantown."

"Morgantown! You mean you drove there and back already? What time did you leave?"

"I was here at five o'clock this morning and Danny was ready," said Emily smiling broadly. We will not be sharing a room or an apartment, Mrs. Goody-Two-Shoes." She and Danny gurgled with laughter at Lucinda's bewildered look.

Jason came into the kitchen and stood beside Lucinda. "I don't know how you managed that, but Lucinda would have cried all day if I hadn't called and drove over here."

"Her eyes look like she's cried all day anyway," said Danny suspiciously.

Jason looked down at Lucinda. "We both did some crying, but they were cleansing tears." Lucinda looked up at Jason and could hardly believe that her Jason was standing here beside her. She smiled.

"Well, I have cried some, but I feel all clean on the inside and happy," said Lucinda as she looked at Danny.

"Your Mom is the happiest I've ever been in my life except the moment you were put into my arms."

Danny gathered her close in his arms. "Mom, I'm so glad. We both had to live on edge for so many years." Danny looked up at Jason. "You'd better be good to her, she's had enough abuse."

Jason grinned. "I'll be good to her if she will let me. Your mother is a very wary woman, Danny."

"If you'd been abused every . . ." started Danny, but was interrupted by Lucinda.

"Hush, Danny. Some things are better left unsaid." Lucinda walked over to the table and pulled out a chair. "Well, sit down and tell us what you've worked out. I can tell that both of you are bursting at the seams to tell us."

Jason came to sit beside Lucinda and Danny took a seat beside Emily on the back side of the table. "I called Grandmother Washburn last night and we were talking about housing. I told her that Danny and I would like to get a room in the same building so that he could take me to school and be close at night," said Emily. Then Danny took over the story.

"Mrs. Washburn said she had a cousin who was thinking of taking in boarders. She said the woman lived in Morgantown. I asked her to call the lady. Her name is Margaret Handler. She's in her seventies, but spry for her age. Anyway, she has two extra bedrooms and she offered to rent them to us provided we would help around the house." Danny was smiling broadly.

Jason looked at Lucinda. "I know Mrs. Handler and she was always a nice lady, but she didn't seem to be the kind of person to hand out freebies."

"We have to pay rent, Dad, but not as much as we would have had to without being willing to help," said Emily.

Lucinda sat listening, but she somehow didn't feel like the details were important. Jason was sitting here beside her and everything had taken on a dreamlike quality. *I'm worse than a star-struck teenager*, she thought and tried to jerk her mind back to her son.

Jason must have had the same problem since he soon had Lucinda's hand in his and couldn't take his eyes from her face. "Well, all that sounds wonderful to me, but she didn't spell out what she meant by "help" around the house did she?"

"Yes, she did. I'm to do the laundry and any ironing and Danny is to mow the lawn and do the trimming, but she has all the modern equipment," Emily gloated.

"Well, Mom, does this meet your moral standards? Mrs. Handler's bedroom is in the hall between Emily's bedroom and mine and each room has its own bathroom," said Danny with raised eyebrows.

Jason squeezed Lucinda's hand beneath the table where their hands were clasped. "We are very proud of the both of you. That was a very mature thing to do, wasn't it, Lucinda?"

Lucinda pressed Jason's hand and looked up at him with glowing eyes. "Danny, I'm glad you got the scholarship, but some colleges want their freshmen to live in the dorm the first year. Did you and Emily ask about that?"

"No. We didn't have to. Mrs. Handler knew the Dean and she told him we were relatives and were going to live with her so it's all settled. So now we're both going to WVU and everything is going to be fine. That's where Dad always wanted me to go, isn't it, Dad?" asked Emily.

Jason nodded as he grinned at Lucinda. She smiled back at him and said, "Well, I think this is just wonderful. I agree with what Jason said and I think this is better all around. You won't be living with total strangers and a house is safer than an apartment, or I always thought it was, and also WVU is a very good school and you will neither have to live in the dorms."

Jason grinned. "Whatever she says, I agree. Now, that you've eased Lucinda's mind about your sleeping arrangements we can drop that subject. Now, for tonight, I don't know your and Emily's plans, but I'm taking Lucinda to Beckley for the best dinner they have in the classiest restaurant in town."

Emily giggled. "You two are so sweet and silly. Look at them Danny. They are like teenagers on their first date. Maybe we should go with them as chaperones."

"Oh no, Miss Prissy Boots, nobody is going with us tonight. I've waited a long time for this and I think Lucinda has too," said Jason, looking down at Lucinda who nodded happily.

"Well, Emily I guess you and I will have to go back to Welch and eat at the Sterling Drive-In or fix a sandwich at the house. Since we're the grown-ups now I guess we'd better try to pack some of your things for the move to Morgantown. You two go on and have fun, but remember you need to be in no later than twelve," said Danny and then burst out laughing at the look on Lucinda's face.

"What's so funny?" asked Lucinda as if she had suddenly awakened.

"It's your face, Mom. You look like you've been hit with a brick or something. Why are you looking like that?"

Lucinda dropped her clasp on Jason's hand and stepped away from him. "You've just made me realize that I am a mother and you are my first responsibility. I've been acting like a silly teenager."

Danny grabbed her by the shoulders and shook her gently. "I was kidding, Mom. I'm glad to see you acting like a teenager."

"I'm too old to act silly." Then looking over at Jason she said, "I'm sorry, but I don't think I can go out with you this evening."

"Why not? You were okay with it a moment ago. What suddenly changed you?"

"If Danny's going away, I should be helping him pack instead of going out on a date."

Emily broke in with, "I'll help Danny pack and he is going to help me pack. He isn't a little boy anymore and we don't need you to help us." Seeing Lucinda's crestfallen expression, Emily quickly put her arms around her. "Listen, I didn't mean that to be harsh, but we really are both adults and we can pack and do things like that for ourselves. Please don't be upset."

Lucinda turned and walked toward the living room. Jason followed her and when she took a seat, Jason sat down across from her. "I know this is hard for you, Lucinda. It's hard for me, but I think it is probably harder for a mother. Let's go out to dinner and try to get used to adult children instead of dependent children."

"I guess you think I'm just being silly, but Danny and I have been through so much together. We've depended on each other for emotional support and sometimes physical support," said Lucinda thoughtfully. "I . . . It is really hard to just abruptly think differently."

"Emily was the one that saw me through when Janet died. I felt so guilt-ridden that had it not been for Emily I don't know what I would have done," said Jason as he studied Lucinda's face and thought, *she still looks so young except in her eyes. Such sadness shows in her eyes. I wonder what life with that devil was really like.*

Suddenly Lucinda looked at Jason and smiled. "If you still want to take a silly old woman out to dinner, I'll go pretty up."

"You'll have time since I have to go back to Welch. I was in such a hurry to get over here this morning that I didn't take time to put on socks. See," he held out his foot and sure enough he wasn't wearing socks.

Lucinda grinned. "You're always showing me your ankles. At least you aren't wearing that fireman's short pants today."

Jason got to his feet, grinning also. "We should have gotten a picture of that, shouldn't we? I could show it to Mom, but I wouldn't want her to have a heart attack."

"She'll have more than a heart attack if she learns that you have taken me out to dinner," said Lucinda.

Jason raised his eyebrows. "No, she won't. She knows what will happen if she ever acts or says one word negatively about you or to you. We had it out when I found those letters and I have not been a frequent visitor since then."

Lucinda put her hand on Jason's arm. "I'm sorry, Jason. I certainly don't want to be the cause of disruption in your family."

"Lucinda, you didn't cause it. My mother and Janet caused it, but I blame Mom more than Janet. Janet wasn't as class conscious as Mom."

"Well, you'd better go on home if you want to dress up. It's already five o'clock and you heard Danny. We have to be in by twelve," Lucinda said as Danny and Emily came into the room.

"You mean you are still harping on that. Gosh, Mom, I didn't realize you were that easily upset," said Danny.

Lucinda went to him and put her arms around him. "I was kidding, Mr. Marshall. It will take me a while, but I've already started sawing on the apron strings.

Danny hugged her and so did Emily. "Good! Now you two get all dressed up and go have fun."

CHAPTER 6

That evening begin the courtship of Lucinda Harmon Marshall and Jason McCall after a twenty-one year hiatus. They soon learned that, as Jason had proclaimed, 'they were never bored.'

During their dinner in Beckley they discussed their children, sometimes arguing and sometimes agreeing. "Do you think they will marry, Lucinda?" asked Jason.

"Of course they will. They were meant for each other. I've known that since they were in that spelling contest in Beckley," answered Lucinda.

Jason's eyebrows went up. "Oh, yes. I'll not ever forget that. Janet fussed all the way home. I think she suspected that I had planned the whole thing in order to see you."

"I wish fussing was all that Jeff did. He started to hit Danny and I grabbed up Danny's trophy and threw it at him. The trophy is gone for good. I think he would have hit me if Howard, his brother-in-law hadn't intervened," said Lucinda, wincing painfully at the memory.

"That man must have been a pure devil," said Jason in an angry voice.

Lucinda moved the salt shaker around and around in a thoughtful pattern. "I've already told you he had an emotional problem. If he took his medicine and remained calm he was good to me in most ways. Well, he would have thought in all ways, but he wasn't."

"Did he sexually abuse you, Lucinda?" asked Jason solemnly.

Lucinda gasped. "That's too personal, Jason. You have no right ...."

"Okay, okay, don't get upset. That can wait until later. According to Danny, he was terribly jealous. Is that true?"

Lucinda drew in a long breath. "Yes. He was extremely possessive. I was afraid to raise my head or speak to any man when Jeff was present. If my principal hadn't been an old man I think he wouldn't have allowed me to teach."

Jason reached across the table and took Lucinda's hand. "He surely knew that you would never break your marriage vows. Without trust one cannot truly love, or at least I don't think they can."

"I tried to tell him that and he always said that he trusted me, but didn't trust the men," said Lucinda, smiling tiredly. "He was hard to live with, but in his own way I think he loved me."

"Most people love their possessions," said Jason, caressing her hand.

"Let's talk about something else. The past can't be changed, but we can work on our future," said Lucinda with a smile.

"Together, I hope," said Jason with eyebrows raised in question.

Lucinda looked at Jason and knew that she wanted to spend the rest of her life with him and not in her dreams only. She was afraid, however, and said, "I don't know, Jason. We've both changed and we never really knew each other before."

"Yes, we have both changed, but we never forgot each other. That tells me something and then too, we both dreamed about each other, didn't we?"

Lucinda looked at Jason and couldn't hide her feelings. Suddenly Jason jumped to his feet and grasped her hand. "Let's get out of here, Lucinda. We need to talk . . . I mean really talk."

Lucinda didn't say a word as Jason walked with her out the door and to the car. Jason got in and still not speaking started the car and went careening out of the parking lot.

"Jason, slow down! Are you trying to kill us both?" squeaked Lucinda as they pulled onto the highway.

Jason slowed down, but kept a steady sixty as he drove down the highway until the blue lights of a police cruiser flashed behind them. "Well, I'll be damned," said Jason as he pulled to the side of the highway and stopped.

Jason rolled down his window. "Yes, officer, I guess I was speeding. Is that why you pulled me over?"

The officer looked inside the car with his torch. "Why were you in such a hurry? Was there an emergency?"

Jason grinned mischievously. "Yes, her son said we needed to be home by twelve since this is our first date."

Lucinda gasped, but didn't say anything. However, she was glad the policeman couldn't see her face.

The trooper grinned. "Did you know that one of your taillights is out?"

Jason looked stunned. "You mean that I confessed to speeding and you were only stopping me to warn me to get my taillight fixed?"

Now the trooper laughed and shook his head. "Young love, first date and all. Since this is your first date let this be a warning. Get the taillight fixed and slow down. Take your time, man, because it won't last."

Jason looked at the officer. "Thanks Officer, but I believe this will be a life time story."

"You must be a real gambler, but I hope you're right. Good night!"

Jason said, "Good night, Officer." Then rolled up his window and pulled out onto the highway once again. He looked across at Lucinda, "I'm sorry I scared you, but it's your fault."

"My fault! I didn't do anything. What are you talking about?" asked Lucinda in bewilderment.

"I can see that you don't know what I'm talking about. You seem just as innocent and naïve as you were at sixteen. Don't you realize how attractive you are to men?"

Lucinda turned red, but glared at Jason. "I don't do anything to attract anybody; especially men and I never have."

"You aren't doing anything, but being you, Lucinda. There's just a certain appeal about you that men gravitate toward," said Jason as they pulled into Lucinda's driveway.

"That's a bunch of garbage. Nobody has said anything to me and every man I've met has treated me with respect," said Lucinda as she angrily hit the door handle.

"My God, Lucinda," said Jason as he sprang from the car and stomped to her side of the vehicle. He grasped her shoulders. "Listen to me. I didn't mean that men thought you were immoral or indecent. I meant there is an innocence and vulnerability about you that brings out the protective instincts in men."

Lucinda jerked away from his grasp. "Why don't you just go home? I've never had anybody to talk to me like this before. I don't understand what I'm doing that causes this . . . whatever you're talking about."

"No, I'm not going home. Lucinda, you and I are going to have our talk so let's not give your neighbors a free show."

Lucinda unlocked the door and they went on into the house which was now sparsely furnished. "Danny must have moved some more furniture after we left," said Lucinda since the room looked barer than it had that morning. Most of the furniture had already been stored in an upstairs room over Sam and Jill's garage. Lucinda turned as Jason flicked on the overhead lights.

"The couch is still here so sit down if you want to. I'll make some coffee if you would like a cup," said Lucinda as she took off her sweater and placed it on the counter.

"There are still chairs in the kitchen, so let's sit in there. This room looks so empty that it makes me feel uncomfortable," said Jason following her into the kitchen.

Lucinda soon had the coffee perking and produced a cake from a cake pan on the counter. "I bought this Friday evening so I think it's still good."

Jason sat watching her and not speaking. When she had two cups of coffee poured and on a tray with cream and sugar she brought them to the table and sat down. Jason kept his eyes on her as he put cream and sugar into one cup. He still sat looking at her.

"What? Why are you staring at me? You're making me nervous."

"I'm just amazed at how little you have changed," said Jason as he picked up his spoon and stirred his coffee. "Look at me! I'm gray-headed around the edges and have lines and wrinkles, but you look just like you did at sixteen, except you have cut your hair. It looks nice, though." Jason angled his head to the side still looking at her. "Cute and pretty, maybe even beautiful." Jason squinted and angled his head the other way as if trying to get a better view.

Lucinda grinned as she put her elbows on the table and rested her chin in her hands. "I don't see any lines and wrinkles. You still look just like Jason to me."

Suddenly Jason said, "Lucinda, do we have to go through all this? I've loved you since the first time I saw you and I believe you feel the same way about me, so why are we doing this?"

Lucinda knew he was telling the truth, but still was afraid. "I . . . I'm afraid, Jason." Her eyes were wide and tears were ready to spill over."

Jason arose and came to her side of the table. "I know, dear. I know you are, but you have no need to be." Taking her hands he drew her to her feet and into his arms.

Lucinda felt as if she had come home at last and she rested her head against his chest and sobbed. After a minute, Jason pulled out his handkerchief and mopped her face. "Okay, now that's over with, we can go back to the sofa and talk about what we want to do.

When they were seated side by side on the sofa Lucinda asked, "What do you mean when you say, 'what we want to do?'"

"I mean, that I don't see any sense in us wasting time acting like we are two other people who don't love each other. We do love each other and we know that we will get married, so what are we waiting on?"

Lucinda sat up on the edge of the sofa. "Do you mean we should just go get married right now?"

Jason looked at his watch and then turned to her grinning. "Well, not right now. Most preachers are in bed by now, but I think we should go tomorrow and get married." Then he grinned wickedly. "Of course, I could stay with you tonight so we could get an early start in the morning."

Lucinda saw his grin and jumped up. "I don't think so, especially on that last part." Then she smiled smugly.

"You can sleep here on the sofa if you really want to get an early start in the morning."

Jason didn't jump up but rose slowly to his feet. "Lucinda, I'm serious. Will you agree to get married tomorrow if we can?"

Lucinda looked up into his face and solemnly nodded her head yes."

Jason pulled her into his arms and kissed her like she had never dreamed a kiss could be. When she pulled back and stood looking at him with an amazed look on her face, Jason said, "What? You look like you've just discovered something."

With love shining from her eyes she whispered, "I have. I've just discovered that . . . ." She didn't get to finish because she was back in Jason's arms and she didn't mind at all. She didn't mind when they sank to the sofa together. This was the Jason she had dreamed about almost every night of her life and she was now in his arms. When Jason's hand moved down to her hips, however, Lucinda shivered and jerked away so suddenly that Jason tumbled to the floor.

"What's the matter? Why did you shiver and shove me into the floor?" asked Jason as he slowly rose to his feet.

Lucinda was standing beside the sofa, but she looked as if she was ready to faint. She was trembling and her face was ashen. "I thought you were different."

"You thought I was different. I don't think I understand what you mean. How am I supposed to be different?"

Through chattering teeth, Lucinda said, "I thought I could hug you and you wouldn't start putting your hands all over me. That's the way Jeff acted and I ended up . . ., she shivered again. "It was awful."

Jason stood looking at her without saying one word. He really didn't know what to say. Lucinda was a grown woman, but she seemed to think that she could hug and kiss and that was all. When he heard her words though and saw her trembling like a leaf, he realized that her husband must have been very uncaring or something. He raked his hand back through his hair, pursed his lips and walked toward the kitchen.

"Was there any coffee left?" he asked as if nothing had happened.

Lucinda didn't move back as he passed her, but she stood watching him to see what his reaction would be.

"You're angry, aren't you?" she asked.

Jason turned. "Angry! No, I'm not angry, but I am frustrated. What got you into the state you're in? We didn't do anything, but you are acting as if I was trying to rape you."

"That's what you would have done!"

Jason's face turned red and Lucinda could tell that he was enraged. "Lucinda, I have never touched a woman who didn't want me to touch her, so don't ever accuse me of something like that again."

Just then car lights flashed through the windows as Danny's car pulled into the driveway. Jason, who had been standing in a rigid position, suddenly relaxed. "Lucinda, you and I need to have a heart to heart talk."

"You're home early," said Lucinda as Danny came through the door. He looked at his watch.

"Well, two a.m. is early in the morning, but I've been on a long date and it seems like you have too," said Danny, grinning when he saw his mother's red face.

"Danny, Lucinda and I were thinking of getting married tomorrow if we could find a town where people can marry in one day. I don't guess you have heard of a town that allows that, have you?" Jason asked as he looked at Lucinda, trying to gauge her reaction to this comment.

Danny grinned. "Yes, as a matter of fact, I do know of such a town. How much are you willing to pay for the information?"

Jason smiled. "I promise to be the best thing that ever happened to your mother and I'll try to be a good step-father."

"Just be good to my mother. I want her to be happy. This friend of mine and his girlfriend got married last week. They married on Friday and left for Chicago, Illinois the very next day."

Lucinda was still standing by the sofa, but was turned toward the kitchen where Jason and Danny had now taken seats at the table.

"What's the matter, Mom? I'm not going to chastise you for wanting to get married. Come on and sit with us since this is your life," said Danny, grinning widely.

Lucinda walked hesitantly toward the kitchen, but her eyes were on Jason. "I can't talk about getting married yet. I'm not ready." Her eyes were pleading with Jason for understanding.

Jason grinned at her and turned to Danny. "Isn't that just like a woman? Earlier this evening, she agreed that there was no point in us waiting since we already know we love each other. Now she's changed her mind."

Danny looked at Lucinda thoughtfully. "She may need to get some false ideas out of her head. I told you she hadn't been very happy with my father."

"I realize that now, Danny. I think our plans to marry will have to be put on hold, but not by me," said Jason as he looked at Lucinda solemnly.

"Don't rush me," pleaded Lucinda. "Both of you give me some time to think."

Jason left not knowing how long he was going to have to wait, but decided something needed to be done.

CHAPTER 7

For the next week Lucinda did a lot of soul searching since she knew that her fears were unrealistic. "Every man can't be judged by one man," she repeatedly told herself. Even though Jason called she had refused to go anywhere with him or anyone else. She didn't even talk to anyone on the phone. She intermittently read the Bible, tried to pray, and ended up crying.

Danny and Emily were together every day trying to get things ready before the last of August for their move to Morgantown. On Friday evening Danny came home to find Lucinda sitting in the kitchen just staring out the window.

"Mom, why are you sitting here in a practically empty house? You won't answer the phone, you aren't eating, and you're not doing anything. This is not like you. Jason is worried sick and so am I," scolded Danny.

"I can't make up my mind, Danny. Jason wants to get married, but I keep remembering how it was with your dad and I get afraid," Lucinda explained.

Danny hugged her. "Mom, I don't really know what personally went on between you and Dad, but I did hear you crying at night. I've always believed that he was abusive. You were a trained counselor, Mom, so why don't you hearken to your learning and see a counselor yourself."

"I always made excuses, Danny. Your dad was ill and I felt that since I was trained as a counselor that I should have been able to help him."

"Mom, he needed psychiatric help and medication, but he wouldn't listen to the doctor. You'd get him to go for a short while, but you know how he tricked you about taking his medicine, that time."

Lucinda jumped up. "All right! All right! I'll call Dr. Wilkins since he knew your dad so well. He told me to call if I ever needed him."

Danny grinned. "Good! I'll call Jason."

"Call, Jason? Why? It's none of his business," said Lucinda angrily.

Danny pursed his lips. "He loves you, Mom."

Lucinda dropped her head and said in a near whisper, "I know, Danny, and I love him too."

The next morning she made an appointment for the following Monday with Dr. Wilkins. He knew most of her difficulties with Jeff already and she felt she wouldn't have to rehash all the sordid details.

Later in the morning a car pulled up in front of the house and Lucinda looked out the window to see Jason getting out of his car. She drew a long breath and went to open the door.

Jason just stood looking at her. "Aren't you coming in?" Lucinda asked as she turned back toward the kitchen.

Jason followed her on into the kitchen after closing the door behind him. "You've about drove me nuts this week, Lucinda. I thought you loved me."

Lucinda turned and stood looking up at him. "I do love you, Jason. I'm just so mixed up, right now."

"Danny said you have an appointment with a psychiatrist. Who is he and where is his office?"

"He has an office in Charleston. Jeff used to go to him. He's very good, but Jeff wouldn't do what he said."

Jason sat down at the table. "It's about time you decided to get some help before we all fall apart." He looked at her intently. "You've gotten thinner. You haven't been eating, have you?"

"I haven't wanted anything. Mavis came down twice and brought soup. She wouldn't leave until I ate it. She's been a real friend to me ever since I moved here," said Lucinda.

"Will you allow me to take you out to dinner or I can cook here, if you will let me," said Jason in an almost pleading voice.

Lucinda stood looking at Jason. You know what I'd like more than anything?"

Jason stood up looking at her quizzically. His lips parted in surprise when she walked into his arms. "I just want you to hug me. I've been so afraid, Jason."

Jason stood with Lucinda encircled in his arms and rocked back and forth. "I hope you know that I will always be here for you, Lucinda. I know also that you are afraid of intimacy." Lucinda jerked out of his arms and stood glaring.

"What's Danny been telling you?"

Jason shook his head. "Lucinda, I'm a doctor and a doctor has to know something about the human psyche as well as the human body. Danny didn't tell me anything. Remember your reaction the last time I was here? That was enough to let me know that you had some concerns."

"Jason, I'm sorry. I'm going to see this doctor and I will do what he tells me. I don't want to be afraid especially not of you," said Lucinda and went back into his arms.

Jason stood holding her for a few minutes, but then stepped back. "Let's go get something to eat. I'm starved. You've worried me so much that I was beginning to lose my appetite."

Lucinda grinned. "That'll be the day! You're like the commercial about Mikey . . . you'll eat anything."

"Right now, I could. Go on and wash your face or whatever you want to do and let's go somewhere and get a good meal."

Soon Lucinda was ready to go and walked in front of Jason out the door, which he locked behind him. Turning he stopped. "Oops! Do you have your key? If you don't I've locked you out of your house."

Lucinda was dressed in jeans and a t-shirt and was not carrying a handbag. "Why did you do that? I didn't bring my purse. Now, we'll have to break a window to get in," she said in an agitated voice.

"I'll call Danny and tell him you're locked out. He can come home early. I have always locked my door and checked it and I think I just automatically did it. I'm sorry, Lucinda."

Lucinda grinned and then laughed as she ran her hand into her jeans pocket and pulled out her key. "That's why I came on out. I wanted to see if you would check the door."

"Is that important? I mean does it matter whether a man checks the door when he leaves or not?" asked Jason.

Lucinda didn't answer until she was seated in the car. "It is an indication that a man is protective. If a man is dependable and someone that can be relied on he will make sure that the surroundings are secure."

"Now where did you get that bit of information? I don't think I've heard that before," said Jason, giving her a speculative look as he started the car and backed out of the driveway.

"I've learned a few things sent I first met you," said Lucinda.

Jason grinned. "You're just like a kid, Lucinda. Are you sure you love an old man?"

"You're not old, Jason. You're just right," said Lucinda as she slid across the seat and snuggled close. "Where are we going? There's a country diner in Oceana that has good home-cooked meals."

Jason grinned and turned north toward Oceana.

Before the evening was over Jason had gained permission to take Lucinda to Mount Zion meeting on Garland Mountain on Saturday and Sunday as well as taking her to see Dr. Wilkins on Monday. Jason hadn't touched her except to help her in or out of the car. He had decided to let Lucinda call the shots on any kind of intimacy. Lucinda didn't know this, but she was glad that Jason was just being friendly and caring.

On Saturday morning when Jason came for her Lucinda was ready, but when she picked up her purse he took it from her and said, "Wait."

Lucinda looked up in surprise. "Wait! Why?"

Jason put his hand in his coat pocket. "Lucinda, you have agreed that we both love each other and I think we should become engaged, don't you?"

"Engaged! What difference will that make? What do you mean when you say we should become engaged?"

Jason looked at her warily. “Well, I bought a ring hoping that you would wear it. I’d like for people to see that we are serious about each other.” He started to pull his hand from his pocket but Lucinda stopped him.

“No, Jason. Let’s wait until I’ve talked to Dr. Wilkins. I don’t want to commit to something I can’t keep.” Jason’s shoulders drooped but he nodded and handed her purse to her.

“They arrived on the church grounds and were not able to get out of the car before people gathered to greet them. Jason had not yet met Preacher Tommy Adair, who Lucinda loved and now she introduced them. She could tell that Jason was impressed with this soft-spoken man with the twinkling blue eyes.

When they were finally left to find a seat in the church house, Lucinda whispered, “Preacher Tommy is a doctrine preacher. Some people don’t understand doctrine and they think his talks are dry. I like it though because I learn from him.”

Jason squeezed her hand and nodded his head. The service was good and the singing was beautiful. Jason and Lucinda were leaning forward in rapt attention during the opening and prayer by Elder Whitten Sparks. When Elder Sparks lifted his head and cast his eyes heavenward, Lucinda felt like he was seeing something that only he could see.

They heard a rich baritone voice join in on the next song and Lucinda quickly turned since she recognized Danny’s voice. Jason turned as well. Danny and Emily were sitting across from them, but one row farther back. Jason looked at Lucinda and smiled. She snuggled her hand into his while smiling contentedly. The four of them attended the service both Saturday and Sunday.

After service on Sunday, they decided to drive into War, WV to eat. “They do still have a restaurant over there, don’t they?” asked Jason, since he hadn’t been to War in a long time.

"The drugstore makes really good sandwiches and milkshakes. Emily and I went there to a movie one night and then ate at the drugstore. It was good, wasn't it Emily?" said Danny, looking to Emily for corroboration.

He was right and they all enjoyed their meal in a true drugstore atmosphere, an experience gradually passing into obscurity.

When they arrived in Welch, Jason asked Lucinda if she would stop at his house and stay for a while.

"I'll take you home. Remember I am protective and Danny may drive too fast," said Jason, grinning.

Once they had all arrived, Emily said, "Why don't we all play Monopoly? I'll pop some corn and fix some drinks. What do you want, Lucinda?"

"Do you have any Sanka coffee? I'm afraid to drink regular coffee if I want to sleep tonight."

"What about hot chocolate? Emily is a whiz with that," said Danny.

They all agreed even though Lucinda complained that chocolate contained caffeine as well. They spent three pleasant hours together before Lucinda looked at the clock on the wall and jumped to her feet. "Gosh! It's ten-thirty and I have to be in Charleston by eleven tomorrow. I have to go home."

Jason immediately arose. "I guess you two will have to clean up the mess. This lady needs to go home."

CHAPTER 8

Jason arrived at nine o'clock the next morning to find Lucinda ready to walk out the door. "What's the rush? It only takes an hour and a half to drive to Charleston from here," said Jason as she got into the car.

"I don't know if I can remember where his office is located. I do know it is on the airport road, or it was. I should have asked Dr. Wilkins when I made the appointment," said Lucinda.

"You have the number, don't you? If we can't find it, we'll call and ask for directions."

Lucinda relaxed and rode along deep in thought. Suddenly she said, "Jason, you are a doctor and should know. Are all men made . . ." she suddenly stopped and turned red. She shook her head. "Never mind!."

Jason looked at her red face and knew it was something about the male anatomy, but didn't know what. "Most men have the same parts unless they are deformed or have had an accident. Is that what you want to know?"

"No! Just forget it."

"Lucinda, you say you love me and if you do, don't you think it would be easier to ask me things like that than it would to ask a stranger?"

"Dr. Wilkins isn't a stranger. He knows me and he knew Jeff really well."

"Okay. I'm just here to help, if I can," said Jason and pointed across the river at some new construction. "What do you suppose they are building that near the water?"

Lucinda turned thankfully to gaze in the direction he was pointing. "It looks like a train station, doesn't it?"

"It may be a glorified boat dock, since there are no tracks for a train."

They were now entering the city and Jason had to slow down and was stopped by several red lights. Finally Lucinda said, "The next right takes you to the airport and that's the way we always went."

Jason took the exit and soon Lucinda saw the building ahead. "There it is. It looks the same. I hope Dr. Wilkins is as nice as he used to be."

Jason pulled into a parking space near the front entrance and Lucinda quickly got out and shut the door thinking that Jason would remain in the car, but he didn't.

"You can't go in with me, Jason. He'll think I'm awful bringing another man in there," said Lucinda.

"Well, you can't very well bring Mr. Marshall with you since he is dead. I don't know why I shouldn't come in with you. I'd like to meet this doctor myself." Jason walked to the steps and took Lucinda's arm. She dropped her head and walked with him up the steps and into the foyer.

Soon, Dr. Wilkins opened his door and stopped with a surprised look. Then he smiled, "Hello, Mrs. Mar . . . It is still Marshall isn't it?"

Jason arose from the chair he had taken and extended his hand. "I'm Dr. Jason McCall and I'm trying to change her name, but Lucinda has some issues that she needs to get cleared up before we can do that."

Dr. Wilkins clasped Jason's hand. "Nice to meet you, doctor. I've heard a lot about you."

When he heard Lucinda gasp, Dr. Wilkins quickly said, "Not from Lucinda, but I certainly did from Mr. Marshall. You don't look as much like a devil as he painted you." Dr. Wilkins smiled and turned to Lucinda.

"Are you ready, Lucinda? I think you've made a wise decision. In fact, I've thought about you ever since I learned about the fire that took your husband."

Lucinda turned and went into the office with Dr. Wilkins behind her. She walked over and sat down in a Queen Anne chair that she hadn't seen the last time she was in this office. Dr. Wilkins saw her gazing around and explained that some renovations and redecorating had been done in the past three years. He pulled up a chair in front of her, but at an angle.

"Have the last three years been bad for you or were you relieved?"

Lucinda hesitated for a moment as if to gather her thoughts. "Bad." When, Dr. Wilkins just sat waiting Lucinda continued. "I was pregnant. I lost the baby the night Jeff died." She drew a deep breath and sighed. "He slapped me, but I don't know if that caused me to lose my baby or not. I don't know if he knocked me down or I lost my balance and fell. Anyway, I lost my baby and that was difficult. The doctor said I would have probably lost it anyway, but I didn't want to hear that."

Dr. Wilkins sat quietly for a minute and when Lucinda didn't say anything else, he asked, "Why did you want to see me, Lucinda? To be honest, I hoped you would have called me before now. I thought you would blame yourself for what happened."

"I did, until I learned what had happened to cause Jeff to drink again. I don't think he really intended to drink anymore." Lucinda went on to tell Dr. Wilkins the part that Jeff's mother and Geneva Clary had played in bringing about his death.

"How do you feel now? Are you still blaming yourself?"

"No, or at least I don't think I am. I wish I could have helped him and I did try, but I couldn't keep him from being jealous." Lucinda dropped her head. "I've thought that perhaps if I could have liked intimacy he would have been different." Lucinda shivered in revulsion. "I just couldn't like something like that."

"Jeff said you did when you first married. He thought you changed after you met Dr. McCall that time in Bradshaw and fainted."

Lucinda twisted her hands together and wouldn't lift her head as she said, "At first, I took nerve medicine and Jeff was gentle and kind then, but meeting Dr. McCall that time didn't change me. Jeff did that." Lucinda looked at Dr. Wilkins solemnly, "After that Jeff became harsh and abusive."

Dr. Wilkins had such a look of compassion as he said, "I suspected as much. He became angry when he mentioned Dr. McCall."

Lucinda arose from her seat and turned toward the window, but immediately turned and sat down again. "Dr. Wilkins, . . . Jason, I mean Dr. McCall, wants to marry me and I would like to marry him, but what if it is the same way. I know it was probably partly my fault, but I couldn't make myself like something like that. I don't want to go through that again."

Dr. Wilkins heaved a heavy sigh. "Jeff never did talk to you about his problem, then. I tried to get him to bring you in and let me talk to both of you, but he kept telling me that he would explain things to you. I can see that he never did."

"Do you mean Jeff had some kind of problem . . . in that way?"

"Well, yes and no. He wouldn't have had a problem if he had talked to you and used other methods than constantly trying to make you respond." Dr. Wilkins went on to explain to a red-faced Lucinda that Jeff had not been as well endowed as he wanted to be and when she didn't respond he felt more inadequate. "I told him repeatedly that thousands of men would love to be as well off as he was, but he never believed me."

"You see, Lucinda, none of this was your fault. You had never been with another man and had no idea about Jeff's frustration. Your husband would have still had a major problem, but this seeming inadequacy exacerbated that problem. He also used it as a basis for his jealousies which helped him shift the blame to you and to all men. He saw other men and especially Dr. McCall as a threat to taking away his possession . . . you."

Lucinda's face was still red, but she was hearing something that made sense. Now, she had a reason for those all night abuses that she had endured for twenty years. Sometimes, she was even glad when he drank since he went to sleep much sooner. She didn't look up, but did ask, "You mean that all men aren't like that?"

Dr. Wilkins smiled. "No, Lucinda they aren't. To a woman, the wooing is more important sometimes than the copulation and that has nothing to do with size, but only the desire to leave one's mate satisfied. Unfortunately, Jeff was so self-centered and had so many problems to deal with that he didn't consider you in that respect."

Lucinda sat deep in thought, but still with her eyes cast toward the floor.

"Lucinda, did Jeff ever try to talk to you about intimacy at all?"

"No! He always said that if I really loved him I would enjoy it as much as he did. I tried, I really did, but it got worse and worse as time went on. Sometimes I just lay and cried."

"I'm so sorry that your young life was so shattered with false beliefs and this kind of trauma. Many a wife would have left him. Why didn't you?"

"He would have killed me before he would have allowed me to leave him. I was his, in his mind."

"Yes, that's true. I knew that, but I didn't really know what you had to go through with during your marriage. I'm sorry, my dear. There's no reason why you shouldn't marry again and have a happy and healthy life."

"Unless, the next man would be the same way," said Lucinda and turned red again.

"Lucinda, I don't think you'd even consider another man unless it would be this Dr. McCall and I really don't think you would have a problem, but if you wouldn't mind I'd love to have a talk with him," said Dr. Wilkins.

"I don't think he'd want to do that, and I don't know how that would help. I'm the one with the problem, not him."

"But, if he understood the situation, it would make it much easier for him to help you. It wouldn't hurt to ask him, if you will agree," said Dr. Wilkins.

"You can ask him, but I'll be embarrassed to go home with him."

"Lucinda, he is a doctor and I'm sure he has dealt with situations much worse than yours. If he is anything like I assume him to be I don't think you have anything to worry about."

Lucinda arose from her seat. "All right, if you think it would help, you can talk to him if he agrees."

Dr. Wilkins walked her to the door and opened it. He followed her out and walked over to Jason. "Dr. McCall, I'd like to talk to you for a few minutes. Are you agreeable?"

Lucinda didn't look at Jason, but went over and took a seat and picked up a magazine. She heard Jason agree and then follow the doctor into his office.

Lucinda sat as tense as if something was looming over her head that she couldn't avoid. "What if Jason doesn't want to marry me after Dr. Wilkins tells him how I am?" she thought which made her feel sadder than ever.

CHAPTER 9

That wasn't the case, however. Jason was with Dr. Wilkins for what seemed to be hours for Lucinda, but was only thirty minutes. He came out looking pleased, but didn't say anything to Lucinda. Dr. Wilkins, however, came over to her and said, "Lucinda, I'm so glad you came today and I think you have a rosy future ahead of you. I'd like to see you when you come back from your honeymoon."

Both men laughed as Lucinda turned rosy red and sputtered. "I haven't decided to marry yet."

"Well, when you do, send me an invitation," said Dr. Wilkins.

Jason spoke up then. "I hope we can have a quiet wedding and leave immediately afterward for an extended visit to Ireland or wherever Lucinda wants to go. So, if I get my way, you will see the notice in the papers, but there won't be any invitations."

When Lucinda heard Ireland she looked up in pleased surprise. "I didn't know you wanted to go to Ireland."

Dr. Wilkins grinned. "That got her attention, Dr. McCall. I think that's where she'd like to spend her honeymoon." He turned to reenter his office saying, "Well, you have my blessing and wishes for a long life and happiness."

Lucinda was still seated and Jason said, "Are you ready or would you rather stay here and read last month's Reader's Digest?"

"He didn't say when he wanted to see me again. I guess he forgot. I'd better ask," said Lucinda, rising from her seat.

"Yes, he did. He said he wanted to see you after our honeymoon." Jason grasped her hand and walked a stunned Lucinda toward the door.

Once in the car, Jason asked where she would like to go for lunch. "It's one o'clock and I'm hungry, aren't you?"

"I'm not hungry, but wherever you want to go is all right with me," then Lucinda giggled. "I think I'll just start calling you Mikey since you seem hungry all the time."

"I didn't take time to eat breakfast this morning, since you wanted me there at nine o'clock. Remember, it was one this morning before I got to bed after driving back to Welch from your place."

"I didn't eat breakfast either, but not because I didn't have time. I just couldn't eat. I guess I was nervous and I still feel jittery on the inside," said Lucinda.

"Your blood sugar has probably hit rock-bottom. A big breakfast will straighten that out," said Jason as he got into the line of traffic. Soon Jason pulled into the parking lot of a Shoney's restaurant. "They serve breakfast foods all day, I'm told and that is what I want."

When Lucinda only put a spoonful of egg and one piece of bacon on her plate, Jason stopped her. "No, you don't my friend. Here, take some fruit, more egg and another piece of bacon. You need a biscuit and some butter and jelly also," he said and put each item in her plate.

"You're wasting food. I can't eat all that. I never eat that much," scolded Lucinda.

"I know you never do, but I have to get your strength up for all the walking we will do in Ireland," said Jason as he turned with her toward their booth.

When they were seated Lucinda said, "You're kidding aren't you?" At Jason's raised eyebrows she said, "You know, about going to Ireland. You didn't really mean that, did you?"

"Indeed I did, if that is where you'd like to go on our honeymoon. In fact, I'd like to visit Ireland again, myself."

"I didn't know you had been there. Did you and Janet go there on your honeymoon?" asked Lucinda who had suddenly lost all her enthusiasm for the idea.

"No. I was in Ireland with some friends from college. We all got drunk. The Irish have good whiskey and they can certainly drink lots of it."

"Where did you take Janet on her honeymoon?"

Jason looked solemn. "I took her to Niagara Falls for five days and wouldn't have done that if our grandparents hadn't already reserved rooms and paid for the whole thing. I was back at the university and doubling up on my studies in order to take the ophthalmologist's position offered to me in Welch. I felt like I didn't have time to make any trips right then."

"That wasn't fair to Janet."

"I know it wasn't and I felt guilty about that until I found all your letters in her closet. I was so angry with her and mother that I wanted to strike out, but Janet was already dead. I don't feel like I wronged Janet anymore than she wronged me and I'll never have the feelings for mother that I once had."

They were soon finished with their lunch and on their way back to Lucinda's house. "Lucinda, did you ever ask yourself what life would have been like if we had married when we first met?" asked Jason.

Lucinda looked at Jason thoughtfully, before saying, "Jason, perhaps the Lord knew that I felt too inferior, uneducated, and shy to be your wife, back then. Perhaps we both needed this growth period to be true husband and wife to each other . . . well, probably you were ready, but I don't feel that I was and the Lord knew that."

Jason drove more slowly deep in thought. "I don't know about that, Lucinda. I know that if I had gotten your letters I would have married you if you agreed. It seems to me that we have wasted so many years and we need to get married and get on with our lives."

"No, the years weren't wasted, Jason. You have Emily and I have Danny and I feel that the Lord has a purpose for both of those young people," said Lucinda seriously.

Jason turned to look at her and smiled. "I guess you're right . . . I know you're right, but my heart longed for you all the time. Lucinda, I don't think one day passed that I didn't think of you."

With tears rolling silently down her cheeks, Lucinda whispered. "I know, Jason. It was the same for me. I called your name when Danny was being born. I didn't know it, but the nurse in attendance told Jeff and he wouldn't have anything to do with Danny for the longest time. When people kept telling him how much Danny looked like him, he did a little better."

"Danny doesn't look like the man I remember from that Bradshaw incident," said Jason adamantly. "I think he looks a lot like Burb Harmon . . . same laugh, same high cheek bones, and he doesn't have that ruddy complexion that Jeff Marshall had."

"Danny does look like Daddy and his voice sounds like Daddy, especially when he says 'pon-my-honor'." Lucinda smiled. "He started saying that when he was two years old and it was his favorite expression."

Jason laughed. "I'll have to get him to talk like Mr. Harmon sometime. Danny has a droll sense of humor and he is fun to be around. Is Mr. Harmon like that?"

Lucinda grinned. "Dad's a big cut-up. He loves to pull pranks on people, but he doesn't like to be on the receiving end. He's fun though and well-liked in the community."

"Only by Republicans, I'll bet, especially around election time."

"Everybody at church likes Dad and some of them are Democrats. But, of course, Dad doesn't talk politics at church, or I don't think he does. I know he doesn't on the inside of the building, but I don't know when the service is over. I have seen him talking quietly to different ones, but don't know what he was talking about."

"If he was talking quietly you know he wasn't telling jokes," said Jason as he laughed merrily.

Lucinda laughed also. "You have a point there."

By this time they had arrived back at Lucinda's house and without asking Jason got out and followed her inside. Lucinda placed her purse on the counter and said, "I'll make some coffee if you are going to stay long enough to drink it."

Jason walked behind her into the kitchen. "I'm going to stay until you agree to marry me."

"Well, sit down over there and give me time to think about it," said Lucinda nervously.

Jason let out a roar of laughter. "Are you going to decide while you make coffee?"

Lucinda went right on preparing the coffee without making a reply. In gathering the coffee and water she became more and more agitated. After she dropped a cup and it shattered she whirled around. "If you want coffee you can make it. I'm . . . I can't do it."

Jason came to her rescue, but instead of cleaning up the shattered cup he took her in his arms. "Lucinda, look at me. I'm the man who has loved you for over twenty years. You don't need to be nervous about anything you want to say to me . . . and I do mean anything . . . good or bad."

Lucinda did look up at him. Then tears welled up in her eyes and she dropped her head and buried it on Jason's chest. Jason held her tenderly and didn't say anything. Finally she seemed to be calmer, but when she started to talk it came out in a breathless rush. "Jason, I can't marry you. You wouldn't stay with me. I . . . don't like sex."

Jason still held her and swayed as if dancing a slow dance. Finally he lifted her chin and looked steadily into her scarlet face. "Lucinda, I want to marry you and I will stay with you, and we'll work on this problem you think you have."

"But Jason, I was married for twenty years and I . . . didn't like it. In fact I hated for night to come and hated to be alone with Jeff in the daytime also." Lucinda shivered and Jason held her more tenderly.

"What if I told you that I don't think you have a problem? I think there were lots of things that contributed to that feeling and I believe we can overcome them. Will you give us a chance? Please, Lucinda!"

CHAPTER 10

Before Jason left that night he had a promise from Lucinda to spend time with him every day for the next two weeks. "This is to give yourself the chance to test your feelings," said Jason. Suddenly he turned back into the room. "Will you become engaged now? You said to wait until you'd seen Dr. Wilkins, remember."

Lucinda smiled. "I did say that, didn't I?" Then she became thoughtful. "How do you mean for me to test my feelings? I'm not going to sleep with you without being married, so don't even think that. "

Jason glared angrily. "Do you think sex is the only thing on my mind? You sure have some pretty warped ideas."

Lucinda looked bewildered. "Well, isn't that what's on your mind when you hug and kiss me?"

"Hell no! I don't mean I don't want you, but when I hug you, most of the time, I just love you and want to comfort you.

Lucinda stared as if she just had an epiphany. "You truly mean that, don't you? I can see it in your eyes."

"Yes, Lucinda, I truly do mean it. I love you and I truly want you to be happy. I know you can be happy with me, but you don't believe that right now."

Lucinda stood in the warm circle of his arms and felt so safe and secure. *Lord, please help me to accept the love of this good man. I do love him and I want to marry him and be happy*, she prayed silently.

Suddenly Jason said, "I guess one of us is going to have to clean up this mess, if we want any coffee."

Lucinda jumped back as she looked up in guilty alarm. "I'm sorry. I'll clean it up."

"Don't look like you're scared to death. I won't beat you for breaking a cup," said Jason, starting to laugh, but stopped when he saw the look on Lucinda's face.

"You were terrified of that man, weren't you, Lucinda?"

Lucinda grimaced. "I never knew how he would react. Sometimes he'd laugh and tease me when I made a mistake and sometimes he would go into a rage. I don't think I was afraid he'd hit me, but I dreaded the rage that came out of him. He only hit me that one time, but he held me and I couldn't get away many times." She quickly bent down and started picking up the pieces of the broken cup.

Jason turned to the counter and started preparing the coffee. "It's a good thing I can't meet that man right now. I think I'd have to beat him senseless."

"Physical violence never solves anything, Jason. I'm glad you can't meet him," said Lucinda, turning to dump the cup into the garbage.

"You're right. I'm mostly a compassionate person, but sometimes you run into somebody that you can't reason with. I know, according to Dr. Wilkins that Jeff Marshall was a very disturbed man and ordinarily I would have wanted to help him. Right now, however, I'm just glad he isn't around."

Soon the coffee was made and Lucinda took a pie from the refrigerator. "Do you want a slice of this banana cream pie?"

Jason rubbed his stomach. "No. I want to know if you are going to take my ring or do I have to return it to the jewelers? Besides, do I look like I need to eat anything else?"

"You're not fat, but if you don't want it, that's fine," said Lucinda and opened the door to the refrigerator. She turned around. "Well, where's that ring you keep harping about."

"Wait! Don't change your mind. I'm going to the car and when I come back we'll both eat some pie." Jason hurried from the room, slamming the door as he went.

Lucinda stood not even thinking. When he walked in with his hand closed into a fist she looked startled. "Did you lose it?"

Jason opened his hand to reveal a beautiful fire opal ring encircled with diamonds. Neither of them spoke, but Jason picked up her left hand and placed the ring on her finger.

Lucinda looked down. "It's beautiful, Jason. How did you know my size?"

"Danny bought you a mother's ring last Christmas, didn't he? He told me the size. Now, may I kiss my bride to be?" Lucinda tilted her face and Jason placed a chaste kiss on her lips. "Now, if you'll eat a slice of that pie, I will too."

"I don't want anything else to eat, tonight. I think you want me to get fat," said Lucinda.

"Well, I would like you to gain a few pounds. You are really thin, Lucinda."

She grinned and put the pie back on the counter. "Okay. Get two plates and I'll eat a slice if you will." She sat looking down at the ring on her hand. "Jason, this doesn't mean I have agreed to marry you tomorrow, you know. They were at the table eating pie and talking about what they wanted to do the next day when Danny came home.

"Hey, save me some of that pie. I'm starved." Danny went to the sink and washed his hands, but suddenly looked at Lucinda. "I know. I know . . . I'm supposed to wash my hands in the bathroom, but I'm hungry."

Lucinda smiled. "I'll let it go this time, but in my house people wash their hands in the bathroom."

Jason raised his eyebrows. "This looks like a place you're camping out in, not a home. How long are you planning to stay here, anyway?"

Danny turned from the coffee pot with a cup in his hand. "Yeah, that's what I'd like to know. Emily and I will be leaving a week from Friday and I don't want you here in an empty house by yourself." Suddenly the ring caught his eye. "Hey, what's this? Have you finally decided to marry Jason, Mom?"

Lucinda smiled. "It means I will someday. I can't make up my mind as to what I want to do, Danny. I know I have to be out of this house in fifteen days. That's what the contract says, but I really don't want to move in with Dad and Mom and . . . Well, I just don't know what I want to do."

"Why don't you stay in Emily's room at Jason's house for a few days until you make up your mind," said Danny since you all are engaged already.

Lucinda gasped. "Danny, my name would be mud. I'll certainly not do that."

"Mom, it would be the same if you and Jason went to a hotel and got two separate rooms. You would both be staying in the same house, only in separate rooms," said Danny as if he thought Lucinda was dense.

"You're wasting your time, Danny. Your mother has very old-fashioned and strict ideas about conduct between men and women."

Lucinda rose from the table to gather the plates. "I may have, but there it is. I am what I am and I've survived this far on those ideas."

Jason looked at Danny and raised his eyebrows giving Lucinda a wry look. "That you have my dear that you have." Both he and Danny arose to help clear the table.

"Well, since that idea is out, what will you do? A contract says you move, but you have to decide where." Jason said as he wiped the counter and proceeded to hang up the dish towel.

Lucinda heaved a long sigh. "I'm staying here the rest of this week, but I'm not sure about next week. I may get a room in the Carter Hotel in Welch, but I don't really want to."

They all moved into the living room, but Jason didn't sit down. "I guess I'd better get on home, but stopped and looked speculatively at Lucinda. Suddenly he said, "Will you go somewhere special with me tomorrow?"

"Where?" Lucinda asked, looking as if she were about to refuse, but Jason stopped her.

"We've already made a deal. We were to spend time together every day for two weeks anyway. Have you forgotten? Engaged people do see a lot of each other you know."

Lucinda shook her head in exasperation. "You're rushing me. I'm so mixed up I can't think straight."

Danny laughed. "We can see that. If you were thinking straight you'd go ahead and get married. Emily and I can't come back as soon as we get to Morgantown and I thought you would want me in your wedding."

"We aren't going to have time for an elaborate wedding. We want to see Ireland before winter. It is so beautiful this time of the year," said Jason, smiling at Lucinda.

Lucinda's eyes lit up, but then she sobered. "You're trying to bribe me, Jason McCall. That isn't fair."

"All's fair in love and war, my dear and I'm pulling out all the stops."

Danny laughed merrily. "I wish Emily would offer to take me to Ireland for a honeymoon. I'd marry her tomorrow.

"I think it would take less than that, Danny," said Lucinda.

"You're right, Mom. If I was through school and could get a job, we'd get married this week. I'm going to double up on my classes and go summer and winter until I get my degree."

Lucinda looked worried. "You'll make yourself sick. Patience has its own rewards."

Jason walked to Lucinda and bent to kiss her cheek. "I'm having a hard time keeping my patience in check, so please make up your mind."

"I don't believe that doctor helped you, Mom. Are you still feeling afraid?" asked Danny worriedly.

"He must have thought he'd helped me. He wants me to come back after our honeymoon. I don't know what Jason told him." Lucinda looked up at Jason, "What did you tell him?"

Jason grinned. "I just told him, I was perfect for you since I'm kind, patient, and a great lover."

Lucinda turned red, but grinned impishly. "I guess time will tell, won't it."

"You'll never know unless you give him the chance, Mom. If you don't marry Jason you will always wonder what you missed," said Danny and laughed at Lucinda's gasp.

"I'll be over around nine o'clock in the morning unless you would like to drive over to my place. I wanted to take you to a place in Virginia that I heard about," said Jason, turning once again toward the door.

"I'll come over there. There's no sense in you driving over here when you plan to go another way. Can't you tell me where we going?" asked Lucinda.

"You'll find out when we get there. It is a special place so dress pretty." Jason went on out the door and soon his car lights flooded the living room.

Danny plopped down on the sofa. "Why don't you just go ahead and marry Jason, Mom? Look at that beautiful ring he just gave you. I know he loves you very much and I know he will be good to you. That would take a big worry off my mind. You have no idea how much I worried about you when Dad was alive."

Lucinda sat down beside Danny and kissed his cheek. "I'm sorry, Danny. I never knew that you heard me crying. I tried to be quiet."

Danny looked at Lucinda. "Mom, I have waited outside your door with a baseball bat. If I had heard him curse you or hit you I would have tried to kill him."

Lucinda put her arms around Danny. "Oh honey. I'm so sorry. I didn't want you to not like your dad. I tried to keep everything as calm as I could."

"I know, Mom and most of the time, you did. One night I wanted some milk and I sneaked up to get it. For some reason I crept close to your bedroom door. I didn't know what was going on, but I did hear you crying."

CHAPTER 11

The next morning at nine a.m. Lucinda rang Jason's doorbell. She was dressed in a light blue sheath dress with a full-length silky lace coat over it. Jason opened the door and stood smiling in appreciation.

"Well, well. When someone tells you to dress in something pretty you really do, don't you. Gosh! Lucinda you look beautiful. Come on in so I can get a really good look instead of standing gaping in the doorway," said Jason, holding the storm door wide.

Lucinda turned red, but walked in and stopped to take off her shoes at the entrance.

"Don't take your shoes off. Put them back on. I want to see the whole effect, high heels and all," said Jason, walking around her and gazing in a speculative manner. "Everything fits together and you look as if you've stepped out of a fashion show."

"Stop it, Jason. You're embarrassing me."

Jason jumped back and held up his hands. "Okay! Far be it from me to upset you today. I want this day to be perfect, so shall I say you look awful? I'll lie if it will make you feel better."

"If you don't stop I'll go right back home. I've had this dress for a year, but it's the nicest one I have. You talked like we were going somewhere special."

Jason grinned. "I'll not say another word. We are going someplace special and I want us to be dressed special. Now, let me go get the rest of my outfit on and we'll be ready to go. You know where the other bathroom is if you need to use it and you know where the coffee is if you want coffee. Give me ten minutes."

Lucinda went to the bathroom and came back into the kitchen. She didn't want any coffee, but she did want a drink of water. She was opening cabinet doors to find a glass, when Jason came back in.

Lucinda thought he looked so handsome. He wore a navy suit, light blue shirt, and dark blue tie. "You look nice, Jason," said Lucinda and then snickered as she walked all around him. "It's a big improvement over that fireman's suit."

Jason laughed and encircled her in his arms. "I'm glad you think I look nice, for an old man."

"You aren't old. In fact, I think you are just right," said Lucinda looking up at him in adoration. She'd tried to hide this for so long, but now she loved him so much she couldn't hide it.

Jason groaned and softly kissed her lips. "Lucinda, please. Let's just get married. That way you won't have to decide where you want to live."

Lucinda slid her arms up around his neck. "Oh Jason, I love you so much."

Jason pulled her closer to him, but was afraid to hold her as close as he wanted to. "I love you too, dear. I don't even have words to tell you how I feel about you." Then he kissed her again, but not softly.

Lucinda didn't pull back. She felt as if she wanted to be a part of Jason and snuggled closer as she returned his kiss.

Jason raised his head and looked down into her eyes and knew that she felt the same passion as he was feeling. His impulse was to savor the moment, but feared he would stifle what he had in mind for their day. So he kissed her softly again before saying, "I think we'd better do something else, don't you?"

Lucinda stared at him in surprise and then turned red, before dropping her arms and turning away. *Jeff wouldn't have stopped. Maybe Jason doesn't love me, after all,* she thought and then chided herself because she had complained to Jason about hugs and kisses leading to other things. She stepped back and smiled. "Are we supposed to be there at a certain time?"

Jason straightened his tie and smiled. "No, but I'd like to get there before twelve if we can."

Soon they were on the road out of Welch to pick up Route 83 on Premier Mountain. "I think I'll go by War and over Stony Ridge since that is the quickest way to reach 460. We could have gone up by Gary and over Horsepen Mountain, but there are so many coal trucks traveling that road that we'd be three hours getting to 460. "

Lucinda agreed. "That road is awful anyway, especially after you pass the golf course. Danny and I went to Richlands on that road and I just knew our car would be torn up before we got to Stony Ridge."

They drove over Coalwood Mountain without speaking, but Jason was humming softly. Lucinda felt so free and . . . happy, no exhilarated or something. She started singing softly. "I hear singing and there's no one there. I smell blossoms and the trees are bare."

Jason looked over at her and grinned. "'You're not sick, you're just in love,' and it makes one feel great doesn't it?"

Lucinda laughed. "I didn't realize I was singing that song. We used to listen to that on your car radio. Remember the time we were going up Bradshaw Mountain and big soft snowflakes were drifting lazily down. That song was playing then. I felt like heaven couldn't be better."

Jason reached across and grasped her hand and tugged her across the seat to sit beside him. "I do remember that time and all the other times and the other songs. Do you remember Nat King Cole singing, 'Too Young' on the night we went out to the little park up Browns Creek?"

Lucinda nestled her head on his shoulder, but looked up at him smiling. "That's one of my favorite memories. If that owl hadn't scared me I wouldn't have ended up in your arms. I love owls," she said, laughing happily.

Jason's arm tightened around her. "I like owls as well. You were so skittish that I wondered if I'd ever get to hold you."

They rode on into War reminiscing about their previous time together. "Jason, my family thought that what I felt for you was 'puppy love' and would pass, but it didn't. Mom told me that you were a grown man from the city and were just dating me to have something to do to keep from being bored."

Jason grimaced. "I'm sure they told you that I only wanted one thing from you also. Didn't they?"

Lucinda nodded. "Yes. Everybody said that, except Daddy. He may have thought it, but he never said it to me. Of course Daddy wouldn't have talked about anything like that to one of his daughters."

"Well, maybe it is like you believe. The Lord wasn't ready for us to be together back then. I can't see that at all, though. I believe the Lord created us all in Wisdom and gave us all gifts, but it is up to us how and when we use those gifts. So, I think, for one reason or another, we let circumstances get in our way," said Jason philosophically.

Lucinda thought about it. "I agree with what you've said, but still I know that, at that age, I was too immature and uneducated to fit in your world," and *perhaps still am, she thought.*

Jason laughed. "We would have had a lot of hurdles, that's for sure. I thought the old Baptist beliefs were a bunch of backwoods fallacies and you would have fought me tooth and nail on that subject."

"I hadn't united with the church when we dated."

"I know, but you still defended the Baptist beliefs like a mama tiger with her cubs," said Jason laughing merrily. "Of course, now that I believe the Baptist doctrine myself, I'd be the same way. I bet you thought I was pretty stupid for an educated man, didn't you?"

Lucinda raised her head and looked at him. "No, the stars got in my eyes and I couldn't see or think about anything else." She lay back again and sighed happily.

"Lucinda, I . . .," Jason stopped.

When he didn't continue Lucinda raised her head again. "What? You started to say something or ask me something. What was it?"

Jason's brow was furrowed as if bothered about something. "Not now. I'll tell you later."

They were now on 460 heading toward Richlands. "Are we going to Richlands? What's there that you want me to see?"

"Nothing! We'll be passing Richlands," said Jason mysteriously.

"I know! You're taking me to the Martha Washington Inn for lunch. How sweet! How did you know that I've always wanted to see inside it?"

"I didn't know, but if you would like to eat there we can do that," said Jason before continuing with, "Maybe have dinner there, this evening."

"With all these treats in store, I'm getting really excited. Where are we going this morning?"

By this time they were nearing Belfast and Jason was driving more slowly. They reached Belfast Elementary School and Jason made an abrupt left turn up that road. Lucinda sat straight up in her seat and gazed around startled." Where does this road lead to? This is farming country or maybe I should say cattle country."

Jason pulled over in a wide spot by the roadside which was shaded by a gigantic oak tree. He killed the engine and then turned to look at Lucinda. "I want to talk seriously to you, so will you please hear me out?"

Lucinda gave him a puzzled look since he looked so serious. "What's wrong? Has something happened? Have I done something wrong?"

"No, Lucinda, you haven't done anything wrong." Jason pulled her back into his arms and sat quietly for a few seconds. "Lucinda, you and I both are sure we love each other. We both belong to the same faith, our children are grown and love each other, I'm lonesome and you're lonesome or at least at loose ends. You don't know what you want to do with your life or where you want to live, so with all that in mind will you go with me into Lebanon and get married today?"

Lucinda sat feeling so safe, secure, and as if she belonged with Jason. She knew that everything he said was true and also Dr. Wilkins had assured her that being married to Jason would be different. She pulled back and heard Jason sigh dejectedly. She looked up at him and saw such sorrow in his eyes that she could have cried. "Don't look like that, Jason, please. I'll marry you, but I don't ...."

She couldn't finish since Jason was crushing her to him and mumbling, "Thank you, Lord, Thank you." Lucinda sat watching as tears crept down his cheeks. Then she was crying as well, but laughing also. Time stood still as Jason kissed her, but she returned the favor until Jason took out his handkerchief and wiped his face and started to wipe hers, but she stopped him.

"You'll wipe all my make-up off. I probably have streaks down my face already," said Lucinda pulling the visor down to look in the mirror.

Jason grasped her chin and turned her face toward him. "Let me see. Right here," he said and kissed her cheek.

She laughed and pushed him away. "Okay, that's settled. I'll have to find a bathroom to mend the damage."

Jason looked at his watch. "We need to hurry. We'll go to the hospital and get our blood tests and, no let's go to the courthouse first and get our license, then go get the blood tests."

Lucinda's eyes blared widely. "You mean we are getting married right now? We can't just go into town and get married, can we?"

Jason grinned. "Oh yes we can. I've already checked it all out." He started the engine and pulled out. "Your make-up isn't splotched, so don't worry about it. You look beautiful."

Soon they pulled into the parking lot at the Russell County Courthouse in Lebanon. Jason took her hand and they went up the steps and into the Clerk's office. "We want to apply for a marriage license, please," said Jason, beaming at the girls who were all staring.

The clerk brought the form over and explained that they had to have a blood test and find a minister in the town to marry them if they wanted to marry today. "We need to marry today since we plan to leave for Ireland tomorrow," said Jason, squeezing Lucinda's hand.

"Are you taking her to Ireland for your honeymoon?" asked one of the girls in a voice full of wonder.

"Yes, I am. I've waited for this woman for twenty odd years and right now I'd give her the moon if I could," said Jason, looking at Lucinda in a way that made her pulses leap.

With the license carried carefully in a long brown envelope, they dashed back to the car and left for the hospital. When he told the receptionist what he wanted she smiled. "We'll make an exception for you and send you straight to the lab. I'll call Wilma and I don't think you'll have to wait to have the blood taken, but there may be a wait to get the results. Let me talk to Wilma for you?" She picked up the phone and dialed. "Wilma, I have a man and woman here wanting a blood test so they can marry. Can you please rush it for them? You'll see why when you meet them. Okay! They are Jason McCall and Lucinda Marshall."

She hung up the phone and pointed to the left. "Down that hall three doors and make a left. You two make me happy just to look at you. God Bless you both."

Both Jason and Lucinda smiled as they thanked her and hurried down the hall. As soon as they walked in the door, a short heavyset woman with a mannish haircut arose from her seat and smiled. "Come right in, folks. We're waiting on you." They soon had filled out all the information needed and each had their arm stuck and blood drawn. "You'll have to wait until two o'clock to get the results since the lady who runs the tests won't be back until one- fifteen."

"That's fine, just as long as we get married today. Tell us where to go to find a minister. I know there are several churches here in town and it doesn't matter what denomination," said Jason.

"You can find Preacher Virgil Hale at the Baptist Church out at the end of town on the right and Preacher Floyd Davis at the Methodist Church if you make a left by the statue of the confederate soldier just out the street. They are both usually at their churches after lunch most days," Wilma explained.

They thanked her again and left the hospital holding hands and smiling like two teenagers who have gotten their favorite request. "Do you want to find something to eat? We could go and locate these churches and then look for a restaurant," said Jason.

Having made her decision, Lucinda seemed so relaxed and happy. She walked along in a euphoric state, smiling at everyone she met. "I'm not hungry, but we have to wait, so I guess we may as well eat."

When they stopped at the Baptist Church there was a sign informing visitors that Pastor Hale would not be in today due to illness. "I hope the other one is in. If he isn't we'll go all over this town if I have to, to find a minister," said Jason worriedly.

Lucinda smiled up at him in a dream-like voice. "He'll be there. Don't worry Jason. We're getting married today."

Jason hugged her there on the Baptist church steps in full view of any on-lookers. Lucinda didn't mind, but hugged him also. "Well, we'll find a preacher somewhere, since I plan to marry you today, Lucinda."

CHAPTER 12

Reverend Floyd Davis opened the door of the Lebanon United Methodist Church just as they reached it. "Don't go yet, please." Jason almost pleaded.

"I'm not going anywhere except to get some lunch. I'll be back by one o'clock. Is this something urgent?"

"Well, sir, as long as you are here at two o'clock, it isn't urgent. We want you to marry us, if you will. Our blood tests won't be checked until then," said Jason.

Reverend Davis smiled pleasantly. "This isn't your first marriage is it?"

"No, sir. We've both been married before. Our spouses are now dead and we've found each other again. However, we've loved each other for over twenty years."

Jason looked down at Lucinda for approval and she nodded her head, smiling broadly. "I met him when I was sixteen years old and I've loved him ever since."

Reverend Davis smiled. "That sounds like an interesting story, but right now I have to meet my wife for lunch. You two have to eat as well so you could go to lunch with us and continue the story."

Lucinda looked up at Jason and he turned to Reverend Davis. "Thank you Sir, but today we want to be alone. I hope you understand."

"I do. I certainly do and I'm not one bit offended. I'll see you back here at two o'clock."

"We may be a little later than that if they haven't finished with the blood test results. We'll be here as soon as we get it," said Jason and clasping Lucinda's hand he turned away, but stopped to ask, "Where is some place that serves fish in this town?"

"There's a K & G Restaurant out in the Russell County Shopping Center, there's also a Long John Silver's in that area as well as a Bonanza restaurant. You should be able to get fish at any of those places, I think."

Jason thanked Reverend Davis and he and Lucinda left holding hands. Reverend Davis stood watching them and smiled. Later he told his wife, "They acted like two teenagers in love and they're certainly not teenagers. You should come back with me for the wedding. They'll need a witness anyway."

Meanwhile Jason and Lucinda were sitting in the car trying to decide where to go eat. "I don't care if we just get sandwiches and go find a shade tree somewhere and eat," said Lucinda, who now that she had made up her mind seemed to have dropped all her fears.

Jason smiled. "Well, we don't want to get your beautiful wedding dress mussed up. I guess we'd better go somewhere and get a seat back in a corner. How's that sound?"

"Let's go to Long John Silver's then. I love their fish," said Lucinda and soon they were seated in the last seat in the second room of the restaurant, which had very few people anyway.

Later Lucinda would remember everything they said and all the details of every minute of that day, but now she was in such a state of mind that her world had become a dream. Her eyes were shining and her face had taken on a rosy glow. Jason sat looking at her and thought she was more beautiful every time he saw her. When they had finished, Jason looked at his watch. "It's ten minutes past one. They might be finished with the blood test. Let's go see."

Although Jason had thought and in fact told Danny and Emily that they would get married and leave that same day for Ireland, he now realized it would be impossible. He didn't mention this to Lucinda, however, since he hadn't told her his plans fearing that he couldn't get her to marry in one day. *I'll just play it by ear,* he thought as he parked at the hospital once again.

It was one-thirty by the time they parked and walked up the hill. When they walked in the door the receptionist looked up and smiled. Then she looked toward the gift shop and nodded, but turned back to them with a bigger smile. "You can't wait, can you? Go on back, they may have finished early."

As soon as Jason and Lucinda walked through the door several of the girls started humming the wedding march while Wilma held out her hand and said, "twenty dollars, please," as she waved a paper high in the air.

Jason grinned and pulled out a fifty- dollar bill. "Here, just take out for the bill and then you girls go out and spend the rest."

Wilma grinned and passed the test results to him. Since there was nobody waiting, they followed Jason and Lucinda back to the waiting area. The receptionist was standing in front of her desk with a large bouquet of flowers. "Here, we thought you should have flowers for your wedding."

Jason and Lucinda were so surprised. Lucinda had tears in her eyes as she said a wobbly thanks, but Jason pulled out his wallet again. This time he put twenty more dollars into Wilma's hand. "Add this to the other and all of you have a party for our wedding."

They all yelled thanks and good wishes as Jason and Lucinda hurried back to the car. Five minutes later they were parking in front of the church. Jason got out and came around to open Lucinda's door, but she just sat there. "Come on dear, the preacher is waiting. There's his car."

Lucinda looked up with wide frightened eyes. "Jason, what if I've not changed? What if it doesn't work out?"

Jason bent down and kissed her softly. "I promise you, it will work out. Lucinda, I'll do everything in my power to see that you have a happy life. Please don't back out on me now." He looked so worried that Lucinda's heart melted. She got out of the car and hand in hand they walked into the church.

Reverend Davis and his wife were sitting on a sofa in the church office, but they came out when Jason and Lucinda opened the door. "I told my wife that you two would be here before two o'clock."

Jason said, "Yes Sir. We want to be on our way to Ireland tomorrow, if at all possible."

Mrs. Davis smiled. "What a nice honeymoon trip. Were you high school sweethearts?"

"No. Jason was already a doctor when I met him," said Lucinda proudly.

"She was sixteen and the prettiest girl I'd ever seen. I've loved her since the first time I saw her, but we've had to wait over twenty years so please do the ceremony before she changes her mind," said Jason, trying to smile.

"Well, let's place you two in front of the altar. My wife can act as witness if that is all right."

"Wait! I left my flowers in the car," said Lucinda, turning to go out.

"No, you stay here. I'll get the flowers," said Jason, rushing out the door. He was soon back and Lucinda held the bouquet in her hand as she and Jason walked to stand in front of the altar.

"I have a camera. Would you like for me to make some pictures?" asked Mrs. Davis.

"That would be wonderful," said Lucinda, trying to smile, but found she was so nervous that she was trembling.

Then Reverend Davis began: "Dearly Beloved, we are here today to unite this man, Jason Henry McCall, and Lucinda Harmon Marshall in holy wedlock." He continued on and Lucinda shook worse by the minute. When Reverend Davis started the part of the ceremony about the rings Lucinda raised startled eyes to Jason's face. Jason smiled and opened his palm to show a large gold circle and a smaller one with similar designs. Lucinda trembled as she tried to put the ring on Jason's finger. Then Reverend Davis asked them to kneel with him to pray, and Jason had to help her down and almost lift her back to her feet after the prayer.

Then Reverend Davis said, "And now I pronounce you man and wife, Mr. and Mrs. Jason Henry McCall. You may now kiss the bride."

With tears streaming down her cheeks, Lucinda looked up into her new husband's face. She saw tears shimmering in his eyes as well, but he smiled as he bent his head and gave her a lingering soft kiss that felt like a promise.

Jason thanked Reverend Davis and handed him several bills, but Lucinda didn't know how much. "I don't charge this much, Dr. McCall."

"It's a donation to your church after you take out your fee and the cost of the film that your wife used."

Reverend Davis filled out the marriage certificate and told Jason to take it to the courthouse to be filed. "They will mail you your copy to put on display, but they will make you a copy of this one if you want them to."

"We'll want one and thank you again," said Jason as he turned with Lucinda to go out the door, but Mrs. Davis stopped them to give Jason the roll of film she had used.

When they were seated in the car, Jason breathed "Thank you, Jesus, and thank you, my darling Lucinda. You've made me the happiest man on earth."

Lucinda looked at him, and seeing the love and joy on his face, she dropped her head in her hands and cried. Jason pulled her into his arms. "Are you sad because you married me?"

"No, Jason. I . . . I think I've dreamed of this so long, but didn't really believe it would ever happen and now I'm just overcome."

"Well, it's real and we need to thank the Lord for hearing our prayers. I'm so very thankful, aren't you?"

Lucinda raised her head. "Yes, I am, Jason. I'm not acting much like it though, am I? What do we do now?" Lucinda pulled out some Kleenex and wiped her eyes.

"First we take this license to the courthouse and file it, but get a copy. Then it's up to you. I thought I might take you to the Martha Washington Inn for dinner. We could see a show at the Barter Theater after dinner and stay at the Martha Washington tonight or wherever you want to stay."

"Could we go back to my house tonight? No, I guess that would be too late after we have dinner and see a show. Maybe, we could just go back to your house," said Lucinda looking at Jason uneasily.

"Let's just go get this done at the Courthouse and then we can decide, okay."

They decided to go on to Abingdon, but still hadn't decided where to spend the night. "Jason, see if you can get Danny on your cell phone. I'll bet he'll be surprised."

"No, he won't. I told him and Emily what I hoped to do today. I didn't want you to see either of them this morning. They were so excited that I feared they'd give it away." Jason grinned. "I'll call them though, but we may have to wait until we get to a land phone. I could call the house, but they won't be back there until late. They were taking some more of their things to Morgantown today."

Suddenly Lucinda said, "We have to call Mom and Dad. If they should call the house and not find me they would worry."

Jason pulled her over closer to him. "Stop worrying, Mrs. McCall. We'll call anybody you want to, but we have to get someplace where we can."

Lucinda looked at Jason and suddenly smiled. "This is really true, isn't it? We are really together. Oh God, I hope it works because if it doesn't I couldn't stand it."

CHAPTER 13

Lucinda had never been to the Martha Washington Inn and she just couldn't believe how historically correct it seemed to be. She loved the ambience which was like an aura of a bygone era in every room. "Jason, this place is beautiful."

Soon they were seated in a spacious dining room with crystal and silver very much in evidence. Lucinda was in such awe that she was very careful about everything she touched. "Relax Lucinda. This is a restaurant, even if a bit grand, but the idea is to relax and enjoy your meal in this atmosphere."

"Already you are finding out how gauche I am. Aren't you sorry that you've married a girl with so few social graces?"

Jason grinned. "You just haven't been exposed. You just wait, my dear, you are going to learn fast. We'll go on the grand tour and see the world."

"See the world! I thought we were just going to Ireland."

"We are for our honeymoon, but that's just the beginning. We're going to enjoy ourselves. We're going to spend the rest of our lives just enjoying being together and making each other happy. It will make me happy to show you the places I have seen," said Jason with a broad grin at the look on Lucinda's face.

Jason ordered the dinner and also champagne. "Jason, we're church members. We shouldn't be drinking wine," cautioned Lucinda.

Jason's eyes blared. "Well if Jesus wasn't too good to drink wine, then I don't think church members should act as if they are better than Jesus."

Lucinda was stunned by an idea she had never heard espoused before and felt out of her depth in trying to refute what he had said. She'd been raised in the Baptist faith and they didn't believe in drunkenness or brawling, but she also knew that wine was served in their communion services.

Jason sat watching the different emotions flit across her face. "Lucinda, don't you think it may be a matter of excess? If church members are to keep themselves unspotted from the world then certainly they shouldn't go to wild parties and get drunk and carouse. Having a glass of wine with one's dinner, however, is a far cry from drunkenness."

Lucinda smiled. "You know, I don't think I've ever heard that subject discussed in those terms before. Grandpa often said that gluttony is a sin and I suppose that would apply to anything one overdid, wouldn't it?"

Their food was served and Lucinda ate orange roughy with some sauce that she'd never tried before, but it was delicious. The dessert was some sort of crème Brule, so Jason said, since Lucinda had no idea what it was. She did know she liked it, however. Then much to Lucinda's surprise a small wedding cake was brought to their table with the champagne. Everyone in the dining room stood and clapped as together they sliced the small cake.

Lucinda looked at Jason with such love in her eyes. "Jason, stop being so sweet or I'll break down and bawl right here in front of everyone."

Jason picked up his champagne glass and raised it aloft. "Friends, if my wife cries don't think she is sad. She cries when she's really happy and right now she seems to be happy."

Everybody laughed and then people started coming over to their table to congratulate them. One woman came tugging her husband along and stopped beside of Lucinda. "Honey, don't be embarrassed. I do the same thing," she looked at her husband and said, "Of course I often cry because I'm sad as well." Then she laughed and so did others who apparently knew her.

The champagne had given a rosy glow to an already dreamlike day and evening and when Jason looked at his watch and said, "Dear heart, we must leave if we want to see the play at Barter Theater." They thanked everyone again and then hurriedly left the restaurant.

The play being performed that night was a comedy entitled "Lend Me a Tenor." Lucinda and Jason along with everyone in the theater were soon consumed with laughter. "Jason, I've laughed so much that my sides are sore," complained Lucinda and then went into whoops again.

When they finally exited the theater it was eleven o'clock. When they reached the car, Jason helped Lucinda inside and closed the door then while walking around to the other side he did some urgent, though silent, praying. He didn't know how to approach Lucinda as to where they were to spend the night. He realized it would be foolish to drive all the way back to his house and even then Lucinda may not want to stay there. He opened his door and got in, but didn't start the engine. "Okay, Mrs. McCall, it's your call. Do we get a room here at the Martha Washington or do we drive back to my house?"

Lucinda drew a long breath. "I don't have any night clothes with me. I don't have a tooth brush or clean clothes for the morning either. I don't see how I can stay anywhere but at home."

Jason sat quietly thinking. "If you had those things would you stay here tonight?"

"That's a senseless question since I don't have them. I didn't know I would be getting married today."

"Still, would you stay here if you had those things?"

"It's a dumb question, but yes I'd stay here tonight. It is a long way back to Welch or Pineville and it is late."

Jason picked up her hand as it lay in her lap. "You remember that I said I had told Danny and Emily what I hoped to do, well, I also told them to pack you an overnight bag. It's in the trunk as is my overnight bag, but it may not be what you would have chosen."

"You tricked me, Jason. You got me to agree to stay here tonight knowing that you already had the answer," argued Lucinda, but Jason could tell she wasn't angry.

Jason put his arms around her and whispered. "Yes, I did, my dear. I have to learn to be with you. Right now, I'm scared."

Lucinda pushed back so she could see his face. "You scared! I can't believe it. You're not afraid of anything."

"Oh yes I am. I'm afraid that I might upset my beautiful wife because I haven't gotten to know her yet."

"Okay, you're scared and I'm scared so we'll just be scared together as we go try to get a place to sleep for the night," said Lucinda, clamping her lips together with a satisfied smirk.

They not only got a room, they got the bridal suite and Jason carried Lucinda across the threshold before he went back to get their luggage. When he came in and closed the door he found Lucinda exploring. "This is like a small apartment, isn't it? Is this like the apartments people have in penthouses?"

"Sort of, but those are as large as some houses and not just a suite of rooms," said Jason as he put their bags in the bedroom. When he came back in the room he had an ice bucket and a bottle of champagne. "I thought we'd drink a toast to our future. Will you join me, Mrs. McCall?"

Lucinda accepted the glass he poured her and raised it to her lips, but Jason cautioned her. "Don't gulp it, dear. Champagne is meant to be sipped."

"Oh, excu-use me, sir. I'm sorry if I offended you with my lack of social etiquette."

Jason set his glass down and turned to the window saying, "Come here, Lucinda. I want to show you something."

Lucinda walked to his side and he put his arm around her. "Now, look at that star, the one that is brightest. That star is just like the stars that seem to have lesser light. The only difference is that it is nearer the earth in its orbit. What I'm trying to tell you is that you are no better or no worse than the most polished hostess in New York or any other city. If you want to, you can gain all the social graces that you think you lack, but always remember, I fell in love with you as you are and I don't give a damn if you never become a social butterfly. I love you just the way you are."

Lucinda looked up at him and smiled. "Thank you, Jason. You say the nicest things." His arms tightened around her and he kissed her gently.

"Do you want to watch television, talk, dance or what?"

"I want to take a shower and get this rig off." She kicked off her high heels and scooted her feet along the floor. "Ooh that feels so good. We've walked fifty miles today."

"That we did. You can have the shower first. I feel scruffy myself. I think I'll listen to the news and try to call Danny and Emily. It's too late to call Burb Harmon since his curfew was always eleven o'clock."

Soon they were both showered and dressed in their night clothes. "Let's have a night cap before we call it a day, shall we?" Jason walked to the table and picked up the champagne bottle.

"Do you want me to be drunk?" said Lucinda, remembering all the nerve pills she had taken such a long time ago.

Jason came over and took her in his arms. "No, dear, I do not want you drunk. I want you to remember the first night you and I spend together for the rest of your life." Then he tipped his glass with hers and they both drank to their future. Jason lowered the glass to the table and then kissed her.

Years later the children would find Lucinda's memories of the most beautiful night that anyone could have ever had. In the present, however, she wouldn't talk about their wedding day to anyone. Oh, she gave the facts as to who married them and in what church, but her thoughts and feelings were never discussed., When asked about their wedding night she only turned red and smiled as if she was shielding a marvelous secret. She knew that she didn't have words to describe the feelings of being united in body, soul, heart, and mind with the person she had loved all her life. That's why she only smiled.

Lucinda awoke the next morning with Jason's arms around her and she felt so loved and cherished. "Good Morning! I thought I was going to have to shake you to get you awake," said Jason as he leaned over and kissed her gently.

Lucinda turned red but snuggled closer to Jason and whispered. "I feel . . . I feel like a bright, shiny penny that has just been minted."

Jason grinned impishly. You look like a rosebud just ready to bloom and I feel ten feet tall."

"Well, you're not, so we'd better get out of these rooms before we are charged for another night," said Lucinda, pushing at Jason.

CHAPTER 14

The next two days were a frenzy of activity for not only Jason and Lucinda, but Danny, Emily, Burb and Nancy Harmon, and all of Lucinda's brothers and sisters who still lived in McDowell County.

When Jason and Lucinda left the Martha Washington, Jason had already revised his plans. He realized that Lucinda would not leave home without seeing Danny and her parents. Now, that they were married Jason realized that he also needed to rethink his hasty get-away. *I need to secure the house, put the phone to sleep, and tell the Post Office to hold my mail,* thought Jason as they drove back to Welch since he had plans to make their honeymoon an extended trip to England and Germany.

Danny and Emily were helping to get the rest of Lucinda's furnishings packed and taken to Sam's garage. Lucinda took the clothes and other keepsakes she wanted to keep to Jason's house. Kyle and Rita Bender promised to keep an eye on Jason's house while they were away. Jason had to cancel the phone, electricity, newspaper, and magazine service while at the same time Lucinda had to do all that for her place in Wyoming County. Jason did his on a temporary basis, but Lucinda's was final since her house was sold.

Burb and Nancy wanted to have a big dinner on the evening before they were to leave and have all the family there. Lucinda went to visit Margie and Jill, Jeff's sisters, for several hours. She packed and unpacked two suitcases several times until Jason in exasperation closed the lids and dared her to open them again. "If you've forgotten something we will buy whatever it is. You're making yourself a nervous wreck and me also just watching you."

Lucinda jumped up and thumped him on the chest. "All right, Mr. Money Bags, if you want to spend money on things I already have, so be it."

This caused a wrestling match in which Lucinda was the loser, but she soon decided that losing was more fun anyway and didn't mind at all. Of course this made them later getting everything packed and the house emptied. Danny came in after taking a load to Sam and Jill's and stood in the door grimacing, "I thought you two were going to have the bed taken apart and be ready. Instead it looks like you've had a wrestling match."

Jason grinned. "We have and I won. I couldn't get your mother to quit packing and unpacking her suitcases so I had to wrestle her down. I didn't like it one bit either." Lucinda hit him in the stomach on her way to the bathroom.

Danny shook his head in amazement as he turned to Emily who had just come in, "These two haven't done one thing. They've been wrestling instead of working, or so they say." Emily turned red as she looked at her father and saw his satisfied smirk.

Without much help from Jason and Lucinda, everything was finally moved from the house. A cleaning service was hired to come in and clean the entire house. Mavis Hylton, Lucinda's long-time friend, was given money to pay them and was asked to see that they did a good job.

"If they don't clean it right they won't get any money from me," she said looking amazed at the amount Jason had given her. "In fact, I think I'll take a supervising fee from this myself. This is too much money just for cleaning a house this size."

This caused everybody to start laughing. Lucinda and Danny because it was so unlike Mavis to kid, especially around people she didn't know very well. Jason and Emily laughed because this nice old lady thought she was being asked to do all this for nothing.

"Mrs. Hylton, you take a hundred out of that for your help. I intended you to have it anyway," said Jason, smiling warmly.

"Charlie Hylton would have my head if I took a penny from Lucinda. She's like our own daughter," countered Mavis.

"Yes, I know, and I thank you, but this is for me. You see if I can't get you to do this, I won't get Lucinda away from here until the new people are ready to move in," said Jason. "So, please accept it and you'll be doing us a big favor."

By seven o'clock that evening there was nothing else left to do. Lucinda hugged Mavis who whispered, "Be happy, honey. God knows you deserve it."

Lucinda finally rode away from the house she had lived in for many years. It had been a good neighborhood, but a house of anguish and she knew she'd never miss it. She would miss Mavis and Charlie Hylton though and waved at Mavis until she was out of sight. "I don't know what Danny and I would have done had it not been for

Mavis and Charlie Hylton. They were like parents to me and grandparents to Danny."

"You can come back to see them, dear. I suppose our home base will be in Welch."

"What do you mean by home base? Are we going to be vagabonds and roam the earth?" asked Lucinda tiredly. "If that's what you think you can count me out. I'm too tired to do much roaming."

Jason looked across at her smiling fondly. "Well, I thought we'd visit some places, but always come back to McDowell County. Of course Abingdon has become a favorite place of mine in the last few days."

Lucinda slid across the seat and snuggled against Jason. She yawned. "I have a great fondness for it as well, especially the Martha Washington Inn."

Jason smiled as he slid his arm around her. "I told you so, didn't I?"

Lucinda sat up. "Well, how was I to know that . . . well that things could be so different?"

By this time they were over Indian Ridge and nearing Welch. Jason drove slowly as they passed the little park that held such poignant memories for both of them. "Do you want to stop and look at the moon?" asked Jason.

Lucinda looked out the window. "There is no moon. It's as black as ink. I can't even see a star."

They pulled into Jason's driveway. "Gosh, we're at your house already. That was a quick trip."

"It isn't my house, Lucinda. It is our house . . .your house and mine."

"I'm not used to saying that. It has always been your house and Janet's. I always looked every time I passed here, but I had to be careful or Jeff would have found out it was where you lived. I don't know what he may have tried if he had known where you lived."

"If you feel you won't be comfortable living here, we'll sell the house and buy or build another one," said Jason as he opened his door. When they were in the house he looked at Lucinda steadily. "I mean that, Lucinda. If you'd rather not live in this house we'll get another one."

"I don't want to think about that right now. Anyway, I only mentioned what Jeff's reaction would have been if he'd known where you lived," said Lucinda.

"Let's forget about that man, okay. Thinking of him is very unpleasant. I'm tired, hungry, and need a shower, how about you?"

"I just want a shower and then bed. I feel like I could sleep a week," said Lucinda as she plopped down on the sofa.

"Let me wash my hands and I'll fix us something to eat. "How's that sound?" asked Jason.

Lucinda looked up at him sleepily. "Are you going to cook? I don't want anything, but I'll fix something for you."

"No, you won't. You can take a shower, a nap, or watch television, but I'll fix us something to eat. We had lunch at eleven o'clock and it's now eight o'clock. I believe in eating more often than that. You go on and do whatever you want. I'll find you when the food is ready."

Lucinda looked at him in puzzlement. "You mean you really are going to cook?"

"Yes, I'm really going to cook. I've been doing it for several years now. I cooked before Janet died. Don't look so stunned. I'll let you help me mow the lawn. I believe in shared work," said Jason, laughing at the look on Lucinda's face.

Lucinda didn't know what to think so she wandered into the bedroom and gathered a clean nightgown and robe before heading to the bathroom. When she came out of the bathroom ten minutes later the most wonderful aroma drifted through the door.

She went back into the bathroom and brushed her hair and put cream on her face. "Hey, woman how long are you going to be in there. Food is ready to put on the table," yelled Jason as he came into the living room.

"What have you cooked? It smells wonderful." Lucinda sniffed. "Is it some kind of chicken?

Jason met her halfway through the living room and put his arms around her and swung her into the air. "Um you smell better than the chicken, but yes it is a chicken pasta dish that is quick and both Emily and I like it. Come on," he said as he swung Lucinda around again and danced her into the kitchen.

When Emily and Danny came in they had just finished eating. "Hey, did you two save any food for us?" asked Danny, eying the table hungrily.

"There's enough left. I expected you two to be hungry since Lucinda and I wrestled instead of helping you," said Jason as he put two new plates on the table. "Emily you can get your drinks. I have to take a shower. Since my wife is all clean and smells so good I want to return the favor."

Both Emily and Danny stared at Jason and then Lucinda as if they didn't know what to think. "What is it?" asked Lucinda, looking puzzled. "You're both staring as if Jason and I are Martians or something."

Danny came over and put his arms around Lucinda. "Mom, I'm just amazed at the change in you and in Jason. You both walk around as if you have 'the world on a string' to use a cliché. I've never seen you like this in my life."

Lucinda hugged Danny and looked up at him. "I'm happy, Danny. I'm so happy. I don't know what to do with myself sometimes. I want to pinch myself because I can't believe this has happened to me."

Jason stood looking at Lucinda with a look on his face that made Lucinda's heart leap for joy. "Danny, you wanted me to be happy and Jason has made me happy. Just be glad for us and you and Emily try to find what we have. We'll pray that God will grant you two the kind of love he has blessed us with."

Emily came over and put her arms around Lucinda. "Mama . . . may I call you, Mama, Lucinda?

Jason laughed. "Mama Lucinda, that sounds good to me. How does it sound to you, Lucinda?"

Danny laughed. "Do you mean Emily is to call Mom, Mama Lucinda? I think it fits. What say you, Mama Lucinda?"

Lucinda looked at Jason and smiled then hugged Emily close. "I love it, Emily. I'll try to be a good mama to you."

Jason turned toward the bathroom. "Okay, that's settled and I'm going to take my shower. All of us are scheduled to eat with the Harmon family tomorrow, so you two had best get some food down you. Lucinda and I will clean up after you're finished since we didn't really help much today." He laughed and left the room.

Soon Emily and Danny were seated at the table with filled plates. "Mom, we've decided to leave for Morgantown when you and Jason leave on your trip. Is everything settled about the house?" asked Danny.

Lucinda had poured a glass of milk and now took a sip. "The money for the house is in the bank. I put your money for college in your account, and all the deeds are signed. We have furniture in the room over Sam's garage and if you need any of it you have the key. Yes, I believe everything has been done."

Emily looked up at Danny. "I don't have to ask Dad. He made a list and didn't stop until every detail was as he thought it should be. One thing I can tell you, Mama Lucinda, is that Dad is a stickler for details."

Lucinda grinned. "Good! Now I won't have to worry about forgetting something I'm supposed to do."

They were discussing their living quarters in Morgantown when Jason came back in tying the sash on his dressing gown. "Dad, I told Mama Lucinda that I knew you had everything taken care of here already since you're such a stickler for details," said Emily, smiling fondly at her father.

Jason pulled out a chair beside Lucinda and sat down. He put his arm around her and closed his eyes sniffing appreciatively. "What? Oh, yes I have everything in order. Why? I certainly can't just lock the door and walk away without making arrangements about the house and other business, like some people I know. Danny, my dear daughter will leave the lights on, the stove on, and forget her house key if you don't keep an eye on her."

Emily jumped up. "Daddy, you know I'm not that bad. I've never left the stove on . . . Well, I did one time, but that was right after we came back here after Mom died."

Danny saw that Emily was hurt and he said, "I've found Emily to be very reliable. I don't think I'll have anything to worry about."

Jason got up and pulled Lucinda up with him. "I was kidding you, Emily. You and Danny better get ready for tomorrow while Lucinda and I clean up the kitchen. That's another thing. Tomorrow evening we'll have to clean all the food out of the refrigerator and turn everything off. That means we'll have to get breakfast somewhere else in case you hadn't thought of it."

They all laughed. "See, didn't I tell you Dad was a stickler for details."

CHAPTER 15

The four of them piled into Jason's car at ten thirty the next morning heading over the mountains to the dinner at Burb Harmon's place. The drive was spent with Danny regaling them with stories about the trips he and Lucinda had made over the mountains to see his Papaw.

"He shocked me when he suddenly said, 'Pon my honor, Papaw loves me,'" said Lucinda laughing happily. "He hadn't been putting many words into sentences. That's what shocked me."

Emily snuggled close to Danny in the back seat. "I'll bet he was a cute little boy, wasn't he?"

Lucinda turned her head to give Danny a loving look. "Yes, he was. I'm shocked that he's turned out to look so much like his papaw."

"Didn't you want him to look like his papaw?" asked Emily.

"Sure, I'm glad he looks like Dad, but the shock is because everybody always said he looked so much like Jeff, and he did, at first," said Lucinda frowning in puzzlement. "I don't know when he changed, but I guess one can get a shock or be startled when you realize you've been wrong."

"I'm glad Danny doesn't look like his father. I don't like that man," said Emily. "If I were you I'd be glad Danny changed instead of being shocked."

"There are many kinds of shock, Emily," said Lucinda. "I didn't mean shock in that sense. I only mean that I was startled when I was first made to notice how Danny had changed. "

"Let me tell you about shock," said Jason. "Lucinda is right. There are many ways to be shocked because that wasn't the kind of shock I received. I mean I wasn't shocked because I realized I was wrong, but because I knew I was doing something wrong. I knew I shouldn't be going to Bradshaw hoping to see Lucinda, but I really didn't think I would see her. I did though. I almost knocked Lucinda down with the door as I came out of the drugstore. I'd been driving to Bradshaw almost every week and had almost given up seeing her. Then I flung the door open and there she was at my feet," said Jason, chuckling as he took Lucinda's hand. "Now, that was a real shock."

"I'm surprised you didn't get a black eye," said Lucinda.

"Yes, Mr. Marshall would have tried it, but he was too busy trying to get you away from me. He did use a few choice words as he shoved me away," stated Jason, scowling.

Not wanting to tell Danny and Emily things they didn't know, Lucinda interrupted as they passed Number

One Bartley camp. "Emily it was at this mine that ninety-one miners were killed in an explosion."

From there the talk was about how coal had been the cause of the building but also the cause of the desolation in the area. "It's like the two sides of a coin, isn't it?" said Emily thoughtfully. "One side builds things up and then the coin is flipped and everything goes downhill."

Several cars were parked below the house when they reached Burb and Nancy Harmon's place. "Well, it looks like the whole family has shown up, Mom," said Danny eagerly.

Lucinda looked at Jason and laughed. "Danny knows he's going to get royal treatment from all the family."

Danny had already gotten out, but turned to Lucinda. "Now, Mom, you know I don't let that bother me, but I do love every one of them and not because of their treatment, either."

Lucinda didn't have a chance to reply since family members rushed out to meet them before they could get into the yard.

"Well, Pon my honor, Danny, if you ain't brung your Mommy and her new husband," said Burb, giving Danny a hug before turning to Lucinda. He opened his arms wide and Lucinda walked into her father's embrace. He hugged her close and looking over her head at Jason, he said, "You be good to my Cindy, Doctor McCall, or you'll have to answer to me."

Jason smiled and put out his hand. "I'll do that, Brother Harmon, since I don't want to have to answer to you."

Burb looked contrite as he shook Jason's hand. "I'm sorry, Brother McCall. That wasn't a brotherly greeting was it?"

"No, Brother, it wasn't, but I understand your concern. I don't think you'll ever have any cause to be upset, though. I don't want to own Lucinda. I just want to share my life with her," said Jason, gripping Burb's hand.

Emily went over and hugged Burb. "Papaw, you and Dad quit being so formal with each other. You should be Brother Burb and Dad should be Brother Jason since you belong to the same church."

Burb hugged Emily. "You're right, little Sister Emily. I guess I'm not used to seeing Lucinda with a man. That first one wasn't near what I thought he was."

Lucinda was soon encircled by her sisters, her mother, and Gordon who were all talking at once. Lucinda reached out her hand to Jason and pulled him to her side. "In case you people haven't met him, this is my husband who, if you recall, was too old for me and just wanted someone to pass the time with since he was lonely."

When Lucinda saw their stricken looks she gurgled with laughter. "It's all right. I was kidding anyway. Jason, this is Odell, Oprey, and Ellen, my sisters, and this is Gordon, my brother. Faye, Nathan, and Benjamin live too far away to get back very often." Jason smiled and shook hands with all of them and they all trooped inside to find Danny already there hugging Nancy, his grandmother.

Nancy pulled away from Danny and came to Lucinda and Jason and put her arms around them both. She looked up with tears in her eyes. "I've prayed that this day would happen for three years." She wiped her eyes on her apron. "Be happy and be good to each other."

Jason hugged Nancy again. "Please don't worry, Mrs., I mean Sister Nancy. I promise that I'll do everything in my power to make Lucinda happy as long as I live."

Nancy stepped back and looked up at him solemnly. "I believe you will, son. I truly do."

Dinner was on the table and every seat was soon filled, but the children all filled plates and took them out on the porch.

"I hate to see them young'uns havin' to eat out there," said Nancy, looking through the window with a sad look.

Odell looked at her mother. "They're tickled to death to get out there together and talk teenager talk. They don't want to have to listen to us old fogeys."

"Well, I resent that, Aunt Odell. Emily and I aren't exactly old fogeys," said Danny.

"We put you on that special place beside of Poppy. Don't you remember asking for that seat every time you came over?" asked Odell.

Danny grinned and slid closer to Burb. "We're the two best looking men here, aren't we, Papaw? So, we deserve the best seat, I think."

Burb laid down his fork and looked sideways at Danny. "Well, pon-my-honor, you not only look like me, you've got a big head like I have, ain't you? We can't help it though, it was the Good Lord that made us sech fine lookin' fellers, and we had nary thing to do with it."

Lucinda laughed. "You two do look alike, that's for sure."

"They don't just look alike, they act alike also," said Gordon from the other end of the table. "I know Dad feels proud since none of his sons really looked that much like him."

Soon everyone was finished and left the kitchen to congregate in the living room. With sighs of comfort they all settled in their chairs as Burb spoke up. "I hear you're taking Cindy across the ocean for a honeymoon, Brother Jason. Why do you want to go so far?"

Jason looked at Lucinda and raised his eyebrows. "That's the only way I could get her to marry me. Every time I mentioned Ireland you should have seen her eyes light up, so I took a chance and promised that we'd go there."

Lucinda leaned over from her perch on the arm of Jason's chair and hugged him. "Ye-s-s, and we already have the tickets. I'm so excited. I'm going to kiss the Blarney Stone and Jason will take my picture doing it."

Jason looked up at Lucinda and smiled. "See what I mean. It was a honeymoon in Ireland or no wedding."

Burb looked astonished. "Well, pon my honor, Cindy, I never heard you mention anything about Ireland before. Did you always want to go there?"

Lucinda grinned. "I kept a lot of things to myself, Dad, but yes, I always dreamed of going to Ireland. That's not the reason I married Jason though."

Burb got up to turn on the television since it was time for the six o'clock news. "We all know that, Cindy. Every one of us has always knowed you loved that doctor from the day you first set eyes on him. I'd have to say, though that you tried to be a good wife to Jeff."

Nancy butted in. "I reckon she did. She nearly killed herself trying to keep him peaceful. We didn't know how he was, but we knew something was keeping Cindy skinny, and run-down." She looked at Danny and grinned sadly. "Course, Danny dropped a few hints along the way, so we knew things weren't like Cindy wanted us to believe."

Jason stood up. "I'd rather not talk about that man, if you folks don't mind. I don't want to spend my opinion of Danny's father."

Lucinda jumped to her feet as well and took Jason's arm. "Come on, I want to show you the trees that Grandpa and I always loved."

When Jason and Lucinda went out, all eyes were turned to Danny. "We should watch what we say, I guess," said Odell.

"Dad isn't angry, Aunt Odell. It's just that he loves Mama Lucinda so much and he can't stand to think about how Danny's dad treated her," said Emily.

"Emily's right. Jason isn't upset with any of you. He's a really nice man and if ever a man loved a woman, Jason loves my mom," said Danny with assurance.

"I wish I was going to Ireland," said Oprey. "Heck, I wish I was going to Florida or even to Bluefield once in a while."

Odell laughed. "I don't know, Oprey, living in Michigan hasn't done me much good. Well, yes it has. It has given my children the opportunity to attend college. I don't think we could have made enough to send them, living back here."

Jason and Lucinda came back hand in hand, laughing like two teenagers. "Danny and Emily, I think we'd better go. My wife has some strange ideas of what's fun. I don't think I'm ready to climb apple trees."

"Climb apple trees! Why in the world does she want to climb apple trees?" asked Gordon.

Jason looked at Lucinda and grinned wickedly. "I don't know exactly, but it was something about 'me Jane and you Tarzan'."

Lucinda turned red and punched Jason on the shoulder as she walked past him on her way to the bathroom.

Jason had Danny and Emily ready and as she came into the living room, he said, "Well, dear, if we want to catch a six o'clock plane in the morning I think we should get back to Welch, don't you?"

Lucinda made the rounds of farewell hugs for all her sisters and her brother, but almost broke down when she hugged Nancy and Burb. "Daddy, you and Mommy be happy for me, please. I know it is a long way off, but when I lived in Michigan I had no way of getting back. With Jason, he would see that I got home some way if I was needed. I'll send post cards and write."

Jason interrupted. "We'll call when we arrive in Ireland, and like Lucinda says, I'll see that she gets home if anything happens."

This didn't keep the tears from clouding Nancy's eyes, nor Burb's voice from sounding husky as they said their good-byes, even though they bravely smiled as their youngest daughter drove away with her new husband.

CHAPTER 16

The alarm woke Lucinda at three-thirty the next morning. She jerked up and pushed her tousled hair out of her eyes. Jason was coming out of the bathroom. "Okay, sleepy-head, it's all yours. Get a move on. We have a long drive ahead of us."

Lucinda swung her feet over the side of the bed. "We should have gone to Charleston last night. I'm so sleepy I'll probably drown."

"I'll come back and shower with you, if you want me to," said Jason suggestively.

Lucinda grinned. "Not this time, mister. You go make some coffee. I'll manage on my own."

They were soon on the road, but still with their coffee in the cup holders anchored to each door. Lucinda stretched. "Why didn't you insist that we go to Charleston last night? I'm still wooly headed."

"You would have cried your eyes out if you hadn't gotten to spend last night with Danny. It was hard enough to get you away, this morning." Jason stopped when he saw the tears running down Lucinda's cheeks.

"Now, Lucinda, you know both Danny and Emily wanted us to go and besides they are leaving for Morgantown this morning. I hope to God they remember to turn the water off and lock the doors," said Jason worriedly.

Lucinda wiped her cheeks and took a drink of coffee. "You can call Rita. If they forget Kyle will see that everything is safe. I didn't see the need of turning the water off. If we aren't using any the bill won't be any higher."

"It will if there's a leak left undetected for any length of time."

Lucinda didn't reply since she had already learned that Jason was very frugal about many things that she wouldn't have even thought about.

An hour later they pulled into the parking lot at Yaeger Airport. Jason went to the office and signed some papers, relinquished his keys, and then went to get their boarding passes. He noticed that Lucinda was pale and very quiet, but thought it was because she was still thinking of Danny and didn't comment about it.

They were soon checked through security and ushered on board their plane on the first leg of the trip that would take them to Idlewilde Airport in New York. Lucinda was seated beside a window and Jason on the aisle side next to her. He reached over and fastened her seatbelt just as the stewardess came through, requesting that everyone should fasten their seat belts. Jason clasped Lucinda's hand and smiled. When the plane began to move Jason felt Lucinda flinch and turned to look just as the plane lifted off the runway. He gasped as he saw Lucinda slump toward him.

He summoned the stewardess. "Do you have some smelling salts and a coke? My wife has just fainted."

The stewardess hurried away and soon returned with the requested items. Lucinda moved her head and pushed at Jason's hand as he waved the smelling salts beneath her nose. "Don't. That smells awful," she mumbled and opened her eyes.

Jason handed the smelling salts to the stewardess and pulled Lucinda upright. "Here, drink this coke. You fainted. I didn't know you were feeling ill. Why didn't you say something?"

Lucinda looked up at him and through trembling lips she whispered. "I couldn't. I'm too scared." She started struggling to get up. "I'm going to be sick."

Jason quickly unfastened his seat belt and hers and helped her to her feet. Then he hurried her to the bathroom, where she was sick. Finally, Jason mopped her face. "Stay here. I'm going to get my bag. I have something for motion sickness, but I believe this is a panic attack. Has this happened before?"

Now Lucinda was crying. "No. I've never been on a plane before."

Jason gasped in surprise. "Why didn't you tell me? I could have given you something before we boarded the plane."

"Then I wouldn't have gotten to go to Ireland," she wailed.

"Stay here and don't move," said Jason as he hurried away. Lucinda knew someone was waiting outside the door, but she didn't care since she felt sick again.

Jason came back just as she stopped vomiting. He expertly slid a needle into her arm and rubbed the spot. "Okay. You'll feel better in a little bit. Are you able to go back to our seats? Three people are waiting to use the restroom."

"I'll try. Jason, I'm sorry." Lucinda stepped out, holding onto Jason's hand and looked at the other women standing in line. She mumbled. "I'm sorry."

Jason kept her on her feet until they reached their seats. Once she was seated and had a pillow placed behind her head she was nodding off. Jason smiled at her tenderly and kissed her forehead.

An hour later they landed at Idlewilde Airport and Jason had to waken her, but she was still so drugged that she walked like a robot.

Later Lucinda wondered what people thought as Jason sleep- walked her to a seat. He sat with her leaning against his shoulder until their next flight was called and then sleep- walked her again through security. "I'm a doctor and my wife has never flown before. She had a panic attack when we first became air-borne from Charleston, West Virginia and I had to sedate her." He pulled out his credentials to be inspected. Doing this while trying to keep Lucinda on her feet, must have been hard and looked worse. He ended up having to show their passports, their marriage license and their flight tickets to Belfast International Airport in Belfast, Ireland.

The clerk looked up at Jason and smiled. "Everything seems to be in order, except your wife. Did she faint or what happened? I've seen lots of panic attacks?"

Jason grinned. “She’d never ridden a plane before, but she wanted to go to Ireland so badly that she didn’t tell anybody.”

They were nearing land in Ireland when Lucinda awoke again. She raised her head and looked at Jason. He smiled. “Hello, Mr. T.”

She squeezed her eyes together as if trying to think. “Oh! The A Team! Mr. T couldn’t ride a plane without being knocked out, could he?” Lucinda smiled sleepily. “Where are we?”

“We’re over Ireland and will be landing in about five minutes. How do you feel?” asked Jason, looking at her closely.

“I’m still sleepy, but I feel all right otherwise. What did you give me?”

“I gave you a nerve medicine that is mild and has no side effects in that dosage. I had to give you something since you were so sick and we hadn’t been in the air ten minutes,” said Jason.

Lucinda squeezed his arm and said, “Thank you, Jason. I’m sorry I’m such a bother.”

“I could have saved you all that sickness had I known you’d never ridden a plane. No harm done, though. We’ll know on our flight home,” said Jason just as the seatbelt light came on and the captain announced they were coming in for a landing.

Soon they were in the airport and waiting by the carousal to retrieve their luggage. A young boy with a kilt and a sash across his chest approached them.

“Mr. and Mrs. McCall, I have a taxi waiting to take you and your luggage to your hotel,” he said in that lovely Irish dialect that Lucinda had always loved.

When they were seated in the taxi and speeding down the highway on the wrong side of the road, Lucinda said, “How did that boy know who we were?”

“When I purchased our tickets I told them I wanted all the amenities, so I suppose that is part of it,” said

Jason, looking around him. Lucinda was looking from right to left like a kid turned loose in a candy store.

"He's driving on the wrong side of the road isn't he? Oh I forgot. That's the side they use in Europe isn't it?" asked Lucinda.

Jason agreed but told her that they drove on the right side in Holland. "I can't remember right now if any other countries in Europe use the same side as we do in the states, but England sure doesn't."

The taxi pulled up under the portico of the magnificent Hastings Culloden Hotel and soon they found themselves in a suite of rooms on the second floor so opulent that Lucinda caught her breath. She turned around and around looking up at the Louis XV chandeliers. She realized all the furnishings were antiques and she wondered how they dared to display such beautiful paintings since she knew they were very valuable. "Jason, this must be the royal suite. You can't afford this, can you?"

"This is their honeymoon suite and yes, I can afford it. I'll never get to take you on our first honeymoon trip again and I want it to be the best honeymoon any woman could ever have," said Jason as he swept her into his arms and danced around the room and stopped at the window. "We are looking at the Belfast Lough or Lake as we say in America. Quite a view, isn't it?"

Lucinda stood in the circle of his arms and gazed in wonder. She hugged Jason tightly around the waist as if she feared this would all end. She looked up at him with her soul bared. "Thank you so much, Jason. I love you with all my heart."

Jason bent to kiss her. "I love you too, darling, and also with all my heart." Lucinda suddenly didn't feel nearly as tired, but that didn't matter for just then the doorbell rang. Jason opened it to reveal a porter pushing a trolley loaded with food as well as champagne.

The porter popped the cork and poured two drinks and then smiled. "Compliments of Hastings Culloden Hotel! Welcome to Belfast."

Jason placed some money in his palm which brought another big smile to his face before he left. Jason looked at Lucinda. "I'm almost too tired to eat, aren't you?"

Lucinda nodded wearily. It was four o'clock in the afternoon and they had now been up and about for twelve straight hours. They quietly ate their food, or at least some of it, took showers, and tumbled into bed. Suddenly Lucinda jumped up. "Jason, we didn't call Danny and Emily or Mom and Dad."

Jason shook his head. "They don't need this call as much as I need some sleep, but I'll call them. Otherwise, neither of us will get any sleep. What's your Dad's number?"

After Lucinda and Jason had talked to her parents, Lucinda sat waiting until they got Danny on the phone. When she found that they were already in Morgantown and really liked their landlady, she turned and flopped back on the bed. Jason settled the cover over her shoulders and pulled her close. They both fell into a dreamless sleep.

Lucinda awoke with Jason's arms around her. "Good morning, my beautiful wife."

Lucinda leaned up and kissed him. "Good morning, my handsome husband. How long have you been awake?"

Jason kissed her and said, "Just long enough to thank God for allowing me to finally marry you."

Lucinda got up on her knees and looked down at him. "Oh Jason, you say the sweetest things."

"I'm not just talking, dear. I truly mean it. You are the best thing that has ever happened to me and I know I have God to thank for it."

Lucinda looked down with tears in her eyes. "I know . . . I thank God all day long that HE has given us this opportunity. We are truly soul mates, aren't we?"

Jason pulled her down on top of him, and crushed her to him. "Yes, my soul, you are my mate. God intended for us to be together and we would have been sooner if other people hadn't meddled in our lives."

Lucinda paused deep in thought. "No, I don't think so, Jason. Remember I told you before that I think we needed to grow to who we are now before we could be what the other one needed."

Jason grinned. "You may be right and speaking of needs . . ." and then there was no further talk for a long time.

CHAPTER 17

That started the first day of a honeymoon that words could never describe for its beauty, its romance, its glamour, and its complete happiness. From the time they arose in the mornings their itinerary was scheduled. "I wanted you to see everything I'd heard you mention so I called the tour service and told them what you wanted to see," explained Jason.

Even though it was scheduled it wasn't a rushed schedule. They stopped where they wanted to and stayed as long as they wanted to. Lucinda did kiss the Blarney Stone, which was at the top of a 15th century castle. They had to climb up a steep slippery spiral staircase to get to it. "If I'd known I had to almost lie down on my back to kiss the darn thing, or how scary it was going to be I wouldn't have been so eager to do it," said Lucinda when her feet were back on solid ground.

Jason laughed. "I was holding you. I wouldn't have let you fall."

"You seemed to be just holding my legs. The rest of me could have fallen," complained Lucinda.

"No, you couldn't. I was holding your hips and legs and the tour guide had his hands under your back. You were just so scared you didn't feel them," said Jason. "When I put you back on your feet you were as white as a ghost. I think I've married a coward."

"Me, a coward! I didn't see you lying on your back under that big rock," said Lucinda.

"I had no desire to kiss a rock. I talk quite well enough already," said Jason smugly as he took her hand. "Come on we haven't toured the castle yet."

They walked along the Giant Causeway listening raptly as the guide told them the legend that explained its presence. Lucinda had a handheld recorder and recorded the story. That night she transcribed the tape and faxed a copy of the legend to Danny and Emily.

Every day they visited something new such as the Old Bushmill's Distillery, the home of Irish malt whiskey. Even though Jason said it was really good, Lucinda still shivered when she took a sip. They also toured Dunluce Castle, located one hundred feet above the ocean on a solid basalt rock. They had to cross a twenty-foot chasm to get from the coast to the castle. "Some of the castle ruins date back to twelve hundred A.D.," explained the guide.

That wasn't the only chasm or deep gulch they had to cross though. Lucinda would never forget their hair-raising walk over the Carrick-a-Rede Rope Bridge which led to the Carrick-a-Rede Island. She took one look down and almost dropped. They were walking across a twenty-three meters deep chasm. Once they reached Carrick Island there was a fantastic view of Rathlin Island and Scotland. Lucinda, however, was so terrorized that she didn't really enjoy any of it. Her only thoughts were about having to return across that swinging rope bridge.

Jason became more and more concerned about Lucinda's pallor as they made their way back across the bridge. Once back on the other side, he said, "You were terrified the entire time and yet you went right on, didn't you? You should have just refused to go."

Lucinda was afraid to move or even raise her head since she felt bile rising and suddenly she began vomiting. Jason held her head, wiped her face, and then pulled out a flask which held Irish Malt Whiskey and put it to her lips. She swallowed and then pushed it away and sank to the ground. "Just let me rest a while," she whispered through trembling lips. Jason sat down beside her and put his arm around her.

"Here, darling lean back against me and try to relax. We'll not visit any other place that has this kind of access, I promise. I wouldn't have gone this time, but I thought you wanted to," he said as he wiped her face again.

They had been in Ireland three weeks and every day and every night until very late they had visited different sites, eaten in different pubs or restaurants. One night they stayed in a Bed and Breakfast owned by an elderly couple. Lucinda loved that even if it was difficult to understand much of what the couple said. Their English was mixed with Gaelic and sounded lyrical, but made very little sense to Lucinda.

They returned to their hotel in Belfast on Thursday of their third week in Ireland and promised each other that they would just loll around and rest the next day. They intended to take a tour to the Cliffs of Moher which jutted out into the Atlantic Ocean and then take in an Irish music festival and a few other sites before they returned to the States. Jason had plans to stay several weeks in England and then make a side trip to Germany, but he hadn't told Lucinda.

Those plans were changed however. On Friday afternoon just as they came in from swimming the phone rang.

Lucinda's eyes widened as she gasped. "That's Danny, Jason."

Jason turned puzzled eyes to Lucinda as he picked up the phone. "Jason, this is Danny. I don't want to upset Mom, but Papaw was rushed to the hospital last night. Emily and I are leaving now. Aunt Odell called us a few minutes ago."

"Danny, you tell the family that we'll fly out tonight and should be in the States sometime tomorrow. We'll try to get a flight into Charleston or even Bluefield if we can get there quicker. You call us back as soon as you find out what happened," said Jason and putting down the phone turned to Lucinda.

"Your Dad's in the hospital, dear, and I know you'll want to go home, so you start packing and I'll see about tickets and flights," said Jason since he knew that Lucinda would handle this news better if she was forced to stay busy until the shock wore off.

Lucinda grabbed Jason's arm. "What's wrong with him, Jason? Dad has never been sick."

"Danny didn't know, darling. Odell has just called him and he immediately called us. You remember that I told him to call us if any member of your family or mine became ill while we were away."

Jason hugged her close. "Be brave, dear. It may be appendicitis or something minor, but we'll go home anyway. That's what you want isn't it?"

Lucinda nodded and wiped the tears from her eyes. Then she pushed out of his arms. "You get us a flight and I'll get the packing done, but first I'm going to shower. The chlorine in the water makes my skin feel awful and we'll need to shower before we leave anyway."

"I'll get our flight and then shower. That way, I can help you get everything packed," said Jason as he released her and patted her shoulder.

All while she was taking her shower she was praying, *Lord, please take care of Daddy. He didn't want me to come to Ireland, but I wanted to come so badly. I have been so happy with Jason, Lord. Is it wrong to love some man so much that one forgets about their family? Please, please Lord, let Daddy be all right. If I've done wrong, punish me, but please let Daddy be all right.*

When Jason finished his calls and came to the bedroom he found her sitting forlornly on the side of the bed weeping copiously. "What's wrong, dear? I know you are worried, but don't think the worst. It may be gastritis or something that's easily cured. Come on now, if you keep this up you'll be sick before we can get home."

Lucinda looked up at Jason and then began crying harder. "Jason, I've been so happy that I haven't given my family one thought. I've not even been praying for them. In fact I've not remembered to pray at all. Oh Jason, I'm so afraid. I fear the Lord is punishing me through Daddy's illness."

"Lucinda, what kind of believe is this? The Lord isn't that petty. There is nothing wrong with being happy and besides that, you've called twice a week and spoken to both your parents and also Danny and Emily. Why are you beating yourself up for nothing?" asked Jason in frustration.

Lucinda got up from the bed and started toward the bathroom. She turned, "Well, don't act like I'm stupid. I can't help the way I feel. You don't live inside my skin."

Jason stood and took her in his arms. "Who controlled you with guilt? Is this left over from that ogre you were married to? You have no reason to feel guilty. We all do things we probably shouldn't, but we aren't saints. Lucinda, we are mortal beings, made of a material subject to sin and vanity and I fear we will exercise both vices occasionally even if we don't intend to. The Lord doesn't make another person ill to punish you. You are just punishing yourself."

Lucinda's mouth opened in stunned protest, but then closed it again and went on into the bathroom. She washed her face thinking about what Jason had just said. *Am I punishing myself? I know that Jesus came that we may have life and have it more abundantly, but that of course refers to our life in the spirit, or at least I always thought so.* Her brow furrowed. *Perhaps it means naturally and spiritually. Grandpa always said Jesus wanted me to be happy.* Lucinda smiled. *I've certainly been happy since I married Jason and Jesus sent him back to me when I had given up all hope that he would.*

She went back into the bedroom to find Jason seated on the bed with the Bible open on his lap. He looked up warily as she came in as if to judge whether she was angry or not. "Lucinda, I'm sorry. I shouldn't have been so harsh with you."

Lucinda sat down beside of him. "You have nothing to be sorry about, Jason. Instead of being thankful for the love Jesus has sent my way, I'm trying to go back to beating myself up and feeling guilty when anything goes wrong. I'm not Jesus. I can't bear everyone's sins on the cross even if I castigate myself daily. Thank you for reminding me."

Jason's expression cleared and he took her in his arms. "I'm glad Jesus put us together. We are good for each other. You help me to have more compassion and I help you by talking you out of guilt trips." He hugged her tightly and kissed her, but suddenly released her. "I'd better quit this and get my shower if we want to catch a six A.M. flight."

Lucinda jumped up as well and pushed him toward the bathroom. "I'll finish packing while you take your shower. Six o'clock will be here before we know it."

CHAPTER 18

Upon Jason's insistence Lucinda took the nerve pill he handed her just before they boarded the plane. This was at seven o'clock the next morning and as before, she slept all the way across the Atlantic, only rousing as they came in to land at Idlewilde International Airport. "Gosh! How long did I sleep?"

Jason grinned. "Longer than I did. We were on a 747 and it only took a little over five hours. You'll still suffer from jet lag, so don't expect to feel fully awake for a while. Keep your eyes open though, since I have to leave you to get us on another flight to Charleston, if I can."

Jason soon came back with tickets to find Lucinda nodding. He shook his head in exasperation. "Lucinda, wake up. I can't carry you to the plane."

Lucinda looked up at him with eyes blared like an awakened owl. “You made me take that nerve pill and now I can’t get myself to wake up.”

Jason grinned tiredly. “Well, hang on to my arm.” Lucinda did, and before she had really gotten her bearings they were landing in Charleston. “Our car is here already, Lucinda, so we may as well pick up our luggage and drive on home. Your dad is in the hospital in Welch anyway and we should be at the hospital in about three hours.”

Lucinda didn’t care how they got there. She just wanted to see her dad. “I think Daddy sensed that something would happen before we left. Do you remember how uneasy he acted?”

“I saw that he was afraid for you to fly. I think that is normal for most people who have never ridden a plane or even some that have,” said Jason looking solemnly at Lucinda, as he picked their luggage from the carousal.

Three hours later Lucinda and Jason walked into room two-twenty-six at Stevens Clinic Hospital in Welch. They found the room full, and Burb Harmon sitting propped up in bed. “You don’t look sick, you old fraud,” said Lucinda as she leant to hug him.

Her dad hugged her close. “It got you home, didn’t it? That was the whole idée, since I could tell from your letters that you had really took a liken’ to them leprechauns or whatever them little wee people are called,” said Burb with a weak chuckle.

Nancy got up to hug Lucinda saying, “If you’d seen him when we brung him in here you’d a knowed it wouldn’t no act.”

“They took out his gall bladder, Mom,” said Danny.

“Was it diseased?” asked Jason coming to shake Burb’s hand.

“They said it was. That doc said something about it had some sort of duct blocked, but I don’t know nothin’ about medicine." I just knowed I was sick as a dog and somethin’ had to be done,” said Burb giving Jason’s hand a squeeze. “I see Cindy brung you back in one piece.”

"It's more like Jason brought me back in one piece, Daddy. I'm like Mr. T from the A Team show. Jason had to knock me out when the plane lifted off the ground," said Lucinda laughing now that she knew her dad was all right.

She found that Danny and Emily had taken Nancy and Odell to Jason's house at night and Danny had stayed with his Papaw, which pleased them both.

"Has the doctor said when he will release you Brother Burb?" asked Jason.

"If I don't have a temperature tonight and have used the toilet the nurses say he will probably let me go home tomorrow."

Jason nodded his head in agreement. "Well, Lucinda and I are suffering from jet lag and really need to go home and rest. So, if Danny is going to stay with you tonight, the women can come back to the house and stay with us. They may find us asleep but Emily knows where everything is."

"We'll go back with you, Dad and get us all some supper. Papaw needs to rest," said Emily looking at Odell.

"I'm with you Emily. Poppy does need to rest. He's had company all day," said Odell as she picked up Nancy's handbag. "Here's your moneybag, Mommy. You may as well go with us. You need some sleep too."

So, Lucinda, Nancy, Emily, and Odell were soon gathered around the kitchen table. "Mama Lucinda, I'm going to fix some bacon and egg sandwiches. Is that all right for supper?"

Lucinda looked up at Emily wearily. "That sounds like the answer to my prayer, honey. Do you need me to help?"

"I'll help her," said Odell getting to her feet. "You look ready to drop. What time did you leave Ireland?"

Jason looked at his watch. "We left Ireland at six o'clock this morning and it is now twelve midnight so that means I haven't been asleep for eighteen hours and with jet lag it seems twice that long." He looked at Lucinda sitting in a wide-eyed stupor and grinned. "Lucinda slept all the way, but we are both still worn out."

"That sounds almost impossible," said Odell bustling around energetically.

Jason explained that they were lucky to have gotten changed from a regular jet to a 747 which left out earlier and made their trip faster. "I had to fork out some extra bucks, but we didn't know how bad her dad was and Lucinda is such a worrywart that I thought it best to get here as fast as we could."

After almost eight hours of sleep Jason and Lucinda showed up in Burb's room at eight thirty the next morning and stayed for an hour. They were back again, after lunch, just as Dr. Stevens arrived. Jason introduced himself and asked about Burb's condition, to be assured that Burb was great and was going home. "I've heard about you," said Dr. Stevens. "You were the ophthalmologist at Doctor's Memorial before it closed, weren't you?"

Jason nodded. "We've just arrived home from our trip to Ireland and this morning I heard that Stevens Clinic was going to close as well. Is that true?"

Dr. Stevens nodded grimly. "I'll never be able to sell my house, but I'll be moving to Atlanta the first of next month. I have hired Wade Watson's law firm to sell it for me."

"Where's your house located? I might be interested in it. How much land is with it?" asked Jason and Lucinda sd looking at him in wonder.

They learned that the house was on the road to Pineville, near Indian Ridge. "It is sort of isolated, but there's two acres of land," Dr. Stevens explained.

"Right now we live on Browns Creek Road above the bowling alley, but we may want to get another house," said Jason. So, we may talk again.

Soon, Odell had Burb ready to go home. "We'll come over to see you this weekend, Dad. Of course, if you need us before then just call. We didn't have the phone cut off in Jason's house. It was just "put to sleep," according to

Jason. I didn't know you could do that," said Lucinda looking up at Jason. "This man knows everything, Dad."

"Don't tell him that, he'll think he's smarter than I am. We can't have anybody in the family thinkin' like that," said Burb wincing as he tried to laugh.

When they were in the car headed back into town Jason said, "Lucinda, we don't live in Jason's house. We live in our house. Aren't you comfortable in the house?"

Lucinda sat thinking. "Jason, I don't want to upset you, but that house will always be your house or rather Janet's house. I can stay in it, but I don't think it will ever be home to me." She put her hand on Jason's arm. "I guess I'm being childish, but you asked me and I . . . you said we needed to be honest with each other."

"No, you're not being childish and thanks for your honesty, but houses are inanimate structures, you know. They can be redecorated and they don't take on the character of their former occupants," said Jason in what Lucinda took to be the voice of someone talking to a dim individual.

"I'm not stupid, Jason. I know objects are inanimate and I also know they don't take on the character of their previous owners. The tone of your voice leaves the impression that my feelings shouldn't be taken into account. So, like I said, I can live in it, but it will never be home to me. You can think me stupid if you want to, but I wonder how you would have liked living in the house where Jeff and I lived," said Lucinda giving him a keen look.

"I . . . Okay, I wouldn't want to live there, so we'll go look at the house that doctor has up for sale. Will that be home to you?"

"Yes, but only if it's home to you also, Jason," Lucinda stated assuredly. "I'm glad you recognized that we are who we are because of the experiences in our lives. We can't turn those off and on just because it isn't logical. We feel the way we feel about certain things and certain times and logic has nothing to do with it."

Jason tugged her toward him and she gladly slid to his side and snuggled close as his arm went around her. Suddenly she jerked up. "You can't drive around these curves with so much traffic with only one hand." She pulled his arm from around her and put his hand back on the steering wheel. Then she put her arm around him and sighed contentedly.

They didn't talk much on the rest of the ride home. Lucinda thought about how she hoped Dr. Stevens' house looked. Jason was busy thinking about selling the house he now lived in. As soon as they came in sight of his house they realized that Danny and Emily were there and they didn't know whether to mention moving or not. Just as they pulled into the driveway Lucinda asked, "Are you going to tell Danny and Emily that we are going to look at another house?"

"Sure, but it's none of their business. It's my house and I can sell it or keep it and nobody tells me what to do with something I've worked out," said Jason sternly.

Uh-huh, thought Lucinda. *He thinks of this house as his whether he admits it or not. If we stay here it will always be his house instead of our house. I knew it all along.*

Jason didn't mention his plans, but Lucinda told Danny and Emily that Jason was thinking of moving.

"Are you going to sell this house, Dad? Emily asked.

"Well, Dr. Stevens, the doctor that took care of Lucinda's dad, wants to sell his house and I . . . rather Lucinda and I will probably look at it. If we both like it we may buy and move out there."

"I think that's a good idea, Dad. Except for Uncle Kyle and Aunt Rita most of our old neighbors have moved away. It just doesn't seem the same," said Emily thoughtfully. "I never did really like this house. Did you know that?"

Jason looked puzzled. “No, Emily, I didn’t know that. You always seemed happy as you grew up. Why didn’t you like it?”

Emily looked thoughtful. “I don’t really know. Mom complained about it all the time to me. I guess I blamed the house, but now I know she just didn’t like living here in McDowell County. This county was ‘Hicksville’ to Mom. I’m surprised that she didn’t turn me against it, but I love it.”

Lucinda sat listening. *That’s why she always looked haughty to me,* thought Lucinda, while trying to judge Jason’s reaction.

Jason sighed. “I knew that, Emily even though your mother tried to hide her feelings around me. I heard several conversations between Mom and Janet as well as between Janet and her mother, so I knew she would use any method she could to get me away from here.”

CHAPTER 19

Lucinda lay awake that night, long after Jason was sleeping soundly. *I wonder if Jason thought she was faking her illness at first because she wanted to leave Welch so badly. If he did, then he would have felt terrible when she truly did have cancer. Maybe that is why he felt so guilty*, thought Lucinda, but then realized she felt guilty about Jeff and he didn’t have cancer. *Of course, the disease he had was just as bad . . . he died because of his illness too.* Her thoughts were so chaotic that she turned over restlessly and then sat up in bed.

“What’s wrong, Lucinda? You’ve turned over three or four times in the last hour,” said Jason as he also sat up in bed.

“I started thinking about Janet and that made me think about Jeff. They both died from their illnesses and you and I have lived with guilt ever since.” Jason made no comment and Lucinda continued. “Jason, do you think people have a certain time to die? I think I would feel better if I knew Jeff would have died when he did because he had a predetermined time. If that is so, then there's no need to feel guilty," said Lucinda hesitantly, as if feeling her way through a mine field.

"I think this is a hell of a time to be having this conversation." Then suddenly he laughed. "I swear you are the strangest woman I've ever met, but I love you anyway."

Suddenly Lucinda flung herself against Jason's chest and encircled his chest with her arms. "I'm so glad you love me, Jason. Please don't ever stop."

Jason hugged her close. "You don't have to worry about that, Lucinda. You may soon make a really old man out of me, but I'll love you along the way." He pulled her back down in bed with her head on his arm. "Now, let's unravel this eternal question that you've posed in the middle of the night."

"Well, I have been puzzled over this predestination thing and what Emily said tonight about her mother not liking to live here got me thinking."

"Halt! Stop right there. How did Emily saying Janet didn't like it here evolve to this question of predestination?"

"Because you've already told me that you felt guilty, especially when Janet was so ill and I felt guilty when Jeff died," said Lucinda slowly. She was unsure about how to put her thoughts into words. "So if they had to die at that time anyway, then we wouldn't have to feel guilty. Then nothing we did or didn't do would have prevented their deaths."

Jason burst out in a loud laugh. "That is utter nonsense, Lucinda. You studied science in college didn't you? Genetically speaking, our bodies contain the genes for everything, but how we care for our bodies, or the risks we take will affect how long our bodies can operate. That has nothing to do with how anyone else feels, guilty or otherwise. Janet had the gene for cancer as does everyone else, but hers became activated. Jeff wouldn't listen to his doctor, nor take his medication and thus was in the wrong place."

"Do you mean, that you don't believe we have a predetermined time to die?" asked Lucinda thoughtfully.

Jason lay for a minute before he answered. "I believe that we have a 'biological clock' and it is set and will continue to tick until we damage our bodies so much that it cannot sustain life any longer, or it ticks until our bodies wear out."

"That's still means it's predetermined, though. I mean if we have a biological clock that is set to tick so many times then our life is predetermined, isn't it?" asked Lucinda.

Jason sighed. "You sure can ask hard questions in the middle of the night. I guess you are right in the respect that we have a time to die, unless we are destroyed in a fire, accident, or even illnesses caused by our life styles such as tobacco and drug use. I certainly don't believe we have a certain way to go. I personally think that our time to die is always ready."

Lucinda sighed. "Well, I'm not going to walk out in front of a car to test it out, that's for sure."

Jason yawned sleepily. "Are you ready to stop asking deep questions and go to sleep?"

"I know that if I did wrong in my marriage to Jeff, the Lord didn't cause me to do it, but I do know he forgives. He knows I didn't deliberately do wrong, but I couldn't stop loving you, Jason. I just couldn't. I tried so very hard to put you out of my mind."

Jason turned toward her and hugged her fiercely. "Lucinda, I know that God is love and loving another person is not wrong. Neither of us should have married someone else, but we did. The Lord did not take Janet and Jeff's lives so that we could be together, but since they are gone, and we had nothing to do with the causes of their deaths I think we should accept God's forgiveness and put the guilt aside for good."

Lucinda hugged Jason. "I guess we both need to pray that our sense of guilt be taken from us." She lay quietly for a moment. "I also think we need to pray for understanding of the scriptures. I think my thoughts were immature and foolish and your thoughts were too analytical. The only way we'll be satisfied is if the Lord gives us spiritual eyes to see and interpret the scriptures."

Jason yawned. "We'll worry over things and then perhaps go to church and some elder will be blessed to preach out what we have been pondering on. That's what often happens to me."

Lucinda grinned. "It couldn't happen very often. You haven't been a member long enough."

"That's true," mumbled Jason and Lucinda realized he was half asleep so she turned over and silently prayed for guidance and understanding before she too slept.

Lucinda awoke to the smell of bacon frying. *I wonder who's cooking breakfast?* She pushed her hair back out of her eyes as the door opened.

"You'd better get up sleepyhead. Our children are ready to leave and I thought you'd like to tell them good-bye," said Jason standing with the door half-opened behind him.

Lucinda jumped up and started toward the door then turned back and grabbed her robe at the foot of the bed. She looked at Jason in exasperation. "Why didn't you wake me?"

Jason grinned. "Well, unlike you. I am much too considerate of your feelings. I'd never wake you out of a sound sleep to probe imponderable questions."

Lucinda stuck out her tongue. "You didn't act like you minded and it sure didn't keep you awake very long."

She went past Jason through the door and on into the kitchen. There she found Emily and Danny eating breakfast, but both in their pajamas. She turned to look at Jason.

"I thought you said they were ready to leave. You've caused me to come in here looking like the witch in The Wizard of Oz."

Jason brought a plate with toast, egg, and bacon and put it on the table. "Sit down, Mrs. Witch. Your breakfast is getting cold. I had to get Danny and Emily up as well since Danny said last night that they wanted to leave by eight o'clock this morning."

Lucinda looked at the clock above the corner cabinet. "I'm sorry, Jason. I should have gotten up myself, but I forgot to set the clock."

"It wasn't your responsibility, Mama Lucinda. Danny and I should have set our clocks. I guess I have gotten too accustomed to Dad keeping me on time. I'll have to do better than this, won't I?"

"We'll both have to do better Emily, but I sure appreciate Jason this morning. We both have classes this afternoon," said Danny as he swallowed his last sip of coffee and arose from the table.

Lucinda started to get up as well, but Danny pushed her down. "Go ahead and eat. We have to brush our teeth and load the car.

Lucinda turned back to her breakfast just as Jason sat beside her. "Did I do the eggs to your liking, madam?"

"Yes, you did, Rochester. Thanks very much also for calling me a witch," said Lucinda turning toward him with a scowl.

"You said you were a witch, so I thought that would please you. Anyway, you don't look like a bad witch. You're the good witch from the east who gave Dorothy the ruby slippers," said Jason as he leaned over and kissed her cheek.

Lucinda looked at him and grinned. "You're working on brownie points aren't you? I wonder what you expect as a reward for them."

Jason raised his eyebrows with a wicked leer, "I have some ideas. Would you like to hear them?"

Just then Danny came hurrying through the room with his suitcase and an armful of books. Lucinda jumped up.

"Here, Danny let me take the books for you."

"He can carry them, Mama Lucinda. He's a big boy now," said Emily as she came out of her room with her suitcase.

Lucinda turned red. "He's still my son, Emily."

Emily put her suitcase down and put her arms around Lucinda. "I know. I was a little smarty, wasn't I? I don't mean to be hateful. I just say things so bluntly. I wish I was different. I'm a lot like Dad and so I'm afraid you're going to have to get used to both of us." Emily hugged her again and stepped back. "Of course, you don't have to live with me, but Dad's been at this being abrupt much longer than I have."

Lucinda remembered last night when Jason had said, "This is utter nonsense." *So, I'll have to get used to speeches like that*, she thought as she looked at Jason.

Jason didn't blink or look away. "I never said I was perfect. I said I would be good to you and love you all the days of my life, but I didn't say I wouldn't be abrupt with you." Lucinda's eyes narrowed.

"That's right you didn't, because it never came up. I guess I'll have to remember that you don't like to discuss anything in the middle of the night."

Jason started to reply, but Danny came back in the door. "Oh! I was just coming to get your suitcase, Emily. Is this all you have?"

Emily laughed. "Yes, and I think we'd better leave since I may have started a fight between Frankie and Johnny. Right now, I don't think they are sweethearts.

Lucinda laughed. "That's a first. We've been called 'teenagers' 'lovebirds' and 'honeymooners', but never two hoodlums."

Jason came around the table and put his arm around Lucinda's shoulders. "Don't worry you two for as soon as you leave we'll kiss and make up, won't we, dear?"

Lucinda stepped away from Jason and hugged Danny and then turned to Emily. "Thanks for filling me in on one of your father's character traits." Then she hugged Emily close and whispered. "Take care of Danny for me."

Emily kissed her cheek and whispered also. "I promise I will."

Soon they were both out the door and Lucinda stood rooted to the spot until she heard the car back down the drive.

CHAPTER 20

"Lucinda, I called Dr. Stevens earlier and he's going to show us the house this evening about five-thirty," said Jason as he began to clear the table.

An image of Jeff telling her he had found the house in Rock, West Virginia flashed through Lucinda's mind. She felt hurt then and she felt hurt now. "What if I have something else to do at that time? You could have asked me," said Lucinda frowning.

"You said this house would never be home, so I'm trying to buy you another house, but you're upset. I don't understand you. Don't you know what you want?" Jason looked like he was aggravated and was trying to deal with a child.

He's acting just like Jeff. All the furniture I ever had Jeff went out and bought it. Even that house in Rock wasn't of my choosing, thought Lucinda as she put the dishes in the sink.

"Don't sulk, Lucinda. I need to know what you want."

"I'm not sulking and stop treating me like a child. You haven't asked me, not once, if I would like to look at the house. You told me about it, but you didn't ask my opinion. If you make all the decisions about things then they are yours, they won't be ours."

"Well, I'll be damned. I do everything I can to make you happy and. . . . Okay, Lucinda, do you have time to look at a house this evening at five-thirty?" Jason stood looking stonily at her as he waited for her answer.

"You're not supposed to curse. You are a church member now," said Lucinda as she wiped off the table and put the placemats back in place.

"Oh, I'm so sorry, Saint Lucinda. I shouldn't have offended your delicate ears," said Jason as he strode toward the living room.

At first, Lucinda was angry and then realized that it really didn't matter as long as she had Jason. Then she broke out in peals of laughter. Jason turned to stare in amazement. "Jason, how big is that sore on your rear?" she asked with a straight face, but couldn't contain it when his eyes widened in astonishment.

Lucinda bent over the table and laughed until tears ran down her cheeks. Before she could control herself she felt Jason's arms around her.

"You, little minx! What's a man to do with you? You have me so frustrated that I don't know what to do and now here you are laughing like a mad woman."

"It . . . It's so silly. We both want the same thing and instead of listening to each other, we quarrel. We're acting like children. I used to have mock trials to settle school yard differences. Do you want to have a trial?" asked Lucinda as her arms crept up around his neck.

Jason's arms tightened around her. "No, I don't want to have a trial. I just want to love you for the rest of my life. I'm too old to accept change easily, Lucinda, so be patient with me, please."

Lucinda stepped back until she could look at him. She smiled impishly. "So, you admit you were wrong."

"Yes, I admit that I should have talked it over with you. I've done things exactly the way I wanted for the past few years and I just didn't think about you being offended."

Lucinda grinned and then on tiptoe leaned up and kissed him. "You're forgiven, since you didn't really ask, but you did say you were wrong."

Jason picked her up and swung her around before putting her down. “Don’t think I’ll always give in to you, Lucinda. I love you, but I have strong opinions.”

Lucinda pulled out of his arms and turned toward the living-room. “So do I, Jason. I think we’d better decide how we are going to handle differences since we both know we want to be together as long as we both live. Or, at least that’s what I want and I thought you did too.”

Jason followed her as she made for the bedroom where their bathroom was located. He grasped her shoulder and turned her around. “I intend to be with you as long as we both draw breath. So, you’re right. We need to decide how we’ll handle our differences.”

Lucinda gave him a penetrating look. “Let’s not work it out right now. I need to get ready to go out. We need some groceries and then I want to look at that house this evening.”

“Whew! That’s finally settled. Now I can go shopping with you and we both want to look at the house.” Jason hugged her again and went whistling out of the room.

Soon Jason was pushing a grocery cart through Goodson’s grocery which was a new grocery store located on Route 52 going out of Welch. “This is organized better than Kroger’s, isn’t it?” said Lucinda as she chose fresh spinach for a salad.

“It’s nice, but I can’t understand why it was built. There’s no work in the area. I guess there are enough welfare recipients to support this store, though,” said Jason in his usual voice, and a woman with a heavily loaded cart glared at him and angrily almost shoved her cart into him as she passed them.

Lucinda looked up at Jason with widened eyes. He shrugged his shoulders and grinned nonchalantly. “I wasn’t talking about her.”

When they were outside Lucinda breathed a little easier. “Jason, you’re going to have to stop spending your opinion so loudly. I thought that woman was going to shove that cart right into you."

"I didn't know her, and I didn't use any names. Besides, this is a free country and I can speak what I think."

"Grandpa always said that there was a time and a place for everything, but you picked the wrong place today."

Jason loaded their groceries in the trunk and closed the lid. "That woman paid for that load she had with food stamps so I didn't care if she did hear me. My taxes paid for what she bought."

Lucinda didn't say anything until they were both seated in the car. "Jason, you sounded like a Republican or a conservative. I'm surprised."

He started the car and backed out of his parking place. "If I am then I'm a social conservative, I guess." Before he pulled into the highway, Jason asked, "Do you want to eat out or do you want to go home for lunch?"

"I'd like a grilled cheese sandwich. What do you want?"

"Can you put lettuce and tomato on it? If you can, that's what I would like as well."

"Well, let's go back to the house then. I make a mean grilled cheese sandwich."

Soon they were seated at the kitchen table with grilled cheese sandwiches and chips.

Lucinda, what do you want in a house? I don't know what kind of house you would like and unless you like Dr. Stevens' house I won't buy it."

Lucinda sat thinking. "I'd like an eat-in kitchen and dining room combined, a living room, three bedrooms with bathrooms, plenty of closet space, a laundry room, and a spare room for crafts, library or whatever we need it for. Oh! And I'd like a full basement."

"Do you want all this on one floor, except the basement, of course?"

"No, some of the bedrooms could be on another floor, I suppose. In fact I've always dreamed of an upstairs in a house. When I was a little girl I always daydreamed about a house with upstairs. I'd lean out the window and my house always had a balcony that looked into the woods and I'd sit there and watch the little animals." Lucinda laughed. "I'd forgotten about how I used to dream about that house."

Jason finished first and arose from the table, taking his plate and glass to the sink. "I can just see you looking off into space with eyes alight with dreaming. I'll bet you were a pretty little girl."

Lucinda pushed her chair back. "I was a fat little girl and I laughed a lot. Grandpa always said I was either laughing or crying, but I don't remember crying much until Grandpa died."

Jason took her plate and glass from her hand and put them in the sink, but Lucinda turned on the water. "What are you doing?" asked Jason.

"I'm going to wash these dishes. I don't like to leave dishes in the sink."

"That's wasting water. Wait until after dinner tonight and we'll wash them all at one time," said Jason turning off the water.

Lucinda reached around him and turned the water on again. "I don't like to leave dishes. The kitchen looks so messy and somebody might come in and see a sink full of dishes."

"I always wait and wash dishes once a day. It keeps the water bill down and who do you think is going to show up here without calling?"

Lucinda looked at him stonily. "Well, I wash my dishes as I use them and that is what I'm going to do, so get out of the way, please."

Jason sighed in resignation. "Don't use three gallons of water. That meter ticks over pretty fast."

"For God's sake! If you're that stingy I'll pay part of the water bill," said Lucinda wrenching the faucet to off.

"Humph! There's more in saving than there is in making it, woman. I'm not stingy and I don't want your money, but I don't believe in wasting either."

Jason picked up a towel and began to dry the plates she had already put in the drainer. Neither of them spoke as they finished the dishes and Lucinda started to pull the plug to drain the water.

"Do you want me to save this water to flush the toilet?" asked Lucinda.

Jason looked at her as if she'd lost her mind. "Why . . . ." Jason let out a roar of laughter. "You're doing it again. You're punching holes in the fabric of my life. Here I was being frugal and serious and you come up with some off- the-wall comment. You make it sound like we're the Clampets from The Beverley Hillbillies."

Lucinda giggled. "Well, I was just trying to help you save."

Jason pulled her to him. "You see how old I am. I sound like I'm seventy and you sound sixteen."

"Oh Jason, no. You'll never be old in my eyes." Lucinda put her arms around him and hugged him close. "You are my prince in shining armor and I love you more than anything on this earth."

CHAPTER 21

That evening at five-thirty they saw, for the first time, the house that would be their home in West Virginia for the rest of their lives. It didn't have a laundry room on the first floor, but it did have a full basement, and there were three bedrooms upstairs as well as a balcony. When they were inspecting the rooms Lucinda whispered, "How much would it cost to take out this partition? I don't really want a formal dining room, do you?"

Jason looked at the wall between the dining room and the kitchen and knocked on the walls with his fist. The sound brought Dr. Stevens back into the room from the outside deck. "Did someone knock on the door?" he asked.

Lucinda grinned. "No, but my husband knocked on the wall."

Dr. Stevens turned a puzzled look at Jason. "I was trying to determine the construction of the inside walls. Do you have any idea of whether the walls are two by sixes or two by fours?"

"No, I don't. Does it matter?" asked Dr. Stevens anxiously even though he was trying to hide it.

"It does if someone wanted to take out a wall. Sometimes the walls are the only support for the second floor. Who built this house?" asked Jason.

Dr. Stevens gave him the name of the construction company and their address before they left. "I'm going to talk to this company and if I get the right answers I'll call you back. We like most of the house, but I need to check a little further before I commit myself," were Jason's parting words.

When they were in the car Jason turned to Lucinda. "You liked the house, didn't you?"

"Yes, I love it, except for the dining room and really part of that could be turned into a laundry room, couldn't it?"

Jason thought about it. "I believe it could since one end is near the kitchen sink which would make it easier to run the water lines for a washing machine."

Lucinda sat dreaming all the way home. The house was up on a small hill which leveled out at the top. The land ran back into a boundary of woodland and another small hill. She knew that little animals would be down to investigate. "Jason, we may have some deer come to visit if we buy that house," said Lucinda in a wistful voice.

Jason chuckled. "Yes, and panthers and bears also. Won't that be nice?"

"Aw, there aren't any bears around in these parts, or at least if there are I haven't heard of any," replied Lucinda.

"At one time, there were too many people and there was a mine operating in most of these hollows which kept the bears away. Now, however, most of the mines are closed and the forest is taking over again, so I wouldn't be surprised if we saw some."

Lucinda shivered. "I'd be scared out of my wits if a bear walked into my yard."

"If they get hungry bears will break into houses, but I don't think we're at that stage yet," said Jason.

"You're trying to scare me out of wanting that house, aren't you?"

"No. You brought it up about seeing some animals and I just added a few to the ones you named," said Jason as they pulled into the driveway.

Lucinda looked at him and saw that he was smiling. She hit him lightly. "You're playing dirty, Jason. You know how cowardly I am. That's all right though. If a bear comes I'll get behind you so he can have a better meal."

They went into the house laughing and kidding each other but stopped when they heard the phone ringing loudly. "You answer it, Jason. It's Emily," said Lucinda. Jason turned to look at her with a puzzled frown.

Jason picked up the receiver. He turned with widened eyes and said, "It is Emily."

"Hello, Little Bit, are you settled in?" Jason stood listening as he began to frown. Lucinda could hear Emily's voice which sounded agitated." I don't know, but I'll ask Lucinda." Jason turned to Lucinda. "Have you been in Emily's bedroom since they left?"

Lucinda hadn't, but Jason told her to go look for a brown billfold. "Emily has lost her billfold and she hopes she left it here."

Lucinda came back with a worried look on her face. "I couldn't find it. I looked under the bed, in all the dresser drawers, and behind her desk. I may have missed it, but I don't think so."

"You didn't leave your billfold here, Emily. I've told you a thousand times to keep your billfold in your pocket or purse, but you never listen," scolded Jason. "You'd better stop payment on all your checks, and called DMV about your driver's license." Jason grew red in the face. "Do you mean you didn't make a copy of any of those papers like I told you to? Well, it serves you right . . ., and stop that bawling. That won't get your billfold back."

Lucinda had stood listening to Jason raking poor little Emily through the coals and it was breaking her heart. Without thinking she plucked the phone from Jason. "Emily, don't cry, dear. Everybody makes mistakes, except your Dad, I guess. Can I call the DMV for you?"

Jason jerked the phone from Lucinda's grasp, almost causing her to fall. "Don't ever do that again, Lucinda. This is my daughter and I'll handle this."

Lucinda looked up at him in astonishment. She had never seen him so angry, but he was wrong to browbeat Emily like he was. *I can't do anything about it*" thought Lucinda. *He's right, Emily is his daughter, but I can't stand to hear a man talking like that to a woman, especially a young girl like Emily,* thought Lucinda as she walked out of the room.

Needless to say, the atmosphere was certainly strained, when Jason hung up the phone. Neither of them spoke and Lucinda went back to do a more thorough search of Emily's room. This time she went over every inch of the room; even under the bed and in the waste basket, but found nothing. She started out of the room, but suddenly thought, *I didn't check in the bed coverings.* She turned to the bed and threw back the covers, but didn't see anything. She was so disappointed. The fitted sheet was wrinkled, so she decided to just take all the covers off and remake the bed. When she pulled the bedspread off there was a soft plop on the other side of the bed. Lucinda's eyes lit up as she hurried to the other side. She yelled, "Yes! Thank you, Jesus," then grabbed the billfold and ran out of the room.

"Jason, Jason, I've found it," she called as she entered the living room, but Jason wasn't there. She went into the kitchen and it was empty also. She walked to the window and looked out and he wasn't outside, and then she went to the kitchen door and looked out into the carport. Jason's car wasn't there.

He's still angry with me, she thought as she plopped down in a kitchen chair. She sat for a moment before jumping up and reaching for the phone. *I can at least make Emily happy,* she thought. She dialed Emily's number, but Danny answered the phone.

"Jason, if you called back to further upset Emily I won't let you talk to her," said Danny solemnly.

"Danny, I found Emily's billfold," said Lucinda and heard a long sigh from Danny. "Can you hold on just a minute, Mom," said Danny.

Soon Danny came back on the phone. "I can't get her to stop crying. Can I call you back, Mom?"

"Tell her that her billfold is here and everything is all right. It was caught in the bed covers," said Lucinda with misty eyes since she knew how Emily must feel. *She was already scared to death and then Jason telling her off like that, made it much worse,* thought Lucinda.

Before the phone rang again the headlights of a car flashed through the window and Lucinda knew that Jason had returned. *Surely he won't be drunk* thought Lucinda remembering how Jeff was when he went away angry. The door opened and Jason walked in.

He stood looking at Lucinda and she sat looking at him; neither of them spoke. Finally he walked over to the table and sat down across from Lucinda. "I messed up again, didn't I? Darling, I'm so sorry. I should never have acted that way with you. Can you ever forgive me?"

Lucinda felt so sorry for him. He looked so tired. "Jason, I shouldn't have interfered. Emily is your daughter, but I truly love her too, and I understand what it is like to make a mistake. More than that, having her dad light into her the way you did, was, in my opinion, being much too hard on her. She's so young."

Jason dropped his head. "I know. I'm going to call her. I've been trying to think of ways to get everything straightened out for her. I couldn't think of anything but how I had talked to you, though. I don't know how I could hurt you like that when I love you more than anything."

"I don't like to be threatened, Jason, but like I said, I shouldn't have took the phone from you. I just couldn't stand to hear a man talking like that to a woman, especially to your own daughter. I had to take that kind of talk for so long that now it upsets me terribly," said Lucinda. When she looked up at Jason he looked so miserable that she could have cried.

"I hope you can forgive me for interfering, but I also hope you stop to think before you rake Emily through the coals again. Besides, I found her billfold. I ran in here to tell you and you were gone."

Jason's head jerked up. "You found her billfold! Where?"

"I went back to her room to look again after you got upset and I turned that place inside out, but didn't find it. I started to leave and then for some reason I thought that it could be in the bed. I threw the covers back and didn't see it. I was so disappointed and started to leave, but saw how untidy the fitted sheet was and decided to just remake the entire bed. I pulled off the bedspread and heard a soft plop on the other side. The plop was Emily's billfold."

"I'd better call her. She'll be beside herself since she was so upset," said Jason.

"She knows, Jason. I don't think she can talk right now. She's been crying ever since she called you."

"How do you know? Did you call her?"

"Yes, but I got Danny instead of Emily. He's supposed to call me back. I think they're both rather upset with you, right now," said Lucinda.

Jason got up from the table and came around to Lucinda's side. He crouched down low to look into her eyes. "I'm not concerned about them, right now. I need to know if you will forgive me if I promise to never talk to you in that way again."

Lucinda leaned over and kissed his cheek. "I will forgive you anything, Jason, but I won't stay with you if you abuse me; physically or emotionally. I've had enough of that."

Jason rose to his feet and pulled Lucinda up into his arms. "Thank you dear. I guess I've been acting like a dyed- in- the- wool bachelor. Help me learn to act like a husband should. I realize that I must have been bossy with Emily ever since Janet died. I think that because you're so young I've been treating you like I do Emily."

Lucinda snuggled close. "All right, Grandpa, I'll forgive you this time." Then she giggled and looked up at Jason mischievously. "I know it is hard on old people to make long trips, but could we take Emily's billfold to her?"

CHAPTER 22

They made the trip to Morgantown, staying three days, and visiting several of Jason's former professors. Lucinda felt they should go on to Pittsburgh and visit Jason's parents, but since he didn't mention it neither did she. Jason apologized to Emily and they parted with everybody promising they would be together for Thanksgiving and Christmas.

When they were back in Welch, Jason and Lucinda became caught up in remodeling and redecorating the house on Indian Ridge. Even though they worked every day except Saturdays and Sundays they weren't finished by Thanksgiving. Danny declared that he and Emily could only stay for two days anyway.

"We could have had it finished but, we've been to ch . . . meeting , which is what Lucinda says we must call it, every weekend. I'm glad we did though. I've learned that the saying, 'the more you put into something, the more you get out of it,' is so right. The more I go to meeting the more I want to go," said Jason with a smile.

"Danny, can you and Emily stay with us at Papaw Burb's house for Thanksgiving and attend meeting there at Bee Branch on Saturday and Sunday?" Lucinda asked when they first arrived.

Danny looked at Emily. "Do you have a test the following Monday? I know I don't."

"I do, but I'll take my book and sneak off without doing dishes and study. I want to go to meeting so much. It seems like ages since we've been," replied Emily.

So, it was settled and they went together, as a family for the first time, to spend Thanksgiving with Lucinda's parents.

By Christmas, they were in their new house and the old house was advertised as a rental. Their first night there, Jason built a fire in the giant fireplace in the living room and they snuggled close together on the sofa and watched Miracle on Thirty-fourth Street . Lucinda cried several times and unlike Jeff, Jason did not laugh at her.

After Christmas Jason, became once again involved with the school board. "Lucinda, you should get involved with the Womans' Club or some organization. Don't you like being with people?" asked Jason in what she took as his authoritarian voice. That was the one thing about Jason that bothered her. He always acted like he knew everything and she shouldn't even question him. *It's not that he's mean. He just seems to think he should be listened to*, thought Lucinda.

"Yes, I like people, but I don't want to be a part of some organization which meets to eat and doesn't really have a purpose. I'm not saying the Womans' Club doesn't have a purpose, but I don't know any of those people."

"According to Danny you were always involved with some project in Wyoming County. We live pretty close to Pineville. Go over there and get with some of those people," said Jason as if that solved the problem.

"Jason, I'm enjoying my new home and I'll know when I should venture into something else." She was already involved in something else, but she didn't want anyone to know about it. She looked so forlorn that Jason eyed her in a speculative manner.

He smiled and hugged her. "I'm not meaning to pressure you, but it seems like you never get out. You don't like to shop and there's not much to do as far as recreation is there?"

Lucinda grinned. "I guess not, but you forget that I'm used to being alone and entertaining myself."

Jason began to notice that Lucinda was getting up earlier than he did which was new. He commented about it, but in a joking way, and Lucinda laughed it off. A few weeks later he realized that Lucinda was much thinner than she had been.

"Lucinda, you're losing weight. How much have you lost? Are you not feeling well?" he looked at the dark circles under her eyes and came to a conclusion.

"There's something wrong and you are going to see a doctor. What doctor do you see?" *There he goes telling me instead of asking me*, thought Lucinda.

"I don't have a doctor. I've never been sick since Jeff died. I guess I could go back to see Dr. Wright, but there's no need. I'm not sick."

"Lucinda, people don't lose the weight you have without some cause. Do you know this Dr. Wright's number?"

"No. Besides he's in Logan. If I have to see a doctor, I'll see someone here in Welch. You know most of the doctors. Who do you suggest?"

"I knew all the doctors at Doctors Memorial and most of the doctors at Stevens Clinic, but most of the ones I knew have left the area. I hear there's a Dr. Ross Patton, working at Tug River Clinic that is very good. I'll get you an appointment with him." Lucinda saw that Jason was so concerned that she agreed.

They both liked Dr. Patton as soon as they met him. He and Jason talked for short while after the introductions, while his nurse registered Lucinda in, did her blood work, and had her undressed and into a paper gown. Even without seeing a doctor, Lucinda felt sure she knew what was wrong with her. When Dr. Patton had finished his examination and she sat up he smiled. “Well, I’m sure you know that you are pregnant, don’t you?” He gave her a very serious look.

“I thought I was, but I’m almost forty-two years old. I thought it may be something else.”

“No. it isn’t something else. I’d say you are about two and a half months. How have you been feeling?”

“I’ve been all right, but I’m worried. You see Doctor Patton, the last time I was pregnant I had something called placenta previa or something. Anyway, I lost that baby and nearly bled to death, or so I’m told. I guess I worry that the same thing will happen again. That’s why I haven’t told my husband,” said Lucinda.

“You’ll need to tell your husband. I’m sorry to tell you, but you have the same condition again,” said Dr. Patton kindly.

Lucinda dropped her head to hide her tears, but her shoulders shook. Dr. Patton walked to the door and called Jason inside. Jason saw Lucinda and turned white as a sheet.

“What’s wrong with her? You shouldn’t have told her until I was with her.” He gave Dr. Patton an angry look and put his arms around Lucinda.

“Dr. McCall, your wife doesn’t have some life-threatening disease. She is pregnant, but I don’t think she can carry it. She has placenta previa.”

Lucinda really began sobbing then. She looked up at Jason. “That’s why I lost my other baby.”

Jason held her close. “I thought you were on birth control pills. Haven’t you been taking them?”

“Jason, I’m almost forty-two years old. I didn’t think I would get pregnant anymore. I have a grown son.”

Dr. Patton grinned. "You don't look forty-two and the reproductive organs only do their job. They pay no attention to age at all. When you quit ovulating then you won't get pregnant anymore, but until you do it is wise to use precaution unless you want a baby."

Lucinda looked up at Jason with such love in her misty eyes that Jason bent to kiss her. "I would love to have Jason's baby. It would be our baby. Is there nothing I can do that will help me carry it?"

Dr. Patton looked at Jason and then smiled at Lucinda. "It seldom happens that a woman with that condition carries and delivers a healthy baby, but who knows? We'll take all the necessary precautions, but it still may not be enough."

Lucinda knew she had to accept the situation and just pray that the Lord would bless her to carry this baby. On the way home, she told Jason that they had to pray to that end. He didn't say anything until they arrived home and he helped her into the house. Then seating her gently on the sofa he sat down beside her and put his arms around her.

"Lucinda, I don't want you to get your hopes up. I think we should pray that the Lord helps us to accept his will, whatever it is."

"You mean, we shouldn't pray that the Lord let our baby live? I have to beg the Lord for my baby, Jason. I want a baby of ours. I didn't intend this to happen and neither did you, but it has happened. The Lord has a purpose in all things. So, I'm going to pray that the Lord has mercy on us."

Jason held her quietly and gently rubbed her back and kissed her cheek. "Yes, we'll both pray for mercy. All things are possible if he is merciful."

Lucinda cried quietly knowing she had a sense of dread, but didn't want to doubt the Lord. *Oh God, please, please let me have this baby. It is part of me and Jason, she silently prayed*, but felt no ease.

They decided to not tell anyone. She was not yet three months and it seemed that by not sharing this life they had produced together made it more special and sacred.

"Let's give it a name, Jason. Of course, we don't know whether it will be a girl or a boy, do we? If it is a boy, we'll name him, Joshua Henry McCall and if it's a girl let's call her Phoebe Mariam McCall," said Lucinda solemnly.

Jason kissed her tenderly. "Those sound like good names to me, darling, but I thought you'd want to name a girl Phoebe Marie. You put my middle name to the boy."

Lucinda smiled and told him that they would change the girl's name. "I hadn't thought about it, but if you want to change either name I'm willing."

Jason lived in dread from then on. He watched every move Lucinda made and didn't want her to do anything at all. "Jason, I can't sit on my butt the entire nine months. I'd go nuts," she complained.

When the weekend came Lucinda began to prepare to go to Bradshaw Mountain to church, but Jason said they couldn't go. "Riding over those rough and winding roads won't be good for you."

Lucinda grimaced. "Jason, the Bible says, 'Seek ye first the kingdom and all things else will be added to you.' I think we should go on to meeting just like we have been. Besides, you know that it will cause questions if we don't show up."

"We can pray and worship here. We don't have to be in a meeting house to worship the Lord," argued Jason worriedly.

"I know that, Jason, but it is so much better shared. Besides, Dr. Patton didn't say I would need to restrict my riding in a car."

"Lucinda, let's compromise. "If you'll agree to stay here Saturday, we'll go Sunday. I'm just afraid that two days will be too much. I would go into a panic if we were on Bradshaw Mountain and you started to hemorrhage."

Lucinda agreed since she realized that he was worried sick already. I'm going to put an Easter tree like the Smiths have out on the front lawn, but only if I can get a live tree, like a pink dogwood or something like that. I know that trees and things like that are not the true symbols of Easter, but at least it will bloom every year. That's almost like coming alive again," said Lucinda then laughed. "That's silly, isn't it? I still feel that way, even if it is silly."

Jason smiled. "No. It just means that you don't want anything that even represents our savior to be just a show. I'll buy you a dogwood tree, but not a very big one."

CHAPTER 23

This was the last of February and nothing happened to alarm them for the next two months. They both began to breathe easier. By the latter part of April, Lucinda looked like she had gained some weight, but wasn't really showing. Everybody who knew her said she had a glow about her.

Nancy and Burb went on and on about how good she looked and finally since she was in her fifth month she told her parents.

Nancy's face fell. "Lucy, didn't that doctor there in Logan tell you that you shouldn't have any more children?"

"Yes, he did, Mommy. We didn't intend for this to happen, but it did. I think the Good Lord has a purpose for this baby to be here. I'm really careful and Jason is like a mother hen. He won't let me do anything."

"Your Mam and me are just worried that you'll be sick like you were before, Cindy. None of us want to live through something like that again," said Burb.

Jason had been outside, but walked in about that time. "I understand your worry, Burb. I can't sleep at night for fear that she'll be sick and I won't hear her. So far, though, the doctor says everything is fine. I tried to get her not to make so many trips over here, but she says going to meeting will be good for her."

Burb was in agreement with Jason. "I don't blame you one bit. It ain't smart to be travelin' over these curvy roads in her condition. The Lord give us a brain to use. It ain't like she can't worship the Lord wherever she is. I don't think she ort to make no more trips until that baby gets here." He looked at Jason with a worried frown.

"Thanks, Burb. We'll call from now on, but we'll not make any more trips, even if I have to tie her," said Jason and smiled at Lucinda. This was Sunday morning; Lucinda hadn't been feeling well all day. When they came out of the meeting house she had suddenly turned deathly sick. She stopped and leaned against the church door while Jason stood talking to one of the deacons, and the sickness wore off. She didn't tell anyone about this, so back at the house she didn't argue when Jason made his declaration. *It won't do any good to argue anyway. Dad agreeing with Jason put a seal on curtailing my trips*, she thought as she turned to the kitchen.

Soon after dinner Jason and Lucinda were on their way back to Welch. Lucinda was feeling decidedly worse and had a nagging backache. She rode along praying, *Lord, please let me make it home before anything happens. I don't want to lose this baby, but I feel like something is wrong. Please help us*, she prayed as they traversed one mountain and started on the other one. Jason looked over at her and thought she looked pale.

"Are you feeling all right, dear? You seem pale to me."

"I think I'm all right, Jason, but I'll be glad when we get home," Lucinda replied.

"That means you aren't feeling good, doesn't it?"

Lucinda looked over at Jason with a troubled frown. "I'm not in real pain, but I feel nauseous, and my back is hurting. I started feeling different just as we left meeting today."

Jason glared at her angrily. "You should have told me, Lucinda. We would have left then." Jason speeded up and Lucinda could tell he was upset. "Dr. Patton said to call him at the first sign of distress and here you've been feeling bad for hours."

"Don't fuss, Jason. I know I should have, but I thought I was just tired and that may be all it is. Besides we're not far from Welch."

They were soon home and Jason walked beside Lucinda into the house. "I'm going to call Dr. Patton. He said to report any problems," said Jason hurrying to the phone. Lucinda went to the sofa and sank down gratefully. It didn't help her backache, however. By the time Jason finished the call Lucinda knew this wasn't normal back pain.

"Dr. Patton said to bring you to the hospital," said Jason as he put down the receiver, but turned white when he turned and saw Lucinda. She had risen from the sofa and stood trembling with fluid pooling at her feet. For a brief moment Jason panicked. "Oh, my God, Lucinda . . ." he stopped and took in a deep breath then grabbed Lucinda up in his arms and almost ran from the house. He soon had her lying on the back seat and was in the driver's seat heading down the highway.

By the time Jason arrived at Stevens Clinic Hospital, Lucinda had lost consciousness. Jason pulled into the emergency bay and set down on his horn. The ER people were soon there with a gurney and had Lucinda on it.

When Lucinda opened her eyes again Jason was standing beside her bed and holding her hand. She looked up at him and smiled. "You look funny," she whispered and then closed her eyes again.

The next thing she knew was hearing Jason calling her name. "Lucinda, Lucinda, Wake up darling. Come on wake up."

Lucinda wanted to answer him, but she just couldn't seem to get the words out. She started praying. *Lord,*

Jason is so worried. Please let me tell him that I'm all right. I don't want to worry Jason.

Suddenly she gasped and opened her eyes. "My baby! How's my baby?"

Jason leaned down and kissed her. "Well, you finally woke up. I thought I was going to have to pour water on you." Jason tried to smile, but tears were creeping down his cheeks.

Lucinda tried to lift her hand to touch Jason, but she was too weak. "Jason, why are you crying? Did we lose our baby?" murmured Lucinda in a thin breathless voice.

Just then Dr. Patton appeared at Jason's side and Lucinda realized that he and Jason were dressed alike; in green suits and each had a mask hanging below their chins. The two doctors exchanged guarded looks which Lucinda saw, but was too weak and anxious to care.

Dr. Patton picked up Lucinda's arm and felt her pulse. He looked at Jason and nodded. "That's better. I think we're out of the woods."

Lucinda struggled as if to rise and Jason put his hand on her shoulder. "No, dear lie still. You need to rest. You've had an operation."

Dr. Patton sat down on the edge of the bed. "Lucinda, the baby died. That's why you were feeling so nauseous. Your body was trying to discharge it and that caused the backache."

When Lucinda heard the word died she gave out a low keening wail. "God, why, why? I begged and begged for my baby to live."

Jason put his cheek down to hers and whispered. "Lucinda, the baby couldn't have lived anyway. It was . . . not well. I think the Lord took it so that it wouldn't suffer. You wouldn't have wanted it to live and suffer every minute of its life, would you?"

Lucinda heard him, but it didn't make sense. She just couldn't seem to stop crying. Finally a nurse came in and gave her an injection and soon she drifted off.

She didn't awaken again until six o'clock the next morning. She looked around the room, but stopped when she saw Jason sitting upright in a chair. He was fast asleep. She must have made some noise or something for Jason suddenly opened his eyes. He rose to his feet and stepped to her side. "How do you feel, dear?" he asked and bent to kiss her forehead.

"I would like a drink of water," she whispered.

Jason poured water from a pitcher and lifting her head held it to her lips. Lucinda drank slowly as if savoring the taste. When she lay back she said, "I feel like I haven't had a drink in weeks."

Jason smoothed her hair back from her face and smiled tenderly. "Well it has been twelve hours, so I guess you were thirsty."

Lucinda's eyes grew wide. "Twelve hours! Do you mean that I've been asleep a whole day?"

"Most of it was because you were sedated, but since about midnight you have just been asleep."

"Jason, can you tell me about the baby? I know it is dead. I worried that it wouldn't make it, but since I carried it five months I had begun to hope," said Lucinda in a wobbly voice.

Jason drew in a long breath. "I'm afraid it will get you all upset again. Why don't we wait until you are stronger?"

Lucinda shook her head. "I already know it is dead, but I don't know if it was a girl or a boy. What was it Jason?"

"It was. . . a girl, I think." Jason drew in a long breath. "Lucinda it hadn't developed correctly. I don't know how it lived as long as it did."

Lucinda looked sad. "Then I was asking the Lord to let it live when I shouldn't have, wasn't I?"

"Darling, you didn't know and I didn't know. Dr. Patton didn't know either. He knew it had a heart beat, but he said he always knew it wasn't developing correctly. He thinks now he should have told us, but we wouldn't have wanted to abort it, would we?"

"No. I couldn't do that. God could have corrected things if it had been his purpose. I just don't know why God allowed me to carry it for five months, do you?" Lucinda lay frowning in thought, but looked at Jason expectantly.

"I . . . I think God has a purpose for all things, but he is his own interpreter and only he can make it plain. Perhaps, down the road we may realize the purpose of this, but right now it's too painful," said Jason carefully choosing his words.

Lucinda lay looking pensive. "We'll have a funeral, won't we? I know it wasn't fully developed, but it is still part of me and you."

"I thought we'd have a quiet burial when you get better. It's in the morgue now and Bob Fanning will take care of it for a few days."

Lucinda began to cry softly and Jason became alarmed again. "Lucinda, please don't cry. I thought you were too weak to discuss this anyway."

She put out her hand and Jason took it. "I'm sorry, Jason. There's something wrong with me. I can't have babies like other women?"

"You had Danny and there's nothing wrong with him. So, get that out of your head. Lots of women have placenta previa, but that doesn't mean that they are abnormal. What you need right now is to go back to sleep. You'll feel better when you wake up again." Jason sat down on the bed beside her and sat rubbing her arms softly until she dropped into a normal sleep.

CHAPTER 24

On the last day of April, Lucinda had been out of the hospital two days. With Dr. Patton's approval Jason relented and allowed Lucinda to make the trip to the funeral. The baby was put in a small white casket and taken to the cemetery above Mount Zion Church on Crane Ridge. Elder Tommy Adair went with them to the cemetery and prayed before the burial. Lucinda cried all the way home and on their arrival at home Jason insisted she go to bed.

She didn't immediately go to sleep, but lay thinking that Jason was different. *He has a different tone of voice since I've been sick. He always asks how I feel about things and I don't know . . . he's just different*, she thought.

In the next weeks Lucinda complained about not gaining any strength. "Jason, I'm so weak that I don't feel like doing anything."

"Lucinda, you lost so much blood and the first transfusion wasn't the right type," Jason explained. "I gave you blood twice. That's why I had that green outfit on the first time you woke up."

Lucinda's eyes widened. "I don't know how you were still standing if you gave me that much blood."

"I gave a pint one night and then another the next day. After that you began to improve and didn't have to have anymore. I guess you just needed good blood," he said with raised eyebrows and a quirky grin.

"Thanks, Jason. I hope I never have to return the favor. The sight of blood makes me sick." Lucinda was sitting up in bed and Jason sat down beside her and encircled her in his arms.

"Lucinda, I was terrified. You were bleeding and when the first transfusion we tried caused a reaction I was about to go berserk. Dr. Patton calmed me down with a few choice words. I got angry at first, but then I realized it was his way of giving me the strength I needed to help you."

Lucinda leaned up and kissed his cheek. "I'm sorry, Jason. I have never wanted to worry you."

Jason kissed her tenderly. "Well, that will never happen again. The operation took care of that."

Lucinda pushed out of his arms. "What kind of operation did I have? Did they do a hysterectomy?"

"No. I wanted to, but Dr. Patton said you only needed a tubal ligation (women say they had their tubes tied), but that's the medical name for it. Anyway, you won't get pregnant again, and I'm certainly relieved."

Lucinda thought about it. "I guess I am too. I would have loved to have had our baby, but since that makes two that I have lost, I guess it is for the best." Tears were inching down Lucinda's cheeks, however.

"Please dear, don't get upset. You know, I think the Lord knew that you wouldn't grieve so much if you knew that it wouldn't have been able to live anyway. God knows how tender your heart is and he spared you the grief of losing a normal baby. I thank him for that, don't you?" asked Jason rubbing her back gently.

"I hadn't thought about it, but I guess you're right. If it had been formed until we could have told what it was and we could have dressed it in clothing, I don't know if I could have held up as well. I guess I grieve for what might have been."

Even though it was a slow process, by the first of July Lucinda was almost back to normal. The "almost" was that she often found herself in tears for no apparent reason. Jason explained about the fluctuations of female hormones during menopause.

"Menopause! I'm not old enough for that, am I?" Lucinda questioned in unbelief.

"You're forty-two and that's old enough for the onset of menopause. If you have a lot of trouble we can adjust your hormones and help you with that," explained Jason.

In mid-July they went to Bluefield and saw The Sound of Music and on the way home Lucinda said, "Jason, I'd like to go to Austria, wouldn't you?"

She thought Jason would come back at her question with one of his "superior set-downs" as she called them. In the first weeks of their marriage, Lucinda learned that anything Jason thought was unreasonable or stupid would cause him to give a snide reply. This time however, instead of "sure and let's fly to the moon, also" Jason said,

"I'd love to take you to Salzburg. It is so beautiful and also historical."

"Do you really mean you'll take me to Austria?"

Jason looked sideways at her as he drove. "Sure, I'll take you, but I'd really like to take you back to the Martha Washington Inn for our anniversary. Do you want to go before August?"

"Oh, Jason, you are so thoughtful. I hadn't forgotten that we had promised each other that we would always go to the Martha Washington on our anniversaries, but I thought you had."

"No-o-o, I'll not forget Martha Washington Inn, not in this life. I'd rather take you back there than any place on earth. Our wedding and honeymoon is one of the very special times that I shall never forget. I hope you won't either," said Jason drawing her across the seat to sit beside him.

Lucinda looked up at Jason and was overwhelmed with the strength of her love for him. "Jason, I thank God every day for allowing us to finally be together. I love you more than life. I want to be with you as long as I live and I hope we die together. I know that is selfish, but I don't want to live without you."

Jason glanced down and saw her tear drenched cheeks. "Lucinda, we shouldn't think about what we can't stand. We should concentrate on enjoying every moment of our time together. "

"I know, Jason, but since the Lord brought us together I sometimes think about having to live without you and I think I'd just die. Honestly, I really don't think I could stand it."

"Lucinda, I feel the same way about you, but we have to be realistic. We can't bind God to our will. The scriptures reveal that 'He has his will in the army of heaven and amongst the inhabitants of the earth and none can stay his hand nor say why doeth thou?'"

Lucinda put her arm around his chest and snuggled as close to him as she could. "Then let's pray that the Lord makes us strong and brave so that we can stand or accept his will, for Jason, if God didn't make me strong and I lost you, I think I'd just lose my mind."

Jason hugged her tightly and kissed the top of her head. "We'll make that our nightly prayer, dear since I feel the same way." They were now coming into Welch and since it was on Friday night the streets were crowded. Both hands were needed to drive which dispelled the morbid mood that their conversation had caused.

They never brought up the topic in that fashion again, but they both knelt by the bedside each night, each feeling sure that the other was begging God for strength and courage to accept his will.

The next morning they left early for the Bradshaw area to attend meeting in one of the four churches where Primitive Baptists met. They did this every weekend when they were close enough to attend. This was done on a regular basis ever since Lucinda had lost the baby and had surgery. They usually were invited to the home of some brother of the church for lunch and were often encouraged to spend the night. They seldom spent the night anywhere except occasionally they stayed over at Burb and Nancy's on Saturday night when it was meeting time at Bee Branch Church.

Lucinda loved it when they stayed with her parents. She and Nancy grew to expect Burb and Jason to have a loud discussion on one topic or another, usually about unions or politics.

"Mommy, I think they both like to argue, but I think they really enjoy themselves, don't you?" asked Lucinda smiling.

Nancy hugged Lucinda and smiled. "Somewhere in the Bible it says 'iron sharpeneth iron' and I think that's what they do . . . they sharpen each other."

Lucinda hugged Nancy also. "You're a pretty sharp woman for a mountain woman. Do you know that Nancy Harmon?"

"Well, I ain't got much book learnin' but I didn't just cut my eye teeth yesterday. There's a heap of learnin' in livin' and I've done a right smart of that."

Suddenly Nancy jumped from her seat at the kitchen table. "Let's go out and gather some rhubarb. I've been wantin' to make a rhubarb pie and I won't make it lest I have folks in to help eat it. I don't like for food to go to waste and we don't much like leftovers. Do you and Jason warm up leftovers?"

"We'll eat some things twice in one week, but mostly I just fix enough for two people. When Jason cooks, though he fixes enough for ten people it seems. I divide it up into two dinner sections and freeze what's left," said Lucinda laughing as she remembered how much vegetable soup Jason had fixed that week.

"Jason likes to cook, don't he? I wish Burb could boil water without scorchin it," said Nancy on a laugh as they stepped out on the kitchen porch.

That weekend was wonderful and it wasn't until they were ready to leave that Jason told them that after their anniversary was over he planned to take Lucinda to Austria.

Burb jerked around in his seat in front of the television. "Austria, why that's plum over in Europe, ain't it?"

Jason nodded and Lucinda sat watching the various emotions flit across her dad's face. She saw that he was startled, but caught the sudden faraway look in his eyes as he said, "I've often wondered what it would be like to travel to another country." He sat still for a second then blurted out. "I've not wondered enough to get me in no airplane to get there, though."

"When did you all decide to do that?" asked Nancy worriedly.

Jason smiled and picked up Lucinda's hand which lay on his leg. "We went to see the movie The Sound of Music which is set in Austria and that's all this daughter of yours has talked about ever since. In fact she asked me to take her and I promised we'd go after our anniversary."

"Yeah we've already heard all about your anniversary. Danny called from Morgantown to tell us about it. I told Nan that for two people who hadn't been married no time a'tall it was a big to-do about nothing, but Nan thanks its romantic or something. Anyway, you'uns is setting a bad example for that boy and little Emily. You'll have them wantin to gallivant around and celebrate every few months. They won't have time to settle down to raise a family when they get married," said Burb.

Jason laughed. "Well, Lucinda and I don't have to worry about having a family and Danny and Emily have to finish school before they can marry so we'll cross that bridge as we come to it."

Burb gave Jason a squint-eyed look. "I don't think you'd better bet on them two finishin' school 'fore they marry if my eyes ain't deceiving me."

Lucinda's eyes widened. "What do you mean, Dad? Did they say anything about marrying?"

Nancy spoke up. "No, they didn't say nothing the last time they was here, but they jest had a look about 'em. Me and Burb talked and we thought the same thing. Them young'uns has got the lovesick blues in the worst way."

"They'd better take some cold showers then or they'll find themselves having to quit school and go to work," said Jason winking at Lucinda.

CHAPTER 25

When their anniversary rolled around, Lucinda and Jason walked all over Abingdon during the two days they spent there, but their nights were spent at the Martha Washington Inn, of course. "I like this coming here every year, Jason. I think we should start some traditions in our lives don't you?" asked Lucinda as they packed their bags to leave.

Jason smiled. "I told you we'd spend our anniversaries here, did you forget?"

"I thought you were kidding, but I should have known you wouldn't kid about something that means so much to both of us." Lucinda leaned over and kissed Jason. "Thank you, dear heart. You don't know how much better my life is now and it is all due to you. I've learned so much from you, Jason."

"I've learned from you, too, Lucinda. One thing I've learned for sure is that if one loves somebody, that love overshadows everything else. I know now, that I have always taken it for granted that the way I saw things was the right way. I guess, Janet never questioned that except wanting to move back to Pittsburgh. However, when I almost lost you, I did a lot of praying and soul-searching. God showed me that loving someone is a two-way street and there are always two ways to look at things. Have you noticed that I always ask you what you think about things before I make a decision, now?"

Lucinda looked up at him and smiled. "Yes, I noticed but I didn't say anything. I guess I was afraid that you would revert to being the "all-wise" decision maker."

"Were you going to allow me to continue to be like that?" asked Jason.

"I was trying to figure the best way to get you to see what you were doing. I didn't think you realized you were so domineering. Well, when Emily thought she had lost her billfold and we had that argument, I thought you must have thought about it," said Lucinda.

Jason shook his head. "I got so angry that night when Emily called that I felt I had to get away. But, when I left the house, all I could think about was how I had hurt you. I knew that even if you were wrong I couldn't stay mad at you and I didn't want to hurt you. I didn't come back and apologize because I realized there was something wrong with what I did. I apologized because you were hurt about how I had acted." He took in a long breath and let it out. "I guess it took you being so sick to open my eyes. I'm so sorry darling. I hope I never hurt you again."

Lucinda snuggled closer. "You probably will and I'll probably upset you, but we know we love each other and we know we want to stay together so I don't think our disagreements will amount to much."

Jason grinned. "I already know that I'll never make a liberal thinker out of you, but lately I've caught myself having conservative thoughts, but not frequently."

"Mommy always said, 'A good woman is the making of a man', so I'm trying my best to make a conservative thinker of you," said Lucinda and then giggled at the expression on Jason's face.

By the end of the following week, Jason was busily checking flights and booking hotels for their trip to Austria. Lucinda kept asking about the weather in Austria and the kinds of clothes she should take. The first week in September arrived with a flurry of activity for both of them.

They had planned on a one week stay in Austria and then a leisurely train trip to Dresden, Germany to see the cathedrals, and a little town of Kiefelden in the Bavarian Alps, just to get an understanding of the beauty of the German countryside, then on to Heidelberg, in southern Germany to visit the University because Jason had met a professor from there, and then on to Leeuwarden, in the Netherlands because Lucinda had read so many books by Betty Neals in which Holland was so meticulously described.

"I've read every book she has written. She is so good on description that I think I'd feel right at home to visit one of the homes by a canal," enthused Lucinda about the authoress, Betty Neels.

"She only writes Harlequin Romances doesn't she? I always thought they were very light reading," said Jason.

"They are, but if one wanted to write, I think they could learn how to plot a story from reading her work. Like I said, she also knows how to add description without being redundant," countered Lucinda in a thoughtful manner.

Jason smiled. "If you say so, dear, since you know her and I have never even seen one of her books. I've just heard about them. Do you plan to write a book, sometime?"

Lucinda sniffed and pushed her shoulders back in a haughty manner. "I've thought about it. Why? Don't you think I'm smart enough?"

"Smart enough! I think you are too smart to settle for writing Harlequin romances."

Lucinda looked bewildered. "I wouldn't even know where to start. I don't feel smart enough to write a romance, Harlequin or not. Writing takes a gift and talent and I don't think I have either."

"Well, I think you have. Once, I was in a regional school board meeting and a member of the Wyoming County school board told about this young teacher in Pineville who wrote skits, poems, and news releases that got a lot of attention for Pineville schools. I asked him the teacher's name and he said Marshall but couldn't recall the first name. I asked somebody else and found that it was you. So, I know you can write.

Lucinda's eyes lit up. "Did you really hear that? Jason, I have a box somewhere with a copy of everything I've ever written. I never dreamed that anyone would like my writing well enough to remember it, though."

Jason looked at Lucinda with a speculative gleam in his eyes. "Why don't you buy a notebook and start journal keeping. If you wrote about one thing you will see or experience on this trip it may be worth reading someday. Our grandchildren would probably like to read it and probably many others as well."

Lucinda made no comment, but before they left Welch she did buy a three-ring binder and lined paper to fill it. She hid this away in the bottom of her suitcase for some reason. *I guess I'm afraid Jason may find it and laugh at my attempt at writing.* She pulled herself up short as it flashed through her mind. *I know Jason would never make fun of any effort I made, but I still don't want him to find it,* thought Lucinda and continued to cover it with her underclothing.

Jason found that they could get a straight flight from Charlotte, North Carolina to JFK International Airport in New York and reserved their tickets. "We'll just leave the car there at the airport since I bought round trip tickets from Charlotte, North Carolina to New York. That way we'll be sure to have a car waiting for us when we get back."

"Do they have a safe place to leave the car, there at the airport?" asked Lucinda. "That would cost a fortune, though, wouldn't it?"

Jason grinned. "It may be a fortune to some people, but it doesn't cost, 'an arm or a leg', as your sister, Odell, would say. I'm willing to pay for the convenience."

They were scheduled to leave the third Monday in September and Lucinda was so pleased when Jason told her. "Oh good! This way we will get to attend the church association meetings. I was praying we could, but I didn't want to pester you since you had it all to arrange."

Jason smiled gently. "I'm a member too, you know. I kept the associations in mind when I was trying to get everything scheduled."

They got rooms in Buck's Motel in Clintwood and attended the Three Forks of Powell's River Association all three days, and were anxiously anticipating the next association. Danny and Emily came in for the Elkhorn Association which was being held at the Bee Branch church there on Bradshaw Mountain and that became another marked event in their lives. Neither Lucinda nor Jason knew that Danny had felt the call to preach. They knew that he often started and lined songs and even sometimes dismissed the services. They privately discussed why the other elders had started asking Danny to get involved in that manner.

"I wonder if he has said something to one of the elders," said Lucinda on the second occasion she had been present when he had lined a song.

Jason and Lucinda looked at each other in surprise when, on Saturday morning, Elder Tommy Adair asked Danny if he would open service and pray. Danny sat staring thoughtfully for a moment and then slowly rose to his feet. Lucinda could tell he was very nervous when he produced a handkerchief and wiped his brow. Lucinda grasped Jason's hand and squeezed it. She began to silently beg the Lord to deliver him, if he was called to expound on the scriptures.

Danny started by telling the congregation that he had been troubled for more than six months. "I've been dreaming and waking myself up preaching and I can't find any peace in anything. I finally went to Papaw Burb and he said I should offer myself. That's why you see me standing here. I feel like a very small empty pail and if the Lord doesn't fill the pail and give me something to say, I'll not be before you very long." He went on to talk of his experience in faith and suddenly as if a mighty rushing wind had blown through the congregation a voice became part of Danny and his countenance took on a bright glow. Words came from him with such eloquence and power that the congregation came alive, as fire in sagebrush and leapt from breast to breast. People were crying, shouting, and praising God while hugging each other. Someone started a song and the whole house sang and rejoiced as in one voice.

Non-members who always stayed outside and visited with each other were now hanging in the windows and crowding the doorways. First two young women came to the front and gave their hand to the church and then they were followed by three men who also united with the church.

This was an unusual occurrence since the door was usually opened for the acceptance of members at the end of the services, but this was at the beginning of the service. Danny had no idea how to handle the situation, but Elder Tommy Adair stepped in and by motion and second accepted the inductees as candidates for baptism and then Danny knelt to lead in prayer. His prayer was good, but nothing compared to what had just happened.

At the end of service when the door was opened for acceptance of members it was explained by Elder Tommy Adair that since Danny had not yet been set at liberty to exercise his gift that some other elders would have to perform the baptism. Elders Whitten Sparks of the Washington Association and Wendell Williams of the Three Forks of Powell's River were chosen by the men to baptize them, but the women wanted Elder Stewart Owens of the Washington Association and Elder Roy Flanary of the Three Forks of Powell's River to baptize them. They all requested to be baptized on Sunday after the services were over.

When they gathered beside the river at Whitewood, each of the candidates requested that Danny open the service with prayer. Again, the heavens opened and the spirit came down causing much praise and rejoicing. Two elderly women made their way into the water as the last man was led out and they two were baptized.

A happy group of believers made their trip home that evening with light hearts and satisfied minds knowing that they had been gathered in the spirit of the Lord and had become one body of believers.

CHAPTER 26

On the way home Sunday evening Lucinda rode along in pensive silence. She was nestled close to Jason, but her thoughts were on the wonderful gift that God had bestowed on her son. Tears of thankfulness crept down her cheeks as she silently prayed. *Lord, I have no way of showing how much I thank you, but I do with all my heart. You take care of him, Lord for I know that with a gift such as you've given him, much will be required of him. Please help him and keep him mindful as to from whom the gift came. He isn't the gift, I know, but only the instrument through which the gift is delivered, but he is so young, Lord.*

As if Jason knew what she had been praying about, he said, "Don't worry about Danny, Lucinda. The Lord gave the gift and he prepared the vessel to deliver it. I think that as long as that gift is needed God will preserve Danny. I just hope Danny will treasure that gift and work in it. I'd hate to see his gift taken and given to someone else. Our Association needs that gift so badly right now, I think. Don't you?"

Lucinda raised her head. "Yes, I do, Jason. Right now with Dad and Uncle Dave as strong Deacons, we don't have much to worry about. After they pass away, though, we both know we have some among us who will cause trouble. Without strong deacons a church can be split apart and that would break my heart.

They talked on in this vein all the way home. Danny had decided that he would stay at his Papaw's that night. At first Emily said she would return to Welch with Jason and Lucinda, but when Nancy asked Emily to stay also she eagerly accepted the invitation.

Danny had followed them out to the car. "We have to go back to Morgantown tomorrow, Mom, so we will probably wake you and Jason early. I wouldn't do this, but I really need to talk to Papaw," explained Danny.

"That's all right, Danny," began Lucinda, but was interrupted by Jason.

"Yeah sure! Come as early as you want to Danny. Your mother won't hear the door, but I will. I get up early, but some woman that I know often sleeps until eight or nine o'clock," said Jason laughing at Lucinda's red face.

"She feels guilty when I tell on her. I don't know why, but every time her sleeping late is mentioned she gets embarrassed." Jason laughed, but looked puzzled.

"Do you have any idea why she feels guilty?" he asked Danny.

Danny grimaced. "Yes. If Dad overslept and thought he was going to be late for work he always quarreled at Mom. He always said she roamed around the house all night and kept him awake."

"Danny, your father was a sick man. I wish you'd get over that bitterness you feel toward him," chided Lucinda.

Danny dropped his head. "I don't hate him anymore, Mom, but I still get upset when I remember some of the things he did to you. I try to remember that he was emotionally ill and then I have compassion for him."

Both Jason and Lucinda had nodded in agreement but made no comment. When they were home Jason fixed hot chocolate and they went to the living room to listen to the news while they drank it. During a commercial Jason said, "Lucinda, did Jeff not realize what he was doing to you?"

"I don't know, Jason. I guess he didn't because in his own way, I believe he loved me. Now, I realize how tormented he must have been. His jealousy literarily destroyed him."

Jason sat drinking his chocolate deep in thought. "I think Mom and Janet had the same problem, but to a lesser degree. They kept their jealousy hidden, but Jeff couldn't, I suppose."

"What was your Mom jealous about?"

"Control! I think Mom wanted to be in control of her whole family. I think Dad and Frank were smart enough to let her think she had control, but I crossed the line."

"Are we ever going to visit them, Jason? I don't want to, but in a way I feel that it isn't fair to your Dad and perhaps your mother also."

"I talk to Dad two or three times a week and once in a while I talk to Mom. I had a hard time with hate for Mom and even Janet when I first found those letters. Through your talks and understanding, the Lord has taken the hate away, but I don't want you subjected to Mom's snobbery." He rose to take their cups back to the kitchen. "If you want to, we may make a short visit, after we come back from Europe."

"I dread it, dear, but I would like to see the school you went to, the places you hung out, and I look forward to meeting your dad," said Lucinda also rising to prepare for bed.

Danny and Emily pulled into the driveway at seven-thirty the next morning. Both Lucinda and Jason were waiting for their arrival. "I got your mother up at four this morning. She didn't want to oversleep and miss seeing you before we begin our trip," said Jason seriously.

Lucinda's eyes widened. "He's not telling the truth. I got up before he did, but not at four. We've been up since six-thirty though. I gathered the luggage for both of you since I thought you may have classes this morning." Lucinda smiled at Emily, who stood yawning with half-closed eyes.

Jason walked over and put his arm around Emily. "I hope you don't have to drive, Princess. You're almost asleep on your feet."

Danny stopped with a suitcase in each hand. "She went to sleep as soon as we hit the highway on Bradshaw Mountain and woke up as we stopped for the light at Coney Island. Don't worry I'm not going to let her drive."

Jason gathered up the rest of the bags and boxes they were taking back with them and walked behind Danny to the car. When they came back in Lucinda asked, "Will you have time to eat or have you already eaten?"

"Mom, you know that Nanny and Papaw wouldn't let us leave without eating breakfast. I ate a big breakfast at six this morning, but Emily didn't eat much. She did drink a cup of coffee though." He looked at Emily who still looked sleepy and smiled. "It didn't help her much, did it?"

They all stood for a few minutes as if they didn't know what should happen next. "Well, you two know that we will be flying out on Wednesday from Charlotte, North

Carolina. I booked a straight flight to Hamburg, Germany and from there we'll fly on into the Salzburg Airport W. A. Mozart," said Jason.

"What time does your flight leave Charlotte?" asked Danny.

"Six o'clock Wednesday evening. We wanted to arrive in Hamburg in the daytime," said Jason explaining that it would be easier to get a room in case there were changes in their flight plans. "I try to always plan for contingencies."

Lucinda had been standing quietly by, but now she walked over to Emily and put her arms around her. "Emily take care of Danny for me and Danny, you take care of Emily. We'll call before we leave Charlotte and then again when we reach Hamburg."

Emily hugged Lucinda tightly. "Mama Lucinda, you know that I'll take care of Danny, but really it is always him taking care of me. I wish you wouldn't worry so much about us. We have a wonderful landlady. She's just like a very special aunt and she loves having Danny there. Well, she loves having us both, but a big strong man like Danny makes her feel safe." She looked up at Danny's six-foot-six- inches with so much love in her eyes that Lucinda blinked in sudden recognition. "He makes me feel safe too," Emily continued and turned red when she realized that Lucinda and Jason were both staring at her.

Lucinda stepped away from Emily to be engulfed in Danny's arms. "I'll miss you Mom, but not as much as I would if I didn't have Emily." He stopped and hesitated a moment. "I guess you two know that Emily and I will get married as soon as we can, maybe before we finish school."

Jason and Lucinda exchanged glances. "Not this semester, I hope. We'll be away until the first of November and can't be here to prepare for a wedding," said Lucinda.

"Mom, you don't have to prepare for a wedding. You didn't when you and Jason got married," replied Danny soberly.

"I hope you two consider all the responsibilities you would be taking on to marry so young," said Jason looking from one to the other.

Danny looked at his watch. "We have to go or I'll never make it in time to unload and get to our classes. Be sure to call and don't worry. We are a lot more level-headed than you two give us credit."

Lucinda hugged him again. "Don't you two do anything foolish, but then you were never one to do anything without thinking it through. I don't know why I worry now." She leaned up and kissed his cheek. "Good-bye Danny. Drive safely." She then went to Emily and gave her a hug and a kiss on the cheek and hurriedly left the room.

Jason walked out of the house with them, but Lucinda didn't see him. She was in the bathroom crying heartbrokenly. Jason found her convulsed with tears and sobs. "Why are you crying like that, dear? You didn't get that upset when we went to Ireland."

Lucinda blew her nose on toilet paper and wiped her eyes. "I know, Jason, but I feel like it's different this time, for some reason."

"Well, we are going farther away, but they will be in Morgantown until Thanksgiving anyway. We should be back by then, so it isn't like we would be seeing them any quicker." Jason kept talking to her until Lucinda finally calmed down and went into the kitchen to fix them some breakfast.

Even though it seemed impossible at first but by nine o'clock on Wednesday morning Lucinda was packed and ready to go. They had called Burb and Nancy, Emily and Danny, and had made sure that Kyle and Rita had their key and a list of instructions for emergencies. Lucinda worried that asking Kyle and Rita to watch their place was too much, but Jason assured her that both Kyle and Rita had insisted. "Besides it would only be once each week". .Lucinda looked back as they drove away and realized that she really loved this place that they had created together. It was truly a home of her heart.

Jason looked over at her and smiled. "We're going to miss our evenings on the patio in back, aren't we? In fact, I think we'll miss a lot of things about our home, don't you?"

Lucinda slid over and put her head against Jason's shoulder. "I think just being together makes places special. I never felt like this about any place I lived with Jeff."

Jason put his arm around her. "I know, dear. Janet and I lived in the house on Browns Creek for over twenty years, but I didn't mind leaving it at all. Our home is where my heart is and that's because you are in it.

CHAPTER 27

Even though Lucinda had flown to Ireland and back she still found herself beginning to panic as their flight time drew nearer. *I'll just take a nerve pill before Jason reminds me. Maybe he'll think I've overcome my fear*, she thought with a sneaky smile. She was in the bathroom at the airport and knew that they had another hour to wait before boarding. She took the pill and checked her face and hair before walking jauntily out of the restroom.

Jason was waiting just outside the door. "If you take a nerve pill now, it should take effect before boarding time." Jason opened his extended palm to reveal a small white pill.

Lucinda shook her head. "I feel all right. I believe I can fly without it." She walked past him and he stared in amazement. Following her back to their seats he sat down beside her. "Lucinda, I really think you should take this. What if you get sick and the bathroom is full?"

He sounded so concerned that Lucinda felt sorry for him. She put her hand on his arm. "I've already taken a nerve pill, Jason. I was going to try to fool you. Don't worry. I took it while I was in the bathroom."

Jason sighed with relief. "I wish you could fly without them, but I'd rather take a chance on a shorter flight, wouldn't you?" asked Jason.

By the time their flight was called Lucinda was drowsy, but she made her way holding to Jason's arm, to their seats. Soon they were airborne and Lucinda was relaxed. This time she didn't sleep, however. They watched Gone with the Wind. Lucinda became so engrossed that she forgot about where she was. Their plane stopped at JFK International, but they didn't have to change planes. By the time they landed at Hamburg, Germany she had slept several hours and woke up just as they were coming in to land.

Hamburg Airport was a really nice airport with a truly wonderful gift shop, but Jason said to wait about buying until their return trip. "We'd just have more to carry if we bought things now, and besides the announcer just said we would be boarding for Salzburg in about twenty minutes. I think we'd better get to the right gate since we certainly don't want to miss our flight."

Lucinda was so spellbound with all the new sights and hearing people speaking in a language she didn't know. *I feel like I'm in some kind of fairy tale*, she thought as she followed Jason. Her eyes were darting to the right and left as she touched Jason's arm every few seconds to draw his attention to something that fascinated her.

Jason smiled indulgently, but still hurried her along. They were soon on board another plane and fastening their seat belts. This flight was smooth as well and Lucinda was caught up in anticipating her first sight of Austria.

When the plane set down and they were walking down the ramp Lucinda felt like she was walking on air. In the airport she had to be shuffled along since she wanted to linger at every new sight. While they were waiting for the shuttle to take them to their hotel Lucinda said, "Jason, who would have ever thought that a little hillbilly girl from the top of Bradshaw Mountain would ever be walking the streets of Austria? This is so unbelievable that I feel like an alien from outer space."

Jason smiled down at her shining face and eyes. "Well, if you are, you look so happy that I want to be an alien with you. Let's get away from this airport and just follow 'the yellow brick road' and see if we can find some munchkins. You make me feel like a kid again, Lucinda." He bent and gave her a quick kiss just as the shuttle bus pulled in and Jason directed the porter to their luggage.

They had reservations in the Meierhof with their rooms located on the third level but this level looked out onto the courtyard which had grass and trees. When the shuttle pulled up Lucinda stepped out still staring in what her brother used to call a "goggle-eyed" fashion when they were young and couldn't get their eyes wide enough to see all they wanted to see.

Jason finally got Lucinda and their luggage up to the rooms and decided that they needed something to eat. "Do you want to go out to eat tonight or would you rather have something sent up? I'm really tired. If you don't mind I'll order something to be sent up and we can begin exploring in the morning."

Lucinda looked at Jason and saw that he looked worn out. "Oh Jason, I'm sorry. You've had to put up with my gawking since we left the States and you look so tired. Let's just eat here. I don't want to go out anyway. I just want to call the folks and Danny and then I think I could sleep for two days. She put her arms around Jason's neck and pulled his head down to kiss him. "Thank you Jason for everything. You are so good to me."

Jason hugged her close. "Well, I'm tired, but you didn't cause it. It is jet-lag I guess, but I could use some rest. I want to do things for you, Lucinda. In fact, I like doing things for you and taking you places you've never been. It makes me feel good to have you relying on me. You get so excited that it energizes me, usually, but right now, I confess that I feel my age."

Lucinda kissed him again. "I'd do the same for you, but I don't know how. I don't really need anything to eat if you'd rather just go to bed and rest."

"I'm not that tired. I'll call room service while you take a shower then we'll put in the calls to the States," said Jason as he picked up the phone.

The excitement was still in Lucinda's voice when she talked to her parents and to Danny and Emily. "Mama Lucinda, you sound like a sixteen-year old. You're making me want to visit Salzburg just hearing you talk about it. Once you've been there a week you'll be flying so high that Dad will have to tie sandbags to you just to hold you down," said Emily laughing merrily.

Needless to say, both Jason and Lucinda slept until nine o'clock the next morning. Jason rolled over and as usual gave her a morning kiss. "Good Morning! Fairy princess! Are you ready to try your wings?"

Lucinda kissed him in return and reared up to look down into his face. "If my handsome prince has his winged horse we'll fly away together."

"I know another way to fly," said Jason with raised eyebrows and pulled her down into his arms again. At ten o'clock Jason picked up the bedside phone to call for room service, but Lucinda grabbed the phone from his hand and replaced it in its cradle. "I want to go downstairs to eat," she said scuttling hurriedly to the bathroom.

By eleven o'clock they had eaten and were down in the courtyard going over the city map that the management had provided. "I want to see every place where Maria Von Trapp lived especially the Abbey," was Lucinda's main request.

"Well, if every place feeds like we were fed this morning I think we'll need to do a lot of walking, don't you?" Jason laughed as he looked down to see if his stomach was bulging.

Lucinda patted his stomach. "Don't worry. You'll always be slim. You're not a beer drinker."

"I know lots of people who have a bulging gut who are not beer drinkers, dear. If people take in more calories than they burn off they are going to put on pounds."

Lucinda went to a window and stood looking at her reflection. "Have I put on pounds, Jason?"

"No, but we'd better move along before that young man gazing at you decides he wants to get acquainted."

"You're with me. He knows I'm married," said Lucinda as she turned away to walk beside Jason.

Jason grasped her hand. "You look so young that he probably thought you were with your father."

"Jason, you don't look old. What makes you think that?"

"Lucinda, I'm ten years older than you. I was in the sixth grade when you were born."

They walked on swinging their clasped hands. "I'm so thankful that I have you, Jason. You're all I've ever really wanted." Suddenly Lucinda stopped. "Jason! Look! "Original Sound of Music Tour! Let's take the tour, please."

Laughing, Jason went to purchase tickets still holding Lucinda's hand. Lucinda's face fell when they were told that they were full for the next two days. "Don't get upset, dear. We'll still get to take the tour but it will be two days from now. I'm sure there's much more to see and we want to see it all," said Jason.

They went wandering through the middle of town stopping to look at anything that interested them. Around one o'clock they saw a sign saying Café Tomaselli and decided to have lunch there. When they were inside they were fascinated by the marble and wood décor and the entire wall of 18th century portraits. They were ready to be seated when they learned that there was a nice place where they could eat out in the open if they wished. They chose to go outside and were soon seated in a shaded nook. Lucinda sat reading some of the literature she had picked up as they came in. "Jason, this says that Mozart's beloved Constanze often dropped in here since she lived next door."

"Let me see that for a second." Lucinda passed it over to him and he said, "I thought I'd read somewhere that it was an example of the Vienna Coffeehouse and if that's true I'll bet they have that famous Mocha Mozart Liqueur and Whipped Cream. You know that drink that our breakfast guest was talking about?"

"Oh, that Mrs. Gustav ---something. She spoke English really well, didn't she?" said Lucinda looking thoughtful. "Jason, do strangers here just sit down with anyone if there is an empty spot at their table?"

"I guess so, since that lady came and sat with us this morning. You'll have to admit that it's a good way to get acquainted," said Jason laughing at Lucinda's expression. She looked around to see if they were going to get other uninvited lunch mates, but nobody was headed their way and she sighed with relief.

"Don't you like to meet new people, Lucinda? I thought you liked people."

"I do like people, Jason, but all of this is so brand-new to me that I don't want to have to drag my attention away from all I want to see. You know, when you have guests one feels they should be polite and talk to them and right now I just want to fill my eyes with images."

Jason shook his head, smiling. "You'll never be old. Your mind never slows down. You really should try writing, Lucinda. The smallest thing fascinates you, doesn't it?"

Lucinda looked at Jason with her eyes aglow with excitement. "This is just so unbelievable. Jason, it's like I'm in a dream . . . such a glorious dream. Oh Jason, I wish I could tell you how I feel. I want to spread my arms wide and pull all of this into some secret place so I can take it out and treasure it at different times. I want to touch and feel and smell the different scents and . . . I can't speak my joy, Jason. I just can't find the words."

Jason sat watching and listening to the excitement on her face and in her voice. "You sound like somebody who has just fallen in love, Lucinda."

Lucinda's eyes widened. "That's it! I feel like this about you and I have since I first met you. That was like Cinderella meeting a handsome prince. You know that song, I hear singing and there's no one there, I smell blossoms and the trees are bare, All day long I seem to walk on air, well that's how I felt then and still do." She looked up at Jason and then inched closer to him. "I wouldn't enjoy it if you weren't here, though. You're still my handsome prince, Jason. As long as I have you, I don't have to have all this to be content."

Jason got to his feet. "All right then. I guess we can get the next flight out."

Lucinda's face fell and Jason laughed. "You mean I'm not really enough? I'm hurt."

Lucinda saw the twinkle in his eyes. "Well, could we stay just to do the Sound of Music tour?"

Jason pulled her to her feet and hugged her tightly. "We can stay as long as you want to stay, my little fairy princess, but I don't have a white horse to ride."

Lucinda leaned up and kissed him. "Just always love me, Jason. I meant it though, even if I do want to take that tour. You are all I ever truly wanted. I love Danny, but I didn't want him at first. But, I've wanted you from the first time I saw you and never dreamed you'd ever want to marry me."

They sat waiting to be served and Lucinda had suddenly become very quiet. Jason studied her guilt-ridden expression. "What's the matter? You look like you've killed somebody."

Lucinda looked at Jason with tears running down her face. "Oh Jason, here I am enthusing and trying to explain how much I love you and not once thanking the Good Lord who sent you to me. Jason, I'm letting this . . . travel or seeing new things become more important than my God. How could I be so foolish?"

Jason put his hand over hers on the table. "Lucinda, please don't start loading yourself with guilt again. God lives inside you and you didn't forsake Him. Without God you wouldn't have these feelings of happiness, joy, and appreciation for all the wonders he has allowed you to see. I know that I don't have a pure heart like you have, but honestly dear, I think that God wants us to enjoy this beautiful world that he prepared for us to live on."

Lucinda wiped her cheeks and sat looking thoughtful. "I know that what you say is true, but I got so excited just thinking of how much I love you, and how much I'm enjoying this opportunity that it made me afraid."

"Afraid! My sweet innocent darling, you have no need to be afraid. God made you just as you are and allowed me to spend my old age with a ray of sunshine. God sent you to me and I am certainly a much kinder person because of it."

Jason sat holding Lucinda's hand and Lucinda looked up at him with such wonder in her eyes. "Do you really think that, Jason? I mean do you feel that the Lord sent me to you to make your life happier?"

Jason slid closer and put his arm around her. "Yes, dear, I not only believe it, I know that I am only happy with you and I was never this happy before." He started to say something else to be stopped by the appearance of the waitress.

The waitress dressed in native dress came to take their order and Jason asked about the Mocha Mozart Liqueur with whipped cream. It was the specialty of the house and Jason started to order two, but Lucinda stopped him. "I may not like it. Why don't you just order one and we can share it. I'll bet it costs a fortune, doesn't it?"

When the order came, they both liked this concoction but agreed that sharing was better since they were really too full for any kind of sweet anyway. "We'll come back here another time and get one without a big lunch. It is good, isn't it?" Jason took the last sip and pushed the glass away before they both rose to their feet.

CHAPTER 28

They spent that day and the next seeing the sights all over Salzburg. They made their way back to Siftskeller St Peter for dinner each evening, however, since they were so impressed on the first night. It was located near where they stayed. They only had to walk down a hill into Salzburg central.

"We're going to play like we're natives and have wine with our dinner," said Jason looking at Lucinda. "Don't get all upset. I'm not going to get you drunk. A glass of wine with ones dinner helps with digestion. Didn't you know that?"

"No, I didn't know that and you know I didn't. I'd never had wine until I married you." Lucinda suddenly stopped as she remembered going to the concert in Charleston with Jeff which led to her marriage to him. That wasn't because she got drunk, but because his truck broke down and she'd had to spend the night in a seedy motel on Johnny Cake Mountain.

Jason saw the stricken look on her face. "What! Why are you looking like you've just remembered something awful."

Lucinda swallowed the giant lump that had formed in her throat. "I drank some wine once before and it led to disaster," whispered Lucinda.

Jason slid around the table and put his arm around her. "Did somebody make you drunk?"

Lucinda shook her head. "No, it led to something worse than that."

Just then the waiter came to take their order which Lucinda left to Jason. He ordered a white wine called Gruner Veltliner which Lucinda thought was really good. Later Jason explained that the wine was from the Wachau region of Austria. "The grape from which this wine is made isn't grown in many places. That's why people have told me that this wine is the true Austrian white wine," he said importantly. Lucinda didn't know a thing about wines and when the waiter left she gave Jason a questioning look.

He grinned boyishly. "I've been talking to the natives and learned all about the wines and the foods. While you laze around in the mornings I've been out getting educated.

Lucinda smiled. "I wondered why it took you so long to find a newspaper."

The restaurant was super and they learned that it was probably the oldest restaurant in Europe. "I'm amazed that a business would last that long, aren't you?" Lucinda looked around in wonder at how full it was and how well preserved everything seemed to be.

"They serve fresh caught fish. Let's ask the waitress to suggest an entrée," said Jason as the waiter came back with the wine.

They followed the suggestion made by the waitress and found the food delicious and very satisfying. "Um, that was good," said Lucinda as they rose from the table.

"You're not drunk, either. That says a lot since you had a glass and a half of wine," Jason said, laughing as he took her arm. "I think we should eat here every night. We know they have good food and the atmosphere is just what we were expecting, isn't it?"

"Yes. It's like an older generation, but with a modern touch or maybe I mean modern food. I agree that we should make this our dinner place here in Salzburg."

They were wandering down some street and there was a statue of a lady with water squirting from both bared breasts. Lucinda stopped and stood staring. "What was the sculptor saying by that . . . display?"

Jason smiled impishly. "I don't know, but she has nice round breasts doesn't she?"

"Jason! I know it must be referring to the nurturing of humanity or civilization or something that has to do with abundance of caring. It certainly wasn't created for men to ogle," sputtered Lucinda indignantly.

Jason laughed hilariously. "That is a statue of the Madonna, Lucinda. I shouldn't be kidding about it, but I knew that would get you going. You know, Lucinda, you are a real prude, but innocently so."

"I am not. I just don't think one has to constantly refer to private things," replied Lucinda in red-faced embarrassment mostly because she hadn't recognized the Madonna. "I guess you're learning what an uneducated woman you married, aren't you?"

Jason hugged her close. "Lucinda, you are educated. You may not be versed in some of the art forms or perhaps other areas, but that has nothing to do with intelligence. It has to do with experience." Lucinda looked up at him smiling her appreciation and taking her hand in his they walked on down the street. Suddenly Jason hailed a cruising taxi and told the driver he wanted to go to another small town someone had told him about. The street became narrow as they rode along, but it was paved. They rode for about eight miles along the road and going around a sharp curve they came in sight of a farm. They saw Flamingos, but they were almost white. They had a pink tinge to them but they were not pink as Lucinda had thought Flamingoes were. Further along the road was a fenced- in spot with pigs sloshing around in a 'mud hole' made by their own antics.

"You said those were Flamingos, but I thought Flamingos were pink," said Lucinda looking around her in surprise. "How come this farm is so close to the city? Back home, it's ten miles to Bradshaw from the top of the mountain, but there are no pig lots near the roads."

Jason raised his eyebrows and shook his head. "Beats me, unless the Flamingos get their color from what they eat. As to the pigs, I haven't a clue. The EPA back home would oust them before they got a chance to make a wallowing hole, that's for certain."

When Thursday, the Sound of Music Tour day arrived, Lucinda was on her way to learn about Maria Von Trapp. She was so excited that Jason feared she would be sick. "Lucinda, you need to calm down. Maybe you should take a nerve pill. The bus will be traveling over some winding roads."

Lucinda squeezed his arm. "No, I won't get sick, but I hope some big fat person doesn't block my view. I want to see everything."

Jason laughed indulgently. "I'll lift you up if that should happen, but if we don't hurry to Mirabellplatz, in front of St. Andrew's Church we'll miss the tour altogether."

This calmed Lucinda down a little since she had to hurry to keep up with Jason's longer stride. They made it in plenty of time and stood listening to The Sound of Music being played as everyone gathered. Jason looked down at Lucinda and smiled at her eagerness. "*I hope they give us seats in the front of the bus or she'll be sick the entire trip",* he thought.

The tour guide walked to the center of the group and everyone got quiet. She explained that the first place they would visit would be the Mirabell Gardens which was just across the platz or square. "You'll see all the flowers and choose fruits from the stalls in the wonderful farmers market," said the guide and continued with, "Before we start however, I need to explain the rules for the tour. Everyone must remain seated while the bus is in motion, be courteous, and be responsible for your own things. The complete tour takes four hours." She went on to explain about the various stops they would make. She explained about lunch and the bathroom facilities and asked if there were people with special needs.

Lucinda just half listened to all this since she was so eager to see and hear all about the houses and areas the movie had made so magical. She almost danced as the guide led them across the square to the Mirabell Gardens. In no time at all they turned in at the most beautiful garden or park-like spot Lucinda had ever seen.

"This is the Mirabell Gardens, explained the guide." She went on to tell that the gardens were laid out in the 18th century. "In the movie Maria and the children were seen dancing around this statue of Pegasus, as they sang 'Do-Re-Me.' If you recall, Pegasus was the winged horse praised in Greek mythology."

Soon they had gone all over the Mirabell Gardens, with people buying fruit from the many vendors, Jason being one of them. The guide then hustled them along to the bus to be driven to the Leopoldskron Castle.

Once there, Lucinda nudged Jason, "Are you taking pictures? Don't you dare miss any of this! Can you get the whole front of the castle?"

Jason had not only taken pictures of what they saw but of Lucinda also. To him, her expressions and utter joy that was so overtly displayed were treasures he didn't want to miss. He smiled. "Yes, dear, I am faithfully recording all your joy on film."

"Sh-h," whispered Lucinda as the guide stopped and began her speech.

"The front of the castle was shown as the Trapp family home in the movie. It was on this, the Leopoldskron Lake," the guide explained as they walked toward a beautiful serene body of water, "where the children were boating when they fell into the water."

Lucinda stood looking at the water almost as if she could see and hear the children's happy shouts and laughter. They weren't allowed to go inside the castle that day but the guide told them that the Venetian room was copied from the castle and used as the ballroom in the movie.

Next they went to the Heilbronn Castle, which wouldn't have meant so much if the song, Sixteen going on Seventeen, hadn't been playing as they neared the glass pavilion which served as the gazebo where the oldest daughter took shelter in the thunder storm with Raolf. The guide explained that the castle was really a hunting castle built in the 17th century by Prince-Archbishop Markus Sittikus, but Lucinda didn't care about that. She was only staring in dreamy wonder at the glass pavilion which had been reconstructed because so many fans kept coming back to see it thirty years before.

Lucinda knew that their next stop was the abbey where Maria was a novice. The bus pulled in to a parking space at the bottom of a hill. The guide began her spiel. "If any of you have problems going up steep inclines I think you should wait in the hotel across the strasse or street." Several of the more elderly people went grumbling towards the hotel. Lucinda, Jason, and the others followed behind the tour guide. At the top she stopped so they could all get a good view and take pictures.

Then she started her explanation of the Abbey's history. "Nonnberg Abbey is the oldest convent in the German speaking part of Europe." Lucinda already knew that the scenes where the nuns were going to Mass and Maria came running in late was filmed there and the guide said that the Baron and Maria were married at the same Abbey in 1927 which made Lucinda gaze in awe. "Jason, just think, we are visiting a part of the true history of the Von Trapp family. It makes me tremble inside to know that I . . . I almost feel like I'm taking part in their lives."

Jason squeezed her hand as he put a finger to his lips to get her attention. The guide said, "Of course this is not where the wedding in the movie with Julie Andrews and Christopher Palmer took place. We'll see that in the town of Mondsee where we will also stop for lunch."

Back on the bus an elderly lady asked if she and her husband could trade seats with Jason and Lucinda since she had become nauseous on the previous ride. This was translated to them by the guide and Jason looked at Lucinda. She took one look at the couple and smiled as she nodded in agreement.

Jason smiled at the guide. "My wife is bad to get motion sickness herself, so she will need to sit where she can see out. Perhaps, here behind the driver?" said Jason looking at the tour guide for permission. This meant that the tour guide would have to stand."

The guide and the driver talked for a moment and nodded in agreement before the bus got underway. Jason and Lucinda took the seats vacated by the tour guide which was quite crowded since she had paraphernalia for her job on one of the two seats which left only one seat and part of the other. Still they were able to fasten their seat belts, which was a definite requirement. They hadn't gone but five miles over the crooked, winding, uphill road when Lucinda began to feel nauseous. Jason took one look at her face and unfastened his seat belt and changed to the inside seat, giving Lucinda a better view of the road ahead. It wasn't as good as the seats they had given up to the elderly couple, but by leaning out in the aisle she had a better view. They rode in this fashion into the beautiful village of St. Gilgen located in the Salzkammergut area. On the way the guide explained that the scenery shown in the first part of the movie was filmed at Lake Fuschi as they passed it.

"The Mozart family and every visitor to the area loves the scenery found here," finished the guide just as the bus pulled to a stop.

Jason and Lucinda were the first ones off the bus since Jason wanted to get her into the fresh air before she lost her breakfast. Jason looked at the guide. "We may have to have the same arrangement on the rest of the tour, if it's permissible. We don't want that old couple to be sick and they certainly will on these roads if they sit in the back. How did they make it this far without becoming ill?"

"The Frau . . . woman said that she hadn't been feeling well before she started. She thinks that once she eats lunch she will be fine," explained the guide.

Jason looked doubtful, but made no comment as they all unloaded from the bus. When he and Lucinda were walking behind the guide, however, Jason whispered, "Do you feel all right now? I know you were crowded, but it was the best I could do?"

"Yes, I'm fine as long as I can look straight ahead. It was those curves going up, down, and around that got to me. We'd better let the old couple have our seats, I think," whispered Lucinda squeezing Jason's hand and smiling at his thoughtfulness.

Jason got some really good pictures of Lucinda with scenic views as a background. One of the other tourists took their picture together with Lake Wolfgang as the backdrop. Jason could speak enough German and also using gestures and sign language to make the man understand that he would take a photo of him and his wife if he would like that. The man smiled and pulled his wife to his side, tilted his hat to a rakish angle and stood smiling. Jason took three poses which pleased the pair very much. They kept shaking hands with Jason and then Lucinda. They kept saying something, but, neither Jason or Lucinda could understand until the man leaned over and kissed his wife and held up her hand to show her wedding ring.

"Oh, you mean honeymoon," said Lucinda smiling.

"Ja, ich glaube" replied the man also smiling, although Jason and Lucinda had no idea what he meant except they both had picked up that 'Ja' meant 'yes.'

Hearing this exchange the guide came over. "He's not sure what you said, but he says he thinks so. He wanted to know if you were on your honeymoon. He says he and his wife are on their thirtieth honeymoon."

Jason laughed. "I must really look old. This is only our second honeymoon."

The guide turned to the man explaining Jason's comment. The man turned red and began talking very fast and leaning his head on his hands like a baby sleeping then shaking his head no. The guide smiled as she told Jason that the man was apologizing since he had thought he and Lucinda had just married.

"Danke, Herr . . .," Jason stopped since he did not know the man's name.

The man put out his hand. "Schmidt ich mien name." They shook hands smiling and then turned as the guide ordered them back on the bus.

CHAPTER 29

Jason and Lucinda waited until everyone else was on the bus and then they boarded and as before took their places in the tour guide's seat behind the driver. This time though, Lucinda took the aisle side of the seat and leaned as far out in the aisle as she could. "I want to make sure I don't get sick before we get there," she explained to the tour guide as the bus started.

Their last stop was to be Mondsee Cathedral and the town where they would eat lunch before their return trip. Once lunch was over they would have an hour to explore Mondsee Cathedral and the setting of the famous film wedding of Maria. Lucinda began to get nauseous before they were there. The tour guide either forgot or didn't care because she often stood in front of Lucinda. Just about the time the bus pulled to a stop Lucinda thought, *If she doesn't move she'll have to change her clothes.*

The bus stopped and Lucinda jumped to her feet. The tour guide called, "Everyone remain seated please."

This didn't deter Lucinda however, or Jason either. Holding her hand over her mouth Lucinda pushed past the guide and almost jumped from the bus. She began vomiting as she hit the ground. Jason literally picked her up by the waist and set her on a grass verge a few feet away. Then he pulled his handkerchief from his pocket and proceeded to mop her face.

When the other passengers filed off they looked their way with sympathy, but the old couple stopped. The woman patted Lucinda's arm and when Lucinda looked up she rubbed her stomach and shook her head sorrowfully. Finally the tour guide exited the bus and came to their aid with a thermos of cold water. Jason thanked her and poured some on the handkerchief and washed Lucinda's face and gave her water to rinse her mouth. Finally a very pale Lucinda walked unsteadily, holding onto Jason's arm to a bench on the sidewalk and sat down.

Jason told the guide that he was going to get a coca-cola if possible for Lucinda and entered the café behind the bench. He was in luck and soon Lucinda felt better and wanted to continue the tour.

Everyone else had already gone to lunch in Mrs. Brown's Café and Jason guided Lucinda to the same place. "Jason, I don't think I can eat, right now," said Lucinda as the odor of food wafted through the air.

"Take another drink of your coke, dear. I think you'll be all right once your stomach settles,' said Jason reassuringly. By the time they were seated and she had finished her cola she did feel better, but she was afraid to eat.

"Eggs are less likely to upset you, than anything else that I see on the menu," said Jason giving her a speculative look. "What about a couple of scrambled eggs and some saltine crackers?"

The waitress raised her eyebrows when Jason gave the order, but he pointed at Lucinda while rubbing his stomach and the waitress smiled. "Ja," she said and hurried away.

The eggs were very good and Lucinda had another coca-cola, which she sipped slowly. "I want to take this back with me. Maybe, if I sip on it as we go I won't get sick."

When Jason finished his fish and vegetables he said, "I have to order the crisp apple strudel. I was told that it is the best in the country and is so truly Austrian. I'll ask for another fork and you can take a bite also, or I will order one for you if you want it."

"No, but I'll try a bite of yours," said Lucinda since it had been proclaimed as authentically Austrian.

After lunch the tour guide told the group that they could wander around on their own or she would take them to the sites most requested in other tours. The group opted for the guided tour and followed the tour guide happily from one thing to another until they came to the Mondsee Cathedral. There they were taken through room by room and had the furniture, the paintings, and the décor explained. Once through this it was time to board the bus again.

Oh, Lord please keep me from getting sick again, Lucinda prayed silently as she walked beside Jason with her hand clasped in his. As the line halted to allow one person at a time to mount the steps Jason suddenly said, "I have it. I'll take the old gentleman to the seats in the back and you can share the seat with his wife. That way, you can both see out and neither of you will get sick."

"What if the old man doesn't want to?" asked Lucinda.

Jason called to the tour guide. "Ms. Schuler, will you ask the old gentleman to sit with me in the back and allow my wife and his wife to share the front seat?"

The tour guide looked like she'd been in the dark and someone turned on the light, as Jason spoke. "A splendid idea, Herr Doctor," she said as she turned to the old gentleman who she called Herr Hermann. She explained the request to him and he was very pleased.

So, Lucinda rode back to St. Andrew's Church in the Mirabellplatz not feeling queasy at all. Once in a while Mrs. Hermann would point to something they were passing and say, what sounded like 'ganz schon.' Lucinda thought she must mean 'pretty' or 'beautiful' so she smiled and nodded in agreement. Even though she hadn't gotten sick she was glad to once again have Jason by her side as they exited the bus.

When he took her hand she looked up at him and smiled. "I missed you."

Jason put his arm around her and they started toward their hotel. "It's only four o'clock so we'll have time for a shower and a short rest before we go back to the Stiftskeller St. Peter for our dinner. I don't want to eat before seven, do you?"

"I feel like I stink after all that vomiting I did," said Lucinda sniffing at her shirt. "I want a bath more than I do food, right now. However, I confess to feeling 'peckish' as the British say."

"I can understand that. Two scrambled eggs and six saltine crackers with all the walking we did today would make anyone feel 'peckish,'" said Jason laughing as he recalled the expression on Lucinda's face the first time she'd heard 'being hungry' called 'being peckish.'"

When they came back to the hotel after dinner that night, they both rambled around aimlessly. Suddenly Lucinda said, "Jason, let's go home."

"Go home? Why? We've only been away less than two weeks," said Jason.

"I know, but now that I've seen what I wanted to see, I'm ready to go home. Besides, I've been missing church. Two nights I've dreamed of singing in church. I feel like something is going on that we don't know about."

Jason shook his head in amazement. "You do beat all. How would us not knowing change anything? If something is wrong it will still be wrong when we go back."

"I didn't say that I felt something was wrong. I said I felt like something was going on or happening."

"Well, even if it isn't something wrong, but just something happening we still couldn't get back in time to prevent it." Jason looked at Lucinda keenly. "How, could we make any difference now?"

"I didn't say we could, but I just have a feeling that I'd like to be at home," said Lucinda.

"What about our side trips to Dresden, Kerfelden and Amsterdam? Don't you want to do that?"

"No! I just want to go home, but let's call home and if everything is all right I'll stay long enough to visit Amsterdam for a couple of days. Will that be all right?"

Jason shook his head in puzzlement. "For a woman who complained about wanting to see the world you've certainly cut it down to size." He picked up the phone and dialed Burb Harmon's number.

"Nancy, is everything all right with everyone back there?"

"No, no, Lucinda just felt like something was happening and suddenly decided she'd like to come home. We'd planned to go on to Amsterdam in Holland. Yes, it would only be a short trip from here to there. I agree. Since we are so near, I think we should too. Wait, I'll let you talk to your daughter," said Jason handed the phone to Lucinda who stood listening by his side.

"Mom, it's good to hear your voice. No, I'm not really homesick, but I've been dreaming about the church and hearing singing. I can't remember the details, but they haven't been sad dreams. I really don't know, Mom. I just felt like something was happening in connection with the church or something, Danny and Emily . . . aw, I don't know. It's probably just me, since I'm so far away from everybody and haven't gotten to attend meeting for several weekends now." Lucinda listened with a smile on her face and looked at Jason with raised eyebrows.

"All right, Mom. Since you and Dad are all right I'll call Danny and Emily and once I hear their voices I'll settle down again. I guess we'll go on to Holland for a couple of days. Why? Is something wrong with Danny or Emily? Oh! Why are they having tests in the middle of the semester? Okay then, I'll wait until we get ready to leave Europe. Bye Mom. I love you and tell Dad I love him too."

She put the phone down and turned to Jason with a puzzled frown. "Now, why are they studying for tests in the middle of the semester? Mom, sounded like she wasn't sure she knew what she was talking about, but she said that they were so busy they wouldn't be able to talk if I did call them. Doesn't that sound strange to you?"

"Lucinda, your mother wouldn't know anything about college so I can understand why she sounded uncertain. She would have told you about any happening of importance. She's probably misunderstood what Danny and Emily has told her and wanted to tell it right."

"Well, maybe you're right, but she certainly sounded unsure or something," replied Lucinda worriedly.

Jason took her by the shoulders. "Stop borrowing trouble. Wouldn't you sound uncertain about something you knew nothing about?"

Lucinda held her hands palm up in resignation and then dropped them to her side. "All right! Tomorrow we leave for Holland so let's pack."

CHAPTER 30

They went on to Amsterdam and stayed for a week. Lucinda loved the beautiful old houses nestled beside the canals, the prosperous looking farms, and especially the flower and cheese markets, but she was also glad when they were ready to leave.

As the plane lifted into the air and reached its desired altitude Jason looked down at Lucinda. "This is the first time I've seen you look glad to be in the air. You truly want to go home, don't you?"

"Jason, please don't think that I don't appreciate your wanting to show me so much of the world, but I just know something has happened at home," said Lucinda with such a solemn look that Jason squeezed her hand that he had been holding since they'd boarded the plane.

"Well, dear you are so sure about this that I, too, am beginning to wonder if something is happening, or has already happened." He unfastened his seatbelt and then leaned over and unfastened Lucinda's. "I don't think something bad is happening, however. If that is the case, it is probably just something unexpected."

Lucinda leaned her head against his shoulder. "So, you feel it, too, do you?" she asked drowsily.

Jason put his arm around her shoulders and nestled her more snuggly against him. "Well, no I didn't sense anything. I don't have the 'sight' as Sharon Mac Crumb's 'Nora Bonesteel' did, but I often think you do."

Lucinda sat up with a puzzled crease on her brow. "Why? Do you really think I may have the 'sight?'

Jason looked down into those clear blue eyes that he loved so very much. "Well, you know that often when the phone rings or the doorbell chimes you will say, "That's 'so and so,' answer it will you? Also, lots of times I start to talk to you about something and you answer me before I even get two words out."

"Do I do that?" asked Lucinda with a puzzled expression on her face which suddenly changed to amazement. "I do, don't I? Honestly, I hadn't noticed it. I know who is calling or visiting most of the time, but everybody does that, don't they?"

Jason shook his head. "No, Lucinda, everybody doesn't do that. In fact, very few people do that. The first time I really noticed it was when you told me where I'd put my pocket notebook that time I misplaced it. I knew that you hadn't seen me put it away. Do you remember that?"

Lucinda looked relieved. "I can't stand to see you so worried. That's why that happened and that didn't mean anything except my concern for you."

Jason pulled her head back down on his shoulder. "I know, dear, but that still doesn't account for your knowing I had put the notebook in my topcoat pocket. You did not see me put it there. I know that for a fact, since only Kyle Bender was with me when I put it there. It was raining when we came out of a meeting. I put the notebook in my inside topcoat pocket to keep it from getting wet and then forgot all about it."

Lucinda said drowsily. "I guess I picked up on your worry or something, but it has nothing to do with having the "sight" as you said." She closed her eyes and slept. Jason looked down at her almost childlike features and then gently kissed her forehead while thanking God silently for allowing him to finally marry her.

When they landed in Heathrow Airport in London, Lucinda had roused and walked steadily beside Jason off the plane. He walked her briskly to the bathrooms and pushed her toward the one marked women before turning to the other one. When Lucinda came out she had washed her face and felt much more alert than when she went in. She stood waiting for Jason and looking at the vast array of humanity gathered in one place. She realized that she was seeing apparel worn by people from India, Pakistan, the Congo, America, and Central America. *I wonder if they are just coming to visit England or if they are going back to their homelands?*

Lucinda stood puzzling over this until she saw Jason emerge from the men's restroom and then walked to him and grasped his hand. "How long will we be delayed here?"

"Another forty minutes. Let's go get something to drink. Do you want coffee?"

They walked over to the concession section and Lucinda looked into the glass case in front of her. "Yes, get me a cup of coffee and that oatmeal cookie, right there," she said pointing to what she thought to be the fattest one.

Jason grinned. "That's the one they use for enticement. It's probably been there a week."

Lucinda's eyes widened. "Do they do that? Get me one of the others then."

Jason laughed. "No, they don't do that. At least, I don't think they do. I'm laughing because you are so gullible. I think you believe everything I say."

Before she could answer the waitress said, "May I help you, Sir?"

Soon they were seated side by side each with a cup of coffee and two cookies. They sat munching and watching the actions of various people. "I'll bet that is a mother, daughter, and granddaughter from India, don't you?" asked Lucinda gesturing toward a family of two women and a little girl dressed in what she thought to be Indian clothing.

"Possibly, but that isn't an Indian dialect that I've heard before. They're probably from Pakistan or Afghanistan," replied Jason.

"I thought people in Afghanistan were too poor to travel except on camels."

"Some of them are very wealthy, but I didn't know that their women traveled without a male escort," said Jason looking around. They apparently didn't since a tall bearded man with a turban joined them and he seemed upset.

Their flight was called and they didn't get to find out what he was upset about, but they talked about what it could have been until they were actually on board. Jason always gave Lucinda a nerve pill before she boarded a plane and she had taken it with her coffee while they were waiting for their flight to be called.

They had been in the air for an hour and Lucinda had fallen asleep when the plane began to bob up and down. The stewardess went from seat to seat reassuring each passenger that it was due to a storm,and they must fasten their seat belts again. "This happens sometimes, but our pilot has many years of experience and everything will be all right," she said. This didn't stop frightened squeaks, prayers, and moans from many of the passengers especially as the storm worsened.

The lights came on and the captain came over the speaker. "We are passing through a turbulent electrical storm. Please remain seated and don't panic if the lights should go off. This sometimes happens, but I have been assured that we should soon be clear of the storm and everything will calm down."

Jason had fastened Lucinda's seat belt when asked to. Now he sat clasping her hand in silent prayer for their safety and also thanking God that she was asleep and didn't know what was happening. She didn't stir until the captain's voice came over the speaker again, "We are through the storm and should have a smooth flight the rest of the way."

Lucinda opened her eyes and looked up at Jason with a panic stricken expression. "What's wrong? What's the captain talking about? Why is my seat belt on? I thought you unfastened it."

Jason eased his arm around her. "He just said that the weather looked like it would be a smooth flight all the way to New York. I fastened your seat belt because we went through a storm and I feared you would wake up and get upset. Here, let me unfasten it now. The stewardess is bringing drinks around."

The rest of the flight was smooth and Jason was very thankful. He could see that Lucinda didn't quite believe that something hadn't happened while she slept. *I'll tell her about it someday, but not as long as we plan to travel*, he thought as he made room for the little tray for their drinks.

Their landing in Charlotte, North Carolina was smooth and they were soon in their car heading home. They drove almost out of the city before they pulled into a roadside diner to eat. From there Jason put in a call to Danny and Emily.

Danny answered the phone. "Where are you?" was Danny's first question when he heard Jason's voice.

"What do you mean, where are you? I thought you'd be saying how happy you were to hear from your mother," said Jason turning to Lucinda with a puzzled expression. "We are in a diner in Charlotte, North Carolina right now."

"I don't know. It depends on how tired we are. We landed about thirty minutes ago." Jason put his hand over the mouthpiece. "He wants to know if we plan to spend the night on the road or drive on home tonight. What do you want me to tell him?"

Lucinda shrugged her shoulders as she yawned sleepily. "I'll do whatever you want to do, Jason. Does it matter?"

"We're both tired, Danny so, right now I don't really know. It depends on how we feel by the time we get to Bristol or Abingdon. Is it important for you to know whether we will be home tonight or not?"

Jason looked at Lucinda and shook his head. "Well, I'm sorry, Danny, but that's the best I can do. If we stop we'll call and if we don't we'll be on home. Since you're in Morgantown I don't see that it can make a lot of difference. Why does it?"

Jason raised his eyebrows. "Oh, I see. Well, I suppose. Good-bye, Danny." Jason ended the call and turned to Lucinda. "I can't figure him out. He said he needed to know when we would get home since they had some plans."

"Some plans! What is he talking about?" asked Lucinda.

Jason pursed his lips. "I don't know. He just said he had some plans and he needed a little more time before we got home."

"See, I told you something was happening. I knew it," said Lucinda in a puzzled voice.

Their food came and Jason said, "Well, let's eat and then drive on to Bristol and get a room. I am tired and we'll both feel better with a night's sleep since we're back in the good old USA."

CHAPTER 31

They certainly got a big surprise when they pulled into their driveway the next afternoon. A huge 'Welcome Home' Banner was displayed out front but they didn't see anyone. They pulled into the garage and still didn't see anyone.

"Do you think they left a banner and went somewhere thinking they would get back before we did," asked Lucinda as she got out of the car and slammed her door. Jason was already out, but turned questioning eyes to Lucinda.

"I don't know, but I'm home and does it ever feel good. I'm still tired. What about you?"

Almost hesitantly Lucinda opened the door leading from the garage. Jason was behind her and he too stepped in expecting something. Nothing was different in the boot-room. Out of habit they both slipped off their shoes and opened the kitchen door. The kitchen was clean and empty of people also.

"Oh! Those children. Here we were wary of entering our own house and they've put out a banner and then decided to do something else," said Lucinda hurrying across the kitchen.

When she entered the hall she stopped. Her eyes had caught a glimpse of something at the edge of the living room doorway. She tilted her head back to see Jason and rolled her eyes as she nodded her head toward the living room. She grasped his hand and together they went through the living-room door.

"Welcome home!" was the loud shout heard from all corners of the room as Emily came through the door from Jason's office. She was dressed in a bridal gown and Lucinda turned to see Danny in a tuxedo coming from the entrance foyer. Elder Tommy Adair was standing in front of the bay window with the Bible open and a twinkle in his eyes. Lucinda and Jason stood spellbound as Danny and Emily walked to meet each other directly in front of Elder Adair to stop and join hands.

Lucinda looked around and saw her parents, brothers, and sisters as well as Margie and Jill, Jeff's sisters, their husbands and children. Kyle, Rita and Katie Bender were also present.

Jason, who was still holding Lucinda's hand pulled her to the side and stood waiting. They didn't speak, but the silence was pregnant with expectations.

Elder Adair cleared his throat and began with, "Dearly beloved ...." He continued on with the ceremony until he pronounced them man and wife. Lucinda and Jason still had not uttered one sound.

Burb Harmon broke the spell. "Well, pon-my-honor if they ain't lost their voices. Brother Jason ain't you got nothing to say to your new son-in-law?"

Jason stroked his chin with thumb and two forefingers and then said, "Where's the license? You can't get married without a license."

"Here's their license," said Odell. Lucinda's sister put a framed document in front of Jason and Lucinda.

They looked at it together. "Jason, look! They got married on that day I called home because I 'thought' something was happening," said Lucinda as if to say, "There. Didn't I tell you?"

Everybody started laughing, especially Burb Harmon. "Yeah and Nan almost give it away. If I hadn't pinched her she would have blurted it out."

"Well, I didn't know what kind of excuse to keep Lucinda from calling them. I didn't want to tell an outright lie," muttered Nancy Harmon.

Jason looked at Lucinda and rolled his eyes. "Since it's a done deal I guess we may as well give them our blessing and tell them the bad news."

"Bad news! What bad news?" Lucinda asked.

"I don't think they want to hear that school is out for them after this semester, but now they're on their own."

"Dad, you don't know the circumstances," begin Emily to be stopped by Danny.

"That's all right Jason. We'll finish in summer and night classes. I have a job lined up beginning in January." Danny put his arm around Emily and gave Jason a resolute stare.

"The church will help them, Jason since Danny is to be ordained," blurted Oprey and then clapped her hand over her mouth.

"Ordained!" Lucinda gasped in astonishment. "I know he has a gift, but isn't the church acting awfully fast, Dad?" Lucinda turned to her father with a troubled look.

"Pon-my-honor Oprey, I wouldn't want you to know if I was in trouble with the law."

Oprey turned red, but shot right back at her dad. “Well, the church will help him and it ort to.”

“Aunt Oprey, I don’t want help from the church. I’d refuse it if it was offered. I can work more until Emily finishes and then I can finish as well. We’ve doubled up on our classes this semester already and we’re both taking night classes,” said Danny solemnly.

Seeing that everyone was getting upset Jason interrupted. “Well, since all of you wanted to please me and Lucinda by redoing the wedding I think we should be celebrating instead of quarreling. So, where’s the champagne?”

“I’ll drink to that,” chirped Odell and giving Jason a bear hug. “How are you brother-in-law? You look like you’re worn to a frazzle.”

Jason grinned. “That’s what I get for marrying a young woman. I just can’t keep up with her.”

Lucinda hadn’t said one word. Her eyes were fastened on her tall auburn-haired son. *This child of my heart is a grown-up, married man and is to be an ordained elder in our church*,” she thought as tears crept down her face. Danny looked at Lucinda and suddenly she was in his arms and they both were shedding tears.

“Mom, be happy for me. I’ve been happy for you,” he begged as he hugged her.

“I am happy for you, Danny. This is all such a surprise . . . Well; no it isn’t. I did know something was happening, I just didn’t know what it was.”

Lucinda raised her head and saw Emily standing there in her bridal outfit and opened her arms wide and Emily stepped into her embrace. “Now, I truly have my own daughter. Thank you Emily, dear.”

Soon Jason came to join their hug- fest. “Let me in on this. I’m part of the family too. Welcome to my family Danny. I’m not nearly as rough as I sounded.”

“As long as you are good to Mom, you don’t have to be nice to me, but I hope we will like each other still. I thought I gave enough hints before you two left for Austria that this wouldn't be too much of a surprise."

"We felt it was going to happen, but we thought you would wait until you both had finished school," said Jason.

People were calling for them to come to the kitchen and Danny said, "We'll talk later, Jason. Emily and I have some ideas we'd like to run by you and Mom.

Jason clapped him on the shoulder. "Sure, Danny, because as you say, it will have to be later."

A lavish feast was laid out in the kitchen and everybody was waiting until the McCall and now the Marshall families joined them. Elder Adair said grace and people began filling their plates.

"We don't have any champagne, Brother Jason. We're Baptists you know and we only drink wine at communion," said Burb Harmon with twinkling eyes and a broad smile.

"That's right, Dad," chimed in Gordon, Lucinda brother. "We drink moonshine from a jar, don't we?"

"No, but that's what we're accused of. Course, I'll have to confess that old man Noah Stewart could make moonshine so good that it would a beat that champagne all to flinders."

This raillery went on for another two hours and then everybody decided at once to go home. Elder Adair had driven his own car with Burb and Nancy as his passengers. In all four vehicles were brought from up the street, from behind the garage, and other hiding places and were now all loaded and driven away.

The women had cleaned all the debris in the kitchen before they left which gave the McCalls and the Marshalls a period to rest and settle whatever issues were caused by the early marriage.

Danny and Jason talked while Emily and Lucinda showered and came back to the living room wearing robes. Jason patted the sofa beside him and said, "Sit here beside me, dear. I have a very level-headed son-in-law and so I've decided that we will help them until they finish school after all, if you approve of course."

Lucinda shook her head. "I thought you were kidding anyway. Besides that, Danny has enough money from the insurance on his Dad to pay for their education anyway. I thought you knew that."

Danny grinned. "Well, I am stupid. Emily, you won't have to get a job and neither will I until we graduate. I forgot about that other money. You see, Jason, Mom didn't trust me. She put the money in an education fund when Dad's insurance came through. Then when she sold the house she put that into what I thought was a trust until I was twenty-one or something."

Jason looked surprised. "What did you plan to live on, Lucinda? You gave everything to Danny."

"No, I didn't. I have my retirement from teaching and I never spend all of that each month."

"So, you planned to marry me all the time, didn't you?"

"I what? Do you mean that you think I was trying to trick you into marrying me? I'll have you know, Mr. McCall that I have never asked you to spend any money on me," said Lucinda with a mulish expression.

Jason started laughing. "You're right about that. Danny, your mother has a thing about asking me for money. I have to almost make her let me buy her things."

Danny grinned. "I hope Emily picks up that habit."

"I'll have you know that my Daddy has been paying for everything I buy, Danny Marshall. So, don't you try that with me," said Emily and then punched Danny on the arm. "You're trying to get me upset and I'm not going to let you, so stop it."

It was the next morning when Emily asked, "Dad, do you have to sell the house on Browns Creek or do you just want to rent it?"

"I don't really want to have to bother with renters. Why? Do you want it? If you do and Lucinda is all right with it you and Danny can have it as a wedding present."

Of course it was fine with Lucinda. In fact it was better than fine since that would insure that her son and his family would always be near. She jumped up and hugged Jason who pulled her into his lap where she stayed until they all had to go out on various errands

CHAPTER 32

That next year Jason and Lucinda stayed at home except for their anniversary at Martha Washington Inn, their occasional trips to Gatlinburg, or Pigeon Forge, Tennessee, or to see some national monument or battleground like Gettysburg or Valley Forge.

Jason sometimes wanted to go farther afield, but Lucinda always put him off for one reason or another. She wanted to go to meeting every weekend and then on to visit with her parents.

"Lucinda, don't you think they may get tired of seeing us so often?" Jason asked since he had never thought of visiting his parents that often.

"They don't get tired, Jason. They love it that we are visiting them so much. Older people begin to think that they aren't useful anymore when their children and friends stop visiting. Besides, I feel that I'd better go to see them while I can."

"They seem healthy. Are you worried about them?"

Lucinda sat thoughtfully staring into space. "It's just a feeling, Jason. I'm not really worried, but there's just something. Anyway, you like to hear the preaching as much as I do, don't you?"

Jason nodded with a broad smile. "Danny's preaching really gets to me. That young man is wonderfully gifted, that's for sure. However, I don't see how he keeps his grades up and still come down here every weekend. Of course I'm worried about Emily too. I think she looks really tired. Did you notice her this past weekend?"

Lucinda had noticed and she and Nancy had talked about it as they cooked dinner. "Do you reckon Emily is eatin' right, Lucy? She looks dragged out."

"They're both carrying too many classes, Mom. Emily says she will be able to do her student teaching in September and then graduate in December. That will take a lot of the stress away, if she can last that long," said Lucinda as she carried bowls from the stove to the table.

Jason and Burb held their usual heated discussions about everything under the sun. As they came to the table upon being called, Burb's usual quip was, "I'm shore glad supper's on the table. Jason had me so riled I was about to lose my religion."

"Burb Harmon, do you think you're the only one that gets riled. You won't even try to see reason," said Jason coming in behind him.

"Well, Pon-my-honor if you ain't the beatest man. Come right into a feller's house and accuse him of not being reasonable." Burb went to the sink and splashed water onto his face and hands. When he had dried his face he put his glasses back on and looked at the table. When his eyes lit on the cobbler beside his place he turned with a wide grin. "If'n you act more reasonable I might share this cobbler with you."

Jason looked at Lucinda and winked. "I guess I'll have to act reasonable, Burb since I don't want to miss out on Nancy's cobbler."

Sometimes Lucinda would look out the window and see Burb standing with his hand on Jason's shoulder while talking quietly. She'd stand looking until Nancy would come over and look as well. "They're a lot alike, Lucy. You married a good man and I've got a good man. The Good Lord has really blessed us."

Lucinda always smiled and hugged her mother. "Yes, Mom we are most richly blessed."

More and more often now Lucinda hugged her parents tighter when she left and looked back as long as she could see the house. Jason noted her actions but made no comment since he knew Lucinda felt things that most people did not.

The longer they were married the more Jason realized that Lucinda had a faith that few people had. She didn't talk about it, nor did she go about telling people she was a Christian.

He and Danny had talked about it from time to time and once Danny had said, "Mom has always been an example by her actions. She never tells people they should do this or that, and she's certainly not a 'holier than thou' person. I think people love Mom because of the way she lives her life and it makes people try to be like her. Mom doesn't try, that's just who she is. I think that is the gift the Lord has given her and I'm thankful for it. She has certainly helped me down through the years."

Jason nodded. "I know you're right. She's helped me also. She's so strong and yet so vulnerable and innocent. I want to protect her, but at the same time, it's almost like she has some kind of invisible shield that holds her up."

Danny slapped Jason on the shoulder. "I think we're all better for having her in our lives. I know I'm thankful that the Lord put you in Mom's life. She is truly happy, Jason and she loves you so much. I'd be jealous if I didn't have Emily."

In Lucinda's mind her life couldn't be better except for this something that made her want to be with her parents so often. Then one night about eight o'clock they were relaxing on the patio when the phone rang. Lucinda said, "Jason, that's your mother. You'd better get it."

Jason looked at her with startled eyes, but didn't say anything. He quickly arose and went to pick up the phone. "Hello, Mom, what's wrong?" he asked before she could say a word. Jason stood listening.

"Which hospital is he in? Is Frank with him? All right! Try to pull yourself together. We'll leave here in about an hour. We'll go to the hospital first. Yes, she will be with me. We'll see you in four or five hours, Mom."

Jason turned to Lucinda. "She thinks Dad's had a heart attack. He's in Mellon Institute. How long will it take you to pack a few things, dear?"

Lucinda was packed and ready in an hour. She hung up the phone from calling her mother just as Jason came in with his overnight bag. "Do you need to call Kyle or anyone before we leave?

Jason shook his head. "I called Emily while you were packing. They will probably beat us there."

Four hours later they met Frank walking down the corridor at Mellon Institute. Frank's eyes lit up. "My God! It's really you. How have you been, Brother?" Then they were hugging each other as Lucinda looked on. When they stepped away from each other there were tears in both their eyes.

"Frank, this is my Lucinda," said Jason pulling Lucinda to his side and Lucinda this is my baby brother, Frank McCall.

Lucinda looked up at this tall, broad-shouldered man who was smiling with delight. "She hasn't changed, Jason. She looks just like the woman you described to me and Dad over twenty years ago. Come here sister and give baby brother a big hug." Lucinda walked into his embrace as she smiled at Jason

Jason grinned and looked down at Lucinda with so much pride. "You're right. She hasn't changed, but I have."

Releasing Lucinda, Frank looked at Jason as if giving him a 'once-over.' "Well, you may have some gray in your hair, but you look happier than I've seen you look in a long, long time."

"It's been a long time since you've seen him, hasn't it?" asked Lucinda.

"I saw him last year when he came to WVU. I thought you'd come then. Why didn't you?"

"We had just gotten back from Austria and I was just too tired to make such a short trip. I tried to get Jason to make it longer and go on to see his parents, but he didn't want to."

The two men looked at each other and then Frank nodded at Jason. “Dad’s been asking about you. He’ll be glad to see you and Lucinda,” said Frank. “He’s on the third floor, room 304. Emily and her Danny are there now. My girl friend took Mom home to rest until visiting hours this evening.”

“Where are you going now? You’re coming back aren’t you?” asked Jason.

Frank assured them that he would be back in about an hour and left them waiting on the elevator. Soon they were walking down the corridor to stop at Room 304. Jason looked at Lucinda and smiled before he rapped on the door.

Danny opened the door and Lucinda got her first look at the real-life Henry McCall. *He looks just like that picture on Jason’s desk*, thought Lucinda as Jason walked with his arm around her to his father’s bedside.

Henry McCall turned a misty-eyed stare at Jason and whispered. “It’s about time, Son. Were you waiting to attend my funeral?”

Jason’s voice was husky as he grasped his father’s hand. “No, Dad and I’m so sorry I’ve stayed away these last five years. Talking on the phone just isn’t the same, is it?”

“No, Son it is definitely not the same. I’ve missed you,” Henry McCall wheezed and Emily came quickly to his side. She poured water into a glass on his bedside table and put it to his mouth. “Here, Granddad. This helped you when we came in.”

Mr. McCall took the glass from her hand and lay looking at Lucinda. Finally he took a sip of water, smiled and put out his hand. “So, this is my new daughter. I’m pleased to meet you, Lucinda.”

Lucinda put her hand in his and then impulsively leaned over and kissed his cheek. “I’m pleased to meet you too, Mr. McCall. I’m sorry that we haven’t met before now.”

"As I told you on the phone, Dad, Lucinda has encouraged me to come many times before now. She has been through so much, though, and I didn't want her hurt anymore. I should have listened to her, shouldn't I?" Jason asked solemnly.

"I think so, Son. I know your reasons, but it was something that needed doing and putting it off won't make it any easier," said Henry McCall and started to wheeze again. He drank more water and lay back with a smile. "You're here now, though. This is what I've been waiting for."

Mr. McCall still held Lucinda's hand in his and she stood patiently waiting for him to release it. His eyes twinkled merrily. "The last time I was in the hospital Jason and Frank thought I was asleep. Jason put Frank to sleep describing you, but I listened and imaged what you looked like. Jason's description was accurate and you haven't changed much."

Lucinda laughed. "I was only seventeen when Jason and I first met," she looked around at Jason and said, "Actually I was sixteen the first time I saw Jason." Her face lit up as she recalled Jason stopping to ask if she wanted a ride."

Jason put his arm around her. "She still looks sixteen, doesn't she, Dad?"

Henry McCall squeezed the hand he held. "Not far from it, Son. That's for sure and she's still in love with you, I see."

Lucinda squeezed Mr. McCall's hand and said, "Yes, I am. Jason is my knight in shining armor and has been since I first met him."

CHAPTER 33

Lucinda immediately recognized that she had a friend in Henry McCall, but she quaked inside at the idea of meeting Jason's mother. She had spoken to Elizabeth

McCall right after she and Jason married, but only briefly. On that call, Mrs. McCall had been rigidly polite and left the impression, in Lucinda's mind that she would wash out her mouth once the conversation was over.

Now, Lucinda sat thinking, *I don't know how to handle this meeting. I want Jason and his mother to be friends again, but I am so afraid and know that I certainly can't help.* Jason had been standing beside her when she was talking to his father, but had wandered over to the window and Lucinda had taken one of the chairs against the wall.

Jason came to stand in front of Lucinda. "Are you tired, dear? I can get a room and let you go rest for a while if you want to."

"I'm not tired, Jason," said Lucinda. "I . . . When is your mother coming? I'm so nervous."

Jason pulled her to her feet and turned to Mr. McCall. "Dad, I'm going to show Lucinda around the hospital. We'll be back in about ten minutes."

"Sure Son. You do that, but Lucinda, I think it will be much better than you think." Lucinda's eyes widened as she realized that Mr. McCall knew what Jason was trying to do. She smiled and walked with Jason out the door.

"Lucinda, I know you are terrified of meeting Mom, but don't be. Just be yourself. You are a very special person to me and to others that know you and God made you as he wanted you to be. I'll be by your side and Mom already knows what will happen if she is unkind to you."

Lucinda leaned onto his shoulder. "Jason, I think it would be wonderful if the relationship between you and your mother could be mended. I don't want to make it worse. I can't imagine what it would be like if Mom and I didn't get along."

Jason grimaced. "I wish it were different also, but I can't get through to Mom. Maybe I haven't tried enough." He put his arms around Lucinda since they had reached the solarium at the end of the hall. He hugged Lucinda close and said, “Okay, let’s go back with our minds made up that we will meet her halfway.”

Lucinda slipped her arms around his waist and looked up with a tender smile. “I’ll go more than halfway if it will make you happy. Jason, I love you so very much and I want you to know that I’ll do anything I can to make your life better.”

Jason hugged her more closely and kissed her tenderly. “I know, dear. God has blessed us with that kind of love for each other, but I don’t intend to let anyone bruise or wound you.”

Hand in hand they walked back to the room. The door opened as they reached it and Frank stepped out. “I wondered where you had escaped to.” He looked at Jason and rolled his eyes in question. “Are you ready to get this over with? I think Dad is as uneasy and you both are.”

Lucinda didn’t know what she expected, but the attractive and youthful.looking woman who turned from the bedside to greet them stood waiting with a smile on her face. Jason, with his arm around Lucinda walked forward. “Hello, Mom. You look great!”

Elizabeth McCall clamped her lips together and swallowed while still trying to keep the smile on her face. “Hello, Jason and . . . Lucinda. It is so good to see you both,” she said and stepped toward them at the same time that Jason stepped toward her. They both opened their arms and Lucinda found herself caught in the circle of two pairs of arms.

Jason stepped back first, but he had a smile on his face. “Lucinda, meet my mother, Elizabeth Wentworth McCall. Mom this is my darling wife, Lucinda Harmon McCall.”

Lucinda smiled and put out her hand. “It’s nice to finally meet you, Mrs. McCall.”

Elizabeth McCall kept the smile on her face, but some strong emotion flitted across her face, which gave Lucinda cause to wonder. *Does she still hate me so much that it is hard to speak to me?* Lucinda thought, still retaining her smile

Finally, Mrs. McCall said, "I too, am glad to finally meet you. I've been away from my son, long enough."

Jason spoke up. "Lucinda has encouraged me to visit from before we married Mom. So, don't get the idea that she is in any way to blame for the distance that has been between us."

Lucinda touched Jason's arm. "That doesn't matter, dear. What does matter is that now can be a new beginning. Mothers and sons need to visit and have a part in the lives of each other."

Mrs. McCall turned a gimlet gaze at Lucinda. "I believe you mean that."

Lucinda gave her a sober look. "I do mean it, Mrs. McCall. I think you and Jason should erase the past and start out on a new footing. I promise I will not stand in the way."

Before Mrs. McCall could say anything, Jason interrupted. "I'd like that, Mom, but only if Lucinda is a part of it. Lucinda has my heart and is a part of who I am. Without her I'm just a shell."

"No," started Mrs. McCall to be interrupted by Jason.

"Yes, Mom. Those are my terms and I hope you can accept them."

"Jason, let me finish, please. You were always so head-strong. I accept your terms, but I do need to get the past off my mind, but not right now."

Jason looked down at Lucinda and asked. "Is that all right with you, dear?"

Lucinda grasped his hand and smiled. "I think this is wonderful and I'm agreeable to whatever it takes to have you and your mother to be friends again."

Jason turned to look steadily at his mother for a few moments. "I guess we'll take this as a first step, Mom."

"Yes, Jason. This is a first step," said Mrs. McCall also looking at Jason with a smile. She then turned back into the room and Jason looked down at Lucinda, raised his eyebrows and crimped his lips together as if in question.

Lucinda put her arm around him and smiled as she nodded her head as if saying, "It's a start." Jason hugged her and together they followed his mother on into the room to stand in front of Henry McCall.

Mr. McCall's pale face seemed to glow. He winked at Lucinda and nodded. Lucinda winked back and grinned widely, but sobered as she looked at Mrs. McCall whose brow was creased.

"Well, Dad, now you have to hurry and get back on your feet. We all need to go out and celebrate," said Frank from his position at the foot of the bed.

"I'll try, but let's not go to a disco just yet," wheezed Mr. McCall.

Jason was quick to react to the wheeze. "I think we should all leave and let Dad rest for a while. Mom, are you staying with him?"

"I stay most of the day, but I go home at night and Frank has been coming in then. I know you told Frank you would stay at night, but tonight I'd like for you to come home with me. We need to talk."

"Lucinda and I have a suite of rooms at the Holiday Inn, but we can come for a hour or so to talk, can't we dear?" asked Jason looking down at Lucinda.

"That's fine with me, Jason or if your mother would rather just talk to you I could stay in the rooms until you get back," replied Lucinda.

At first Mrs. McCall's eyes lit up and then she shook her head. "No, I think the both of you need to hear what I have to say."

Jason nodded as he took Lucinda's hand. "We're going to our rooms first. It's six o'clock now. Would seven-thirty be all right to come by?"

Mrs. McCall nodded and walked to the door with them, but turned back into the room after smiling at Jason. "I'll see you at seven-thirty then."

Later, Lucinda realized that their visit with Mrs. McCall and all that she had told them had only sealed her assurance of the dislike Mrs. McCall held for her. She listened calmly and smiled as Mrs. McCall laid the blame for her devious activities at Janet's door. When some of the things Mrs. McCall said couldn't have happened as she said they had, Lucinda thought, *Poor Janet is no longer here to defend herself.* Lucinda continued listening as she said that Janet had come over and gone through the mail each morning, and was amazed. *Who would come to somebody else's house and go through their mail?* "No, that just could not be true" mumbled Lucinda quietly when she had escaped to the bathroom.

Right at first, Jason had only asked questions after stating that he would not allow Lucinda to be hurt. "Mom, you felt Lucinda was beneath you or not in your class of people. If you still feel that way, I think we are wasting our time. Lucinda is one of the finest, most honorable, and loving women that can be found in this world and nobody is superior to her."

Mrs. McCall had paled and swallowed, but straightened her shoulders and tilted her head toward Lucinda in some sort of acknowledgement. "I'm sure you are right, Jason. I think I was so enchanted by the idea of Janet for a daughter-in-law that it colored my thinking. You'll have to admit that Janet had royal lineage, had gone to the right schools, gotten the right education, and really fit into our kind of people, though."

Jason jumped to his feet. "There's that snobbish mind-set that you've always had which has caused all this and it hasn't changed, has it?"

Mrs. McCall arose also and put out her hand. "Wait, Jason, you didn't let me finish. I was only pointing out the ease in having Janet for a daughter-in-law. I didn't know that she was or would be . . . devious when it came to you."

When Jason still stood Mrs. McCall sighed. "Please, Jason. You need to hear me out, if not for my sake, then for Henry's sake. This reconciliation is all he has talked about since he's been in the hospital."

Jason looked at Lucinda. She smiled and nodded. He sat down once more and waited, but this time holding Lucinda's hand.

Mrs. McCall, finally wound down and stopped. "Well, there it is. I know I shouldn't have been so taken-in by Janet. I have no excuse for that. I never visit the Washburns' and they have nothing to do with us, so that is another legacy left by Janet. Olivia and I were once the best of friends."

Those last few words brought a break in Mrs. McCall's voice and Lucinda felt sorry for her. Jason looked at her with compassion also. "I'm sorry about that, Mom. You should just call Olivia and try to bridge that gap."

"I should? I didn't cause the rift. Olivia Washburn has never invited me and she never includes me in anything she's doing. I'll not lower myself to go begging."

Jason shrugged his shoulders. "That's your call, of course. As for all this you have told us, we only have your word, but we'll accept it and put it behind us. Is that what you want, Mom?"

Mrs. McCall gulped and tried to retain control. In doing so she almost became a statue. Finally, she gasped. "Yes, Jason. I want my family together."

Lucinda and Jason stayed for another half-hour and then went back to their hotel. Jason drove in silence and Lucinda felt he needed the time to digest all that had been said and therefore kept quiet also.

CHAPTER 34

Back in the room Jason was first to break the silence. "She didn't tell the truth. Olivia Washburn, is a snob also, but at least she is truthful. Right after Janet's funeral she and I had a long talk. She admitted knowing part of the scheme Mom and Janet had cooked up, but she made excuses for Janet."

Lucinda put her arms around Jason. "Any mother would do that Jason. She just didn't want you to think it was all her daughter's fault."

Jason hugged Lucinda. "Right now, I can hardly be civil to Mom. She may have told herself that it was all Janet's fault so long that she now believes it. I thought that since she seemed so glad to see me it would be different, but as the scripture asks, 'can a leopard change its spots?' I should have realized that Mom could never see herself as she really is and she still can't."

Lucinda tugged Jason to the sofa and cuddled close to him. "Jason, your Mom is who she is, but she is still your mother and she does love you. You may not believe it, but her delight in seeing and hugging you was sincere. Beg the Lord to just let you accept her as she is and try to build some kind of relationship with her. Think back about the good times and cling to those. You don't want to go back to that bitterness you had before we married."

Jason tilted Lucinda's chin and looked deeply into her eyes. "You really want that don't you? We both know that she acted as if you weren't really there, but you still make excuses for her."

"Jason, I kept thinking of how awful it would be if Danny had been estranged from me for four or five years. That would destroy me."

Jason hugged Lucinda closely. "Okay. I'll try to put this all behind us, but you have to know that Mom and I can never have the kind of relationship that you and Danny have."

"No, I don't suppose so, but at least she'll get to see you several times each year, won't she?" asked Lucinda.

"She won't see me without seeing you as well, but if she ever tries to hurt your feelings or does one of her famous put-downs that will end it all."

Lucinda shook her head sadly. “Please, Jason. I’m not that important and my skin isn’t so thin that I can’t take a snub now and then.”

Jason put both hands on Lucinda’s shoulders and shook her tenderly. “Lucinda, you are the most important thing in my life and nobody is ever going to hurt you again if I can help it.”

“Okay, but don’t allow bitterness to take over again. That kind of feelings will destroy you.”

Jason released her and started taking off his coat. “I’ll give her the terms tomorrow and if she agrees we’ll visit about twice a year, unless there is illness that brings us here. I think Dad is on the mend, but he is nearing eighty.”

Walking toward the bedroom, Lucinda turned and smiled. “I fell in love with your Dad, Jason.”

Jason followed her. “By the way his face lit up I’d say the feeling was mutual.”

The next few days proved that to be true, but it also proved that Elizabeth McCall was never going to truly accept that Jason had married a woman so far beneath him. She was always very careful to be polite to Lucinda and when necessary included her in the talk or activities. This caused Jason to be more attentive to Lucinda. *They’re making me feel like a rag doll that is being shoved away on one side and clinched tightly on the other side*, thought Lucinda.

By the time Mr. McCall was released from the hospital Lucinda was more than happy to start home. They left, promising to return again in a few months since Jason was to speak at the graduation commencement at West Virginia University Medical School.

Lucinda didn’t get to attend that engagement with Jason, however. Burb Harmon had been feeling unwell from early spring and just before Jason was to leave he became ill. Lucinda stayed to drive Nancy and Burb to and from the doctor’s office. Therefore Jason wasn’t with her when Burb was diagnosed with stomach cancer.

Lucinda hadn't wanted Dr. Hatfield at the Yukon Clinic to tell her Dad what he suspected, but since Burb had said he wanted to know the truth, he was told. "I want this verified Burb. I'm setting you up for X-rays at Bluefield Community Hospital, just to make sure," stated the doctor.

Lucinda looked at Nancy who had grasped her arm tightly. She whispered, "Are you all right, Mom?"

Nancy nodded but still clung to her arm. Burb had turned paler than he already was, but pushed his chin up, swallowed and said, "I suspected something like this Doc. I've lost a sight of weight this summer. Course, I accused Nan of not feeding me," he said trying to lighten the dismay they all felt.

Lucinda wanted to gather her father in her arms and wipe away the horror she saw reflected in his eyes. "Dad, they may be able to operate and give you treatments. Medical treatments have improved so much. Let's not give up hope yet."

"That's right, Burb. The Good Lord knows how to take care of you. He always has," Nancy said in a firm voice.

Burb nodded his head. "If He's got anything else for me to do here, He'll work it out and if He's through with me this will be His way of taking me home."

"He ain't through with you yet and the church needs you, so that's what we're goin' to remember," said Nancy putting her hand on his shoulder and giving him a steady look.

Burb looked at her for a moment. "Aye, it'll be all right, whichever way it is. The Lord knows best."

During this exchange with her Dad and Mom, Lucinda kept fighting the tears that fought to be released. The doctor had gone to another room to make his call to the hospital. He now came back. "Burb, I have you set to see a gastroenterologist at Bluefield Community Hospital for next Thursday. His name is David Glasco. I know him. He's a good man and very thorough" He handed Burb a card with address and phone number as well as some forms that needed to be presented at the hospital.

They left the doctor's office in a very somber mood. Lucinda wondered if she would be able to hold up or even drive home. *Now, pull yourself together Lucinda, you have to be strong for them,* she scolded herself silently.

The next months were the worst times Lucinda had spent since Jeff had died. Looking back she felt that she couldn't have made it without Jason's support and her faith in God. Burb had been diagnosed with inoperable stomach cancer and only lived three months from the date he'd been informed he had cancer.

Nancy Harmon was a strong woman, but even she was too old and now not able to continue to live on the farm. Jason and Gordon sold the farm and bought Nancy a trailer. When she revisited that painful time, Lucinda thought Nancy Harmon had grieved herself to death since she died in her sleep six months later.

Both Danny and Emily had finished with college and had jobs with the Wyoming County School System. Danny was working at the Wyoming County Vocational/Technical Center and Emily was teaching at Riverview Elementary.

Jason had given the house on Browns Creek to Danny and Emily, but Henry Burbrage, their first child, was born in the big upstairs bedroom in Lucinda and Jason's house on Indian Ridge.

Lucinda and Jason had bought into a gated apartment complex in Pittsburgh after Henry underwent more heart surgery. The care of Henry was mostly left to Frank and Jason, but Henry wanted Lucinda to visit every day. Frank's wife, Audrey was a teacher and could only help on the weekends.

All these family trials curtailed the travels originally planned by Jason and Lucinda. They still had been able to stay at least one night at the Martha Washington Inn in Abingdon on their anniversaries, but often wondered how soon they'd have to forego that pleasure.

Two years later Henry died and Elizabeth McCall suddenly developed Dementia. She gradually became worse and eventually had to be put into a nursing facility where she died a year later.

During all this time, Jason and Lucinda lived haphazardly in first one state and then the other. After Elizabeth McCall's death they lived most of the next year in the house on Indian Ridge. They were babysitters for young Burb and now little John William.

"I don't know how Emily knew what personalities these boys would have, but she certainly named them correctly," said Jason laughing heartily.

"Why? What have they done now?" asked Lucinda coming onto the back patio where Jason had been watching them.

Jason's grey head lifted as he smiled at Lucinda. "Watch Burb and you'll see what I'm talking about."

Lucinda watched in amazement as Burb walked on his sturdy legs to the playpen where little John had pulled himself to standing position and was holding onto the spokes. Burb had an ice cream cone and offered it to John. When John reached to get it he lost his balance and fell. This caused Burb to laugh merrily. As soon as John pulled himself to his feet again Burb went through the process again. This time, however, he was so caught up in his merriment that he slapped his legs which caused the loss of the ice cream for both of them. Burb's look of amazement was so comical that Lucinda laughed aloud.

"He acts like Dad, doesn't he? Who taught him to slap his legs when he laughed?" asked Lucinda.

Jason laughed and pulled her down into a seat beside him in the swing. "I don't think anyone taught him. I think he's a reincarnation of Burb Harmon. He even looks like him."

Lucinda sat looking at the boys closely. "They will probably change, but right now Burb does look like Dad and I think John looks like Mr. McCall."

"He does and he's a peace maker also. That's just like Dad. He always kept the peace at our house," said Jason reflectively.

Lucinda rolled her eyes. "Little John is too little to keep anything. I don't see how you came up with that?"

"If they are in a space close to each other and Burb gets upset just watch how John tries to make him feel better. Dad was always like that and so is Frank."

"You must have been the trouble-maker in the family," teased Lucinda.

"No, But I'm surprised I didn't kill some of them with my medical cures." Jason laughed merrily. "I'm surprised that Frank grew up at all. I used him as my guinea pig."

CHAPTER 35

Thus Lucinda and Jason's travels were curtailed for almost five years. This seemed to give them a longing to travel again and one day Jason came in from his daily trip to town with some travel brochures.

"Lucinda, I'd like to take you to Korea and show you where I worked when I was in the army. Look at this! We could go there and on to Tokyo in Japan at a very reasonable price."

Lucinda had been noticing that Jason seemed aimless and bored or something in the past six months. *Our age difference bothers him and it shouldn't,* she thought and this is one more bit of evidence. "I'll start packing. When do you want to go?" She looked at him with an impish grin.

"I'm serious. Japan and Korea would be beautiful in the spring. We could leave about the middle of April and stay until the first of June. That way we won't miss any of the communion services or association meetings at church."

Lucinda left the iron standing on its end and went to sit at the table beside of Jason. The brochure was well-done and the places displayed looked beautiful. Lucinda had also been in the doldrums when she allowed herself to think about her parents and knew she needed something to perk herself up. She grasped Jason's hand.

"Get the travel plans arranged and let's go. As far as I know Emily isn't pregnant again and Rita and Kyle will help out with the boys if they're needed. We're free, so let's just go."

Jason hugged her close. "That's what I love about you. If you see that I'm feeling down you'd jump off a cliff to get me out of the mopes. I would like to go, but only if you really want to."

"I want to! I want to! Go on get on the phone and start getting our tickets," said Lucinda jumping up and pulling Jason to his feet.

In the next few years they lived away from home so much that Jason and Lucinda made another life-changing decision. After several complaints from Emily about the numerous repairs that had to be done to the Browns Creek house Jason said, "Lucinda, is there any need for Danny and Emily to continue living on Browns Creek when our house is empty three/fourths of each year. They are now repairing their house and seeing to the upkeep of our house."

Lucinda look startled. "Are you suggesting we give up our Indian Ridge home to them? I don't want to do that. I love having my home in McDowell County."

"We could still have a home. We'd just extend or build onto the garage and have our own apartment when we want it," said Jason hopefully. "We don't have the time or the inclination, or at least I don't, to keep up the place even when we are there."

Lucinda remembered last summer when Jason seemed so tired before he finished all the mowing, weed-eating, edging and trimming that needed to be done on the lawn alone. She looked at Jason and smiled. "Let me think about it. You throw these ideas at me, right out of the blue, and I can't decide that fast."

They were planning a trip to Venice, Rome, and Paris for the following spring and Lucinda knew that would leave Danny and Emily to spend lots of time on the Indian Ridge place anyway. The next morning Lucinda had made her decision. "Okay Jason. When are we going to talk this over with Danny and Emily?"

"Let's have them out to supper one evening this week. The boys want me to take them to the pond to fish anyway," said Jason with a fond smile.

So, Indian Ridge became the permanent home of Jason and Lucinda as well as their beloved children and grandchildren. Jason and Danny drew up the apartment plans with Lucinda and Emily arguing for this point and that point. "We'll just get everything ready and the builder can start on our wing while Lucinda and I are on our trip to Europe next spring," said Jason with a big smile.

"Why didn't you just say, 'Danny, you can live in the house, but in exchange you have to get an apartment built for us?'" asked Danny with raised eyebrows, as if he knew Jason had planned it this way.

Jason smiled. "Well, don't you think you're getting a good deal? You'll be getting the money from the sale of the Browns Creek house and only have to oversee the work out here?"

Danny backed away with his hands in the air. "I'm not complaining! I love the idea, but I also know that you want to be away when the work is being done. Really though, Jason, are you and Mom sure this is what you want or is it because Emily fusses about the Browns Creek house needing so much repair?"

Jason looked out the window for a moment. "I guess a little of both. Lucinda and I travel so much and we also stay in our place in Pittsburgh several times each year as well. Besides that, we both also like the idea of the children growing up out here. When we're home we can see them and spend time with them, but send them to your side of the house when we are tired."

Danny grinned and put out his hand. "Let's shake on that Jason. I like knowing that I'll be close should either of you become ill and we also like to have someone to be with the boys if I'm called away to a funeral or an Association."

Emily walked into the room. "We'll also be able to sleep at night and not worry about the roof leaking. If we stay in Browns Creek we'll definitely have to replace the roof." She looked at Danny and continued, "We will also not have an excuse to not take a vacation, will we, Danny Marshall?"

Lucinda came through the door with a little boy tugging each hand. They had been transplanting some bulbs in the back of the house. She released the little hands and dusted her hands together. "Ah Ha! That puts the lid on that and it's about time. Danny's like his grandfather, Burb , who thought taking a vacation was getting the corn hoed for the last time each summer."

Danny looked at his mother with widened eyes. "He did, didn't he, Mom? I remember Aunt Odell saying that is why she got married in April. She said she didn't want to wait until the last corn hoeing and Papaw always cleared his new ground in February. He planted the first time in early May and from then on until the last of August Aunt Odell said she was out in the corn field."

The four of them sat around reminiscing until it grew dark and their nightly serenade of the whip-por-will was heard in the woods in back of the house. "Emily, hear that! That's our sign," said Danny jumping to his feet.

Emily laughed. "Oh yes. When the whip-por-will calls . . . I've forgotten how it goes, but it's something about my blue heaven."

"It's dark outside, Mommy. You can't see whether heaven is blue or not," chirped Burb sleepily and then grinned. "Pon-my-honor it is."

Lucinda swooped down and gathered him into her arms. "Give me a hug, Little Burb before you go to sleep and go home without hugging me." Lucinda received a hug and a kiss for her trouble and turned to place him in Jason's lap.

After all the good-byes were said and the car pulled out of the drive, Jason patted the sofa beside him. "Come here woman. I've shared you with everybody else all day. Now it is my turn."

Lucinda ran to sit beside Jason with arms flung wide. "Okay, you poor neglected man! I'll have to tell those bothersome children they'll just have to stay at home." She laughed and then leaned up to kiss Jason's cheek.

Jason wrapped his arms around her and let out a contented sigh. "You've made my life so complete, Lucinda. The Lord has certainly blessed me with the perfect wife."

Lucinda grinned. "Well, you don't seem to feel that way when you have to knock me out on our plane flights and then almost drag me from the airports."

Jason gave a quirky grin. "Probably I should have said, 'Perfect most of the time' shouldn't I?"

Lucinda put her arm around Jason's middle and snuggled close. "Remember when I used to go to sleep like this while we were watching movies?"

Jason laughed. "I don't think you ever stayed awake all the way through Gone with the Wind, did you?"

Lucinda straightened up. "No, I never did. Let's watch it on our next trip. I think I can fly without being knocked out now."

Jason looked doubtful, but said, "We can try, but don't blame me if you vomit on somebody."

Lucinda shivered in revulsion. "That's what makes me afraid to try. I'd hate to have someone do that to me and I certainly don't want to do that to someone else."

They sat quietly reminiscing until Lucinda said, "Do you want some chocolate before we go to bed?"

"No, not unless you want to watch The Dollmaker with me. You said you wanted to watch it again and I picked it up at the library today."

Lucinda shook her head. "No, it's too sad. I don't like to watch something like that before I go to sleep. I like to go to sleep with happy thoughts."

Jason rose to his feet pulling Lucinda up also. He looked down at her with a lecherous leer. "Well, let's go make some happy thoughts and we'll both sleep like babies."

Lucinda tilted her head to one side and looked up at him with raised eyebrows. "Sounds like a winner to me."

"I think I'd better make the most of what I have considering my age and discrepancy." Jason said as he walked over to make sure the front door was locked.

When he turned back Lucinda stood with her hands on her hips. "Jason, please stop harping on your age. There's not one bit of difference in you since our first stay at Martha Washington Inn. In fact I . . . well, I think you are a better . . . ah, lover now." Lucinda still turned red when speaking of intimacy.

Jason put his arms around her. "Well, I should hope so. I was scared to death."

"After you'd been married twenty years, you couldn't have been scared," said Lucinda doubtfully.

"But, my dear, if you recall I had to take you to a counselor before I could get you to marry me. I certainly didn't want to give the wrong impression on our honeymoon," said Jason as they walked in the bedroom and closed the door.

CHAPTER 36

Looking back, as she sat on the back deck of their house on Indian Ridge, Lucinda often thought that their trip that year was so very special. Now it seemed more special than any of the many trips they had made to spots all over the planet. *I guess it is because it was the last trip we made together*, she thought and then chuckled as she shivered from the cool air on the deck. On their trip to

Alaska, Jason asked if she wanted to take a day trip farther north. But, Lucinda refused to go to the Arctic or to Antarctica.

"I've seen every part of the globe that I want to see, Jason," had been her response while they were in Alaska. "Ice, snow, and bitter cold are not my idea of a pleasant trip."

Lucinda brought out her memories as she grew older. In doing this she was sometimes transported back and could almost feel Jason's presence. Most of her memories were such joy and comfort to her, but not the one she held so very dear, even though it was the most painful. They had just returned from a trip to Korea when Jason awoke one morning, turned over and as usual hugged her close to him. They went to sleep after a last hug at night and awoke to that same greeting each morning. Lucinda lay luxuriating in the love and wonderful life she had until Jason groaned. She laughed. "That's the first time you've groaned when you hugged me."

When there was no reply she pulled out of his arms to look at him. He was smiling that beautiful contented smile that she had grown accustomed to over their fifty year marriage. Lucinda leaned over and kissed his lips and when there was no response she became alarmed.

"Jason, Jason," she whispered and then shook him. This caused him to roll over on his back, but still there was no reaction. Lucinda scrambled to her knees and literally jerked his head up from the pillow to have it fall back as she propelled herself out of the bed. She was screaming inside her head, but no sound came out. She grabbed the bedside phone and dialed 911.

"Please send help. My husband . . . something is wrong. He won't wake up. Please," she was now really screaming and crying.

"Ma'am, are you alone? Please try to be calm and give me your address," instructed the voice on the other end.

Lucinda couldn't answer. She sat down on the bed beside Jason and fell over on his chest, softly crying and mumbling his name. Mary Tibbits, the housekeeper and close friend, had heard the screams and cautiously opened the door. Seeing Lucinda sprawled across the sleeping body of her husband crying piteously, she hurried to her side. Before she could touch Lucinda she saw the phone dangling from the nightstand. She picked it up.

"Hello is someone there?" she asked.

"Yes. This is emergency services. Someone just called that her husband would not wake up."

"Oh my! Yes, I'm Mary Tibbets, the housekeeper, and Mrs. McCall is lying across her husband and he isn't moving." On request, Mary gave the address and said she would have the door open. Hanging up the phone she turned to Lucinda.

"Mrs. McCall let me help you into the living room. The medics are on their way," she said as she pulled at Lucinda but could not budge her.

Mary went to the other side of the bed so she could see Lucinda's face when she bent down. Lucinda was no longer crying, nor had she fainted. She was staring fixedly at something and not seeing anything. Mary thought she was in a coma or dead, but still she grasped her arms and shook her. "Mrs. McCall, you have to get control of yourself. Your husband will need you."

Lucinda blinked and looked at Mary. "No, he doesn't need me now. He's gone . . . farther along."

"No, no, we don't know he's dead. He may have had a stroke. Come on, get up please. I don't know all the particulars to tell the paramedics when they arrive," pleaded Mary as she straightened to help Lucinda to her feet.

Lucinda reluctantly struggled and finally was on her feet, but grasped Jason's hand just as the door bell rang and then the emergency team came through the living room with a stretcher.

They soon determined that Jason had died, but didn't say that since they recognized the state Lucinda was in. "We'll take him to the nearest hospital. They'll know what to do."

Lucinda turned to Mary and calmly said, "Will you please call Burb? He'll want to go to the hospital." She turned to the medics. "Take him to the Mellon Institute. They know him there."

Burb called his father and mother, Danny and Emily Marshall, and his dad said, "Let her stay close to all his things. She's tough. Just let her handle it in her own way. You are driving her down, aren't you? That's good. Is there anything you want me to do before you get here?"

" No, I don't think so, but what about Mom? She loved Gampa so very much. I worry that she'll break down."

"Now listen Burb, your mother is tough like your gramma. She'll grieve and I'll be with her, but she'll pick up the pieces and go right on. As for Mom, don't grieve too much. Those two had fifty years of wedded bliss and your grandfather was ninety-three years old. People can't live forever and he died easy. When I talked to Mom she said he had a smile on his face."

"He still does Dad. It looks as if he is asleep and having a pleasant dream," said Burb in a voice full of wonder. "I worry about Gramma though even if she is tough. She seems to be so calm. Of course she wasn't the day he died. When the doctor at the hospital said Grampa had died they had to sedate her to get her to calm down. Now, though she is calmly silent. But if I try to get her to come to my house she gets upset. She wants to be where he was or at least around some of his things."

"Let her do that, Burb. She'll want to bring everything related to him down here, so you may as well bring your SUV." Danny could almost visualize his mother standing still yet making sure she got her way. He smiled as he turned to tell Emily what Burb had said.

Emily sagely nodded her head. "I knew she would be all right. She is one tough little woman. I didn't think she was when I first met her, but after she married Dad I got to know the real Lucinda. I guess she was even when your dad was alive, but she had so much to deal with, didn't she?" Emily looked up from her seat on the sofa and caught such a look of remorse or anger on her husband's face.

"Danny why are you looking sad, angry, or something?" she asked.

Danny's face changed as if a shield had been erected. "I guess I am Emily, I mean I think I'm sad, angry, and so sorry. I loved Jason. He was so good to my mother."

Emily pressed her lips together, swallowed, and blinked her eyes. "She was good to him too, Danny. Their love story is better than any movie, but it will never be told. Lucinda would never write it, but she could if she wanted to."

Seeing Emily's struggle to remain calm, Danny put his arms around her and smiled. "She's like you. She could, couldn't she? Mom is so talented. Jason always tried to get her to write, but she said she didn't have time. I think she feared it would take some time away from Jason."

Danny kissed the top of Emily's head and snuggled her more closely to him. "I think our love is the kind theirs was, don't you Emily?"

"Of course you big galoot. How could it be anything else? I chased you until I caught you and like Papaw Burb, always said, 'I hogtied you to me'." Emily laughed as tears sneaked slowly down her cheeks and she gave Danny a tight squeeze.

Pulling herself out of Danny's arms Emily straightened her shoulders and with a soft sigh said, "Well, I guess we'd better start making the arrangements on this end."

"Do you suppose we should call Brother Robert Mullins or Sister Sis Short? Somebody needs to go up and check on Mt. Zion church? It may need to be cleaned and we need to see if anything else is planned for the building for the next week. Can you think of anything else?" asked Danny walking back and forth through the living room.

Emily stood thinking intently. "The crypt will have to be opened but I think Fanning Funeral Home will take care of that. As to preachers Dad respected Elder Tommy Adair more than any elder he knew, but he loved your gift in doctrine when you are blessed and he also liked Preacher Whitten Sparks, but I think we'd better get approval from Mama Lucinda before we make that call, don't you?"

At Danny's nod she continued. "I can't think of anything else, Danny, but I'll have to let the sisters in the church know so food will be prepared."

"Emily, you're taking this really well. I know you loved your dad and I worried about you when Burb first called. You must have had a visit from the Lord," said Danny.

Emily nodded and raised her face to Danny's. "He sent me a dream Danny. Last night I dreamed that Dad was walking along a beautiful path beside a wide river. He was smiling but looking across the river at Mama Lucinda who was on the other side. I was pretty far back behind her and Dad yelled, 'Emily take good care of my darling Lucinda, for me' and I yelled back that I would. He waved and went on out of sight." Danny gathered her in his arms and for the first time since they had heard the news Emily leant into his shoulder and cried.

Danny stood holding her and rubbing her back and occasionally kissing her cheek. Finally she raised her head. "How do you always know just what I need? I just needed you to hold me and that's what you did."

"Didn't you know that you married a mind reader?"

Emily smiled and pushed herself out of his arms. "Well, I can't expect the church sisters to prepare all the food. I'd better get my apron on. Burb will be expecting my Italian Crème Cake to be waiting for him."

For the next few days Danny and Emily were busy preparing rooms for the people coming down from Pittsburgh, making calls to the local newspapers, after Lucinda approved of the arrangements, ordering flowers, and cooking dishes that could be frozen until needed.

Even though Danny and Emily had first moved into Jason's old house on Browns Creek road when they graduated, the Indian Ridge house had always felt like their home. They had first resisted the offer from Jason and Lucinda to move into their house, but relented when they realized that their parents really wanted them to live on Indian Ridge. They had moved in promising to build an attached apartment for Jason and Lucinda to use when they were in West Virginia. The apartment was built but Jason and Lucinda hadn't spent much time in it since part of the year they traveled and they also stayed in Pittsburgh several months at a time. Now, Jason was dead and the children didn't know what Lucinda would want to do.

To Danny and Emily the Indian Ridge house was home. Their children Henry Burbrage, called Burb, John William, called John, and Nancy Elizabeth or Beth had all been brought up here and the three of them had each been born in the first room at the head of the stairs.

Welch was the best place for them to live since Emily had gotten a teaching position at Welch Elementary and Danny had become Principal of the Wyoming County Vocational School. This proved to be a very good arrangement when Danny was called to the ministry. His weekends were always free so that he could attend services in churches not only in his association but in the other two associations as well. Now he was the Moderator of the Elkhorn Association and called upon from many fronts.

Welch was still home to them even though the town itself was no longer the bustling coal town that it once was. Kyle and Rita Bender's house was still next door to the house Emily was brought up in. But, Jason had sold his house and Rita Bender had passed away. Katie Bender, Kyle's daughter really took care of her father. She was home almost every weekend and often visited Emily and Danny, bringing Kyle with her.

While all the funeral arrangements were being made in Pittsburgh Danny and Emily's door bell pealed constantly as well as the telephone. Neighbors dropped by with condolences and offers of help.

"Danny, it really touches me that so many people remember Dad with so much respect and fondness," said Emily as she closed the door and walked back into the living room after seeing her last caller out. "That was an old lady that came to tell me how Dad had treated her all one winter when she lived at Bartley and hadn't charged any fees."

"That Mr. Duncan that came by earlier today, told me how Jason had saved his eyesight. He said that some other doctor had told him that nothing could be done, but Jason sent him to the Mellon Institute. From what he said, Jason must have paid for it all since he never received a bill," said Danny.

Emily looked at Danny with tears in her eyes. "Dad never told me or Mom about any of that. We knew he was liked and respected, but we didn't know it was because of things like that."

CHAPTER 37

Meanwhile, Burb was taking care of all the arrangements for his grandfather's movement from Pittsburgh to McDowell County, but it hadn't been easy. Mary Tibbets, the housekeeper, had called him before she called the Rescue Squad, but they had arrived first. He found his grandmother, Lucinda McCall sitting in a chair by the bed dressed only in her dressing gown. She was also holding Jason's hand, even though Burb knew that Jason was dead.

Burb swallowed the tears which threatened to break through. The two people who had meant so very much and been such an important part of his life would now be parted. *God please help her*, his mind kept repeating.

"Gramma you don't need to go to the hospital. I'll go there and see about everything," said Burb.

Lucinda looked up at him from a dry-eyed, but extremely pale face. "You can follow me, but I'm going to the hospital. I'll ride in the ambulance with him."

"Gamma you can't. I mean there isn't room. The EMT's will be working with him and they have all kinds of equipment which takes up space. If you want to follow him, I'll drive you, but honestly I think it would be best if you remained here," said Burb in an almost pleading voice.

Lucinda didn't speak for a moment. "I'll go with him and be with him every minute. He wants me with him." The ambulance men were now ready to lift Jason onto the gurney, but Lucinda didn't move or release Jason's hand.

"Here, dear let me help you up. You need to move so we can lift him onto the stretcher," said the young EMT as he started to take Lucinda's hand away.

Lucinda, with a surprising grip for someone her age, refused to let go. "I want to go with him to the hospital."

"Someone can take you dear, but right now we need you to move so we can take him to the hospital," said the EMT looking at Burb beseechingly.

With gentle urging from Burb, Lucinda finally rose from her chair, placed Jason's hand on his chest, and walked out of the room holding Burb's arm.

Mary Tibbits took Lucinda's arm and urged her into the bathroom to dress in street clothes. "You and Burb will probably beat the ambulance there anyway," said Mary when Lucinda tried to rush her dressing.

Burb dreaded what would occur when Jason was pronounced dead, and with good reason. At the doctor's words Lucinda looked startled. "No, he isn't dead. We always go everywhere together. He won't die until I do." Then she started a keening wail that seemed to penetrate the entire hospital and the doctor had to sedate her.

Burb took her home expecting the same outburst when she again awoke, but surprisingly Lucinda nodded as Burb told her Jason was gone as he sat by her on the bed. "He's gone on before me, but a little farther along I'll join him," she said and turned back to Burb. "Where is Jason's body now?"

"The funeral director is preparing him for the trip to West Virginia, Gramma."

The next two days were a flurry of activity for Burb and Mary. Finally Burb with Lucinda sitting beside him in his SUV pulled in behind the ambulance bearing Jason's body and began the long trip to McDowell County.

They stopped for lunch in Beckley and then drove on into Welch. There Jason's body was taken to Fanning Funeral Home at Coney Island. Bob Fanning, the manager met them at the door, clasped Lucinda's hands and then helped her into his office. Lucinda and Jason were friends of all the Fanning family and now Bob was very solicitous of Lucinda's grief. Still holding her hand he led her forward. "Take this chair, Lucinda and we'll discuss the arrangements. Danny and Emily have already completed everything per your instructions, but if there's something you've thought of on the way down we'll take care of it."

Burb, who was seated beside Lucinda looked at Bob, raised his eyebrows and shook his head as if amazed. "She told them every detail, I think. Can you think of anything else, Gramma?"

"I want to go in by myself when you have him ready and then I don't want to look at him anymore, here. I'll see him again a little farther on though."

Lucinda looked at Bob and Burb with a smile. "Isn't it wonderful to know that we are only parted briefly, although to me it will seem a long, long time. It isn't though. Jason hugged and kissed me before he went to sleep and did the same when he first woke up and then he went to sleep again. He was smiling. Did you know that?" she asked looking at Bob.

"He still is, Lucinda. I'll take you to see him after a little while and we'll both see his smile," said Bob patting Lucinda's hand which he still held.

They sat discussing the trip down and how long they had been on the road. "You must be really tired Lucinda. Why don't you go out to Danny's and rest for a few hours. You can come back later tonight or in the morning and we'll go see him," said Bob.

Since it was already seven o'clock Lucinda agreed and Burb walked with her out to the SUV. Soon they were pulling into Danny and Emily's driveway. "I love this place, don't you?" asked Lucinda.

The outside lights were on and the Tudor house blended perfectly into the small hill into which it nestled. "Yes. I do love it Gramma. Mom said the azaleas were in bloom, but they won't show up tonight," replied Burb as he opened his door and went to help his grandmother out.

Soon Lucinda was folded in Danny's arms. She laid her head on his chest and cried. "I always believed we would go together. That's why I didn't mind the many plane trips, and ocean voyages we took. I knew that should something happen we would be together."

Emily came and put her arms around the both of them. "Mama Lucinda you were together when he died. Just think of the wonderful memory he left you . . . a hug, a kiss, and a smile."

Lucinda backed out of Danny's arms and looked at Emily with a smile. "You're right. He did. Thank you dear for reminding me. Jason died with his arms around me."

"Okay, now that I've given you something to think about you'll need to have something to eat. Your soul isn't the only thing that needs nourishment, you know," cautioned Emily smiling and taking Lucinda by the arm. "Your dinner is in the oven and still good. I just checked it."

"Practical little Emily. You married a treasure Danny," said Lucinda as she walked with her arm around Emily's waist.

Danny had gone to the other side of the table in the kitchen nook. "I decided early on that I only wanted special women in my life, so I have you, Emily, and Beth."

Lucinda took the chair pulled out by Emily and sat down. "You didn't have a choice, except for Emily and I'm not so sure you even had a choice there."

Danny laughed. "I know, I know. The Lord sent me a helpmeet and Emily was it." He looked up at Emily who was placing plates of food on the table. Emily smiled at the love she saw in his eyes.

"Dad was lucky that such a wise choice was made for him. I don't think the Lord has a helpmeet in store for me," said Burb with a laugh.

"I don't think you've been looking, Burb," said Emily smiling at her tall handsome son.

They settled down to eat while Danny and Emily went over all the things that Lucinda had told them to do. "We did everything you said, Mom and a few things you didn't say. The neighbors and friends from all over McDowell County have sent cards, food, donations to St. Jude's in Dad's honor and many have said they would attend the funeral," said Danny.

"You did schedule a wake service here in Welch and also in Iaeger didn't you?" asked Lucinda.

"Yes, it will be three until five here in Welch and six until nine that night in Iaeger," said Emily. "Also, since it is warm weather, the sisters of the church have planned a reception at the church after the funeral. Dad helped so many people all over the county that they are expecting a large crowd."

"Grampa would like that, wouldn't he, Gramma?" asked Burb smiling as he visualized Jason's grin.

Lucinda smiled as well. "Yes, he would. Jason loved people . . . not just the church people. He loved everybody, but he could be mean when he thought someone was unjust."

"Didn't he hit a man in Venice for kicking a dog?" asked Danny.

"He knocked that man flat on his rear and I took my umbrella to him. He had that poor dog tied and was dragging him along. The dog was trying to get away and then the man kicked him. I guess we acted impulsively, but I'm glad we did. We had to spend that afternoon in the police station or whatever they call the police over there," said Lucinda and began laughing. "When that man fell Jason untied that poor dog and then dusted his hands off as if that settled it. Of course it didn't since that man was on his feet ready to pounce on Jason. That's when I hit him with my umbrella."

"I'm surprised that you two didn't land in jail in one of those exotic places you were always visiting," said Emily laughing with everyone else.

"Do you know how many countries you visited, Gramma?" asked Burb.

"I'd have to write them down and count them, but I have pictures from every place we visited. Our life was like a vacation even when we were at home. We went for walks, we swam, we went skiing, sledding, treasure hunting, picnicking, dancing, and most of all we attended church. If we weren't here to attend a church of our own faith we went to some small church in every little town or village we found ourselves in all over Europe and Asia. We toured the cathedrals and thought they were beautiful, but when Sunday came we always found some small church. We didn't believe like they did, but we always met some really nice people." Lucinda had slow tears running down her face and Emily jumped to her feet.

"Come on Mama Lucinda, you need to be in bed. This has been a really long day."

Using the table napkin Lucinda wiped her face and rose from her chair. "I am tired, but I'll need to shower before I can rest."

Soon Emily had Lucinda in a pretty room on the first floor. It wasn't the room that Lucinda and Jason had always used when they visited until the apartment was built, but Emily feared it would make Lucinda sad to use that room. Also that room had been upstairs and Lucinda looked too weary to climb the stairs right now.

Emily turned the shower on and unpacked Lucinda's suitcase. "Here's a nightgown. Is this all right?" she asked holding up a soft silky blue nightgown.

"No dear, I just want to fold that one and put it in my memory drawer. I was wearing it the last time Jason hugged me," said Lucinda and started crying.

Emily gathered her into her arms and held her until she stopped sobbing. "I know it is hard, Mama Lucinda, but just think of all the people that will lose loved ones and not have such pleasant memories."

Lucinda straightened up and looked at Emily. "You're right. You know my Grandpa always told me, 'You have to stand whatever comes along, but you have a choice in how you stand it.' That's so very true and his words have really helped both me and Jason down through the years."

Emily chose another nightgown and Lucinda was soon bathed and clothed. "Do you want a glass of warm milk or anything else before you go to bed?"

"No, Emily I'm fine. Maybe, I'll go to sleep and dream about Jason. I hope I can," said Lucinda as she climbed into the bed.

CHAPTER 38

Lucinda seemed fine the next morning and after talking to Burb and Emily, Danny decided they would take Lucinda to Fanning Funeral Home to have her last look at Jason.

"I really dread this, but it has to be done. I want you two with me. You know how I am about Mom," said Danny and Emily came and put her arms around him.

"Don't worry dear, Burb and I will be right with you and Mama Lucinda," said Emily hugging him close. Soon Lucinda came into the room from her bedroom. She was pale, but very composed and as usual dressed elegantly. Lucinda was never flashy, but she had good dress sense and wore her clothes well.

"You look sharp Gramma," said Burb eyeing her appreciatively. "If I ever find a woman that can look like Gramma no matter what, I'll snatch her as fast as I can."

"If you haven't seen one by now, Burb you may as well stop looking," said Lucinda as she walked over to Danny and laid her head against his chest. She looked up at him. "Let's go, Danny. I guess you have me to look after again."

Danny's arms went tenderly around his mother. "I've never complained, but really it was always you looking after me. So, now you'll have more time to look after me." Danny kissed her forehead. "I love you, Mom."

"I know, Danny. I know, but you have your precious Emily. In fact we both have her, don't we?" Lucinda asked and reached out her arm to draw Emily into her embrace.

"We both love you, Mama Lucinda even if Danny does act like he has the monopoly on love," said Emily hugging Lucinda and looking up at Danny with a smile.

"Okay, folks let's stop all this blubbering and get out to the car if you want me to drive you," said Burb as if they were hindering him from something he was anxious to do.

Soon they were pulling into the parking lot of Fanning Funeral Home at Coney Island. Danny and Emily walked on each side of Lucinda as they made their way inside and Burb followed. Bob Fanning came through the hall before they could get to his office.

"Prompt, as always aren't you, Lucinda? This woman has never been late in her life if she had an appointment. I've served on committees and boards with her and not once was she ever late," said Bob with a smile.

Lucinda pursed her lips and looked up at Danny. "I know that you, Emily, and Burb want to go with me, but I can go alone. In fact I want to be alone with Jason for a few minutes after you children have seen him."

"Mom, I'd rather stay with you. I won't speak or anything," said Danny anxiously.

"No, Danny. I need to spend a few minutes alone with Jason. I'll be all right."

Danny looked forlorn and Burb tapped him on the shoulder and raised his eyebrows and nodded his head. "All right, Mom, but we'll be right outside the door," said Danny quietly and nodded at Bob to lead the way.

They followed Bob through a wide door and on into a vestibule and then back into the morgue proper. "We have this room much cooler than the other rooms, but that is necessary," he said as he walked over to a silvery gray casket on a bier and lifted the lid.

Lucinda swallowed and walked slowly with her children around her to stand by the casket and look down on the face of her beloved Jason. Tears sprang to her eyes and she reached out a trembling hand and laid it on his chest. She looked up at Danny. "I didn't think this would be so hard. I thought we'd go together. I always told him that, but he'd always say I shouldn't expect that."

Lucinda passed her hand down over his chest and straightened his tie. "Coming back on the plane on that last trip, I said, 'Jason, I often wish we'd go down in a plane, but then it would mean these other people would too.'"

Lucinda gripped Danny's hand. "Jason always tried to console me. He'd say, "Lucinda, my love, I'll just be stepping out of TIME . . . like stepping through a door and there will be no time. The next thing I'll know I'll be holding you in my arms again. It'll be just a little farther along."

Lucinda then leaned over and kissed his cold brow and mumbled, "Oh Jason, I so wish I could have gone with you." Lucinda raised her head and said, "If you children want to spend some time alone I'll step out and then come back in."

"No, Gramma we will wait for you outside," said Burb and hesitantly they and Bob Fanning stepped outside the door.

Coming back on the plane Jason had taken a little crystal image of two hands clasped together from his pocket and said, "I bought this for you in Paris. It reminded me of our life together. We've been clasped together for life. Lucinda we've been two people, but we've really been one. You've always tried to bring out the best in me and I've tried to do the same for you. You've been my cheering section, my help mate, my sweetheart, my wife. You've made my life complete and completely happy. I thank you my dear and I want you to keep this as long as we live." He placed it in her hand and closed her fist over it and right there on the plane he kissed her lips tenderly. Now, Lucinda took the little image from her purse and slipped it beneath his hands clasped over his chest. She patted his hands tenderly. "Goodbye for now, my own darling. I'll see you a little farther along," she whispered through her tears and turned resolutely and walked from the room.

Her children were just outside the door and seemed relieved when she opened the door and walked through. They could see that she had been crying, but she seemed calm. Danny took her arm and thanking the now elderly Bob Fanning they made their way back to the car.

Danny, Emily, and Burb talked about it later, but as far as they knew Lucinda did not shed a tear that afternoon at the wake service, nor that night at Iaeger when they had several elders to preach, but she went nowhere near the casket.

They had been late getting away from the funeral home in Welch since Jason had so many friends and the same held true in Iaeger. Lucinda greeted each person with a smile and personal comment of thanks, but by the time they were ready to leave Iaeger she had trouble walking without help. Burb backed the car as near the door as possible and soon Lucinda sank into the seat with a long sigh.

"I hope this weather holds for tomorrow, don't you Dad," said Burb as they drove along Route 52 toward Welch.

"According to Sam Sidote at WELC it isn't supposed to rain for several days," said Danny tiredly.

When they arose the next day the sun was shining brightly and a soft breeze ruffled the leaves of the lilac bush near Danny's back patio. Lucinda walked out on the patio as soon as she awoke and stood looking up into the hills. "Lord, thank you for taking Jason in such a gentle manner. He is still smiling. I don't think I could have borne it if he had suffered from a lingering illness. I didn't realize it at first, but again you've blessed me and I do thank you," she said solemnly. She turned as the door opened and Danny stepped onto the deck.

"Good Morning, Mom. Did you sleep any at all?"

Lucinda turned with a smile. "Yes, I did Danny. I slept really well, but I didn't dream about Jason. That's all right though for this morning our good Lord has given me a thankful heart. My darling didn't have to lay and suffer from a debilitating disease and I'm so thankful."

Danny puts his arms around her. "Mom, God knows the needs of his children and he is always there for us. Sometimes, we think we need something, but the Lord knows what is really good for us." They stood together a few more minutes and then Danny said, "Come on inside. I smell coffee and that means Emily has breakfast ready."

The funeral was to be at one o'clock and since it was a long drive to Iaeger and then up Garland Mountain they hurried to finish breakfast and get dressed. They were interrupted in this by the arrival of their daughter, Beth and their son, John. Emily ran to the door as they pulled up.

"I was getting worried. What held you up?" asked Emily as she hugged them close. Beth was crying. "Mom, how is Gramma?"

"Try not to cry, dear. Your Gramma is great. She, like me, was beginning to wonder if you two had wrecked or something."

Beth wiped her eyes and pointed at John. "Blame big brother here. He had to make sure that Valerie had everything just so before he would leave. He acts like she doesn't have enough sense to come in out of the rain."

John looked suspiciously like he had been crying, but said, "Well, she's not been having an easy time with her pregnancy and I didn't want to leave her. She . . .."

He was interrupted by Emily's shriek. "Valerie's pregnant? Oh John, how wonderful. Why didn't you tell us?"

Lucinda and Danny came through the door before he could answer. "What's all the commotion?" asked Danny bracing himself as Beth hurtled into his arms.

"Daddy, Daddy, your baby girl is home," she said laughing through her tears. Danny hugged her close with tears in his own eyes.

"You are my baby girl, sweet Beth and I love you dearly."

"He's not the only one that loves you. Come give your Gramma a big hug. I haven't seen you since last Christmas," said Lucinda standing with her arms flung wide.

Beth moved out of her father's arms and walked into Lucinda's. "Gramma, I'm so sorry. I loved Grampa so very much," she mumbled brokenly.

Lucinda patted her back soothingly. "He knew, little Beth. He loved you too. In fact, I have a little gift he and I bought for you in Paris. It's at the apartment, though. I didn't think I would be coming down until August."

Lucinda crimped her lips together and loosened her hold on Beth. She looked at John with a smile. "So, you are going to be a papa. That's wonderful, but I'm sorry that Valerie was unable to come down."

John encircled his grandmother in his arms. "She wanted to come, Gramma, but the doctor advised against it. I left her crying, but her mother is with her."

"Well, we're glad you made it. We wanted all the family to be together and we all are except for Valerie. We don't have much time, though. Do you and Beth want anything to eat?" asked Emily.

John said they had stopped in Beckley. "We're ready to move out unless I have to drive. I'm worn out."

"We're going in my SUV. There's room for seven and there's only six of us so that means that I have to drive," said Burb chuckling since he knew that John always complained about his driving on curvy roads.

Soon the SUV was loaded and on its way down Route 52 toward Iaeger with Burb driving and Danny beside him. Emily and Lucinda were in the next seats which left John and Beth in the main back. They hadn't gotten far down the road when John became sick and had to trade places with his dad. Normally Burb would have driven on for a few miles just to pester John, but today he refrained.

The funeral was conducted by Elders Whitten Sparks and Tommy Adair. Elder Timothy Davis read the obituary. Both the elders were well blessed in messages about the special sacrifice Jesus had made for his people. Lucinda, who had been so calm now had tears running down her cheeks while on her face was a beautiful expression of such joy and peace that many people gazed at her in amazement. Her expression stayed the same as Elder Sparks continued.

"In first Corinthian in the fifteenth verse it is recorded 'For as in Adam all die, even so in Christ shall all be made alive.' Then on down it says, 'And so it is written, the first man Adam was made a living soul, the last Adam was made a quickening spirit.' So brethren we are quickened in the spirit here, but when this mortal has put on immortality then death is swallowed up in victory through the blood of Jesus Christ."

Danny who was seated beside Lucinda put his arm around her and she looked up into his face. "I'm so thankful that Jason and I were both blessed in his spirit from time to time. Jesus blessed us with such a wonderful life together, but more than that he left us the promise of meeting again."

Soon the last song was sung and people walked past the casket for a final viewing. When the usher came to Lucinda she rose to her feet and walked out without looking at Jason again. The lid was closed and soon the funeral procession wound its way up Route 52 to Garland and then turned left up Garland Mountain. The passengers in Burb's vehicle made the entire trip in silence only broken occasionally by Beth's muffled sobs.

Once on the mountain they were ushered to the seat before the mausoleum which was standing opened. Elder Timothy Davis gave the last prayer for the family and then Jason's body was lowered into the vault and the heavy marble slab was replaced on the top. Lucinda was helped to her feet by Burb since Danny was occupied with Emily who had been suddenly overcome with grief.

Lucinda stood by the mausoleum and then taking out her handkerchief she wiped the top where some particles of earth had gathered in the moving. Then she walked out of the cemetery with her head held high to hide the awful ache in her heart.

Lucinda Marie Harmon Marshall McCall left the top of Crane Ridge in such an empty state of mind. Nothing seemed to matter. "How, am I going to make it? Jason made my life complete. Everything we did, he made it special in some way. Together we celebrated life," thought Lucinda as she rode down the mountain.

She was seated between Danny and Emily and when Danny looked down at his mother he saw that she was so grief-stricken that she hardly knew what was happening. Over her head he looked imploringly at Emily.

Emily raised her eyebrows in understanding, but shook her head indicating that she was at a loss as to how to help. Finally Danny said, "Mom, are you comfortable?"

Lucinda didn't answer and Danny repeated, "Mom." Lucinda looked up and smiled.

"What? Did you say something, Danny?"

"I asked if you were comfortable," said Danny snuggling her a little closer to him.

Lucinda sighed. "I'm as comfortable as I can be now. Don't get upset if I'm a little quiet for a few days. This is going to take some adjustment. I hope I'll be strong enough to cope."

"Mama Lucinda, you're not the only woman who has lost a husband and you are strong. Also, you know where to turn when it becomes more than you can bear." Emily had spoken before Danny could come up with something to console her.

Lucinda turned from Danny and looked at Emily. "I know other women have lost their husbands and I know I'm not special. I also know that I can turn to the Lord, but sometimes Emily we come to a place where we become numb and we have to give our grief some space to ease."

Emily gasped. "I'm sorry, Mama Lucinda. You're right and we, your children should respect you in that. Is that what you just told me?"

Lucinda smiled tiredly. "Yes, Emily it is. I'll need some time and some space. Nobody can walk this path for me. Jason isn't here to help me. I'm just saying that it isn't going to be easy."

Burb spoke up from the front seat. "You're right Gramma. You take your time and your space, but know that all of us are here and we want you to call on us when you're ready. When you're ready I want you to tell me the story of your life with Grampa. Will you do that?"

Lucinda's eyes lit up briefly. "Yes, Burb. Give me some time and I think I'd like to do that, but let's not talk about it now."

John spoke up from his seat beside of Burb. "Yeah, let's talk about how to get off these crooked roads as fast as we can. I always got car-sick when I was growing up in these mountains and I guess I never outgrew it."

The rest of the trip back to Welch was made in relative silence. However, a few comments about the litter along the highway as well as the condition of the highway itself were passed between Danny and Burb.

CHAPTER 39

Back at Danny's house food, prepared by the neighbors, was waiting. "I know this sounds like I'm an uncaring brute, but I have to have something to eat. I have an ulcer and an empty stomach gives me a fit," said John as soon as he returned from washing his hands.

Lucinda crimped her lips together and then spoke up. "We may as well start now in living the way we'll have to from here on. I think we should all try to eat."

Danny smiled. "You heard the voice of authority, so let's eat."

"We certainly can't let all this good food go to waste, can we?" asked Beth.

Emily put her arm around Beth. "More than that, we don't want to offend our good neighbors who were thoughtful enough to bring it."

Soon everyone was gathered around the table with plates of food before them. "I thought Preacher Sparks was blessed, didn't you Mom?" asked Danny.

"Yes, he was. I hope he's still around when my time comes. I'd like him to conduct my funeral. In fact, I'd like all three of the preachers to be in my funeral. Make my funeral as near like Jason's as you can," said Lucinda.

"I hope the road up the Garland side of that mountain is at least graded before I have to travel over it again," said John and then rose from the table. "I'm going to call Valerie and then take a nap, unless you have something you want me to do, Dad." He looked at Danny.

"Go ahead and take a nap. I'll let you mow the lawn when you wake up," said Danny with a chuckle.

Nobody ate very much, but each member of the family left the table feeling that he or she had taken the first step. They followed Lucinda into the living room and took seats near her. When the silence became troublesome Emily said, "Danny called a contractor to come out and do the alterations to the apartment that you and Dad wanted done before you came down this summer, but it isn't finished yet, Mama Lucinda."

"When did the contractor start?" asked Lucinda sharply.

"About three weeks ago," said Danny. "Jason wanted it fixed just like you'd been talking about and I was glad he did. We wanted it to be exactly what both of you agreed on. Emily and I were hoping that you would spend more time down here as you got older."

Lucinda didn't say anything for a few minutes. "I think Jason would have been pleased. We both love you and Emily and you're both good to us, but neither of us liked staying in someone else's house. Do you remember what a row we had when I wanted us to live with Dad and Mom when we first married?" Lucinda laughed. "You would have thought I had asked him to go to prison."

Danny laughed. "Jason was smart enough to know that he and Papaw Harmon wouldn't hit it off. They would have been yelling and arguing every minute even though they grew to like and respect each other, I think."

"They did. Jason could never get Dad to agree that unions were good when the miners needed help so badly, though. When Dad got something in his head a team of mules couldn't pull it out. Jason said he was stubborn, but Jason was stubborn too," said Lucinda smiling softly.

"What about you, Mom? You will move into the apartment when the contractor finishes won't you? You'd be down here where you know lots of people and could see your brothers and sisters often . . . Well, not Aunt Odell, but the others," said Danny hopefully.

Lucinda rose from her chair and walked over to the mantle. A picture of the entire family circled around her and Jason rested in the center of the mantle. A silver candlestick stood on each side of the picture and Emily had arranged ivy as foliage all along the mantle. "This is a beautiful display, Emily. I don't think I've seen this picture before. In fact I don't remember sitting for it."

"You didn't. Beth used the computer and took pictures we'd taken at different times and put them together. Don't you remember that picture of you and Dad?"

Lucinda walked closer and stood looking. "Why that's the picture we had made in Rome, Italy. This man with a camera had been watching us as we sat by a fountain and finally came over and asked if he could take our picture. We agreed, but Jason told him we wanted a copy."

When he took the picture and went away, I laughed. "Tourists stick out a mile, I guess. That's the last you'll see of your money or your picture."

"You want to bet?" Jason asked. "I told him we were on our honeymoon and I wanted that picture as a memory."

"Jason, why did you tell such a lie? Surely, he could look at us and tell we were too old to be honeymooners."

"No. That's what he thought and I just let him believe it. Besides, I feel like we're on our honeymoon," Jason said and kissed me. Lucinda smiled. "My Jason was the most romantic man. He made me feel so loved." She stopped, swallowed and then turned abruptly and left the room.

Danny started to go after her, but Emily caught his arm. "Don't Danny. You're going to have to let her be alone. I know you love her, but you can't take Dad's place.

Danny dropped his head, but turned back. "You're right, but I hate to see her suffer so much."

"Danny, sometimes I think your childhood with your father left a flawed personality trait in you, especially when it comes to your mother," said Emily softly as she rubbed his arm.

"You mean, because I feel so protective of Mom? That's not a personality flaw, or at least I don't think it is. You didn't have to lay awake every night hearing your mother's sobs and knowing that you couldn't go to her."

"Dad was Grandpa Marshall sexually abusive to Gramma?" asked Burb angrily.

"I don't know. When I'd ask her why she was crying, she would say she had a bad dream." Danny sat staring straight ahead. "One morning though I got up and she was lying on the sofa and I could tell she had been crying. Her face was all red and swollen. At that moment I wished I was grown. I wanted to kill my father."

Emily snuggled close to his side. "Well, you didn't inherit any of his traits and for that we can all be thankful. If you had I would have already killed you," she said grimly.

"Gosh! Let's change the subject. This is too morbid," said Beth who had been listening raptly.

"It sure is. Let's think about Gramma and Grampa's life together. Now, that is something to write about. I've already started writing their story," said Burb thrusting out his chest.

"You have! Where did you start? I think you should start when they first met," said Beth.

"I did, but there are wide gaps in that part. Gramma has to fill in all that for me. Right now I'm working on how they met again at the river when Dad, Mom, and Grampa were baptized.

They heard a loud thump and all turned startled eyes toward the doorway and then made a dash to the hallway thinking that Lucinda had fallen down the stairs. Nothing was there and Danny took the stairs two at a time to the landing. There he found the pot of flowers that had stood on a table by the window had blown over and fallen to the floor. They all breathed a sigh of relief and after cleaning up the mess Danny walked softly back down the stairs.

"Gramma must be out like a light since that noise didn't wake her," said Beth.

Danny looked at Emily. "Should I go check on her? That was a loud noise."

"No, Danny. Stop thinking the worst. Mama Lucinda was absolutely worn out and also she had a fan on in her room. If she had heard it she would have been out of her room before we got halfway up the stairs."

CHAPTER 40

The next morning found John and Beth ready to pull out for their trip back to West Virginia University. John lived and worked in Morgantown and Beth attended school there at the university.

Emily followed them to the door. "I wish you could stay longer, John, and I so hate for Beth to leave."

"I'll be back for the Thanksgiving holidays and you'll be heartedly sick of me before I leave," teased Beth as she gave her mother one last hug and turned to her father as he stepped out onto the porch.

"Is Gramma asleep? She looks so lost. It breaks my heart, Dad. Will she be all right?" asked Beth with a worried look.

Danny put his arms around his daughter. "Don't worry, little Beth. Your Gramma may be little, but she has more faith than most people. She'll be lonely and she'll grieve, but she'll also get up every morning and keep on going."

John yelled from the driveway. "Get a move on Beth. We have a long drive ahead of us."

Beth hurried to the car but put her head out the window and looked back until they went out of sight down Browns Creek road.

Danny and Emily went back into the house arm in arm to find Lucinda coming out of her bedroom. “You know, it is better, I think, to say good-bye quick like Jason did. The more one lingers the harder it makes it.”

“What do you mean, Mom?” asked Danny taking a seat in a chair across from the sofa where Lucinda had taken a seat.

Lucinda sat looking at Danny before she spoke. “Well, remember how it was with your grandfather Marshall. He was sick for so long and we thought he was at death’s door six or seven times before he actually died. We felt so sorry because your Aunt Margie and Aunt Jill were torn up for days after each episode. It was almost like he died that many times. I hope I’ll be like Jason who went to sleep and never woke again. That way of going doesn’t cause so much grief.”

Emily spoke up. “That was a terrible time for Aunt Margie and Aunt Jill, but Grandmother Marshall didn’t grieve because she didn’t know any of us by that time.”

Lucinda sat in pensive silence as did the others until Burb said, “I’m glad Grampa went just the way he did aren’t you, Gramma?”

“Yes, Burb, I am. Watching Beth’s lingering departure made me think about Jason. He awoke and gave me my morning hug and that was his final good-bye. It was a shock and I wasn’t prepared, but we never are. Thank God I didn’t have to see him lay and suffer, and that’s a great blessing.”

Danny looked at Emily with a silent appeal to change the subject. “I think we’d better decide what we need to do today? I know we have to do the thank-you cards and you and Danny will have to go to the bank, I guess. You could wait a few days if you’d rather,” said Emily looking at Lucinda.

“No, we’ll get everything done today and tomorrow. Burb and I need to head back to Pittsburgh.”

"Why? Burb has two more weeks of vacation. Why can't you both stay here until he has to go back?" asked Danny almost pleading.

Lucinda leaned over and clasped his hands. "Danny, I need to go back to Pittsburgh. I know that Pittsburgh isn't home to me. It wasn't home to me and Jason, either. We traveled so much that the apartment was mostly a stopping off place, but for a time I need to stay there. I don't know how I'll feel six months from now, but right now I need to be there."

Danny sat holding his mother's hands and longed to keep her with him, but knew he couldn't. Neither could he bear this burden of grief that she was now carrying, even though it broke his heart to think he could not help her.

Lucinda saw the love and sadness in his eyes and shook her head. "Danny, Danny, I know you love me, and I know you want to shelter and care for me, but you can't do this for me. There are some things that can't be explained in words. They are the things the heart feels; pain and joy, both unspeakable, and it's a great blessing if one can experience them both."

Danny sat with tears in his eyes. "I know you've experienced the pain. I know all about that. I hope you've experienced the joy. I know you have in the spirit, but I think you mean in just living the life we're given, don't you?"

Lucinda smiled. "Oh yes, Danny. My Jason gave me so many unspeakable joys. He gave me a new meaning to life that I could have never even imagined had he not been in it. He gave me fifty years of unstinting love and never once held back on something that he thought would bring me joy." Lucinda swallow as tears crowded her throat and then abruptly got up.

Danny jumped to his feet. "I'm sorry, Mom. I didn't mean to get you upset. I'll not try to keep you down here, but promise me that after a time you will consider coming back here to live."

Lucinda had walked over to the picture window and stood looking out onto the street. “I’ll think about it, but not now. One can’t go back, though, Danny and nothing stays the same. All things either, grow and change or they stand still, and either get in a rut, or they die. Of course there are some people who seem satisfied to just exist, but that isn’t living and I don’t want that. So, I’ve already asked you children to give me some space and now I’m repeating that request.”

Danny grinned. “Okay, Mom. I get the point, which is ‘shut up, Danny and mind your own business.’ That’s what you mean, isn’t it?”

Lucinda turned back into the room and smiled. “Yes, it is. I’ll be fine, and it isn’t like I’ll be all alone. I have Mary there with me and Burb can be there in ten minutes.”

“Not, in evening traffic, Gramma,” said Burb laughing and looking so much like his Grandpa Burb Harmon that Lucinda blinked her eyes in wonder.

“You’re right about that. I don’t know where all those people come from, pon-my-honor I don’t,” said Lucinda making them all laugh at her imitation of Grandpa Burb.

Before lunch Danny and Lucinda went to McDowell County National Bank and got a cashier’s check for Fanning’s Funeral Home. While there, they also opened a safety deposit box that Jason had set up when they first married. Lucinda had the key, but had never opened it since she depended on Jason to take care of all the business. Giving everything a quick glance Danny suddenly stopped.

“Mom, do you know how many CD’s Jason had purchased?”

“No, Danny, I don’t. I know he made lots of investments and we both drew so much retirement income besides our Social Security, but I never bothered with asking him anything about it.”

Danny shook his head. “I don’t know the amounts, but I counted ten while just scanning through these papers.”

"I guess we'd better talk to that lawyer, Wade Watson, isn't it? You know the one Jason hired or used while we lived down here. I'm sure that's who Jason said it was that he went to see every time we came down. Just before we went on that last trip I recall Jason calling him one evening. They talked for hours, it seemed," said Lucinda reflectively.

Danny called Wade Watson's office and was told he could see them the next morning at ten o'clock. "That means we'll have to make a trip to Bluefield, doesn't it. Burb and I can go in his vehicle and you and Emily can come in yours and once our business is done, we can go out for lunch together. That way, Burb and I can get an earlier start back to Pittsburgh," said Lucinda organizing everything to her satisfaction.

Danny didn't like her leaving so quickly, but refrained from saying anything. By the look on her face Danny knew that she had already decided and would not change her mind.

When they were back at the house Burb and Emily were updated as to Lucinda's plans. Burb grinned. "You don't let the grass grow under your feet, do you Gramma? It's fine with me. In fact, I totally agree, since we are going anyway, and that will get us into Pittsburgh around dinner time. I want to try out that new restaurant on Shady Avenue. It's called Garconniere's Bistro and I'm told that the food is out of this world."

Lucinda smiled. "I guess that means you want to eat alone, since garconniere refers to bachelor quarters doesn't it?"

Emily started laughing. "Where did you learn French, Mama Lucinda?"

Lucinda grinned happily. "I knew a few words that Jason taught me, but when he realized that I had a desire to know and speak a foreign language he insisted that we take a course in French in one of our longer stays in Pittsburgh."

Danny, Emily, and Burb shook their heads in amazement. "How many more things are you going to surprise us with about you and Grampa?" asked Burb smiling broadly.

Lucinda grinned. "Jason learned French and could even speak it pretty well, but I only learned to understand it most of the time. I kept getting my verbs in the wrong place and we laughed ourselves silly when I tried to speak French."

"I can just imagine what you would do with Mandarin, then," said Danny which sent Burb off in gales of laughter.

"Gramma would be offering herself as a Geisha girl without knowing it, wouldn't she Dad?"

"No, I wouldn't. I was very careful about the company I was in before I aired my French. Of course, once in Germany, I did ask these people if they would come to our place for a mess of knives," said Lucinda laughing merrily.

"Where was this Gramma?" asked Burb.

Lucinda sat reflectively for a moment. "Oh that was in Bremerhaven, Germany. That's an army base city. Jason was stationed there once during his stay in the army. He knew these people, Elsa and Horst Riems. We stopped there and Jason looked them up. They invited us to a cook-out and it was wonderful. Wanting to return the favor I pulled out my German phrase book and thought I had it all worked out, but the word for a meal is Essen and the word for knife is Messer, so I goofed up again. We all had a good laugh anyway."

Lucinda smiled at the memory and then suddenly rose to her feet. "We'll never get anything done if you people get me started. What's for breakfast Emily? Or as Jason always said, "Is it a 'fix your own,' morning?"

Emily arose also. "No, you won't have to fix your own, but I'll have it ready before you are dressed."

Lucinda tilted her head and looked at Emily narrowly. "You want to bet on that?"

Emily grinned. "I'm pretty fast, aren't I, Danny?"

"Yes, you are, but so is Mom, so I think Burb and I had better make ourselves scarce," said Danny pushing Burb toward the patio door.

CHAPTER 41

Their plans had to be changed once they reached Bluefield since the lawyer was away. Two days later Burb and Lucinda left for Pittsburgh. "Remember, Mom, you have to be down here in November to do whatever you decide to do on those stocks that Jason held," said Danny as he helped her into the car.

"Since we want the whole family for Christmas, why don't you just stay while you are here, Mama Lucinda?" asked Emily.

Lucinda sat thinking before she closed the door. "I'll think about it. Right now, I just can't make any far-reaching plans." She smiled and closed the door.

Emily and Danny stood waving until the suburban went out of sight along Browns Creek road toward Pineville.

Lucinda rode along looking to the right and left, remembering every turn in the road which she had traveled so often while she was married to Danny's father and living in the community of Rock. When they passed the Wyoming County Vocational/Technical School however, her mind leapt to the most horrible incident of her life. This incident led to her losing her baby and subsequently her first husband, Jeff Marshall, being burned to death in a motel fire. She shivered and pushed the terrible images out of her mind.

Seeing her shiver, Burb said, "What's wrong, Gramma?"

"I just remembered the connection the Vocational School had to my miscarriage and to your grandfather

Marshall's death. That was a terrible time, Burb and I think it has left a lasting imprint on your Dad."

"I'd like to know about that, Gramma. I know Dad never liked Grandfather Marshall and was actually glad when he died, but Dad doesn't like himself for feeling that way."

"I wish he could just understand that his dad had an emotional problem. If he had taken his medicine and followed the doctor's orders he could have dealt with it, but when he began feeling better he always stopped his medication. I know now, that your grandfather Marshall was bi-polar and had a possessive personality. This led to his jealousy and it got worse as he aged, especially if he drank." Lucinda shivered as she now recalled some of his abuse. "Let's just put that out of our minds. It's too unpleasant to dwell on."

Burb leaned over and patted her hand. "Sure thing, Gramma, but I wish you would write all of that down sometime, if you can stand to do it."

"I'll try to, Burb but I don't know when. Sometimes it is easier than at other times. I'll pick a good time, though and get it down, but I wouldn't do that for anyone but you," she said and laughed. "You'll nag me to death if I don't."

Burb laughed. "Well, I want that story, of course, but really I want the story of your life with Grampa Jason, more than anything else."

Lucinda smiled. "Burb, honey it's hard to put pure love and joy into words. There are things that no words can ever express. I know people looked at me and Jason and saw that we loved each other, but they couldn't see the oneness we felt together." Lucinda sat thinking about the many times that she would start to say something and Jason would finish it or she would do the same for him.

"Jason and I were truly soul mates, and yet we differed on numerous things. We would argue and I would get huffy. Jason would walk off and then later he would come and find me. He would be laughing and soon I was laughing too. You see, Burb, we both knew that we had something very precious and we wouldn't let petty differences ruin it."

By this time they were on the Robert C. Byrd highway in Beckley and nearing the ramp to get on Interstate 77. "Do you want to stop in Beckley, Gramma? If you do, tell me before I get to the entrance ramp," said Burb.

"No, I don't want to stop today, but someday I'd like to come back and look at the high school where Danny was in the spelling contest with Emily. I wish you could have seen them, Burb. I truly believe that they fell in love with each other that day."

Burb smiled. "Yes, I know about that. Dad swears he let Mom win because she was so pretty."

"She was certainly pretty, but I don't know about Danny letting her win. I think he just couldn't spell the word, but since you mentioned it, he could have let her win. If he did he must have really been smitten. He was so afraid of his daddy that it would have taken a lot for him to deliberately lose to someone else," said Lucinda thoughtfully.

"Was Grandfather Marshall physically abusive to Dad?" asked Burb.

Lucinda grimaced in pain at the memories this question evoked. "No, except for that one time and he didn't get to hit Danny then. I threw Danny's trophy at him. Of course, it broke the trophy, but Jeff didn't hit my son." She sat reliving that scene almost in tears until Burb asked, "What happened to the trophy?"

"I don't know. I don't remember ever seeing it again . . . not even the pieces. I assume that somebody picked up the pieces and threw them away, but I know I didn't."

Burb, now on the Interstate, drove along deep in thought until Lucinda said, "Why did you want to know what happened to the trophy?"

"Well, it just doesn't sound like something that Dad would discard. Even if something that important was in pieces, Dad's the kind of person who would have painstakingly put it back together. I've seen him work for hours to restore something that we broke."

"You're right, Burb. I don't know about the trophy, though. Why don't you ask him? He may have it somewhere. He was eight years old at the time and already pretty set and determined about his likes and dislikes."

They drove on into Parkersburg where they stopped to eat and rest. When they got back in the vehicle Lucinda put a pillow behind her neck and soon dropped off to sleep. Burb looked over to see a smile on her face and thought, *I'll bet she's dreaming about Grampa.*

That is exactly what she was doing, but the dream included Lucinda's father Burb Harmon. She was dreaming of Burb Harmon and Jason walking beside a river together. However, they weren't into one of their frequent arguments in the dream. Lucinda was smiling at the beauty of the river by which they were walking and also the beauty of their expressions. Suddenly, Lucinda was awake and sighed happily.

"I've just had the most pleasant dream. Your Papaw Burb and Jason were walking together beside a river and not disagreeing at all. You know that could only happen in a dream, of course," said Lucinda as she laughed merrily.

Burb laughed also. "You're right, Gramma. I don't remember a time that they were together without them arguing about something. They liked each other though. Do you remember how they'd be arguing hot and heavy, but if somebody brought up something else they'd immediately side with each other against that person."

Lucinda smiled. "I always told Jason that he and Dad whetted each other's intellect. Jason didn't exactly agree, but he did say that Dad was a smart old bugger even if he didn't have any education."

"I know Papaw really knew the scriptures. I used to sit and listen to the talks he and Dad had on various points. I remember him saying that the Lord revealed things in this generation that people in his generation could not have handled. That puzzled me at the time, but I know that Dad is blessed to preach out things that nobody has touched on before," said Burb thoughtfully.

Lucinda and Burb spent the rest of the drive into Pittsburgh talking about the relationship between Papaw Burb and Jason McCall. Both Lucinda and Burb had wonderful and unforgettable memories of times spent in the presence of these two amazing men.

"I'm glad Dad lived to see his namesake, Burb. He strutted like a peacock when we told him what Emily and Danny had named you. He even said that he could tell that you were going to 'favor' him. That's what people said in Dad's generation instead of saying a child looked like someone. They would say, 'that young'un favors his daddy, that's for shore.'" Lucinda said with a tender smile.

When they pulled into the gated complex where Lucinda's apartment was located, Burb helped her out. Before she could take a step Carl Burrows, the supervisor of the complex hurried to meet her.

"Mrs. McCall, it's good to see you. I was afraid you wouldn't come back to Pittsburgh."

Lucinda shook his hand. "I'm going to stay here for a while, Carl. I've not really decided where I will make my permanent home. In fact, I'm not ready to even think about that right now."

Burrows nodded in understanding. "We hope you'll stay with us, but anyway, as long as you are with us I want you to feel free to call on me if you need help with anything."

Both Lucinda and Burb thanked him and then entered the elevator which soon deposited them on the second floor entrance to Lucinda's apartment. As soon as Burb opened the door the smell of baked chicken wafted from the kitchen. Burb looked down at Lucinda and grinned.

"I called Mary when you went to the restroom in Beckley. She said she'd have dinner ready."

Entering the apartment without Jason had been a trial, but Lucinda had lifted her head and determinedly smiled her appreciation. “Did you tell her what to fix?”

Burb raised his eyebrows. “Well, I did tell her how much I liked her baked chicken. I don’t know what she puts on that chicken and she won’t tell me, but Mary makes the best chicken I’ve ever eaten in my life.”

Mary came through the door smiling. “Did I hear somebody call my name?” Going to Lucinda, Mary impulsively hugged her and Lucinda smiled as she returned the hug. “Good to see you Ms. McCall? Are you too tired to eat? “

Lucinda grinned. “No, I’m not really tired, but since Burb didn’t offer to stop and feed me, I am hungry.”

Burb shrugged his shoulders and gave Mary a droll look. “I offered to go through the drive-through at Wendy’s and Hardy’s but you refused.” Both Mary and Burb knew how much Lucinda disliked eating in a car.

Mary chuckled and Lucinda shook her head. “You wouldn’t dare, Burb Marshall.”

Soon Lucinda had put down her handbag and gone to the bathroom. She was gone for several minutes, but came out smiling. Burb and Mary silently breathed sighs of relief since she had to go through her bedroom to reach the bathroom. They had thought it would be such a painful reminder of Jason’s death, and it had been, but Lucinda clamped her lips together and with head erect she marched through and back out again.

CHAPTER 42

Mary put the food on the table and Burb stayed to eat with Lucinda, but he also told Mary to eat with them. She declined, however, since she had already eaten. As soon as he was finished Burb rose from the table. “Gramma, I’ll have to run along home now. Will you be all right?”

Lucinda raised sleepy eyes to his face. “Yes, Burb. Go on home and don’t worry about me. I’ll be all right here. Mary is like a guard dog and if I snore she will be checking on me.” Lucinda turned to look at Mary, who was gathering up the dishes, and smiled. “No offense dear. I just meant that I was in good hands while you are around.”

“I know, but I would rather have been referred to as an angel instead of a dog,” said Mary laughing merrily.

“I don’t blame you, Mary. You look more like an angel to me,” said Burb looking at her with raised eyebrows. He turned to go and turned back. “I don’t know about Gramma, but I missed you.”

Mary looked up at Burb doubtfully and then slowly smiled. “I’ll bet you did.”

Lucinda looked from one to the other and realized that some message had been passed between them. Lucinda yawned widely and rose from the table. She turned sleepy eyes to Burb. “See you, tomorrow, I guess. Good night.”

Both Burb and Mary said good night and Lucinda walked sedately into her bedroom. “If my acting was good enough they won’t check on me until in the morning. I have to get used to this on my own,” thought Lucinda as she stood staring at the bed.

She walked hesitantly over to the bed and stood for a moment and then sat down on the bed. She sat as she had seen Jason do every night that they had spent in this apartment. Gradually she reached over and placed her hand on the pillow on which his head had lain. Slowly she moved her hand in a circular fashion over the pillow. Then she arose from the bed and jerked back the covers and rubbed her hands all up and down the side of the bed always used by Jason. Slowly she straightened herself to standing position and looked down at the bed in disgust.

Lucinda turned and looked all around the room as if searching for something. Finally she grabbed a gown from the top drawer of the chest and headed for the bathroom.

That room also received a thorough search before she stepped under the shower.

Back in the bedroom she walked to the mirror over the dresser and looked at herself in dismay. "*I thought I'd feel his presence here to greet me*," she thought as she combed her hair and turned to the bed. From habit she went to her side of the bed and lay down.

Her thoughts were about Jason. In her mind she traced his eyebrows, the laugh creases beside his eyes, and the little mole which had appeared on his upper lip about a year ago. Then she allowed the tears to flow. "Oh, Jason. I miss you so. Why couldn't I just go with you? What am I going to do, now?" she murmured aloud.

She couldn't stop the tears and was beginning to think she'd have to go to some other room when suddenly she felt Jason nestled up to her back. She had always lain on her right side and they had slept spoon-fashion all their married lives. Her tears dried and a smile stretched her lips as she snuggled back into his embrace and dozed off to sleep.

An hour later Mary cracked the door quietly and from the shadow of the hall light she saw Lucinda sleeping peacefully. She let out a relieved sigh and just as quietly closed the door. Going back to the kitchen she picked up the phone and dialed Burb.

Burb answered on the first ring. "Is she asleep? Good. I was afraid she'd stay in there and cry all night. I don't think she is as brave as she pretends, but I don't know of any way to help her. Do you?"

"No, Burb, I don't. I think everybody has to deal with sorrow in their own way. All we can do is to let them know we are there and willing to help if they need us," answered Mary.

"Did you see Paul while we were down in West Virginia?" asked Burb since he knew that Mary's ex-husband had been trying to persuade her to take up where they had left off.

"He came by one night, but I didn't answer the door and he finally left."

"How did you know it was him?"

"I was looking out the window and saw his car pull into the parking lot across the street. I waited and when he rang for admittance I didn't answer the ring."

"Did you want to, Mary?" asked Burb.

"I did, but I didn't at the same time. It just wouldn't work. I wish he'd just let it go and stop bothering me."

"Why don't you go out with me? We'd go to some place he frequents and he'd see you are interested in somebody else," said Burb.

"I don't want to get you involved in something that is no concern of yours."

"Maybe it could be a concern of mine, Mary."

"Now, Burb, I know and you know that you take in every stray or needy person in the area and I will not be an extra burden to you."

"I don't …."

Mary interrupted him. "Yes you do, Burb Marshall. You're just like Jason McCall. You want to make life better for everybody."

"I don't think of you as a needy person, Mary. Why don't you give us a chance?"

"No, Burb. I've been many things, but never a charity case. You go to bed and get some rest. You'll use better judgment in the morning. Good night."

Burb hung up feeling let down but also pleased. To be likened to his grandfather was a great honor, but he was still puzzled as to how he could get Mary Tibbets to recognize that he was interested in her. He had liked her looks the first time he met her. Then she had not been separated from Paul and he tried to put it out of his mind, but she and Paul had been apart for almost a year now.

When Lucinda awoke the next morning she felt refreshed. She stretched and turned over to find Jason's side empty. She inched her hand over to see if his side of the bed was warm. Of course, it wasn't and she quickly jerked her hand back and sat up in the bed. She felt ready to scream when it seemed as if Jason spoke to her. "Lucinda, you have to let me go. I stayed with you last night."

Lucinda put her hands over her face and wept, but soon swung her feet over the side of the bed and reached for a tissue. *Oh Jason, if you can only stay with me a few more nights*, she pleaded in her mind then stood on her feet and headed for the bathroom.

When she entered the kitchen she found Mary there. "Why, Mary, what are you doing here so early? What time is it anyway?"

Mary looked at the clock on the wall. "It's nine o'clock. I came early today since I want to clean the cabinets inside and out and if it's all right with you I want to take tomorrow off."

"You know it is all right with me, dear. I am glad you let me know, however. Sometimes, I have things to do in town and I like for you to drive me, but they aren't urgent," replied Lucinda.

"Whenever, you want me, you know I'll be available," said Mary and feeling that Lucinda needed an explanation Mary said, "I made up my mind, last night to finally file for a divorce from Paul. Do you think divorce is wrong?"

"No, Mary, I don't. I know that you have tried for years to keep your marriage together. You stayed with him longer than most women would have, I think," said Lucinda thinking about her troubled first marriage. "I've often wondered if I caused Jeff's early death by trying to keep a marriage together."

"According to Burb, you tried everything you could, but your actions did not cause his death, Mrs. McCall."

Lucinda smiled wearily. "Mary, you are still a young woman and from what I've learned from Burb and your mother, Paul has been like a yo-yo as well as being unfaithful. So, don't waste the rest of your young life hoping for him to change."

Mary dished up the bacon, toast, and scrambled egg that Lucinda had always liked and talked pleasantries as Lucinda ate and she cleaned up the kitchen. Just as she was ready to leave Lucinda stopped her. “Mary, you’ve been working for me for five years and I think it’s about time you drop the Mrs. McCall and call me Lucinda, don’t you?”

Mary turned with a smile. “Yes, I do. I’ve not thought of you as Mrs. McCall for a long time. You feel almost like a mother to me.”

Lucinda smiled. “That wouldn’t be bad, you know. I could use another daughter.”

Mary turned red, but made no comment as she finished wiping the countertops. “If you don’t have anything else, uh-Lucinda,” I’ll be off. Wish me luck.”

“You know I do, and making a decision is the hardest part. It’ll be fine and you know you have my support as well as Burb’s, if you want it,” said Lucinda giving her an impish grin.

Mary stopped. “Did you know that Burb has been asking me to go out to dinner, but I won’t as long as I’m married to Paul? I believe one should be faithful to their vows, don’t you?”

“Yes, I do, dear. You and Paul have been separated for a year haven’t you? I think that since there are no children and the separation is a year in length you shouldn’t have a problem,” said Lucinda while thinking *unless Paul contests it.*

Lucinda spent the rest of that day addressing and stamping thank you cards to all those friends who had sent flowers and other condolences. She often stopped and wiped her eyes as she thought about Jason’s connection with so many people. Even Olivia Washburn, Jason’s first wife’s mother, now ninety-seven had sent the most beautiful card and a check to St. Jude’s Hospital in Jason’s name.

CHAPTER 43

The next few days and weeks were like a blur in Lucinda's mind and for many months afterward she lost all interest in life. Burb took her home with him from the hospital, but she refused to stay after the first night. "I want to go back to our place. We were going to stay there a few days and then go back to McDowell County. "

Lucinda had felt that she would be closer to Jason if she stayed in the apartment in Pittsburgh, but she wasn't. After that first night when she'd felt Jason's arms around her all night, she'd not sensed or felt his presence anywhere again. *I'm more alone than I've ever been in my life*, she thought forlornly. Each day seemed harder to get through than the next. She didn't want to eat, see anyone, and lately didn't want to talk on the telephone.

Mary cooked things that she knew Lucinda had always liked, but little of it was eaten. Finally she called Burb, even though she had planned to avoid all contact with him until her divorce was final. Burb came over that night.

When he saw his grandmother he was shocked. "Gramma, what are you doing to yourself? You look like a ghost."

Lucinda almost threw herself against his chest. "Burb, I just don't want to live without your Grampa. I thought I'd feel closer to him here in Pittsburgh, but I don't." She was crying so hard that her whole body began to tremble.

"Gramma, I'm going to call Dr. Chambers. He'll come and give you something to get you back on your feet."

"I don't want to be back on my feet. I want to be with Jason. There's nothing left here for me. I have no reason to live."

Burb pushed her back from his chest and putting a finger under her chin he said, "Listen to me, Gramma. You can't go to Grampa until the Lord wants you to. Grampa would be so disappointed in you and so would Papaw Burb. Remember what he told you. He said, 'you have to stand whatever comes along. You can cry, scream, throw a tantrum, or even make yourself ill, but when you get through doing that, you still have to stand it,' so straighten your backbone and decide to stand it."

Lucinda stood looking at him from a white face and tear dimmed eyes for what seemed an eternity to Burb, but was only a few seconds. Then she stepped back and turned away but her back was a little straighter and her walk much more purposeful. She left the room in that fashion and neither Mary or Burb tried to stop her.

When she was in her room with the door closed Burb let out a heavy sigh and picked up the phone. He punched in Dr. Chambers' number. He explained Lucinda condition and Dr. Chambers said he would stop by sometime that evening.

"She'll be really upset with you, Burb," said Mary worriedly.

"I know, but I can't just stand by and watch her waste away to nothing. She can't die just because she thinks she wants to. Life is for living and she's given up on it. If Dr. Chambers will give her something to get her over the cusp of the hill I think she'll be okay."

Mary turned toward the kitchen. "I hope you're right, but I wouldn't want to be in your shoes until then."

Lucinda remained in her room and Burb slumped into the recliner always used by Jason. Mary stayed in other parts of the apartment, not wanting to talk to Burb, fearing he'd ask about Paul.

This is how Dr. Chambers found them when he showed up an hour later. When Dr. Chambers knocked she turned toward the door and said, "Come in." Lucinda was seated in a chair by the open window. She opened her eyes and glared angrily. "What are you doing here, Dr. Chambers? I invited you in thinking Burb had knocked. He wasted your time. I've been sitting in here thinking and I've made up my mind to move back to West Virginia."

"Do you think that will help? I can see that you've lost weight and I've been told that you've become a recluse. Those are both symptoms of depression. I called to see if you would try a medicine for depression for a short time."

Lucinda shook her head. "No. I need to go back to West Virginia and attend church services again on a regular basis. I haven't been to church for almost three months."

"Are you sure? There are many more medicines today to treat mild depression than we once had. You may need something for a month or two until the edge of your grief is dulled," said Dr. Chambers in a cajoling voice.

Lucinda rose from her chair. "Come into the kitchen and Mary will give you coffee. A change of scene and going to church will solve whatever problems I have. Everybody has grief and sorrow. I'm not special. I have to learn to live with it, and the hills have always had a calming effect on me."

As they walked into the living room Burb sat up from his reclined position. "Have you talked any sense into her, Doc? She's as stubborn as a mule when she wants to be."

Lucinda glared at him. "I'd already made up my mind, thank you. He didn't have to talk me into anything. You don't have to worry about me anymore since I'm moving back to West Virginia."

Burb's eyes blared. "You mean that you've shut yourself in that room all day long and had me worried to death when you'd already decided what you were going to do?"

"No, I hadn't decided. Dad, decided for me. Thanks for reminding me of one of the best things he ever said to me. I've decided it will be hard, but I have to stand it. Since I have to live alone I want to do it in West Virginia where I can attend church." She gave Burb a gimlet gleam and continued, "Don't start patting yourself on the back. I awoke this morning with the move on my mind, but until you played your Papaw routine I was ignoring it."

Mary came in and stopped when she saw Lucinda and Burb glaring at each other. She looked from one to the other and turned toward the kitchen again. "Wait! You called Burb, didn't you?" asked Lucinda.

Mary turned back. "Yes, I did. I have been fixing everything I can think of to entice you to eat and have had to throw it out. You've had me worried. You know I didn't want to call Burb." Mary was pale and teary-eyed.

Lucinda went to her. "Forgive me, dear. I know, you didn't, but it's all right. I promise that I'll eat if it chokes me. I just told Burb that I'm moving back to West Virginia and then neither of you will have to worry about me."

"Gramma, neither of us wants you to move, but we don't want you to stop eating and isolate yourself from the world either. I want my Gramma back, not the ghost of Gramma," said Burb pulling her into his embrace.

Dr. Chambers, who had entered the apartment in a somber mood, now stood smiling. "Well, if Mary will give me a cup of coffee I can charge my usual fee for nothing."

As if suddenly recalling that someone else was present they all turned to the doctor in surprise. Lucinda laughed weakly. "Now, see what you've done, Burb. You bawled me out and it's now costing me a doctor's fee to get you to leave me alone."

Lucinda called Danny that night and told him to get the apartment cleaned and whatever else it needed. "Get me some groceries in. Emily will know what the basics are, like milk, sugar, shortening, meal, and flour. Just tell her to get what I will need for a week. Oh! Tell her to get me a dozen fresh brown eggs from that man Kyle buys them from."

"Mrs. . . No, Lucinda, do you plan to give up this place?" asked Mary, who had worked and practically lived in the apartment ever since Jason and Lucinda had purchased it.

Lucinda stopped and looked thoughtfully at Mary. "If you . . . I'm going to talk to Burb about it. He may want to take it over. The deed is free and clear, but the security fee has to be paid once each year."

Mary smiled. "I was hoping you'd say that. I don't think Burb likes where he lives now, so he may be glad to be able to move in here."

When Lucinda called Burb his reply was, "I need to talk to somebody else before I make a decision, Gramma. What about if I tell you sometime this week? Is that soon enough?"

Lucinda grinned, mischievously. "Can't you get Mary to make up her mind?"

"No. She won't try to get her divorce from Paul. I've about given up hope. She knows he'll never change, but for some reason she keeps hanging on."

Mary had told Lucinda about her divorce proceedings, but Lucinda didn't tell what had been told to her in confidence.

"Well, it will take all this week and part of next week to get everything squared away. I hope your affairs will be that easily settled," said Lucinda before she hung up

CHAPTER 44

Two weeks later Lucinda was settled in her own apartment in McDowell County. Danny had made all the changes that she and Jason had told him they wanted before Jason died. The two bedroom apartment was connected to the main house which had been her home with Jason. It was now the home of her son, Danny Marshall, but her own apartment was separated from Danny and Emily by a breezeway.

Until her near breakdown she just couldn't decide where she wanted to be and she hadn't asked about the apartment at all. Danny and Emily, however, constantly mentioned it to her.

"Mom, Burb works every day and is often out at night. What if you needed somebody and couldn't reach him," had been Danny's plea to be joined by Emily and eventually agreed to by Burb.

"Gramma, you always told me to make good memories and they would always be mine. You and Grampa made wonderful memories and you have them whether you are here or in West Virginia. I'd say you made more memories down there anyway," Burb reasoned.

So, Lucinda finally relented knowing that Burb spoke the truth. *I'll move to the apartment and start putting together all my memories,* she thought and then before she could change her mind called Danny to tell him she had decided to move.

She looked around her. "I'm all settled in, but Jason isn't here," she mumbled sadly. She winced at the pain this kind of thoughts caused and quickly began looking through the recipe book she had opened. All her other stays in the apartment she had not been alone. That had been her home with Jason when they had no trips planned, but it looked different since Danny had added the extra bedroom, put new windows in the office, and built a deck on the back.

She and Jason had always arranged their schedule so they could be in McDowell County each year for their anniversary and for the three church association meetings.

So all of August and September was taken up with union and communion services and the three church associations and now it was October.

"Danny, where is the best place to buy a computer," she asked as she came through their door one morning dressed to go out.

Danny turned from the stove where he was frying bacon. "A computer! Now, what kind of bee do you have in your bonnet?"

Lucinda grinned. "I can't garden and dig in my flowers this winter so I thought I'd buy a computer. I will probably have to learn to use it all over again."

"You used to use a Mac computer when you were counselor, didn't you?" Emily came into the kitchen with a towel around her head and wearing a short terry robe.

"I'm told that Microsoft Word is the best program and I know nothing about it, so I'm going to take a night class up at Mount View High School," replied Lucinda.

"You won't have to go all the way up there. They teach computer classes at the library," said Danny as he placed a plate of bacon on the bar.

"Mama Lucinda, I think that is a really good idea. In fact, I'll take the class with you," said Emily. "I know how to use WordPerfect, but I'd like to know about Microsoft Word. What's the newest version of that, Danny?" Emily turned inquiring eyes to Danny.

"I have Microsoft 7 in my office, Emily," said Danny and motioned to Lucinda. "Come and eat with us, Mom and then you and Emily can go down and enroll in the next class. I'll talk to our computer guru at the Vo-Tech school and see what we can do about getting two new computers since the one we have here is slow and old. Jason had one, but I haven't seen it in the apartment. Do you know what he did with it, Mom?"

Lucinda laughed. "He traded it for a Laptop, but we left it on a canal boat in Amsterdam. Jason said he'd rather buy a new one as to try to find that one."

So two weeks later Lucinda and Emily were enrolled in a class to learn Microsoft 7 and Danny said that two new computers had been ordered. Both women were very excited and talked constantly about how much they had learned. Danny often left his reading of the scriptures and sat in his office listening to their happy chatter.

The computers were delivered in early November and Clay Parsons from the Vo-Tech school came over and set both computers up.

"Now, Mrs. McCall, I only live on the other side of Indian Ridge and if you run into any problems feel free to call me," was his parting comment.

Lucinda looked at Danny. "I believe he really meant that. He seemed so content while he was setting up my computer."

Danny shook his head. "He did mean it. He is happiest when he has computer parts all around him and he is trying to solve some problem."

Lucinda stood looking at the computer screen, the tower, and the printer and groaned. "Lord have mercy on him, then. I hope he keeps that attitude for the next year."

Emily came out of her little nook off from the dining room where she had her computer installed. "I'm really excited. I can create lessons to help my students and even do greeting cards. I'm going to love this."

Danny stood and stretched widely. "Well, I assume I may as well take over lots of chores that you two have been doing so I'll start by making some coffee. Will you stay and drink a cup with us, Mom?"

Lucinda stayed and they had a pleasant evening talking about the many nice helpful people that still lived in the Welch area. "I need to go see Kyle and Katie Bender. I know they are lonesome with Rita gone, but our weekends are tied up and both Emily and I are taking that class," " said Lucinda as they discussed how much Kyle had aged since Rita's death.

Lucinda had only been to Mount Zion Church once since she had moved back. The associations weren't held up there now and they only had communion service once each year. Danny was moderator of four churches and Mount Zion wasn't one of them. Lucinda didn't drive any place except from their house to town anymore so she went to whichever church Danny and Emily were attending each weekend.

Gradually Lucinda adapted to living in her little apartment and life took on an even keel even if lonely at times. Burb called from Pittsburgh once each week and it seemed that he and Mary were getting closer to making a decision.

She mentioned this to Danny and his reply was, “Burb’s already made his decision, but Mary is having a hard time. I don’t know how much longer he is going to hang around waiting for her to decide.”

Mary also called Lucinda and what she’d said in confidence Lucinda was unable to comment on. “Well, I hope he understands that everybody can’t or doesn’t act in the same way on every issue.”

“I think he’s been pretty darn patient. I don’t understand what’s so difficult about getting rid of a drunk,” opined Danny but then looked at Lucinda. “You stayed about twenty years with Dad though, so I guess women are wired up differently than men.”

Emily and Lucinda finished their first class on the 15th of December but everyone was so involved with Christmas preparations that neither of them did much on their computers until January.

Emily knocked on Lucinda’s door in early January and when Lucinda let her in she spread the newspaper out on the counter. “Mama Lucinda, look! A Desktop Publishing class is starting Wednesday at the Library. Don’t you think we need to take that class? That’s all either of us would ever need to do what we want to do with a computer. If we learn Desktop Publishing we can do book covers, greeting cards, banners, and oh just lots of stuff.”

Lucinda heaved a sigh. “If I’d known I’d have to go to school for years to keep abreast with all the programs for the darn thing I probably wouldn’t have started it. I don’t like to get out in the cold.”

“It’s just one day a week. We need to get out of the house some anyway. You remember how Dad always insisted that we get out since we needed the Vitamin D from the sun?”

Lucinda smiled. “Yes, he used to almost pull me out. I hate cold weather and the older I get the more I hate it.”

They did take the class and by May they were both fairly proficient in the uses to be made with the program.

When they received their certificates Lucinda hugged hers to her chest and smiled at the teacher. "I'm going to take this home and frame it and after that I'm going to promise myself to never let Emily talk me into taking another class."

Now, Lucinda had her computer, knew how to do Microsoft Word and Desktop Publishing. So without mentioning it to her children she began on her memoirs. She had gone to Sam's Club in Bluefield with Danny and Emily where she purchased an entire box of computer paper, some folders, sharpies, and paper clips.

When she met Emily at the check-out counter she saw the amazed look on Emily's face.

"What! You look shell-shocked, Emily.

"Well, I guess I am. What do you plan to do with an entire box of computer paper? You must be going to write a book."

Lucinda was startled but she covered it by dropping her purse and bending down to retrieve it. "I figured that as many mistakes as I'll be a making, I'd have to be running to the store every few months to get paper, and besides this is on sale. You should get a box for you and Danny."

Emily smiled and turned just as Danny came up. "Mama Lucinda says the computer paper is on sale. She bought a box and I think I'll buy us a box."

Danny smiled. "Hurry then. I'm hungry."

The very next morning Lucinda sat down in front of the computer, but didn't put her fingers anywhere near the keyboard. *How does one tell things that are too dear and precious to explain?* She asked herself silently. She sat there as memories flooded her mind, but finally she began. "I met Dr. Jason McCall way back in August of 1950."

Then her fingers seemed to move on their own volition as that first meeting played before her eyes. It was so poignant that she found tears in her eyes as she wrote it, but she wiped them away and continued since she knew that would happen in all the memories of her times with Jason.

Sometimes she stopped typing and let the tears flow and at other times she laughed until tears flowed as well. *Lord, thank you for giving us such a wonderful life together*, she often thought and would then stop and sit reflecting back to some particular memory that she didn't want to share.

When she hadn't been over to see Danny and Emily for two days she was startled awake at eight o'clock the next morning.

"Mom! Mom! Are you awake? Let me in," ordered Danny rattling the door knob.

Lucinda had been typing at one o'clock that morning and didn't feel like she had been asleep very long. She opened her eyes wondering who was banging on her door. Slowly the noise penetrated the sleep and she swung her feet to the floor and yelled. "Wait just a minute, Danny. I was fast asleep." She slipped on her house slippers and robe and plodded to the door.

As soon as she opened the door Danny came through with a look of relief on his face. "I've been worried about you, Mom. We haven't seen you in two whole days and nights. Are you ill?"

Lucinda shrugged her shoulders. "Well, it makes me ill to be startled awake this early in the morning."

"Have we upset you about something? I know you've been up and about since we could see your lights, but we kept getting a busy signal on your phone. Who have you talked to so much?" Danny had come on in and sat down on the arm of a chair near the door.

Lucinda grinned. "I thought we weren't supposed to meddle in one another's lives. I'm not going to tell you who I've talked to."

Danny shook his head. "We're not meddling, but we felt you could at least have called and told us you didn't wish to be bothered. We happen to love you and were concerned."

Lucinda walked to Danny and leaned down to kiss his forehead. "Okay, I understand and I'm sorry. I had the phone off the hook because I didn't want to talk to anyone."

Danny stood up and put his arms around Lucinda. "Mom, are you upset about something? You know you can be honest with me."

Lucinda patted his cheek. "No, Danny, I'm not upset with anyone, but I don't want to be expected to solve Burb and Mary's problems, nor anyone else's. I've been trying to think about what I want to do with the rest of the time the Good Lord has for me to stay here."

Danny dropped his arms and turned toward the kitchen. "Well, that settles it. Burb can just get himself down here for his summer vacation and take you about."

"He won't come down here right now and to tell the truth I don't really want him to until July," said Lucinda. "Besides, you and Emily are worried over nothing. If it will make you feel better I'll call every night and today I'm going to work in my flower beds."

Danny grinned and hugged her again. "Want to come over for breakfast? Emily is making pancakes and sausage."

Lucinda's eyes lit up. "Give me twenty minutes and I'll be there."

CHAPTER 45

From that time on Lucinda called every night and made sure that Danny saw her outside at least once each day. Also Burb came down in July and they agreed that he would come down every July and take her up to the cemetery by Mount Zion Church.

"Burb, I sometimes miss your Grampa so much that I feel I can't bear it, but then he'll come to me in a dream or something and tell me that it is only a little farther along. I'll wake up happy again. I believe the Good Lord sends Jason back to me in dreams to comfort me." Lucinda smiled and wiped her eyes but she didn't look sad.

This pattern was kept up for five years without fail until they'd had the cancer scare over Emily and then the following year Lucinda had her fall which had altered their ritual. Lucinda could tell she wasn't as strong as she had been. *What should one expect at eighty-nine years old? Jason has been gone seven long years and I'm sometimes as lonely as I was the morning he hugged me for the last time on this earth, she thought sadly.*

Her memories were now a volume of three hundred pages and she often found herself going a full week without adding to it. Burb was due to come down in two weeks and she was eager to make her pilgrimage again to the cemetery.

Burb arrived late one evening and the next morning Lucinda awoke early to cook his favorite breakfast of biscuits, eggs, and gravy. He must have heard her for he soon came through the door into the kitchen.

"Gramma, what have you done? You shouldn't be up cooking at all; especially not a big meal like this." Burb came over and gave her a hug and then sniffed. "Gosh it sure does smell wonderful, though. Thank you!"

While he was eating Lucinda told him she wanted to go to Mount Zion and with a big smile Burb agreed. "I thought maybe you had an ulterior motive behind this feast.

They decided to leave early and get back in time for a late lunch at the Sterling Drive-In. Before nine o'clock they were on the road and arrived on the top of Crane Ridge at ten- thirty and made their way into the cemetery.

"Watch it, Gramma," said Burb, grabbing Lucinda arm as she stumbled. "If you fall over that bank you'll not stop rolling until you hit Dry Fork River." Burb laughed as he righted her and held onto her arm. They were walking from the cemetery across the road from the Mt. Zion Primitive Baptist Church.

Lucinda hadn't been to Mt. Zion church or the cemetery for two years now. Danny attended the other churches and even Mt. Zion when he could, but most of the time he left it in the care of young Elder Timothy Davis.

Lucinda stopped, blew her nose, and wiped her tears away. "It's all changed, hasn't it?" She gazed off to the far hills on the other side of the deep hollow in which Raysal, Bartley, and Atwell had once thrived.

Burb stopped beside her and also looked around. "It sure has Gramma. Grampa loved it, though, or at least he loved this mountain, didn't he?"

"We both loved this mountain. It holds a lot of memories for us. Here at this church house is where your Grampa found peace after your grandmother, Janet, died. We were married again on our fifth anniversary at this same church but your Daddy performed the ceremony. We loved our wedding in Lebanon, but after the church ordained Danny we, for some reason wanted Danny to marry us even though we'd already been married five years. We'd even traveled to Ireland for our honeymoon. Did you know about that?"

Burb grinned. "Yes, Gramma, I did know. Papaw told me a thousand times how your son and Jason's son-in-law had performed the ceremony while Jason's daughter and your daughter-in-law had been Maid of Honor."

"Emily was pregnant with you when we remarried, so I guess you were the ring bearer," said Lucinda smiling.

"Mom said you and Grampa waited three years after Grandmother Janet died before you ever met again. Why did you two wait that long? You always loved each other, didn't you?" Burb asked since he had always been curious.

Lucinda stood breathing deeply of the fresh mountain air and looking off to some far horizon. "Janet's death was so hard on Jason. I wish I could have been there to share his grief," said Lucinda as she started walking on. Then she turned to look up at Burb.

"We needed to get to know each other. We disagreed on many things that we thought, at the time, were so important. We learned better, and found that being able to love each other in spite of our differences was much more important.

"You met, Grandmother Janet, didn't you, Gramma?"

"Yes, a couple of times, but I didn't know her. She didn't like me, but then your Gandfather Jeff didn't like your Grampa either. Jeff didn't like any man that looked at me, though. He was so jealous . . . It was a sickness that he just couldn't help. He wasn't all bad, though," said Lucinda solemnly.

"I don't think Dad is as forgiving as you are. He doesn't have any pleasant memories . . . or at least very, very, few. Why did you stay on with him, Gramma?" asked Burb.

Lucinda stopped. Walking made her tired anymore. "I've asked myself the same question, thousands of times. I think it was because I realized he had a problem and I believed divorce was wrong."

"Wrong! You mean you think it's wrong to get away from someone who abuses you?" Burb was astonished.

"When I got married I vowed to love, honor, and obey until parted by death. Dad raised us all to live up to our commitments and also I was afraid that God would punish me if I broke my vows."

"Somebody like Grandfather Marshall couldn't be classified as a good husband. Dad said he heard you crying almost every night of his life until Grandfather died. The God I believe in would not want you to live like that. Dad doesn't think so either." They had now reached the door of the church building and stopped. Lucinda breathed a sigh of relief. She didn't want to talk about her life with Jeff Marshall.

"I guess it's locked. Try the door Burb. I'd like to see inside. I know I can't get up here to meeting since your dad seldom gets the chance to attend," said Lucinda and stood waiting until Burb tried the door. It swung open and he helped her inside.

Lucinda shook off Burb's grasp on her arm and walked slowly toward the front. She stopped at the second row back and took a seat. She turned as if looking at someone sitting beside her and smiled. Burb took a seat on the other side where he could be close and yet out of her line of vision. His grandfather, Jason McCall, had died in July, seven years before and his grandmother, Lucinda had asked to be brought to his grave many times, but especially in July. Since school was out in the summer, Burb, who was a school principal, usually brought her.

Each time they came he learned something new about his grandparents' story. Everyone that knew anything about them always said, "Their story is just like a movie." Burb's answer had always been, "Nobody but Gramma could ever tell it like it was."

After a few people had said that to him, he had begun to keep a record of each new thing she told him. He had gone way back to the beginning in 1950. Burb sat thinking, *Dad always said their love story reminded him of Ruth in the Bible, he thought.*

Now he looked across the aisle at Lucinda. Her head was angled to the right as if she was listening to what her imaginary companion was saying. Slowly Lucinda arose from her seat and as if taking someone's arm she walked toward the front. There she stopped and rubbed her hand along the edge of the pulpit, looked up at her silent companion, and nodded her head. Then in a clear but elderly voice she sang. "Farther along we'll know all about it. Farther along we'll understand why. Cheer up my darling, live in the sunshine. We'll understand it all by and by."

Lucinda stopped singing and turned to Burb with a beautiful smile. "Let's go back now, Burb. I'll just have to wait."

Emily, Burb's mother, had told him that Grampa and Gramma had changed the words to that song, but hadn't told him what they were. "I don't know what the words are.

They would never tell any of us. I just know it had some special meaning for them," Emily had explained.

Burb stood, and walking forward he took his grandmother's arm and walked slowly with her back to the car. He carefully seated her and then suddenly said, "Gramma, I forgot. I have my camera. Do you want me to get a picture of the church house?"

"Yes. That would be good. Then if I can't get up here I can at least look at the picture."

Burb reached into the back seat for his camera and walking a little way back from the building he took the picture just as the evening rays of the sun glinted off the tall spire above the door. He walked back to the car. "I think I have a once in a lifetime picture, Gramma. Here, look how the sun makes that spire look."

Lucinda looked and shook her head. "What in the world will be invented next? I used to wait days to pick up my pictures after the drugstore had sent them away. Now the pictures are instant. That's just amazing."

Soon they had turned and were making their way slowly down Atwell Mountain. "Gramma, do you remember the version of that song, Farther Along, that you and Grampa changed the words to?"

Lucinda looked over at Burb. "Who told you we changed the words? Emily's been telling secrets."

"No, Gramma, she didn't tell me. She said neither of you would ever tell anyone else the words."

Lucinda smiled. "That's right. Jason never would tell her and I'm not going to either. It was just our song, especially after we got older." She settled down and leaning her head back against the seat closed her eyes.

Burb thought she was asleep, until going over Caretta Mountain she began to hum. He couldn't hear all the words, but he did catch "Farther along we'll meet . . ." then she opened her eyes and said, "Oh I hope it isn't too much longer. My heart is so lonely."

Burb patted her arm. "You still miss him a lot, don't you Gramma?"

She turned tear-filled eyes toward her grandson. "Honey, when half of oneself is taken away, the other half has no anchor. I try, but I know I'm a worry to you children, especially your mother and daddy."

"Now, Gramma, don't start playing a sad song. You know that Mom and Dad don't think of you as a bother. In fact they tell me that you seldom come into their part of the house. What are you doing in that apartment that keeps you so busy?" asked Burb with a quizzical smile.

Lucinda smirked. "I don't ask them what they do in their house and it's none of their business what I do in mine. That goes for you too, young man."

Burb grinned. "Well, I guess that puts me in my place, so I'll not tell you that Mary and I plan to set the date."

Lucinda turned to him with gleaming eyes. "Did she finally get her divorce?"

"Gramma, we didn't call and tell you, but Paul was killed in a car wreck two months ago. Mary was pretty torn up for a while. I asked Doc Chandler to talk to her and now she realizes that Paul was going to drink whether she was with him or not. They'd been separated since before Grampa died, but every time she would decide to make it official he would call her with some sob story and she'd put it off. Several times, I almost gave up, Gramma," said Burb.

Lucinda looked at Burb steadily for a moment. "Don't ever give up on somebody you truly love, Burb. Believe me when I say 'that one is worth waiting for.'"

"I know that, Gramma, but I sometimes thought that Mary didn't love me enough to make a commitment," Burb replied.

"We can't see inside someone else's head and because of that we usually judge them by our own yardstick. Does that make sense?" asked Lucinda.

Burb grinned. "Do you ever come up with these things unless they make sense? You're pretty smart for a young chick."

CHAPTER 46

They did eat lunch at the Sterling Drive-In and Lucinda seemed to thoroughly enjoy being with Burb, but she was tired when they arrived back at her apartment.

Burb spent the afternoon with his parents. "Dad, Gramma seems so much frailer than she was last year. Am I just imagining it or is she flagging?"

"She is, Burb, but I don't know if she's ill. She doesn't complain, but she moves slower and isn't interested in everything like she has always been. Emily and I have been trying to think of some way to get her to go in for a check-up," replied Danny with a worried frown.

To their sorrow, a plan did not have to be worked out. Two months after Burb's visit Lucinda was taken to the hospital. Emily had seen Lucinda leave her apartment and go into her flower garden while she was doing her breakfast dishes. This was something she did most mornings in the summer and Emily went about her work without thinking about her. She did think about her, however, when a sudden rain storm which turned into a short hail storm lashed the windows of the house.

Emily looked out the window and not seeing Lucinda assumed she had gone back inside, but to make sure she dialed Lucinda's number. After the third ring she looked out the window again. She dropped the phone back into its cradle and ran out the door. Through the rain she had seen a splash of red near the rosebushes.

That splash of red was Lucinda's robe. Emily found her lying on her side; not moving. "Mama Lucinda, Mama Lucinda!" whispered Emily as she bent over the inert body.

Lucinda moaned and Emily reached down to lift her up. Lucinda winced in pain, but sat up. She was drenched and clammy cold.

"We have to get you inside. Did you fall? Are any bones broken?" asked Emily.

"I don't think so," murmured Lucinda trying to sit up, but firm hands pushed her back down.

"Mom, wait! You may have broken your back," said Danny with a quake in his voice.

Lucinda pushed at his hands. "No. I didn't fall. I just got weak and couldn't stand. I guess I fainted."

Danny scooped her up in his arms and almost ran to his house with Emily in front to open the doors. Once inside, Emily quickly began to strip off the wet garments, but Lucinda stopped her.

"Go get me some dry clothes and I'll take off my own under things," said Lucinda in a no-nonsense voice.

Emily stepped back and looked at Danny. Danny rolled his eyes and motioned for Emily to do as she asked. When she was dry and dressed Danny said, "Now, we're going to see Dr. Patton."

Lucinda looked alarmed. "Dr. Patton! Why? I told you that I fainted."

"Mom, you don't know that, so if I have to tie you up and carry you we are going to see Dr. Patton." Danny was adamant and Lucinda knew he would do just what he said.

She shivered. "Well, get my coat. I'm cold."

Danny called Tug River Clinic and was told that Dr. Patton was at Stevens Clinic Hospital and was given the number. Dr. Patton was paged and Danny was told to bring Lucinda to the hospital.

Lucinda was helped to her feet by Emily and when she heard hospital she turned stormy eyes toward Danny. "I'm not staying in a hospital so you may as well wait until Ross Patton goes back to Tug River."

"He's just going to check you over, Mom. He didn't say you had to stay."

"Mama Lucinda, please don't be stubborn. You know you need to be checked. People don't faint without some reason," pleaded Emily knowing that Danny was scared that something terrible was wrong with his precious mother.

Dr. Ross Patton did want Lucinda to stay in the hospital for tests but she refused. "Do whatever tests you need to do now because I intend to stay in my own house tonight," she said regardless of what Danny, Emily, or Dr. Patton proposed.

They took her home after chest x-rays, and blood work with the admonishment that should she start sneezing or chilling she had to return to the hospital.

"I'm feeling fine and I sleep better in my own house and in my own bed. You young people don't understand what being in one's own place means to older people."

Lucinda seemed fine after she had eaten supper with Danny and Emily and about nine o'clock she arose from the sofa. "Danny, I'm going over to my place to sleep. Do you want to walk over with me?"

Danny and Emily both jumped to their feet. "You can't go over there tonight," said Danny.

Lucinda put her hand on his chest. "Danny, I love you better than anything on earth and I don't mean to worry you, but I really feel fine and I want to go home."

Knowing that they had an intercom connected to Lucinda's bedroom from their bedroom, even though Lucinda wasn't aware of it, Danny shrugged his shoulders and helped her on with her coat.

Meanwhile in Pittsburgh, Pennsylvania Burb Marshall and Mary Tibbets were busy packing suitcases and doing the usual things to close down a house for an extended stay away from home.

The week before Burb had given up the lease on his apartment that had been his home for ten years, but he had stayed there until that morning, which was also the morning Lucinda had fainted. However, he and Mary had no idea about anything going on in West Virginia.

"Gramma will be so surprised and pleased, sweetheart," said Burb, giving Mary a quick kiss as he passed her on the stairs.

Mary giggled. "I can just see her face, now."

Burb grinned. "She'll say. 'Pon my honor, if you two don't beat all.'"

Regardless of how hard they worked it was still twelve midnight before they closed and locked the door to Mary's apartment which had been Lucinda's old apartment. When Lucinda had moved back to West Virginia she had told Burb that Mary should be allowed to live there.

"I may want to visit and will need to have someone taking care of the place."

This pleased Burb since he had wanted this arrangement all along. He felt that if he could keep Mary away from where she may run into Paul it would be easier for her to divorce him.

They pulled out of Pittsburgh laughing like two teenagers who were going to give someone they loved a wonderful surprise.

"Won't Lucinda be surprised to find that we've come down to West Virginia to marry and also that we are planning to move there as well?" The excitement in Mary's voice was contagious.

"She'll also be pleased that we'll ask Dad to perform the ceremony, but when we ask her to give you away she'll be 'all in a twitter' to use one of her expressions."

"Burb, are you sure that we won't get there before Lucinda's usual arousal time," asked Mary worriedly. "Sometimes, I think all of you forget how old your grandmother is."

Burb smiled pleasantly. "I guess we do forget. Gramma certainly doesn't act like she's ninety years old and she definitely doesn't look that old."

Mary laughed. "I wouldn't want to be awakened at six o'clock in the morning and I'm not half that old."

Burb reached across the gear console and squeezed her hand. "It takes seven hours to drive down there regardless of how fast you think I drive. It will certainly be later than six when we get there."

They pulled quietly into the driveway at seven o'clock and shut off the engine. The main house was dark and so was Lucinda's apartment.

"See! What did I tell you? They're all asleep," scolded Mary sleepily.

Burb quietly opened the door as he put his finger over his lips to make sure Mary acted in like manner. They eased out of the car and walked on the grass verge along the drive to the apartment. Burb took out his key and just as quietly opened the door. They stood listening just inside the door and not hearing anything Burb took Mary's hand and walked stealthily through the living room and stopped just outside Lucinda's bedroom door.

Burb leaned close to Mary and whispered. "When I open the door let's both say, 'Surprise'."

Mary shook her head and whispered. "No. We may scare her and I won't do it."

Burb put out his hands palm upwards as if to say, okay and then gently turned the knob. The door swung open, but Lucinda was not surprised.

Burb and Mary were speechless as they stood staring at Lucinda Marie Harmon, Marshall, McCall. She was lying slightly propped against two pillows. Her head was angled to the left toward the nightstand and tissues were scattered on the floor and atop the nightstand. One arm had fallen over the side of the bed and was dangling while the other arm lay across her chest with a sheet of paper clasped beneath her hand.

Mary and Burb stood staring in slack-jawed astonishment and then Burb almost jumped to Lucinda's side. "Gramma! Gramma! Wake-up!"

When there was no response he almost yelled, "Mary, call an ambulance."

Before Mary could call Danny came hurtling through the door. "What is it?" Seeing Lucinda, Danny stopped in his tracks.

"Oh God! Mom! Mom! Oh God, my sweet mother. I didn't hear a thing. I thought I would. I put an intercom in here." Danny was mumbling and crying brokenly.

By that time Emily came through the door and seeing Lucinda as well as Danny's condition she put her arms around him and by pushing and pulling got him into the chair beside the door.

Mary had gotten the ambulance service and was told they were on their way. Nobody had yet touched Lucinda. *This is like a movie set with all the performers in place, but without a script*, thought Mary who was also frozen in place.

Soon the shrill scream of the siren broke the stillness of Indian Ridge. The noise startled the deer and the myriad of birds that came to feed each morning on the salt licks and feeders scattered around the perimeter of the grounds.

Danny had become very still and now Burb noticed the box which had been on the end of Lucinda's bed all along. He walked over and picked it up.

"Who put this box here? How did it get on her bed?"

Before anyone had answered the emergency crew came through the door. Burb put the box down on the floor beside the bed. Soon they were examining Lucinda and when the paramedic lifted Lucinda's eyelids he turned back to the room. "We'll have to take her to the hospital, but Mrs. McCall is dead."

The other man came to help and when he lifted her dangling arm to place it on her chest he noticed the sheet of paper. He slipped it from beneath her hand. Without turning it over he placed it on the bedside table and continued with preparing Lucinda for transport to the hospital.

Before they left they turned to Danny for instructions. "I know you want her taken to Stevens Clinic Hospital and I suppose to Fanning Funeral Home, don't you?

Danny arose from his chair. "I'll follow you to the hospital. I want to know what happened to her. She was all right last night. Dr. Ross Patton examined her yesterday evening there at the hospital. Her x-rays didn't show anything."

An hour later Danny, Emily, Burb, and Mary sat in stunned unbelief when Dr. Patton told them that she had died from quick pneumonia. "I didn't get her lab work results until a few minutes ago, but she did have acute viral pneumonia and she was already weak. I'd say she tried to cough and sneeze. I think she must have had it when she fainted yesterday morning and the drenching she got when she fell increased the effects."

Emily spoke up. "She ate dinner with us last night and walked over to her place by herself. She looked pale but she never said one word about feeling bad or hurting. Danny went with her and she seemed as normal as she ever did, didn't she Danny?"

"I had an intercom connected between her bedroom and our house and if she ever made a sound it had to be very quiet. The first thing I heard was Burb calling her name," said Danny from stiff lips.

Dr. Patton turned to Burb. "What were you doing at her place that early in the morning?"

Burb grasped Mary's hand. "My fiancé and I were coming down to get married and we wanted to surprise Gramma. We left Pittsburgh at midnight and pulled into her driveway at seven this morning. I have a key so we let ourselves in. When she wasn't up I opened her bedroom door and found her."

Danny and Emily gasped in surprise. "Mama Lucinda said last night when we begged her to stay with us that she expected you down and she wanted to be home when you came. We thought you had told her you were coming down, but she said you hadn't told her anything."

Danny sighed. "Mom knew things that others didn't understand how she knew. Jason always laughed and said that his Lucinda had 'the sight.' She did have some special talent, but I don't know what it could be called."

Dr. Patton began filling out the forms necessary before calling the funeral director. When he noticed Danny's hands shaking he stopped. "Danny, I'm going to write you a prescription for some mild nerve pills to help you through this. In fact both you and Emily can take them." He looked up at Burb. "You may need one or two yourself, young man."

Danny started to protest, but Emily stopped him. "Give me the prescription Dr. Patton. I'll see that Danny takes one tonight, at least." Burb looked at Emily and nodded his approval. He knew that not many mothers and sons had the kind of relationship that his dad and his grandmother had.

Bob Fanning's son came with the ambulance to pick up Lucinda's body. He hugged Danny, Emily, and Burb and in a voice choked with tears told them how sorry he was.

"Why don't you wait until tomorrow to come by and make the arrangements, Danny? It will give you a little time to sort things out and get your bearings," said Mr. Fanning.

CHAPTER 47

Back at the house nobody went to Lucinda's apartment. They gathered in the living room of the main house and sat in silence until Emily jumped up. "Mama Lucinda would be ashamed of all of us. I'm going to make some coffee and cook some breakfast and we are all going to eat."

"That's right, Mom. Gramma would say, 'You can mope, cry, and bang your head against the wall, but when you get through you still have to stand this, so get on with living," said Burb.

Mary smiled. "Yes, that's exactly what she would say. I'm going to help Emily if she'll let me. I suggest that you men get some pens and paper and start taking care of arrangements."

"Mary's right and I do need her help. There's paper in my little office and pens as well. If you can't do that, then go put food out for the deer and the birds. Sitting here grieving won't help the situation at all," scolded Emily as she grasped Mary's hand and headed for the kitchen.

Danny and Burb stopped in the mud room as they went out the kitchen door to pick up bird food and some carrots which Emily and Lucinda always wanted to give the deer. "We could never have an outside garden. The deer and other critters always knew when everything was big enough to eat," said Danny.

"If they didn't know I could see Mom and Gramma out here with carrots or something trying to entice them," said Burb chuckling.

"I dread going in and taking care of Mom's things. I knew this would happen someday, but this is so unexpected that I confess that I'm . . . I'm so, I don't know . . . I guess lost is as good a word as any. I know, an elder in the church shouldn't be like this, but since you've seen me, I'll confess that I feel more alone than I ever have in my entire life," said Danny with lowered head.

Burb put his arm around Danny's shoulder. "You may be an elder, Dad, but you are still just a man. Right now, we're both men experiencing a great loss. Gramma was almost as dear to me as you and Mom are and I feel like a little boy who needs somebody's lap to cry in."

Danny looked at his tall son and grinned. "I used to do that, you know. When I was hurt or didn't understand something I'd sit down beside Mom and lay my head in her lap. I'd tell her all about it and she's ruffle my hair and talk me out of whatever bothered me. She always seemed to know exactly what to say."

The next morning the four of them went together to Lucinda's apartment. There wasn't anything to do in the other rooms, and they dreaded going to the bedroom.

Finally Emily said, "We've put it off long enough. Let's get it over with."

Silently, they opened the door and went in. Mary and Emily went into the bathroom and started putting everything in order. They saw tissues lying about and a still damp wash cloth on the counter top.

"She must have been too warm and tried to wash her face," said Mary as she picked up the cloth and hung it to dry. When they went back to the bedroom Danny and Burb were sitting on the bed with a box between them and both had tears running down their cheeks.

Emily went to Danny and put her hand on his shoulder. "What is it, dear?"

Mary walked past Emily and Danny to stand in front of Burb who had his face buried in his hands. "Burb, I've never seen you like this. What brought this on?"

Danny and Burb both pointed to the box. "This is their story. Mom wrote the story of her life and it's all right here in this box."

"That's what she's been doing when you two were so worried because she didn't call or come over," said Burb when he finally raised his head.

Mary let out a sigh. "What a wonderful legacy! Burb has begged her ever since Mr. McCall died to write their story, but she always said she couldn't. Do you suppose she was already writing it?"

Burb shoved one of the pillows out of the way. "Here, Mary, I'll make room here beside me. Sit down."

"I remember seeing this box when we first came in. It was on the foot of the bed. I thought you did something with it, Burb," said Emily.

Mary saw the sheet of paper that the emergency medic had put on the night stand and reached over to see what it was. She read a few words and put it in Burb's hand. "Look at this, Burb. This was lying on her chest under her hand, when the emergency people started working with her."

I guess we must have been too shocked to pay much attention, but now I do remember she had one hand on her chest and there was something under it," said Emily.

"It's that song, Mom. You remember telling me that Gramma and Grampa had changed the words to that song, Farther Along, but would never tell you the words. Well, I think she must have been trying to sing that song, for here are the words.

FARTHER ALONG

Farther along we'll meet again dear
And never will we part again
Together we'll meet our sweet Jesus
Our blessed Savior and our Friend

Farther along we'll cross the river
And when we reach that other shore
There we'll see our friends and loved ones
And parting pain is felt no more.

Farther along we'll sing his praises
Hand in hand we'll meet our king
And with a band of heavenly angels
In his presence we will sing

Farther along the door will open
And one of us will go before
Leaving the other sad and lonely
But it will only be one step more

ACKNOWLEDGEMENTS

This being the last book in the Lucinda Harmon Saga series I feel so very thankful. My feelings are best stated in the fifth chapter of Ephesians as to whom thanks is due. "Giving thanks always for all things unto God and the Father in the name of our Lord Jesus Christ," and this I hope to have done in these four books as well as in all my other writing. I can state with assurance that the books would never have been written without my using the gift given to me by our blessed Savior. Therefore, I can take no credit unto myself, but only be thankful for the unmerited gift which has been bestowed on me.

Many people contributed to the material in this book and I hope I leave none of them out. I'll first begin with Darrell Fleming and his precious wife, Kathy, who lent me their notebook of notes and pictures from their vacation in Ireland which helped me very much. Thanks my friends.

Everything about Salzburg, Austria was told to me or sent to me in pictures by my dear friend and youthful mentor, Caroline Carpenter. Thanks so much Caroline, and not only for the help you've given me with this book, but the broadening opportunities you provided for me that have become precious memories. You have my undying gratitude. I hope you will be honored by my use of your material in this book.

I wish to thank my natural family as well as my church family for the many things they have said and done throughout my life that helped even though they were not aware of it. They are the people who helped me become who I am and I thank all of them. Through their examples I became rooted and grounded in the Appalachian culture and the Primitive Baptist beliefs which are so dear to me.

My grandson, Travis Davis and his precious wife Cindy Austin Davis are two people in my family who went out of their way to help me by working all of one Sunday afternoon taking pictures to be used as the cover of this book. The artist, Rhonda Whited, who does all the covers for this series painted the picture for the cover using the photograph they supplied. I really appreciate their efforts on my behalf. Thanks Cindy and Travis. I love you both very much.

I give thanks from my heart to my "sister of the heart," Jo Osborne, and her husband, Mike Osborne who is also a dear friend. These two people have been my friends, my support team, my teachers, and my anchor in a world where their kind of friendship is hard to come by. Thanks for being my earthly angels.

A large amount of credit in my writing is due to Rachel Riggsby, my editor and my very dear friend. She tells me how to make my writing better and I appreciate it so very much. I love her honesty and her readiness to allow me to differ with her point of view so that we can have a discussion from which I learn so much. Thanks Rachel.

Due to a bout with pneumonia I probably would not have finished this book had it not been for the friendship and encouragement I received from Linda Hudson Hoagland. This lady is a prolific writer with a heart full of caring for her "favorite adopted aunt." Thanks Linda. Your caring means so very much.

Last but certainly not least I wish to thank my many readers who have encouraged me by their comments and their emails begging me to write another book. It is because of their interest in my work that this four book series has come to fruition. God Bless each of you and thanks so much for your support.

THE LUCINDA SAGA

Here are short Synopses of the Books in this series called the Lucinda Harmon Saga:

Lucinda's Mountain: This is the first book in the series and it introduces the reader to a young mountain girl of Scots/Irish descent. It also portrays all phases of the culture of the Scots/Irish who eventually settled on the rugged mountain peaks in the Appalachian coalfields. These people were rugged individualists, Calvinistic in their religious beliefs, and mostly conservative in their political thinking. Lucinda Harmon is a product of this culture, but she visualized a broader world and dreams of an education far beyond what other members of her family had gotten.

Often in the dialect of her beloved mountain people Lucinda Harmon is used to paint a picture of a place and an era filled with peace, beauty, honesty, and brotherly love.

Lucinda's Mountain is a love story, but it is also an oral history painted in words only used to good effect by these stalwart mountain people. The history is accurate and many of the scenes are taken from real life events.

Lucinda Harmon is the epitome of the determination to move beyond the limited boundaries set for the women from her mountain. Meeting the doctor who came in to treat the people of the area only enhanced that desire and determination.

Jason's Journey: This is the second book in the series about Lucinda Harmon. Each book will stand alone, but people that read one always come back for the others. Jason McCall is a young doctor who agreed to come to the town of Bradshaw, West Virginia to treat the people of the area, especially the coal miners and their families.

Jason is fascinated by the culture not only of the townspeople but more so by the rugged people he met on the various mountain top ridges that meandered around the mountain sides and down the hogback ridges to the creeks far below. He encountered faith healing, absolute predestination beliefs, herbal remedies, and astrological signs, along with stubborn individualism tempered with charitable giving.

Jason met Lucinda Harmon on one of his trips to visit Aunt Sarah (Sarie) Lester. He was attracted to Lucinda Harmon and captivated by the unadorned faith of Aunt Sarie along with a wisdom he had not dreamed of encountering in the hills of West Virginia.

Jason truly made a journey. His journey was of self discovery, of cultural diversity, and of unshakeable faith in the Almighty God. Lucinda Harmon's innocent faith and sincerity was such a potent combination along with her beauty that he could never forget her.

The Beckoning Hills: The third book in the series deals with a much more urbane Lucinda, but also a Lucinda who was a very troubled wife and mother. In this book she marries a coalminer and an avid union member. Not finding work and also to get Lucinda away from any opportunity to meet Dr. Jason McCall, her husband Jefferson Daniel Marshall moves with her to Monroe, Michigan. There Lucinda, after a difficult delivery has a son, Daniel Jefferson, (Danny) who became the one joy of her existence.

Her husband's possessive jealousy and his volatile temper results in a necessary move back to Rock, West Virginia, in Wyoming County. Once again her husband becomes a coalminer and a much stronger union supporter.

Through the pleas of her husband's sister, Jill, Lucinda is allowed to get her degree as a teacher, but only through night classes at a community college. She began her teaching career in the elementary school in Pineville, West Virginia.

Lucinda still had night dreams and day dreams of Dr. Jason McCall and lived with guilt for doing so. She constantly prayed for help in forgetting Dr. McCall, but the more abusive her husband became the more frequent her dreams became.

Realizing that her husband had some kind of emotional problem Lucinda tried in every way she knew how to keep a peaceful atmosphere in her home. Danny, however, grew up fearing and disliking his father even though his father could be very good to him at times.

Jeff's mother and an old girlfriend contrived together a plot to separate Jeff and Lucinda. This culminated in the end of Lucinda's tortured marriage but with devastating results which were difficult to overcome.

AUTHOR'S COMMENTS:

In an attempt to tell the story of the wonderful Scots/Irish people in McDowell County, West Virginia I have borrowed from my own family, from relatives, and from the many wise and long-remembered icons of the community in which I was reared.

Each character in this series will leave the reader either loving them and clamoring to know more about them or hating their very existence. However, even those characters the reader dislikes will touch a soft spot in one's heart for the plight of a human being who is such a disturbed part of God's creation.

Since very few stories about the Scots/Irish descendants who settled in the coalfields have been told, especially from someone who grew up in that culture, I have tried to be as accurate and careful about portraying the multiplicity of the personalities of this wonderful group of people as possible.

The overriding theme is the sure knowledge that true faith and grounded beliefs will be challenged and thwarted by strong personalities and adverse happiness.

31693265R00170

Made in the USA
Charleston, SC
25 July 2014